7'6"

7'0"

6'6"

6'0"

5'6"

5'0"

4'6"

4'0"

3'6"

3'0"

2'6"

2'0"

The Usual Santas

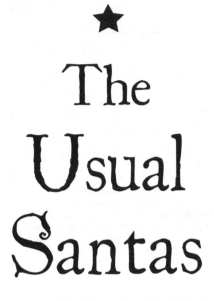

The Usual Santas

· · · · · · · · · · · · · · · · · ·

A COLLECTION
OF SOHO CRIME
CHRISTMAS CAPERS

Published by
Soho Press, Inc.
853 Broadway
New York, NY 10003

Library of Congress Cataloging-in-Publication Data

The usual Santas : a collection of Soho Crime Christmas capers.
ISBN 978-1-61695-775-9
eISBN 978-1-61695-776-6
1. Detective and mystery stories. 2. Christmas stories. I. Title
PN6071.D45 U88 2017 | DDC 808.83'872—dc23 2017011873

Endpaper illustration © 2017 Jeff Wong
Interior design by Janine Agro, Soho Press, Inc.

Printed in the United States of America

10 9 8 7 6 5 4 3 2 1

TABLE OF CONTENTS

Foreword by Peter Lovesey • vii

❄

"I Saw Mommy Kissing Santa Claus"
And Other Holiday Secrets • 247

FOREWORD
Peter Lovesey

Upon the first of all Christmases, St. Luke tells us, the Angel of the Lord appeared at night to some startled shepherds in a field and informed them of the momentous event in the city of David. As if that were not enough of a shock, a multitude of the heavenly host then manifested itself praising God and declaring "on earth peace, goodwill toward men."

The world's religions almost all provide occasions for expressing goodwill toward men—and women—most commonly in midwinter. The Pagan festival of Yule predated Christmas. Worldwide celebrations around the year's end include Hanukkah, Kwanzaa, Pancha Ganapati and the Chinese New Year. Families come together and there is a break from the monotony of work to indulge in ceremony, feasting and the exchange of gifts. Disbelievers like me are only too happy to join in.

Goodwill rules.

But not without exception.

Crime statistics spike at this time of year. The seasonal shopping spree provides rich pickings for thieves and fraudsters. Well-stocked stores become tempting targets for stick-up men and shoplifters. Pockets are picked, shoppers mugged, cars broken into and Christmas tree plantations raided. Cyber criminals relieve the unwary of their savings. Scam emails masquerade as greetings cards. Empty homes are ransacked. Drink-fuelled assaults are common. And even when the run-up to the holiday ends and the streets become more peaceful, domestic violence increases behind locked doors. Family feuds are revived by stressed-out, not-so-merry merrymakers.

All of this is rich material for crime writers. I believe Christmas has inspired more short stories than any other theme. From Sherlock Holmes to Jack Reacher, every crime series character of note has been involved in a festive mystery. It's no surprise that when Soho Press invited its authors to contribute to *The Usual Santas*, the office on Broadway was inundated with stories.

From its beginning in 1986, Soho has set out to publish the best of international crime fiction, so this festive collection is unlike any other in that the writers live in four different continents and have chosen to interpret the seasonal theme in the most colorful and exotic plots imaginable. You will be transported to Sweden, North Korea, Thailand, Ireland, New York City, Utah, Italy, France, Denmark and England. And you will time-travel to Cesena in the era of the Borgias, Bath when Jane Austen resided there, Paris at the close of the nineteenth century, a prison camp in the darkest days of the Korean War and Armagh during Northern Ireland's Troubles. For readers looking for the traditional Christmas, there is snow, Santa Claus (in numbers) and the birth of a child. Those with a taste for noir will find it in the shape of cunningly plotted killing, casual murder, assassination and dismemberment. And still there is room for heart-rending suspense and hot romance between the world's greatest consulting detective and the one he always called *the* woman.

For me, one of the joys of the festive season is the opportunity to give and receive surprises. I won't spoil yours as you turn these pages, but I'd better warn you there are shocks in plenty. Nothing will top the appearance of the heavenly host to those hapless shepherds, but there is plenty here to get your heart thumping.

"JOY TO THE WORLD"

**Various Acts of
Kindness at Christmas**

AN ELDERLY LADY SEEKS
PEACE AT CHRISTMASTIME

Helene Tursten

translated from the Swedish by Marlaine Delargy

 HELENE TURSTEN was born in Göteborg, Sweden, where she now lives with her husband and daughter. She was a nurse and a dentist before she turned to writing. Her books have been translated into twenty languages and made into a critically acclaimed Swedish television series. She is the author of a mystery series set in Göteborg, Sweden, which features police detective Irene Huss, a jujitsu champion, the mother of twin teenage girls, and the wife of a chef. The Irene Huss books are fan favorites because of the way they mingle an icy cold Scandinavian noir setting with the personal life and professional concerns of a hardworking everywoman detective character. The novels include *Detective Inspector Huss*, *Night Rounds*, *The Torso*, *The Glass Devil*, *The Golden Calf*, *The Beige Man*, *The Treacherous Net*, *Who Watcheth*, and *Protected by the Shadows*. In addition to the Irene Huss series, Helene Tursten is the author of the Embla Nystrom series, which begins with *Hunting Ground*, forthcoming from Soho Crime, and of many short stories, including the stories about Maud, the sociopathic octogenarian featured in "An Elderly Lady Seeks Peace at Christmastime."

The churchyard was silent and peaceful so early on the morning of Christmas Eve. Maud couldn't help sighing loudly as she struggled along the snow-covered path. It didn't matter, because she was all alone. At this time of day there wasn't a living soul in sight, and she was unlikely to disturb the others. The rubber wheels of her walker twisted sideways as it plowed through the deep snow, but eventually, after a certain amount of difficulty, she managed to park it next to the grave. She took the special grave lanterns and a box of matches out of the bag in the wheeled walker's wire basket. Two lanterns on the family grave would have to do—one for her parents and one for her sister. Such things were expensive these days.

Her older sister had been named Charlotte. Maud had come along eleven years after Charlotte's birth, much to her parents' surprise and her sister's disgust. Being an only child had suited Charlotte perfectly; a little sister definitely wasn't on her wish list.

Maud thought back to the lavish parties her parents used to throw. She particularly remembered the big party they traditionally hosted on New Year's Eve. She recalled the delicious food, the candles burning brightly in the tall candelabras, the champagne corks popping at midnight, the hum of cheerful voices, the smell of cigars and expensive perfume. And of course the beautiful dresses the ladies wore.

Everything had come to an abrupt end when her darling father suffered a heart attack during an Odd Fellows meeting.

He had collapsed in the middle of a guffaw after someone told a funny story.

For a number of reasons, her mother had very little to laugh about after his death. It turned out that his affairs were "in a bit of a mess," as people said. Once the family lawyer had settled all his debts, there was virtually nothing left. The large property her father had bought several years earlier had to be sold; the only thing the widow was allowed to keep was the apartment they lived in.

Maud's mother was fifteen years younger than her father and ought to have been able to soldier on, but it was as if all the strength simply drained out of her and was buried along with him. Two years later, she too was dead. Maud often thought that the shame of their financial and social disgrace had probably broken her mother. She herself had been eighteen when the fatal blow struck her family; she had just started college, where she was training to be a teacher of English and French.

A year or so before their father died, Charlotte had developed what her mother referred to as "nerves." Apparently Charlotte was "a sensitive, artistic soul." She was thirty years old and still unmarried when the war broke out. Her hypochondria and a growing list of phobias filled her life completely. Charlotte was a trained pianist, but had never performed in public. Nor could she cope with teaching the piano at home.

The limited amount of capital that was left after the sale of the property diminished rapidly during the war. Luckily, the sisters had inherited the lease of the apartment from their mother and were able to live there rent-free. However, they still had to pay for electricity, water, and heating. Maud remembered how bitterly cold the apartment had been during those terrible winters. The ice that had formed on the inside of the windows was so thick they couldn't see out. They lived in the kitchen and the bedroom, keeping the doors tightly closed to retain any warmth. The other rooms were left unheated.

During the war Maud got a job as a teacher at a girls' high school. She loved it right from the start. However, her financial situation didn't improve a great deal because she also had to provide for Charlotte.

The flickering flames of the candles illuminated the worn inscription on the tall gravestone. Charlotte had died thirty-seven years ago. Only then had Maud's own life begun. Better late than never, she thought.

The cold nipping at her toes brought her back to the present. Her boots were warm, but the lining was getting threadbare. Perhaps she should buy herself a new pair.

Laboriously, she began to maneuver the walker toward the path, which had not been cleared. Heavy snow had fallen overnight. When she listened carefully, she could hear a distant rumble that sounded as if it might be a tractor. A harsh scraping confirmed her suspicions; the snow plow was on its way. She congratulated herself on the fact that there was nothing wrong with her hearing. Most of her contemporaries were practically deaf. But not Maud. Which was perhaps a shame. If she had been deaf, she wouldn't have been troubled by the Problem.

Resolutely, she pushed all thoughts of the Problem aside and set off toward the bus stop, which was just outside the churchyard gate; she was quite out of breath by the time she got there, and had to sit down for a while on the waterproof seat of her walker. It was such a handy gadget. Not that she really needed such a thing, but it had been left behind when herr Olsson, the civil engineer, passed away. None of his children had bothered to collect it. They probably didn't even know that the wheeled walker, which was kept just inside the door of the building, belonged to their father. After his apartment had been cleared and sold, it was still standing there, and Maud had simply picked it up and carried it into her own apartment. Last autumn she had twisted her knee when she tripped over a rug, and had reluctantly started to use the walker when she had to go out shopping. The sidewalks were very icy at the time, and she didn't want to risk falling again. She quickly became aware of its advantages: it provided useful support, she could sit on it and have a rest, she was now offered a seat on the bus, people held the door open for her when she went into the stores, and middle-aged female shop assistants started treating her politely and . . . well, they really were quite sweet to her. The walker was a brilliant acquisition.

ONCE SHE WAS SAFELY aboard the bus, her thoughts turned to Charlotte once more. Her sister had crept around their big, gloomy apartment like a restless soul, refusing to go out. Her mental state had deteriorated rapidly during the 1960s. There was no point in suggesting that Maud might get away, even for one day. Her sister would go even more crazy than she already was. Little Charlotte couldn't possibly manage all on her own! Who would cook her meals and make sure she took her medication? Who would be there when the fear dug its claws into her?

The worst thing was that it was all true. As Charlotte's illness gradually got worse, she needed stronger and stronger medication. She spent most of her time in a befuddled torpor; she should really have gone into an institution. Whenever her doctor suggested some kind of residential care, Charlotte always came to life and said sharply, "My sister would never allow such a thing! She and I have always lived together! She looks after me!"

Charlotte had been totally dependent on her sister for her daily care and survival. It didn't look as if Maud would ever have the opportunity to realize her own dreams.

At least until the evening when Maud was standing in the kitchen and suddenly felt a cold draft from the hallway. She hurried out to see what was going on, and found the front door standing open. In her confused state, Charlotte had managed to unlock the door and had wandered out into the gloom of the stairwell. Maud sensed rather than saw her sister moving past the elevator. There was a wide landing with a long stone staircase leading down to the main entrance of the apartment block. By the faint light seeping out from the elevator, Maud was just able to make out Charlotte's thin figure flitting anxiously to and fro. "Hello?" her voice echoed weakly. Slowly she moved closer to the edge of the landing. The stairs themselves were in total darkness. From Maud's point of view, it looked as if her sister was inching toward a black hole. The long, steep stone staircase . . .

The paralysis passed and she rushed toward the open door of the apartment. Charlotte was balancing on the top step. Maud had called out— or had she? She'd definitely tried to grab hold of her sister, hadn't she? She remembered feeling the slippery fabric of Charlotte's checked bathrobe against her fingertips but her sister pulled away and then . . . disappeared . . . down into the depths of the darkness.

Three weeks later, Charlotte had passed away as a result of the severe concussion she had sustained. Maud spent every minute by her bedside. Her sister never regained consciousness.

Over all the years that Maud had been responsible for their

joint finances, she had deposited the whole of her sister's sickness benefit in a special bank account. As time went by, it had grown into a tidy little sum. The day after the funeral, Maud booked her first trip. On the last day of the spring semester, she set off. She traveled by train and bus through Denmark, Germany and France. For the next fifteen years she spent the summer break in the same way, traveling all over the world. She had retired twenty-two years ago, and she had kept on traveling.

THE ICA GOURMET GROCERY store opened at nine o'clock in the morning on Christmas Eve. Maud could see the manager unlocking the door as she stepped off the bus. She plodded over through the slush. The manager waved to her.

"Good morning! You're bright and early!" he called out cheerfully.

Maud smiled back at him. He was the person she spoke to more than anyone else these days.

"I thought I'd get my shopping done before all those stressed-out people start rushing around," she said.

"Very wise, very wise indeed," the manager said with a chuckle as he stacked boxes of raisins into a neat pyramid.

The little store had been there for as long as Maud could remember. To begin with it had sold only dairy products, but then it had expanded to become a minimart. Nowadays it was a gourmet grocery store, selling ready meals that could simply be heated up in the oven or microwave. They were prepared in a restaurant kitchen just a few miles away. The store also sold other delicious foods such as fine cheeses, exotic fruits, fresh bread baked on the premises, and all the other life essentials.

Maud placed two small cartons of pickled herring rolls in the basket of her wheeled walker, followed by a larger pack of herring salad. They were soon joined by a Stilton cheese in a blue porcelain pot, a mature Gorgonzola, a piece of ripe Brie, a packet of salted crackers, an artisan loaf that was still warm, a bunch of grapes, fresh dates, a jar of fig conserve, two bottles of *julmust*, the traditional Christmas soft drink, a small pack of new potatoes from the Canaries, a few clementines and a box of After Eight chocolate mints. She was very pleased to find a portion of Jansson's Temptation, a potato and onion casserole, in the ready meal section, and quickly added it to her basket. Now there was only one thing missing from her Christmas table.

She pushed the walker over to the charcuterie counter. A young man who in Maud's opinion looked as if he was barely out of short pants was fiddling aimlessly with the prepackaged sausages on a shelf in front of the glass counter. Maud stopped beside him and said, "I'd like a small, ready-cooked Christmas ham, please."

The young man pulled out one of his earbuds. "What?"

Patiently Maud repeated what she had just said.

"Ready-cooked?" the boy echoed.

Maud nodded.

"I can, like, cut you some slices of that big one there. All the small ones are gone. There are so many old dudes living around here."

Maud thought his grin had something of a sneer about it. With considerable self-control, she nodded to indicate that she would like some slices of the ham behind the glass of the deli counter. As the boy walked past her he let out a loud yell that could be heard all over the store. The manager came rushing over from his pyramid of raisins, knocking the whole thing down in his panic.

"What's going on?" he wanted to know, sounding horrified.

"The old bat stabbed me!" the boy said, pointing an accusing finger at Maud.

She stooped over the handlebars of her walker.

"What? What's he saying?" she said in a reedy voice.

The manager looked from Maud to the assistant, unsure what to do.

"Go to the staff room and calm down!" he snapped at the boy.

"But the old bat—"

"Don't call the customer an old b- . . . that word!" the manager growled, his face turning an alarming shade of bright red.

"What did he say?" Maud chirped. She was finding it difficult not to laugh. Carefully she closed the big safety pin and slipped it back into her pocket. She had thrust it into that unpleasant young man's buttock with all her strength. It was time someone taught him a lesson about old women! The pin was used to attach a reflective disc on a cord to the lining of her right hand pocket.

"Staff room, now!" the manager repeated in a tone that brooked no disagreement.

As the teenager shambled away, the manager turned to Maud with a strained smile. "Please forgive the boy. He's only been here for a few days. He probably tripped and banged into a sharp corner. What can I get you?"

"I'd like four slices of your cooked ham. It's always so delicious," Maud replied, smiling sweetly.

SHE CARRIED THE WHEELED walker up the wide stone staircase. There was no longer any sign of the bent little old lady who had been so bewildered by all the fuss in the grocery store not long ago. For someone who would be ninety in a few years, she was unusually strong.

A short while later, she was sitting in her favorite armchair with a steaming cup of coffee and a ham sandwich with plenty of mustard. The spiced rye bread flavored with wort smelled wonderful. She put on her glasses and began to read the morning paper.

That was when the Problem began to make its presence felt.

Maud looked at the clock. It was just before ten-thirty. That was unusually early for the Problem. She sighed loudly and decided to try to ignore the whole thing for as long as possible. To her relief, the Problem stopped after a few minutes, and she was able to carry on with her reading.

AT AROUND TWO O'CLOCK, Maud was woken from her afternoon nap. The Problem was in full swing. It seemed worse than ever. No matter how hard she tried, she couldn't ignore it.

The apartment complex was five stories high and over a hundred years old. It was red brick built on a solid granite foundation. The ground floor housed a parking lot and a small number of shops. In spite of the fact that Maud lived on the first floor, her window was almost fifteen feet above the ground. The walls were thick. The only weakness was the system of pipes throughout the building. If Maud was standing in the bathroom, she could hear almost every word from the neighbors on the floor above. Particularly if they raised their voices—then she couldn't avoid hearing their exchanges.

And that was the Problem.

She couldn't pretend she didn't know about it, which was what she would have liked to do: to avoid getting involved in the Problem. All she wanted was peace and quiet.

But the Problem couldn't be ignored. Maud couldn't shut out the sound of raised voices—mainly his voice—and the woman's sobbing. And the heavy thuds when he hit her and knocked her down. *Thump-thump-thud* was the sound that came through the ceiling of Maud's bedroom.

The Problem had begun in the autumn last year, when a famous attorney and his wife bought the apartment above Maud's. They were middle-aged and wealthy, and their children had already left home. According to the rumors, he had kicked up an enormous fuss when he wasn't allocated a parking space, but there was a waiting list of several years, and he just had to put his name down like all the other residents. Meanwhile, he had to park his flashy Mercedes on the street.

After renovations lasting several months, the attorney and his wife had moved in just before Christmas the previous year. "Peace at last," Maud had thought. The noise of the building work had been unbearable.

Over the Christmas period exactly one year ago, Maud had realized that there was a big Problem. Christmas Eve was completely ruined, as far as she was concerned. The attorney had started abusing his wife in the afternoon, and had simply carried on doing so. Maud had been unable to concentrate on the film starring Fred Astaire and Ginger Rogers on TV that night. All she could hear was quarreling and shouting from upstairs.

Early on December twenty-sixth, an ambulance turned up. Maud opened the door of her apartment a fraction. She heard the attorney's well-modulated voice in the stairwell as he spoke to the paramedics:

"She fell down the stairs yesterday. I wanted to call you right away, but she didn't think it was anything serious. But when I saw how she looked today, I just had to call . . ."

Maud closed the door, screwing her face up in disgust. Fell down the stairs! What a revolting man! And he had ruined her Christmas.

After that, things were quiet for a few months. Twice during the spring she heard the attorney abusing his wife again. The week after Midsummer, Maud met the wife on the stairs. It was pouring outside, but in spite of the weather the woman was wearing huge sunglasses. She had wound a big scarf around her head and pulled it well down over her forehead. Her entire face was covered with a thick layer of dark foundation. It didn't help. Maud could clearly see the eye that was swollen shut, and the bruise like a purple half-moon over the cheekbone. They exchanged greetings, and the woman scurried past.

The charming attorney himself was a drinker. That was obvious to Maud whenever they passed on the stairs. He usually ignored her, but she couldn't miss the alcoholic fumes that lingered in his wake long after he had disappeared up the stairs to his apartment.

And now it was Christmas Eve once more, and the Problem was raising its ugly head again. Maud could hear the attorney's furious voice and his wife's sobs. *Thump-thump* came the familiar sound from the floor above.

It was high time she did something about the Problem. Deep down, Maud had already made the decision before the idea began to form in her conscious mind. She went into the bathroom. The voices emerged clearly from the toilet bowl, and the ventilation duct amplified the sound.

"Fucking bitch! You useless fucking . . ."

Bang-bang-thud.

Maud clenched her fists in impotent fury. The anger that flared inside her made her heart beat faster.

"Fix your face. You can't fucking go out looking like . . . to the parking meter," the attorney's voice echoed through the pipes.

Maud heard a sniveling mumble in response.

"I have to do everything myself . . . You are such a disgusting fucking mess . . . I'm going downstairs to get another ticket. You can't even do that right, you useless bitch! You were supposed to get a twenty-four-hour ticket! What do you mean, you don't have any money? Don't you dare . . . ?"

Thump-thump.

Heavy footsteps crossed the floor above Maud's head, moving toward the hallway. She quickly hurried into her own hallway; cautiously she opened the front door and left it on the latch. She pushed the wheeled walker onto the landing and placed it next to the elevator. Anyone coming down the stairs on the other side wouldn't be able to see it, nor would anyone stepping out of the elevator. The stairwell was lit by a brass art nouveau style lamp with a tulip-shaped glass shade. Without hesitation, Maud reached in and partially unscrewed the bulb. Now it wouldn't come on.

As she heard the door open on the floor above, she positioned herself behind the wheeled walker. She gripped the rubber handlebars firmly and waited.

Mumbling and muttering to himself, the attorney stumbled down the stairs. He was playing with the loose change in his coat pocket, trying to scoop it into his hand. He stopped right outside the elevator, fiddling with the coins. Maud could have reached out and touched his right shoulder. His boozy breath made her nostrils flare.

"Not enough cash . . . have to use my card . . . can't see a fucking thing . . ."

Swaying unsteadily, the attorney moved toward the wide marble staircase. Maud tensed her muscles. When he reached the edge of the top step, she summoned all her strength and shot across the landing, cannoning into his calves with the walker.

"What the f—"

That was all the attorney managed to say before he lost his balance and tumbled down the stairs, his arms waving helplessly. The dark, flapping overcoat made him look like a clumsy bat. Or possibly a vampire, Maud thought as she hurried back to her apartment. She did, however, remember to screw the bulb back in place before she went inside. She parked the wheeled walker just behind the door as usual. She didn't bother checking to see whether the attorney was still alive. The heavy thud when he hit the floor at the bottom of the staircase had sounded like a coconut being split open.

ONLY WHEN MAUD HEARD the sirens stop wailing outside the main door of the apartment block did she open her own front door.

The neighbor opposite was standing in the stairwell, looking terribly upset.

"What's going on?" Maud asked, making an effort to appear slightly confused.

"Oh, I'm so glad you're home . . . I was just going to ring the bell . . . it's the attorney . . . he's fallen down the stairs," the neighbor attempted to explain.

A young police officer came up and introduced himself to both women.

"Do you happen to know who the gentleman is?" he asked politely.

He was addressing the neighbor, who was at least twenty years younger than Maud. She told him the attorney's name and where he lived. The police officer nodded and said he would go and tell the man's wife what had happened.

"Those stairs are lethal. My sister fell down them," Maud

said in a weak voice, pointing with a trembling finger. All at once the neighbor looked calmer.

"But Maud, my dear, that was before Gunnar and I moved in. And we've lived here for thirty-five years," she said, giving the police officer a meaningful glance.

She placed a protective arm around Maud's shoulders and steered her toward her apartment.

"Let's get you inside. You're very welcome to join us this evening if you like, but the children and grandchildren are coming over after they've watched Donald Duck on TV, so it might be a bit too noisy for you . . ."

The question remained hanging in the air, and Maud quickly grabbed hold of it and said, "No, thank you. It's very kind of you, but . . . no thank you. I've got my television."

Behind her she heard one of the paramedics say to his colleague, "He stinks like a distillery."

THE AMBULANCE AND THE police car had gone. Someone had come to collect the attorney's weeping wife.

Maud arranged all the goodies she had bought for her Christmas dinner on a tea cart. She poured herself an ice-cold Aalborgs Aquavit to go with the herring. It had been a stressful day, and she felt that she had earned a little drink. The delicious aroma of Jansson's Temptation was coming from the oven. Satisfied with the sight of the laden cart, she pushed it into the TV room and sank down into her armchair with a sigh of contentment.

At long last, the peace of Christmas descended on the old apartment block.

THE USUAL SANTAS

Mick Herron

MICK HERRON was born in Newcastle and studied English at Oxford. He is the author of eleven novels: *Down Cemetery Road*, *The Last Voice You Hear*, *Why We Die*, *Smoke and Whispers*, *Reconstruction*, *Slow Horses*, *Dead Lions*, *Nobody Walks*, *Real Tigers*, *Spook Street*, and *This Is What Happened*, as well as the novella *The List*. His work has been nominated for the Macavity, Barry, Shamus, and CWA Steel Dagger Awards, and he has won an Ellery Queen Readers Award and the CWA Gold Dagger for Best Crime Novel. He lives in Oxford and works in London.

Whiteoaks, the brochures explained, was more than a shopping center: it was a Day Out For The Whole Family; a Complete Retail Experience Under Just One Roof. It was an Ideally Situated Outlet Village—an Ultra-Convenient Complex For The Ultra-Modern Consumer. It was where Quality met Design to form an Affordable Union. It might have been a Stately Pleasure Dome. It was possibly a Garden Of Earthly Delight. It was almost certainly where Capital Letters went to Die.

More precisely, it was on the outskirts of one of London's northwest satellite towns, and, viewed from above, resembled a glass and steel rendering of a giant octopus dropped headfirst onto the landscape. In the gaps between its outstretched tentacles were parks and play areas and public conveniences, and at each of its two main entrances were garages offering, in addition to the usual services, full valet coverage, 4-wheel alignment and diagnostic analysis, as well as free air and a Last-Minute One-Stop-Shop. Cart stations—colored pennants hoisted above them for swift location—were positioned at those intervals market research had determined user-friendly, and were assiduously tended by liveried cart-jockeys. From ten minutes before dusk until ten after daybreak the area was bathed in gentle orange light, the quiet humming of CCTV cameras a constant reminder that your security was Whiteoaks' concern. And in a hedged-off corner between the center's electricity substation and one of four home-delivery loading bays—perhaps the only point in the complex to which the word "accessible" did not apply—lurked a furtive row of recycling bins, like a consumerist *memento mori*.

As for the interior, it was a contemporary cathedral, sacred to the pursuit of retail opportunity. There was a food mall, a clothing avenue, and an entertainment hall; there were wings dedicated to white goods ("all your domestic requirements satisfied!"), pampering ("full body tan in minutes!") and financial services ("consolidate your debts—ask us how!"). There was a boulevard of sporting goods, a bridleway of gardening supplies; a veritable Hatton Garden of jewelers. No franchise ever heard of went unrepresented, and several never before encountered had multiple outlets. Whiteoaks' delicatessens carried sweetmeats from as near as Abbotsbury and as far as Zywocice; its bookshops shelved volumes by every author its readers could imagine, from Bill Bryson to Jeremy Clarkson. The shopper who is tired of Whiteoaks, it might easily be asserted, is a shopper who is tired of credit. During the summer, light washed down from the recessed contours of its cantilevered ceilings, and during the winter it did exactly the same. Temperature, too, was regulated and constant, and in this it matched everything else. At Whiteoaks, you could buy raspberries in winter and tinsel in July. Seasonal variation was discouraged as an unnecessary brake on impulse purchasing.

Which was not to say that Whiteoaks ignored the passage of the year; rather, it measured the months in a manner appropriate to its customers' needs. As surely as Father's Day follows Mother's, as unalterably as Harry Potter gives way to the Great Pumpkin, time marches on; its inevitable progress registering as peaks and troughs in a never-ending flow chart.

For there are only seventeen Major Feasts in the calendar of the Complete Retail Experience.

And the greatest of these is Christmas.

AT WHITEOAKS CHRISTMAS SLIPPED in slowly, subliminally, with the faint rustle of a paperchain in early September, and the echo of a jingle bell as October turned. Showing almost saintly restraint, however, it did not unleash its reindeer until Halloween had been wholly remaindered. After that, it was open season. Taking full advantage of its layout, the complex boasted eight Santa's Grottos—one per tentacle—each employing a full complement of sleigh, sacks, elves, snowflakes, friendly squirrels, startled rabbits, and (counterintuitively, but fully validated by merchandise-profiling) talking zebras. And, of course, each had its own Santa. Or, more accurately, each had an equal share in a rotating pool of Santas, for the eight Santas hired annually by the Whiteoaks Festive Governance Committee had swiftly worked out that no single one of them wanted to spend an entire two-month hitch marooned in Haberdashery's backwater, or worse still, abandoned under fire in the high-pressure, noise-intensive combat zone of Toys and Games, while another took his ease in the Food Hall, pampered with cake and cappuccino by the surrounding franchisees. So a complicated but workable shift system had been established by the Santas themselves, whereby they chopped and changed each two-hour session, swapping grottos three times a day and generally sharing the burden along with the spoils. This worked so well, so much to everyone's satisfaction, that the first eight Santas hired by the Governance Committee remained the only Santas Whiteoaks needed, returning year after year to don their uniforms, attach their beards, and maintain an impressive 83% record of hardly ever swearing at children whose parents were in earshot.

Santa-ing was not an easy undertaking. It was not a task

for sissies. And while the Usual Santas didn't always do things by the book, by God, they got the job done!

And each year, once they'd managed just that—after the shops had lowered shutters on Christmas Eve, and Whiteoaks slumbered, preparatory to the Boxing Day rush—the Santas met in a hospitality room adjoining the security suite, and relaxed over a buffet provided by the grateful merchants of the quarter, and exchanged war stories until the hour grew late, and generally luxuriated in the absence of children.

But however relaxed they grew, they kept their beards on. And remained zipped inside their red suits. And never addressed each other as anything other than "Santa"; and in fact, would have been unable to do so had they wanted, because while they might, for all they knew, be friends and neighbors in civvy street—might drink in the same pub, or regularly catch the same bus to the same football ground—on duty they remained in uniformed character, and always had done. This had started in jest but had quickly hardened into custom. Not long after that, it calcified into superstition. In their dealings with toddlers and hyperactive infants, the Usual Santas had suffered in undignified, frequently unhygienic ways that had bonded them in a manner few civilians could hope to understand, but on every other level they were strangers to each other. And with this, they were perfectly comfortable.

Until, one day . . .

THE BUFFET THAT YEAR was particularly handsome. There were sausage rolls and bowls of crisps; there were slices of ham and fingers of fish; there were rice salads, and things on cocktail sticks, and mince pies, and individual plum puddings. There was a huge plateful of turkey-and-stuffing sandwiches.

There were Christmas pizzas: deep and crisp and even more cheesy. There were eight paper plates, and eight plastic knives and forks. There were eight red napkins with jolly Rudolph patterns. And, most crucially of all, there were several large bottles of brandy and eight glass snifters.

The Santas turned up one by one. Whiteoaks had emptied of punters, but still: it would never do for two Santas to be seen together in public.

The first to arrive poured himself a brandy, downed it in a single swallow, poured another, then helped himself to a turkey sandwich. "Ho, ho, ho!" he said as the door opened behind him.

"Ho, ho, ho! Indeed," the incoming Santa agreed. He too headed straight for the brandy. "What a day," he said. "What. A. Day."

"Christmas Eve."

They both nodded. The words carried a weight a non-Santa couldn't hope to understand.

"You know what happened to me? I was—"

"Ho, ho, ho!"

"Ho, ho, ho!" they both replied as another Santa entered.

Whatever had happened to Santa became lost in a general flurry of opening doors and greetings and fillings of glasses. Joe, the security guard popped his head in too. He wouldn't stop for a drink.

"Let yourselves out through the emergency exit, yes? I'll leave you the master so the alarm doesn't go off. Just pop it through the box when you're done."

"Of course," said Santa. He put the key on the table. "Merry Christmas, Joe."

"Merry Christmas, Santas. Mind how you go with that brandy."

"Ho, ho, ho!"

Joe left.

And Santa arrived. "Ho, ho, ho!" he said.

"Ho, ho, ho!"

"Blimey. Christmas Eve, eh?"

Christmas Eve, they agreed.

Soon the room was full of Santas, bundled round the buffet table; each with glass or plate in hand, and most of them talking at once.

"Blinking cheek of him! Sitting on my knee, bold as brass, says if you're the real Santa, how come your reindeer's plastic?"

"So I said, you know like on *Dr. Who*? You know like this Tardis? Bigger on the inside? So's my sleigh. And *that's* how come it fits all the presents in."

"I don't have a glass."

"I told her, course you don't need a chimney, darlin'. I carry a magic chimney with me. Pop it on your roof, Bob's your uncle. That dried her tears, I can tell you. You can borrow that line, if you like. No charge for a fellow Santa!"

"I don't have a glass."

"The next flamin' elf who tries to tell me Santa's suit should really be green, I'll—"

"Excuse me," said Santa in a loud voice. "But I don't have a glass!"

The Santas' chatter died away.

"Well, someone must have two," said Santa, jovially. "There were eight when we started."

"Nobody's got two," Santa said. "That's the point."

"What's the point?"

"There aren't eight of us here," Santa said. "There are nine."

There was a communal intake of yuletide breath.

"Ha!" said Santa. "I mean, ho! You must have added up wrong."

"I don't think so. You try."

The Santas fell to counting.

Then all started talking at once.

"But—?"

"What—?"

"I—?"

"Ho—!"

At length, Santa quietened the assembly by tapping his glass on the table. "Well," he said. "It seems I owe Santa an apology. One of us appears to be an impostor."

"Pretending to be Santa!" Santa said angrily. "I never heard of such a thing in my life!"

The Santas looked at him.

"Well, you know what I mean."

"Perhaps," Santa said, "we should have a quick roll call."

"What, where you call out 'Santa' and we say 'Present'?" Santa asked. "Did you see what I did there?" he added.

"That's not what I meant, no," Santa said. "I meant, we should all state clearly where we were today. The impostor Santa will have an impossible itinerary."

"Sounds like a plan," Santa admitted. "Who's going first?"

"Well, I was at the food hall this morning," Santa said. "Then electronics. No, then leisure. After that I was at—"

"You can't have been at electronics next," Santa objected. "I was electronics, second shift."

"No, that's what I said," said Santa. "Then leisure, then—"

"I finished up at leisure," Santa said. "Before that, I was at clothing, and before that books. Or was that yesterday?"

"Must have been today," Santa offered through a mouthful of sausage roll. "Because that's what *I* did yesterday."

"Oh, this is hopeless," said Santa. "Could we all just stop milling about?"

"If we all stop *milling about*," Santa said, "the Santas nearest the table will eat all the food."

There was general assent to this. Some of the more suspicious Santas immediately reloaded their plates.

"We need order," Santa said. "We need clarity. Everyone should write down their day's shifts."

"That's right," Santa said, reaching past him for a sandwich. "We should make a list."

"We should check it twice," Santa muttered.

"I heard that."

"Does anyone have a pen and paper?" Santa asked.

Nobody had a pen and paper.

"There's an elf behind this," said Santa. "Mark my words."

The elves were not popular with the Santas. They tended to be disruptive, and argumentative, and frequently indulged in non-traditional banter.

Santa said, "Why don't we take our suits off? See who we really are?"

"Which would help how?" Santa enquired testily.

"I was only saying," Santa mumbled into his beard.

"No, Santa has a point," Santa said. "We'd soon find out if we had an elf among us, if we took our suits off."

"Nobody is taking their suit off," Santa said sternly. "It would be—well, it wouldn't be right!"

"Hmm," Santa said. "That's *exactly* what an elf would say, if he was about to be unmasked."

"I hope you're not suggesting what I think you're suggesting," warned Santa.

"Everyone calm down," Santa said. "It's clear none of us is an elf. We're all far too shapely."

"Quite," Santa agreed. "Anyway, the elves are at their own party. They've gone clubbing."

The Santas shuddered.

"I don't suppose it would do any good to ask the impostor to put his hand up?" Santa suggested. "On an amnesty basis? He's welcome to stay and enjoy the buffet."

"Do you mean that?" Santa asked. "Or do you really think we should beat him up?"

Santa sighed. "Well, he's hardly likely to put his hand up now, is he?"

"Oh," said Santa. "Yes. Yes, I see what you mean. I shouldn't have said that, should I?"

Everyone helped themselves to more food and brandy. The Santa without a glass was making do with a hastily scraped-out trifle dish, though—as he pointed out several times—being last to arrive did not make him the impostor; on the contrary, the fact that he'd had farthest to come—all the way from Gardening—*proved* he was the genuine article, as well as indicating high career-commitment. Since his bowl held three times as much as a glass, and he was emptying it twice as quickly, the other Santas agreed with him, then sat him down in a chair.

"Well," Santa said at last. "Anyone got any ideas?"

Santas hummed and Santas hah-ed.

At length, a Santa spoke. "Suppose . . ."

A hush dropped over the assembly like a cloth on a budgie's cage.

"Yes?" Santa prompted.

'Suppose . . ." said Santa. "Well, suppose this impostor is the *real* Santa?"

A subtly different silence fell.

"Twit," said Santa, *sotto voce*.

"I heard that."

"There's no such thing as Santa," Santa pointed out.

"I can count nine of us."

"A real Santa, Santa meant."

"Who's to say—"

"Don't!" Santa interrupted. "*Don't* say, who's to say what's real and what isn't! Because I hate that sort of nonsense!"

"I was only going to say," Santa continued, "that in order to be the real Santa, our friend would simply need to *believe* that he's the real Santa."

The Santas considered this.

"That's pretty much what Santa told you not to say," Santa said at last.

"No, it's a different thing entirely."

"And anyway," Santa began.

"Anyway what?"

"If there *is* a real Santa—"

"Big if!"

"—or even just someone who *believes* he's the real Santa—"

"Which would make him a bloomin' loony," Santa muttered.

"—then why on earth would he come to Whiteoaks?"

The Santas considered this.

"Why wouldn't he?" Santa asked.

"Because it's a disgusting, crass, horrible place," Santa said. "That's why not!"

The Santas recoiled in horror.

"There!" said Santa. "I've said it!"

"Shh!"

"Quiet!"

"Don't!"

One by one, the Santas looked toward the door to the adjoining security room, where banks of closed-circuit monitors hummed; and where, just possibly, subversive and treasonous opinion was being recorded for later investigation.

"It's all right," Santa said. "We're the last ones here."

The Santas relaxed.

"And besides, it's true."

A delicious guilty knowledge susurrated through the Santas, like a winter's wind adjusting a snowdrift.

"We-ell . . ."

"Well, yes."

"Well, yes, it is."

The Santas nodded, one after the other. It was true. Whiteoaks *was* horrible, unless you liked autonomous commercialism writ huge, in which any suspicion of non-franchised individuality was stamped on before it made waves. The trouble was, the Santas had few alternatives as far as employment went. The local shops they'd once Santa-ed for had closed when Whiteoaks opened.

"But don't you see?" Santa said. "That's precisely why he'd come here!"

Santa said, "How do you mean?"

"Why would Santa bother visiting, I don't know, an orphanage or a children's hospital or a home for waifs and strays," Santa asked, "when the whole *point* of Santa is that he goes where he's needed?"

"Like Whiteoaks? Ha!"

"Ho!"

"I meant ho!"

"Exactly like Whiteoaks," Santa insisted obstinately. "Look at it. It's a soulless temple to rampant commercialism. It wouldn't know the meaning of Christmas if it came with a buy-one, get-one-free sticker. It's crying out for Santa, for criminy's sake!"

"But it has eight Santas," Santa said. "It has us. The Usual Santas."

A pleading note had crept into his voice.

"But it doesn't have the *real* Santa," Santa said quietly. "A Santa to teach it that profit isn't everything."

"That money doesn't matter."

"That it's better to give than to receive."

"That items can't be returned without a receipt."

The Santas stared.

"Sorry," Santa said. "I was thinking about something else."

The Santas fell silent.

Santa picked the last unempty bottle from the table, and passed it round the company. One after the other, the Santas solemnly filled their glasses; by a long-practiced choreography, each pouring an exact amount (except for Santa, who poured exactly three times that amount) which precisely drained the bottle to its last drop. Then each eyed the other morosely.

"If I have to wish one more kiddy a Merry Whiteoaks Christmas—" Santa began.

"—or remind one more parent where to go for all their yuletide needs—" Santa continued.

"—or explain one more time that Santa's gifts are for children with store-validated tokens only—" Santa embellished.

"—I don't know what I'll do," Santa admitted.

Though all agreed that it might involve punching an elf.

Santa by Santa, they raised their glasses; Santa by Santa, they drained them dry. Then, simultaneously, they plonked them down on the table, forming a neat row of eight brandy snifters and a small trifle dish.

"Well," Santa said. "Do I need to spell out our next move?"

"I think we're of one mind," said Santa.

"All for one?" asked Santa.

"And one for all," Santa replied.

"A Santa's gotta do—" said Santa.

"—what a Santa's gotta do," Santa agreed.

"It's a far, far better thing . . ." Santa began.

". . . I can never remember the end of that quote," said Santa, after a slight pause.

"Gentlemen," said Santa. "To the grottos!"

WHAT BECAME KNOWN AS the Great Whiteoaks Christmas Looting was never solved—whoever coordinated the daredevil heist had somehow contrived to get hold of a master key, which not only gave access to every shop on every floor of every avenue of the complex, but also allowed every alarm and CCTV monitor to be switched off. Nor, given the tendency of store managers to estimate losses upwards for insurance purposes, was it clear exactly how much was stolen. Police investigations did suggest, however, that some very big sacks must have been used.

And nor was there any obvious connection between the daring robbery and the appearance, on Christmas morning, of some very big sacks on the doorsteps of the surprisingly large number of children's hospitals, orphanages and homes for waifs and strays to be found in the surrounding countryside. The sacks contained toys and games, and books and clothes, and food and drink, and sporting goods, and any number of DVDs and mobile phones and Wii consoles, and some little sewing kits, and various beauty products, and brochures containing useful information about how to consolidate debt, liquidate assets and set up a trust fund, and the odd item of gardening equipment, and some small brown muslin bags which proved to be full of not-quite-priceless but certainly very expensive jewelry. This, the governors, directors and head nurses of the various establishments concerned swiftly liquidated into cash which they then used to set up trust funds, to ensure that all their charges' future Christmases would be celebrated in an appropriately festive manner. And also to give themselves a small raise because it was valuable and underappreciated work that they did.

Back at Whiteoaks, the only thing approaching a clue that was ever discovered came to light some weeks later, when a truck arrived to collect a recycling bin that was stuffed full of Valentine's Day cards. As it was moved, a large red and white bundle rolled into view. This turned out, on closer inspection, to be made up of nine Santa suits and nine Santa hats.

And eight false bushy white beards.

PX CHRISTMAS

Martin Limón

 MARTIN LIMÓN retired from military service after twenty years in the US Army, including ten years in Korea. He is the author of eleven books in a critically acclaimed mystery series set on the US 8th Army base in Seoul, South Korea, in the early 1970s, at the height of the Cold War, when tensions between Communist North Korea and the US-allied South were at a volatile peak. The series features CID investigator George Sueño, a Mexican American US Army sergeant, who, together with his partner, Ernie Bascom, investigates crimes that involve the American soldiers stationed in South Korea.

The Sueño and Bascom series includes: *Jade Lady Burning, Slicky Boys, Buddha's Money, The Door to Bitterness, Wandering Ghost, GI Bones, Mr. Kill, The Joy Brigade, The Iron Sickle, The Ville Rat, Ping-Pong Heart, The Nine-Tailed Fox*, and the short story collection *Nightmare Range*. He lives near Seattle.

Staff Sergeant Riley slapped his pointer against the flip-chart and barked out the title of today's training session. "Suicide Prevention," he shouted. Then he lowered the pointer and paced in a small circle as if contemplating all the burdens of the universe. He looked up suddenly and aimed the pointer at me.

"Sueño. How many Eighth Army personnel committed suicide during last year's holiday season?"

I shook my head. "*Molla* the hell out of me."

He growled, glancing around the room. There were about thirty GIs in various stages of somnolence slouched listlessly in hard wooden seats. About half were 8th Army Criminal Investigation Agents and the other half MPI, Military Police Investigators.

Riley slammed his pointer on the table in front of him. "On your *feet!*" he shouted.

Slowly, every student rose to a mostly upright position. The last person up, as usual, was my investigative partner, Ernie Bascom.

"Okay, Bascom. Do you know who General Nettles is?"

"He's the *freaking* Chief of Staff," Ernie replied.

"Out*standing*," Riley said. "And do you know how many ways he can screw up your life if he takes a mind to?"

"About thirty?" Ernie ventured.

"At least," Riley said. "He can mess up your life and the life of every swinging dick in this room in about as many ways as you can imagine." Riley paused to let the dramatic tension grow. "And there's no doubt in my military mind that that's exactly what he'll do if the 8th Army Christmas suicide rate doesn't come down and come down *fast*. Is that understood?"

A few bored voices said, "Understood." Then someone asked, "Can we sit back down now?" Riley barked, "Take your *seats!*" Which everyone did.

My name is George Sueño. I'm an agent for the 8th United States Army Criminal Investigation Division in Seoul, Republic of Korea. Riley wasn't telling us anything we didn't know. When you're stationed overseas, pretty much constantly harassed by the pressures of military life, and Christmas rolls around and you're pulling patrol along the Demilitarized Zone between North and South Korea, life can become pretty depressing. Some guys fire a 7.62 mm round into their cranium. Others eat a hand grenade. This, of course, causes quite a bit of consternation back home. Not only do the moms and dads and wives and brothers and sisters complain about the suicide rate but more importantly—as far as the honchos of 8th Army are concerned—Congress complains about it. And Congress controls military funding. So the Department of the Army rolls the shit ball downhill from the Pentagon to the Pacific Command to 8th Army headquarters to the Provost Marshal's office until it splats into those of us working law enforcement on the front lines.

Now that Riley had our attention, he said, "You're probably wondering what law enforcement personnel have to do with suicide prevention." Then he grinned, taking on the visage of a death's head. "The Chief of Staff is initiating a new program. We're going to be proactive. All personnel who seem to be displaying evidence of depression or suicidal thoughts will be placed in the new twenty-four-hour, seven-day-a-week Suicide Prevention Program. They'll be provided counseling and psychiatric treatment if necessary and they'll be kept under observation at all times."

"They'll be locked up," Ernie said.

Riley glared at him. "Not locked up. They'll be provided extra care. And extra training. We want to make sure they make it through the season without harming themselves."

Another of the investigators raised his hand. "Once they're stuck in this Suicide Prevention Program, will they be allowed to leave?"

Riley looked embarrassed and turned to his flipchart. After tossing back a few sheets, he found his answer. "They'll be allowed to leave upon release by medical personnel and the OIC." The officer in charge.

"So they'll be locked up," Ernie repeated.

"Can it, Bascom," Riley told him.

"What about us?" another guy asked. "What are we supposed to do?"

"You'll be picking them up."

"You mean, taking them into custody."

Riley shrugged. "It's thought that since CID agents and MP Investigators work in civilian clothes it will be less obtrusive if you take them in rather than having armed and uniformed MPs make the pickup."

"You want to make it look as if we're not treating them as criminals."

"Which we are," Ernie added.

"I told you to *can* it, Bascom."

Riley flipped through the sheets until he found a map of the Korean Peninsula. Assignments were made based on geography, starting in Seoul, then working south and north. We'd be receiving a list daily as to who to pick up, the name of the unit they were assigned to, and where they worked. Then we were to transport them over to the new Suicide Prevention facility behind the 121st Evacuation Hospital here on Yongsan Compound South Post.

"Any questions?" Riley shouted.

Ernie raised his hand. "What about me and Sueño? You didn't give us an assignment."

"You two are staying on the black market detail."

A guffaw went up from the crowd. Some wise guy said, "Somebody has to protect the PX from the *yobos*." The derogatory term for the Korean wives of enlisted soldiers.

Ernie flipped him the bird.

As everyone filed out of the training room, somebody murmured, "Lock 'em up. That'll help lift their spirits."

WE SAT IN ERNIE'S jeep outside of the Yongsan Main PX, the largest US Army Post Exchange in Korea. With only ten shopping days until Christmas, the place was packed.

"I don't get it," Ernie said. "What the hell are they *buying*?"

"Presents," I said.

"Like *what*?"

Ernie stared at me, honestly wanting an answer.

"Like toys for kids," I told him, "or clothes for the family or decorations for the house. How the hell would I know?"

We were both single, in our twenties, and we both lived in the barracks. About the only things we ever purchased were laundry soap and shoe polish for Korean houseboys who made our beds and kept our uniforms looking sharp. And consumables, like beer, liquor and the occasional meal of *kalbi*, marinated short ribs, or *yakimandu*, fried dumplings dipped in soy sauce. That was about all we ever went shopping for.

Here in the mid-1970s, in the middle of the Cold War,

one would've thought that the honchos of 8th Army would've been primarily concerned about the 700,000 Communist North Korean soldiers just thirty miles north of here along the Korean DMZ and the fact that war could break out at any moment. One would've been wrong. What seemed to obsess the 8th Army bosses most was stopping the black marketing out of the PX and the Commissary.

Twenty years ago, at the end of the Korean War, the economy of the ROK was flat on its back. In Seoul and almost every other city in the country, hardly a building remained standing. Even the rice paddies, which had been plowed out of the fertile earth millennia ago, were fallow and overgrown with weeds. During the fighting that raged up and down the peninsula, virtually everyone had become a refugee. And those were the lucky ones. Estimates varied but it was believed that between two to three million Koreans had been killed during the war, this out of a population of about twenty-five million. Things were getting better. People for the most part had roofs over their head and were employed. However, wages were desperately low, and if you cleared a hundred bucks a month you were doing just fine.

Still, the demand for imported products was growing. Such things as American cigarettes, blended scotch, maraschino cherries, freeze dried coffee, instant orange juice, and powdered milk. The Korean economy wasn't producing those things. Not yet. And it was a crime for GIs to buy such items on base and sell them off base. The official reason was, supposedly, so fledgling Korean industries wouldn't have to compete with cheap foreign products, thereby giving them a chance to grow.

The real reason was more visceral. On a crowded shopping day like today, American officers and their wives hated to stand in long lines behind the *yobo*s, the Korean wives of GIs. Once legally married, the Korean wife was issued a military dependent ID card so she could come on base, and a Ration Control Plate, which allowed her to buy a specified dollar amount each month in the PX and the Commissary. Some of the wives resold what they purchased to black marketeers for twice or even three times what they paid for it. The extra money, for the most part, wasn't wasted. Often they had elderly parents to take care of or younger brothers and sisters to support. The money garnered from black marketing could often be the difference between continued misery for a family versus having a sporting chance to rise out of poverty. However, the 8th Army honchos didn't look at that side of it. They only knew that *their* PX and *their* Commissary was being invaded by foreigners.

It was my job, and Ernie's, to arrest these women for black marketing and thus keep the world safe for Colonels and their wives to be able to buy all the Tang and Spam and Pop Tarts their little hearts desired.

"So who should we bust?" Ernie asked.

We were watching the women parade out of the front door of the PX pushing their carts toward the taxi line.

"Those illuminated nativity scenes seem to be popular this year," I said.

"What?"

"Those." I pointed. "In the large cardboard box. Cheap plastic replicas of a manger and three wise men bowing before Baby Jesus. Just screw in a bulb and plug it into the wall."

"Koreans buy those?"

"Yeah. It makes sense. They can keep it indoors. Makes them seem modern."

"Modern? That happened two thousand years ago."

"Christianity came to Korea less than a century ago."

"They consider that modern?"

"Korea's four thousand years old, Ernie."

"Damn. People have been eating *kimchi* and rice all that time?"

I ignored him and studied the line. "Let's make one bust this morning and another this afternoon. That should keep the Provost Marshal off our butts."

"How about her?" Ernie said.

A statuesque young Korean woman wearing her black hair up in a bun and a blue dress that clung to her figure pushed a cart toward the taxi stand. The wait wasn't long. A black-jacketed Korean cab driver helped her put her bags in the trunk of his big Ford Granada, including one of the illuminated nativity scenes. After she was seated in back, the driver drove off. Ernie and I followed.

THE DRIVER WOUND HIS way through the narrow lanes of the district known as Itaewon and finally came to a stop in front of a wooden double door in a ten-foot-high stone fence. Keeping well back, Ernie stopped the jeep and I climbed out and crept up to the alleyway and peered around the corner. The trunk remained open as the statuesque woman conferred with an elderly woman who Ernie and I both recognized as a well-known black market mama-san. Money changed hands and then some product. I motioned to Ernie and he started the jeep's engine and rolled forward, blocking the taxi's escape. I hurried forward, showed the woman my badge and told her she was under arrest for the illegal sale of PX-purchased goods. Even in the US it's illegal to resell PX goods. The idea is that the shipment and the warehousing of the goods is subsidized by the US taxpayer, to keep prices low for servicemen and their families. To resell under those conditions would be to rip off the taxpayer who is footing much of the bill.

We had no jurisdiction over the mama-san who purchased the goods. We could've reported her to the Korean National Police, but they already knew about her operation and were probably receiving a cut of her profits. We didn't bother. The younger woman was nervous and close to tears but willing to comply. Ernie pulled forward and allowed the cab driver to leave. Then we sat the distraught woman in the back of the jeep and drove her to the 8th Army MP Station.

While I filled out the arrest report, Ernie called her husband, one Roland R. Garfield, Specialist Four, assigned to the 19th Support Group, Electronic Repair Detachment (Mobile). When he arrived his face was grim. His wife, whose name I'd determined was Sooki, nervously fondled a pink handkerchief and dabbed tears from her eyes.

He was a slender man, with moist brown eyes and a narrow face that was filled out by surprisingly full cheeks. I didn't bother to shake his hand. He didn't seem to be in the mood. I showed him the arrest report, had him sign it, and turned over an onion-skin copy.

"You're responsible at all times for the actions of your dependent," I told him.

"I know that."

"You'll retain PX and Commissary privileges but the amount of the monthly ration will be reduced." By about ninety percent, but I saw no reason to rub it in. "Take this form over to Ration Control and they'll issue you and your wife new plates."

He nodded but said nothing. His wife continued to stare at the floor.

"Kuenchana," he said to her. It doesn't matter.

That made her cry more.

After coaxing her to stand, he held her elbow lightly, and they walked out the door.

THE SUICIDE PREVENTION PROGRAM was going swimmingly. After only two days, according to Riley, the original facility was full and more Quonset huts had to be identified to provide housing for the "inmates," as he was now calling them. In fact, the program was going so well that Ernie and I were taken off the black market detail and handed a list of a half-dozen GIs to pick up.

I showed the list to Ernie. "Look at this," I said, pointing.

"Garfield, Spec Four," he read. "Yeah. What of it?"

"That's the guy whose wife we busted for black market a few days ago."

"Oh, yeah. The tall gal in the blue dress."

"Yeah. Her."

"Garfield didn't seem so depressed then. Pissed off, sure, but not depressed."

"Guess you never know."

"No, I guess you don't."

We picked up everyone on the list, saving Garfield for last.

WHEN HE EMERGED FROM the back of the electronics truck, his fleshy cheeks were covered with bruises.

"What the hell happened to you?" Ernie asked.

Garfield glanced around. No one seemed to be within earshot but he said, "Not here."

We'd already given the paperwork to his commanding officer so we had him hop in back of the jeep and we drove him over to the 121st Evac. In the gravel lot in front of the new Suicide Prevention Center he said, "I need your help."

I turned in my seat and looked at him. "What is it?"

"My wife." He hung his head for a few seconds and looked back up at me. "She took the black market bust pretty hard. I told her to forget it but it means a lot to her. The money she was making she was sending to her family. I knew about it but I didn't put a stop to it. Her father's sick and her mother still has a son and a daughter of school age and they can't even afford uniforms, much less the tuition."

Ernie and I sat silently, waiting.

"She went to Mukyo-dong," he said. "Do you know where that is?"

"Sure," Ernie replied. "The high class nightclub district in downtown Seoul."

"Most GIs don't know about it," Garfield said.

"Most GIs can't afford their prices."

"Right. Sooki's resourceful, and good looking. You saw that. She landed a job. Dancing, I think. Maybe as a hostess. Serving drinks and lighting cigarettes for those rich Japanese businessmen. I told her to stop but she said she had no choice. If she stopped sending money home, her brother and sister would have to drop out of school and worse, they'd probably go hungry."

"How about your paycheck?" Ernie asked.

"We're barely making the rent as it is. We can send some but not enough."

"You're not command sponsored?"

"No."

Officers and higher ranking NCOs often are assigned to billets that are considered "command sponsored." That is, although Korea is generally considered an "unaccompanied" tour, if you are command sponsored you can bring your wife and children over here and you're given a housing allowance to help you make the outrageous downtown Seoul rents. Low ranking enlisted men, like Garfield, are seldom offered command sponsorship—especially if they have Korean wives.

"Okay," I said. "Things are tough. I get that. What do you want us to do?"

"She didn't come home," he told me. "For two nights in a row. Last night, I went down there, to the nightclub where she works. The sons of bitches wouldn't let me see her. I tried to push my way in and the bastards did this to me."

He touched the bruises on his cheek and then unbuttoned his fatigue shirt. Red welts lined a row of ribs.

"When the CO saw me this morning he asked me what had happened. I couldn't tell him. I didn't want the entire unit to know what she's doing."

"So he called Suicide Prevention," Ernie said.

"Seems like the popular thing to do these days." He shook his head and re-buttoned his shirt. "I'll break out of this place," he said, nodding toward the Suicide Prevention Center. "And this time I'll take something with me."

"You mean like a weapon?"

"That's exactly what I mean. For all I know, they're holding Sooki against her will."

"Unlikely," I said. "She's probably fine."

"Says you."

Ernie and I looked at each other. He grinned and said, "Hell, I haven't been to Mukyo-dong in ages."

Garfield's eyes lit up. "You'll check on her for me?"

I was of two minds. Getting between a husband and wife always spelled trouble. But we couldn't let Garfield go down there with blood in his eye. By getting beaten up, he'd already proven that he didn't know what he was doing. "All right," I said, "my partner and I will go down there for you.

Tonight. We'll check on her and make sure she's all right. But that's it."

Garfield patted his pockets. "I don't have much money. It's expensive down there."

"Don't worry," Ernie replied. "My partner here is rolling in dough."

Inwardly, I groaned.

"I don't know how to thank you."

"Wait until tomorrow," I said. "Thank us then."

ACCORDING TO SPECIALIST FOUR Garfield, the name of the nightclub Sooki was working in was the Golden Dragon. He didn't know the Korean name, which is sometimes different than the English translation, but I made a guess and asked our cab driver to find a place called the Kulryong or something with a similar name. Mukyo-dong parallels a bustling main road lined with two huge department stores and smaller boutique shops catering to the upwardly mobile elite of South Korea. Down the side streets, barely wide enough for a Hyundai sedan, is where the action is. Especially at night. First, open air chop houses serving noodles and live fish in tanks and various delicacies such as octopus marinated in hot pepper sauce. Then, down even narrower lanes, stone pathways lead to bars and underground nightclubs. Some of them blare rock and roll for youngsters, others are designed for the packs of businessmen in suits wandering drunkenly from one flashing neon sign to another.

The driver stepped on his brakes and pointed down a flight of steps. "Kulryong Lou," he said. The Chamber of the Golden Dragon.

Ernie spotted a shimmering golden serpent. "This must be it," he said.

I paid the driver and we climbed out. Just as we did so, a black sedan pulled up below in a narrow road on the far side of the Golden Dragon. A liveried doorman in white gloves opened the back door and out popped three businessmen in what appeared to be expensive suits.

"Class joint," Ernie said. "They're going to be happy to see us."

Down here, GIs are considered to be Cheap Charlies and our presence only upsets the more free-spending Japanese and Korean clientele who don't necessarily want crude barbarian GIs intruding on their space.

"Front door?" Ernie asked.

"No," I said. "Let's try the back."

The chain link fence behind the nightclub was locked. Inside, in an area about the size of a two-car garage, trashcans were lined up and stacked wooden cases held empty beer and *soju* bottles.

"After you, *maestro*," Ernie said.

I grabbed a spread-fingered hold on the chain link and pulled myself up. The tricky part was at the top. I swung my leg over rusty razor wire and managed by stretching and then twisting like a ballerina to grab a toehold on the other side. Gingerly I swung my crotch and then my other leg after. Once I grabbed another handhold, I dropped to the ground. Ernie climbed over, performing the same procedure in about half the time.

I'm a land animal. Whenever possible, I keep two feet on the ground.

The back door to the Golden Dragon was locked.

"Apparently they've had unexpected visitors before," Ernie said.

So we crouched on either side of the door and waited.

"*KOKCHONG HAJIMASEYO*," I TOLD the elderly cook as we pushed him down the hallway. Don't worry.

He'd popped the back door open carrying a bag of garbage and Ernie'd been on him before he could pull it shut. I continued speaking to him in Korean. "Do you know who Sooki is?"

He shook his head.

"Tall woman," I said. "Only started work two or three days ago."

He claimed ignorance, which figured, because an old man like this doing the drudge work in the kitchen would have little or nothing to do with the elegant young female hostesses.

When we reached the kitchen, I let him go and thanked him for his patience. He stared at me, completely befuddled. Some Koreans have had little or no contact with foreigners and when they hear one of us speak their language, to them it's like hearing a chimpanzee recite Shakespeare. Through a double door, the floor turned from tile to carpet and I knew we were close. Finally, we entered a sizeable hall with an elevated ceiling. On the right stretched a long bar; the wall on the left side of the room arced in a graceful curve lined with high-backed plush leather booths. In the center of the room were a half-dozen tables draped in white linen.

Ernie and I held back, peering over a paneled room divider. He scanned the left, I scanned the right.

"There she is," I said.

"Where?"

I pointed. "In that booth. You can barely see her. She's against the wall, behind those two businessmen."

"We could wait until she goes to the ladies room."

"No way. We're lucky the bouncers haven't spotted us already."

"Then there's no time like the present."

Ernie stepped out from behind the divider and started walking across the room. A few people looked up from their drinks, and then more. The mouths of some of the elegantly dressed hostesses fell open. Apparently, the elderly kitchen worker had dropped a dime on us because hurried steps approached from the hallway behind me. Near the front entrance, two men peered in to see what was causing the commotion.

Ernie stood in front of the booth that contained Sooki, also known as Mrs. Roland R. Garfield, and started speaking to her in English. She didn't look up at him but instead peered straight down at the table. Ashamed.

One of the businessmen seated next to her said, "*Igon dode-chei muoya?*" What the hell is this?

The bouncers approached Ernie and one of them grabbed his elbow. He swung his fist back fiercely and shouted at them to keep their hands off of him. I hurried across the room, holding my badge up and shouting "*Kyongchal!*" Police.

Apparently they weren't impressed. Another bouncer approached me from behind and as I was explaining to him that we were here on police business, Ernie punched somebody. And then they were wrestling, two men on Ernie, and I tried to pull one of them off him and then somebody was on me and in a big sweating mass we knocked over first one table and then another. Women screamed and men cursed and soon I was on the floor.

Ernie managed to keep his feet and was winging big roundhouse rights when the front door burst open and a shrill whistle sounded. Cops. The next thing I knew I was in handcuffs and heading toward the rear door of a Korean National Police paddy wagon.

A crowd of upset customers gathered in front. Some of the hostesses were wide-eyed and clinging to one another. One of them was crying. But Sooki Garfield was nowhere to be seen.

Ernie was shoved into the back door of the wagon and after cussing out his assailants he slid over on the bench next to me.

"Assholes," he said. When they shut the door, he reached in his pocket and pulled out a liter bottle of *soju*. I stared at him with a puzzled look. "Grabbed it on the way out," he said. Then he pried off the cap with his teeth, took a swig, wiped the lip clean, and offered the bottle of rice liquor to me. Grasping it with two hands, I tossed back a glug and then coughed, feeling it burn all the way down.

"At least we know Sooki's all right," Ernie said.

"Maybe," I replied.

"Why? What are you worried about?"

"They're pissed now. And they know she's a *yang kalbo*." A GI whore.

"She's not a *yang kalbo*," Ernie said. "She's a wife."

"Same difference to them."

Ernie raised the *soju* bottle and sipped thoughtfully. "Maybe you're right," he said.

CAPTAIN GIL KWON-UP OF the Korean National Police allowed me to use the telephone on his desk. It took twenty minutes to get through to the Yongsan Compound exchange and two minutes after that I was talking to Staff Sergeant Riley.

"We're going to be late," I told him.

"*Late*? You're supposed to be in this office standing tall at zero eight hundred hours." I imagined him checking his watch. "You have fifteen minutes."

"Like I told you," I said. "We're going to be late. We're tracking down a lead."

He sputtered and before he could form words, I hung up the phone.

"Everything all right?" Mr. Kill asked me.

"Just fine," I told him. "They're very understanding."

We called him Mr. Kill, a GI corruption of his real name, Gil. It made a certain kind of sense, since he was the Chief Homicide Inspector for the Korean National Police. Ernie and I knew him well after working a number of cases with him.

After taking in a GI, normal procedure is for the KNPs to call the US Army Military Police. Last night, I headed that off by speaking to the desk sergeant in Korean and explaining to him that I knew Mr. Kill, and stretched the truth by claiming that we were currently working with him on a case. He was suspicious, but didn't want to risk irritating a superior officer, so he said he'd wait until the next morning to confirm my statement with Kill. Ernie and I spent the night in our own cell, segregated from the raving lunatics in the drunk tank. Special treatment for foreigners. True to his word, the desk sergeant contacted Gil Kwon-up first thing in the morning, and he'd immediately ordered that we be brought up to his office.

"What's her name?" Mr. Kill asked me. I didn't know Sooki's full Korean name. Sooki was a nickname, probably short for Sook-ja or Sook-ai, or something close to that. Her legal name now was Mrs. Roland R. Garfield. He jotted the information down and I gave him her general description.

Then he looked up at me. He'd been educated in the States and his English was excellent. "Why didn't you contact me," he asked, "before almost starting a riot in the Golden Dragon?"

"Sorry," I said.

The truth was, I didn't like to bother him unless I had to. He was too valuable a resource.

He pressed the intercom button on his desk and spoke to another officer. I didn't understand everything that was said but the gist of it was that he ordered two men to go over to the Golden Dragon and pick up the woman called Sooki and bring her in. It was going to take some time. While we waited, Ernie and I sat outside on two hard chairs in the hallway. Ernie was already snoring and I'd started to doze when Mr. Kill appeared in front of us. My eyes popped open.

"She's disappeared," he said.

Once he realized I was fully alert, he continued. "The thugs who own the Golden Dragon are well known to us. We took one of them in and we had Mr. Bam have a little talk with him."

Bam was the lead KNP interrogator.

"According to what he told us, orders came down to pull Mrs. Garfield out of the Golden Dragon and send her to one of their subsidiary operations."

Ernie was awake now. "Subsidiary operations?" he said.

"Yes. A brothel." He handed me a folded sheet of paper. "I won't be able to help you further."

"Why not?" Ernie asked.

Mr. Kill just stared at him, saying nothing. He looked at me, seeing if I understood. I did.

"How high does it go?" I asked.

"Within the police hierarchy," Mr. Kill answered. "Not higher. Which leaves you a certain latitude."

I nodded. "Thank you, sir, for this information."

Then he said, "One more thing. The man in charge of the operation is known as Huk. A Manchurian name. You are aware that Manchuria invaded us a few centuries ago?"

"Yes, sir. I know."

"Be very careful when dealing with him. You'll be on your own. My colleagues and I need to keep our hands off this operation for as long as we are able."

Mr. Kill held eye contact with me until he was sure I understood, then swiveled on the cement floor and strode briskly away.

Ernie glanced at me. Confused.

"What just happened?"

I took a deep breath. "Mr. Kill can't do anything officially," I said, keeping my voice down.

"Why not?"

"Think about it," I told him. "This guy Huk, whoever he is, not only runs the Golden Dragon but also has 'subsidiary' brothels. He makes a lot of money and couldn't be doing that unless he had protection."

Ernie nodded, getting it now. "Somebody high up in the police hierarchy is protecting him."

"Yes," I said, standing up. "Mr. Kill doesn't like it, but that's the world he lives in."

"So Huk's protected," Ernie said.

"Yes. He's protected from the Korean National Police." I paused, thinking it over. "But he's not protected from us."

Relations with the US military are considered to be so important that they are reserved for the very highest levels of government; for President Pak Chung-hee and his most trusted advisors. Whoever was protecting Huk wouldn't have that much pull and therefore wouldn't have a chance in hell of calling off American law enforcement. Mr. Kill was making it clear to me that although his hands were tied, Ernie and I had an open field for action.

I stuck the sheet of paper in my breast pocket and Ernie and I hurried out of the police station.

BACK AT THE CID office, I found the address Mr. Kill had given me on our wall-sized map of Seoul.

"Here," I told Ernie.

"Why'd they send her there?"

"They're pissed. She caused a disruption. Embarrassed them."

"*We* caused the disruption," Ernie said.

"Because of her. And she has a Ration Control Plate. They'll probably work her two ways. Not only in the brothel but probably by forcing her to buy beyond her ration at the PX and Commissary."

"She'll be caught."

"But not for a month or two. It takes that long for the reports to be collated. Only then will the Ration Control violations make their way to Garfield's unit commander."

"And he might not act right away."

"That's what they're hoping for."

"How can they do this?" Ernie asked. "Okay, I get it. The KNPs won't touch this guy, Huk, but why doesn't she look for her own chance and then run away?"

"Because now they know her situation and they know the jam she's in. You can bet that they already have a bead on her mother and her brother and her sister and are using them to threaten her."

"What kind of country *is* this?" Ernie asked.

I shrugged. "It's like most countries. Big money talks. Women are expendable."

"So are GIs," Ernie replied.

RILEY VOLUNTEERED TO BE the first in.

"About time we kicked some ass," he said.

"Easy, Tiger," I told him. "We have a plan, remember? You need to follow it."

"Sure. A Commando raid. I get it."

"No. We're faking an MP bust. That's it."

The midnight curfew would hit in a little more than an hour, and the entire city of Seoul would shut down. We sat in the shadows in a neighborhood near the Han River known as Ichon-dong. Ernie's jeep was parked about a half-block from a dilapidated three-story wooden building that looked as if it had been built on the cheap and would fall down during the next strong wind. So far we'd seen working-class Korean men go in, linger and come out about a half-hour later, and we'd seen women's silhouettes in the upstairs windows. Light from a dirty yellow bulb flooded down a short flight of steps at the entranceway.

Ernie sat behind the steering wheel, I sat in the passenger seat, and Staff Sergeant Riley and the fourth member of our "commando team," Sergeant First Class Harvey, better known as Strange, sat in back. He had a reputation for being a pervert, but on this mission all I required was that he be dressed in fatigues and one of the MP helmets I'd borrowed—and that he be armed with an M-16 rifle. Riley was similarly outfitted. Their job was not to shoot anyone, but to back us up as we ran our bluff.

Ernie and I had come up with the plan this afternoon. We couldn't go to the Provost Marshal and ask for a detachment of real MPs to help us because what we were planning to do wasn't only outside of our jurisdiction, it was illegal. Plenty illegal. So we had to enlist the only two guys we knew who were crazy enough to help: Riley and Strange.

"How about this guy Huk?" Strange asked. "He must be a pretty cool customer."

"Not cool," I replied. "According to Mr. Kill he started as a petty thief after the war and worked his way up to becoming a pimp, and after he landed a few well-placed connections he graduated to becoming a nightclub owner."

"How are we going to recognize him?"

"He has a disfigured nose. 'Mangled' is the word Mr. Kill used."

"Lost it in a knife fight?"

"No. Nothing so glamorous. Not all of Huk's girls knuckle under to him. Apparently, somewhere along the line, one of them fought back. According to Mr. Kill she not only bit into his nose but almost chewed his face off."

"Korean women are *bold*," Riley said, almost in awe.

"What happened to her?" Strange asked.

I glanced toward the Han River. It was only two blocks downhill and glistened in the wavering moonlight. "What do you think?"

After a moment of silence, Riley spoke up. "You sure his office is here?"

"Yes. He never goes to the Golden Dragon or his other properties. Frightens the customers. He stays here in the slums, pulling the strings."

"In the mud where he came from," Ernie said.

"All right," I said. "Everybody has a job to do. Let's go over it one more time."

We did. It was a simple plan, brutal but elegant. If we only had to grab Sooki and return her to her husband, life would've been easy. But it was more complicated than that. We had to assume that Huk and his boys knew about her family, knew where they lived, and they knew how to find them. That was their modus operandi and the secret of their control. Promise the women they trafficked that if they didn't do exactly as they were told, their families would pay with their lives. So we had to liberate not only Sooki, but also her family from the threat of Huk and his gang of thugs.

After the verbal rehearsal, I said, "Okay, everybody got it?" Three nods.

"According to Mr. Kill, Huk's office and his living quarters are on the third floor. That's where I'm going. So don't shoot me on the way down."

Strange waggled his cigarette holder.

"And you better take off those damn shades," I told him.

"What? And ruin my style?"

"To hell with your style," Ernie said. "Do what the man says."

Strange took off his sunglasses and stuck them in the breast pocket of his fatigue shirt. Now I understood why he wore them. His eyes were like desiccated green olives lost in a moist excretion of dough.

We climbed out of the jeep. Ernie took the lead, holding his .45 pointed at the sky. Riley and Strange ran after him across the street and the three of them burst into the entranceway to the Ichon-dong brothel. Once inside, Ernie blasted his whistle and started shouting. Riley and Strange fanned out upstairs to the second floor like we practiced. They were also shouting. It didn't matter much what they said, because English would be incomprehensible to these people anyway. It was their job to make sure that everyone understood that this was a raid by the Military Police and to intimidate the customers and move them out while at the same time herding the girls into a safe place. It was Ernie's job to find Sooki.

My job was to grab Huk.

The central staircase was made of cement. Korean men in

various stages of undress flooded out, frantic to escape before we placed them under arrest. I pushed against the descending crowd, running upstairs two steps at a time. On the third floor, a long hallway greeted me. At first I didn't see any doors. Just flimsy curtains and thin blankets hanging from a network of overhead wire. Inside these makeshift partitions, cots and mats were arrayed at odd angles and female clothing hung from metal hooks. At the end of the hallway loomed a wooden door. A cement wall partitioned this end of the third floor and this had to be Huk's office and living quarters.

I kicked the door in.

He was standing, arms akimbo, staring right at me. He was a small man, wearing blue jeans and sneakers and some sort of red checkered shirt with long sleeves and a collar. If he put on a Stetson, he would've looked like a short Asian cowboy. His face was square, almost wider than it was long and the mangled scars on his face, from eyes to chin, seemed immobile. Dark eyes smoldered through squinting lids. His fists were clenched and he was slightly hunched over, as if prepared to take a blow.

And, to my relief, he was unarmed.

Behind him sat a rickety wooden desk and a diesel space heater and what appeared to be a pilfered army cot. The desk supported a large red phone atop a knitted pad. He reached for the phone. I fired a round into the wall.

Apparently that convinced him I meant business. He held perfectly still.

"Iriwa!" I told him, in very disrespectful Korean. *Come here!*

He hesitated but then stepped slowly toward me. I ordered him to turn around and I cuffed his hands behind his back. Grabbing a knot of his curly black hair, I pushed him outside his office and held the .45 against his back as we stepped downstairs. Ernie had located Sooki. She was crying and covering her face.

Strange and Riley joined us, both of them panting and sweating, their faces flushed red with victory. Mr. Kill had already warned the local KNPs to back off and not respond to any calls that might come from the Ichon-dong brothel. At least not too quickly. Still, I didn't want to press our luck.

"*Kapshida!*" I said. Let's go.

Everyone understood and we ran outside and down the stairs and across the dark street to the jeep.

Ernie drove. I sat up front with Huk kneeling on the metal floor in front of the passenger seat. Every time he squirmed, I kicked him. Riley had left his green army sedan parked near the Han-gang Railroad Bridge. When we pulled up next to the sedan, Riley and Strange hopped out. They took Sooki with them. I thanked them for their help. Ernie warned them not to shoot themselves with their M-16s. As they drove off, Sooki sat in the back seat of the sedan, still crying.

Ernie and I sat alone in the quiet night with Huk, watching the string of lights that spanned the bridge. A slowly rising moon illuminated a few small fishing boats straggling back to their home ports.

"How soon until the next train?" Ernie asked.

"One last train comes in from Pusan just before the midnight curfew. Should be along soon."

We pulled Huk out of the jeep. The expression on his face, such as it was, didn't change. I spoke to him in Korean.

"Sooki doesn't belong to you anymore," I told him. When he didn't answer, I continued. "You will not bother her in the future and you will not bother her family. Do you understand?"

Again, he just stared at me, eyes squinting, mangled face

impassive. Ernie slugged him in the stomach. When he came up for air, the only change in his face was a bubbling gasp from his small round mouth.

We walked him toward the railroad tracks. There was no one out here, just a few abandoned warehouses and what appeared to be cats prowling for rats.

"You understand," I told him. "You can't get to us. We live on the US military compound. You have no power there. Your thugs can't gain entry, and even if they could, it's a big compound and they have no idea where to find us. We're safe from you." I shoved his narrow shoulders and he knelt into gravel. Deftly, Ernie pushed the tip of a short bicycle chain beneath a crosstie and, using the jeep's crowbar, dug a pathway for the chain under the thick plank. Once it was through, he locked the two ends together and then, as Huk stared at his work, he unlocked one of his cuffs and looped it through the bicycle chain and relocked it with a snap.

Huk now knelt in the center of the railroad tracks, like a worshiper waiting for the next train. Ernie switched on his flashlight to make sure Huk could fully appreciate his predicament. A trickle of sweat formed just above Huk's eyebrow. He had yet to speak a word.

I knelt next to him.

"You must promise us not to hurt Sooki, not to hurt her husband, and not to hurt Sooki's family. Once you do that, we will let you go."

Huk said nothing.

"If you break your promise," I continued, "then my friend and I will come after you. We know where your businesses are. We know how to find you. And the next time, we won't be so nice. We will shoot you with one of these." I pressed the business end of my .45 up against the twisted mass of flesh that was his nose. "The Korean National Police won't care. Not about you. And they won't care about us. They don't like to bother the US Army. And their bosses in the Korean government don't like to bother the US Army. No one will investigate your murder. No one will come on our compound to bother me or my friend. You will be dead. Someone else will take your place at the Golden Dragon and at the Ichon-dong brothel. Do you understand?"

His oddly-shaped face still remained impassive and he said nothing.

"Dumb shit," Ernie said and kicked him.

I stood up. I had to admit that he was one tough cookie and I could see why he'd risen to the top of the rackets. I was through wasting breath on him. Ernie and I walked back to the jeep. From this distance, about twenty yards, we watched Huk kneeling on the tracks.

I had no idea what was going through his mind. He didn't yank on the handcuffs, trying to get away. He just knelt there without moving.

Ernie glanced behind us. "Maybe he figures somebody is going to come and save him," he said.

"No way. He doesn't have thugs at the brothel because he doesn't need them. He's protected by the money he pays at a high level."

"Maybe those high-level people will catch wind of this and send the KNPs."

"I don't think so. My guess is that the KNPs are just as pissed about this setup as we are. Mr. Kill warned them off and they'll stay away. Even if the word comes down from on high that they need to save Huk, they'll hesitate. They can always claim that they didn't know where he was; which is true, they don't know."

"So we just stand here and watch him die?" Ernie said.

"That's the plan."

He glanced at me. "Can you handle it?"

"You saw those girls in the brothel," I replied. "Some of them still had their schoolgirl haircuts, just barely out of middle school. Did they have cigarette burns on their forearms? Bruises on their shoulders? I didn't have time to look, but I bet they did."

"They did," Ernie said.

"So I can stand here and watch this creep be run over and smashed into pieces."

Ernie grinned, staring at me, but said nothing further.

In the distance, the train whistle sounded.

THE TRAIN FROM PUSAN emerged along the banks of the Han River on the western side of the district known as Yong-dungpo. The name Yongdungpo is composed of three Chinese characters that mean, literally, Eternally Rising Port. Or, more poetically, the Port of Eternal Ascension. Eighth Army had a supply depot over there for many years and there was a place GIs called the Green Door that old-timers told me was one of the raunchiest brothels in Korea. But that was controlled by a different organization, not Huk's. Whether or not he was thinking about this while the train reached the bank of the Han River and turned east and then about two miles later made the left turn toward the railroad bridge, I didn't know. But when the train did make the turn, we saw the front light of the locomotive shine almost halfway across the bridge. It was heading toward us at about thirty miles per hour, all the massive tonnage of it, and I calculated it would arrive on this side of the Han River in less than a minute.

Ernie and I leaned against the jeep, arms crossed, waiting.

I'm sure he was expecting me to crack first, but as it turned out, it wasn't me, it was him.

"Maybe we should unlock him," he said.

"Why?" I asked.

"This is going to be messy. Blood and flesh and bone splashed all over the place."

"Yeah," I said. "I suppose it is going to be messy."

Ernie studied me. "Are you serious? Do you really want to go through with this?" When I didn't answer, he glanced at the approaching train. A whistle sounded. "We don't have much time."

I kept my arms crossed, my face impassive, and then we heard a choked yell.

"*Okay!*"

It was Huk. Just the one word but that was good enough for me. I ran forward, reaching in my right pocket for the keys. They weren't there. And then I remembered. I'd given them to Ernie.

I turned and shouted. "The *keys!*"

But Ernie was already on it. He ran past me and knelt next to Huk and started fumbling with the handcuffs. The train was only a hundred yards away now, its front light so bright that both Ernie and Huk were illuminated by its fierce glow. A screaming whistle sounded a warning, shattering the night.

Ernie continued to fumble with the keys. I was just about to run forward and snatch them from him and unlock the cuffs myself when I heard the snap. Ernie leapt off the tracks and rolled toward the stanchions on the edge of the bridge. Huk pulled away but for a moment the cuffs caught on something, and then frantically he jerked them up and down until something released and, like the rat that he was, he scurried toward the stanchions next to Ernie. Mesmerized, I realized that I had to back away too, and stepped quickly toward the end of the bridge until I was safely out of the path of the train.

With a great whining and clattering, the train reached us and, like a monster of metal and steam, ground its great iron wheels past, parading the full length of its dragon-like body until it finally pulled away, shrieking regally, into the dark night.

I ran along the tracks, grabbed Huk and retrieved my handcuffs. He remained kneeling on the edge of the tracks, facing the water below, his face and the back of his neck slathered in sweat. As a memento of our visit, I kicked him in the thigh. Hard. Like the tough little shit he was, he took it without a whimper.

We left him there, clinging to the stanchion, staring into the river.

On shaking legs, Ernie and I marched back to the jeep, jumped in, and drove away from the Han-gang Railroad Bridge.

"You're kidding me," Ernie said.

The next morning, we had just stepped through the entranceway to the Yongsan Main PX and stood gazing past rows of consumer goods and milling crowds of shoppers. Against the far wall, a dais had been set up for children to be introduced to Father Christmas.

"Not *him*," Ernie said.

"Yes him," I replied.

"Not Strange."

Sergeant First Class Harvey, also known as Strange, sat on a throne in the center of the dais dressed in a fake white beard and a bright red Santa Claus outfit, greeting the children one by one.

"I guess the Officers' Wives Club doesn't know he's a pervert," I said.

We pushed our way through the crowds of shoppers until we stood in front of the dais. After one of the children hopped off his red-trousered lap, Strange looked over at us, and responded to the quizzical look in our eyes.

"I was *volunteered*," he said.

One of the ladies controlling the tittering line of children sent another youngster up. Strange let out a "*Ho ho ho!*" and lifted the child to his lap.

"Watch his hands," Ernie whispered.

We did. For about twenty minutes. Apparently he was on the up and up. So far.

"I guess children aren't his particular perversion," Ernie told me.

"Let's watch him anyway."

I went back into the PX administrative offices and found a couple of straight-backed chairs. Ernie and I set them out of the way but close enough to the dais so we could keep an eye on Strange.

"So Sooki's all right?" Ernie asked, once we got settled.

"Yeah. She begged me not to tell her husband what had happened. I promised I wouldn't. Not all of it, anyway."

I had told Specialist Garfield that we'd broken Sooki out of the Golden Dragon and that had been good enough for him. He didn't ask more questions. Maybe because he guessed he wouldn't like the answers.

"Huk is a complete shit," Ernie said. "What makes you think he'll keep his word?"

"He knows what I said is true. He can't get to us, not without a hell of a lot of expense and trouble. Even if he managed to take you and me out, he'd face the wrath of the

KNPs and the Korean government, neither of which wants a big-time racketeer messing up their cozy relationship with the United States. Not worth it for a single girl in one of his brothels."

The United States government had not only provided South Korea with 50,000 troops to help in their defense against the Communist army up north but we also gave them millions of dollars in economic and military aide annually. If there was one thing every faction in the South Korean government agreed on, it was keeping the relationship with the United States pristine; without the slightest blemish.

"So if we were bumped off," Ernie said, "the KNPs and the Eighth Army honchos would go after Huk."

"Big time."

"It's like in 'Nam," Ernie told me. "The army treats you like shit when you're alive. But once you're dead, you become a hero."

"Right. They'd probably dedicate a plaque to us."

"The only way we'll ever get one." Ernie thought about it for a minute and then continued. "Okay, so Huk knows he can't touch us. And after that performance on the Han-gang Railroad Bridge, he's also convinced that if he messes with Sooki's family, we'll take him out. So he'll leave her alone."

"It's the smart business decision," I said. "What's one girl, more or less? And besides, nobody in the Seoul underworld knows what happened. He doesn't lose face. As far as they're concerned, the MPs raided the Ichon-dong brothel and he shrugged them off and he's back in business the next day."

"He looks good."

"Right. And if he's smart, he'll leave it that way. Sooki told me that as soon as her husband's tour is up, they'll go back to the States and she'll put in the paperwork to have her parents and her brother and sister join them."

"The sooner the better."

"Right. Because once we're gone, who knows what Huk will do?"

"Once we're gone? What are you talking about? I'm not going anywhere."

"You already have your request in for extension?"

"You better believe it. Riley hand-carried mine over to his pal Smitty at Eighth Army Personnel. How about yours?"

"Already in."

Ernie surveyed the crowd of shoppers, and we watched Strange behave himself as we listened to the schmaltzy Christmas music wafting out of the PX sound system.

"Everybody talks about being homesick at Christmas," Ernie said. "They think that's why GIs off themselves."

"Isn't it?"

"For some," he said. "Maybe for most. For me, I'll only off myself if I end up back in some trailer park in the States and somebody reminds me of Korea."

"Or Vietnam?"

He nodded. "Or Vietnam." He motioned toward the long lines at the cashier stations. "They think buying shit is living. It ain't."

"What is?" I asked.

"This," he said.

I followed his gaze toward the entrance. Sooki walked in, paused, and glanced around the expanse of the busy PX. When she spotted us she smiled, waved, and headed straight toward us.

CHALEE'S NATIVITY
Timothy Hallinan

TIMOTHY HALLINAN, the author of twenty widely praised books, has been nominated for the Edgar, Nero, Shamus and Macavity awards. He currently writes two series. The Junior Bender Mysteries include *Crashed*, *Little Elvises*, *The Fame Thief*, *Herbie's Game* (winner of the Lefty Award for best comic crime novel), *King Maybe*, and *Fields Where They Lay*. His Poke Rafferty Thrillers, set in Bangkok, include *A Nail Through the Heart*, *The Fourth Watcher*, *Breathing Water*, *The Queen of Patpong*, *The Fear Artist*, *For the Dead*, *The Hot Countries*, and *Fools' River*.

The story that follows is set in Bangkok and features a Thai street child named Chalee, a character who first appeared in *For the Dead*. As Hallinan writes, "Christmas for me has always been about children, so the moment I was asked to do a holiday story, I thought of Chalee, with her ever-present pencil and paper, and another street child, Apple, adrift on the gaudy Bangkok sidewalks the night before Christmas."

C halee is drawing.

She's sitting on the sidewalk near the curb with her back to the traffic, trying to solve the technical problem of *sparkle*. If she had her colored pencils, she thinks, she could show it with a mix of yellow and white, a little bounce of tiny lines radiating out from the glowing circle floating above the woman's head. She sees the lines when she squints, which she does frequently because she's nearsighted. She likes the circle better with the sparkle because without it, it looks like what it really is—a fluorescent tube—and she knows it's supposed to be something more mysterious than neon. So she needs the sparkle in the drawing. Problem is she's only got a regular pencil, and when she tried drawing the sparkle lines in black, Apple had leaned over her shoulder, sniffled in her ear, and said, "Is that supposed to be *fur*?" and Chalee had erased the lines.

Which tore the paper, gone all damp because of the drizzle. Chalee has a stack about an inch thick that she'd boosted when she left the shelter, and it's *all* getting damp. That ripples it and makes it more transparent; the black type on the reverse side begins to ghost through. The paper, the blank side of which is prized in the shelter, is donated by a company that shredded it without a thought until a marketing executive realized that they could turn their scrap into television commercials, at essentially no cost, about how the firm makes it possible for homeless children to learn to read and write. "Helping them write the page of their future" is the line that appears at the end, over a picture of some poor kid with his tongue sticking out of the corner of his mouth as he tries to master the curlicues of his name.

If Chalee could read the writing, she'd learn a little bit about some new protocols developed several years ago to test drinking water for insecticides that are thought to cause birth defects. The protocols were loudly proclaimed as an essential step forward by the branch of the government that brags for a living and assiduously ignored by the branch of the government that tests water for a living. The water in Chalee's old home village smelled a little odd when she lived there. Boiling it didn't seem to help.

Apple says, "I'm hungry."

"You're always hungry." On her new sheet, Chalee has sketched the woman's outline again and is using the edge of the pencil's lead to shade the folds in her robe, postponing the glowing circle in the hope that inspiration will tap her on the shoulder. The robe is the blue Chalee remembers from her village, back before her father lost his land to the people who'd been lending him money to grow his rice. The family had rolled downhill to Bangkok like a handful of rocks, leaving only her older sister, who had—

Chalee shakes her head sharply, and the memory of Sumalee rolls back into the slot where she keeps it, out of sight most of the time.

"Let's go back," Apple says, and Chalee turns reluctantly from the woman in the lighted window to look at her temporary companion. Apple is small and dark and disappointed, a mosquito magnet whose face and arms are perpetually bumpy with bites. For the first few weeks, the kids at the shelter had appreciated the insistent hum over Apple's cot as they lay unmolested, but then scabies broke out and the almost-nurse who looked after the shelter's minor complaints had thoughtlessly identified Apple as the probable source. Apple's stock had plummeted to the point that no one would speak to her. After Chalee's only friend, a boy called Dok, had unexpectedly been taken for a trial adoption, Chalee had slipped out one night and hit the street, persuading herself it was good to be back on her own until she turned and found Apple trying to duck into a door half a block behind. That had been five nights earlier.

"Go if you want," she says. "I'm staying."

Apple's lower lip, never out of sight for long, protrudes. She blinks a couple of times, either clearing tears or trying to work them up. Apple cries a lot. She's wearing a boy's plaid shirt that's five sizes too big and a pair of men's shorts that hang well below her scabbed knees and bunch voluminously beneath a belt with a dozen new holes punched in it. Both garments are notably dirty. She says, "If I go alone, they'll beat me up."

"Don't be silly," Chalee says, without thinking. "Nobody wants to touch you."

Apple is blinking again, faster than before. She takes a step back as though Chalee had tried to slap her, and turns away. Chalee thinks she's leaving, but after a long moment she sits on the curb with her feet, in their too-big sneakers, in the street. One of the sneakers has come untied. Her head is so far down Chalee can barely see it above the shirt's high collar. Apple looks like a pile of discarded clothes.

She sniffles again.

How old *is* she? A big eight? A small eleven? If she's eleven, she's not much younger than Dok, who might have been the only person who ever loved Chalee. "I just want to finish this drawing," Chalee says. "Then we'll get something to eat."

Just as she decides Apple won't reply, the smaller girl says, "Promise?"

"I promise." She goes back to her shading, thinking

apprehensively about the glowing circle. The robes worn by the woman in the window are from old times but her face is the same as most of the other women in the store windows, all now so bright and full of things for sale. She looks neither Thai nor *farang*, as far as Chalee can see, but she can't see much because the woman's face is angled down, as though she's looking at the bundled blanket in her arms. There's a baby doll in the blanket, one bright pink arm raised stiffly toward the downturned face. Chalee recognizes the doll, a little girl named Baby Noi that was popular a few years ago, but she's not wearing her *Let's Baby!* T-shirt. In fact, inside the blanket she seems to be naked. The big thing about Baby Noi was that she wet her pants, but the woman who's holding her doesn't look worried.

"Who is she?" Apple asks. She's facing the window again, sitting, like Chalee, on the wet sidewalk. She leans toward Chalee just enough so their shoulders touch, and Chalee can smell her. Apple smells like feet.

"She's, um, you know Santa Claus?"

"Everybody knows Santa Claus." They're both pronouncing it *Santa Claut*.

"This is Mrs. Santa Claut."

"Wow," Apple says. "Her husband is so much *older*."

"And the kid," Chalee says with a certainty she doesn't feel, "is Baby Claut."

"Bet *she* gets a lot of presents."

"He," Chalee says.

"You know everything," Apple says. There's a pause as Chalee evaluates the picture and her story at the same time. Apple says, "Did you ever get presents?"

"I got a new shirt for school," Chalee says. "The year I went to school."

"That's not the same," Apple says. She sniffles again; she has a permanent cold. "Is it?"

"I guess not. What about you?"

"What *about* me?"

"Did you ever get presents?"

"Only when," Apple says, and then she falls silent. Chalee has started to rough in the floating circle when Apple speaks again. "No," she says.

TINY, IRREGULAR ERASURES IN the circle, not much wider than a pencil line, do it. Kind of. The breaks in the circle make it look less solid, airy enough to explain why it doesn't just fall on the woman's head and maybe hit Baby Noi, and when Chalee erases outward, the rubber drags a faint smear of pencil behind it. The smears are better than the lines she drew before because they're soft-edged, more like the sparkle she sees when she squints. Apple's weight on Chalee's shoulder has become permanent, and Chalee has to extend her neck to see around Apple's head every now and then, but she's caught up in her work, and as long as Apple doesn't sneeze on the page, it's all okay.

"Wow," Apple says for the hundredth time in five days, "you can really draw."

"I do it all the time."

"Can you draw me?"

Chalee makes an irritated shrug. "Not now." She's *almost* got the sparkle, and at that very moment she sees what's wrong with the woman's eyes, but she's running out of eraser, and she's already bitten down twice on the tin to squeeze more out.

Apple pulls away and says, "Oh."

"Let me—just let me—" What she saw in the woman's eyes, the thing that had been *missing*, is fading. One time in the village, when she was four or five and fishing with her brother, Chalee had felt a fish's tug for the first time in her life and she'd brought the line up too quickly, snapping it. It came flying up out of the water and spray had hit her face but she barely felt it. She'd seen a sudden flash of silver through the tea-colored water and then another, dimmer the second time, and then a third that might actually have been a memory, and then nothing.

That's what's happening with the thing she'd glimpsed in the woman's eyes, the thing that would have drawn a kind of invisible line between the mother and the baby. She says, "*Shit.*"

"I don't care," Apple says. "I don't want you to draw me anyway."

"Why would I want—" Chalee begins, but she breaks off as she hears her own voice. "I mean, I'm trying to—to—I mean, leave me alone for a minute, *please?*"

"Sure," Apple says. She puts both hands on the wet pavement and gets up. "I don't like your drawing anyway. It's dumb." Chalee is at work on the corners of the eyes, trying to find it again, when Apple starts to walk away. She steps on her flopping shoelace and pitches forward on her hands and knees, making a little *whuff* sound, like someone has punched her in the stomach, and then, for the first time since she leaned against Chalee's shoulder, she sniffles.

"Just a couple of minutes," Chalee says, glimpsing it again.

"Take a year," Apple says. She ties her shoe and wipes her bumpy cheeks, and the next time Chalee looks up, she's gone.

It's there, it's not there, it's not there, it's *there*. She finds it at last, partly in the eyes and partly in the tilt of Mrs. Claut's head, and then she sees that Baby Noi's hand should follow the same line as the mother's gaze. It takes her last tiny bit of eraser, but she makes the fix, and only then does she sit back and take in the whole drawing at the same time. There's a kind of a curve, she's surprised to see, like a crescent moon, that flows from the circle above the woman's head, down through her neck and shoulder and along the bent arm with its uptilted fingers that cradles the baby, and the curve is the most important part of the picture. She studies it in the picture and then looks back up at the window to confirm the accuracy of her drawing, but the curve isn't there. In its place are two irregular angles, like the corners of half-collapsed boxes. The arm is bent so awkwardly it might belong to someone else.

Puzzled, she scratches her head and looks back down at her picture. The curve, the thing that makes the picture seem true, is there. It's as clear to her as the mother's eyes. She shifts her gaze to the window just as the lights inside go out, but she has time to see that the curve, *her* curve, she thinks, isn't there. It's harder to see her drawing now that the window light has been turned off, but it's there, the curve is there, and Chalee says out loud, "I *made* it."

She's known since she was little that she could draw people so other people would recognize her subject, but this is new. Until now, she thinks, she's been able to put what she saw on the page. Now she's put in something that *wasn't* there. Something that was missing.

She wants to show it to Dok, she wants to explain it to Dok. Dok would admire it. He'd look up from the page and smile at her, his two big rat-teeth gleaming, and say something like "Only you could do this, Chalee."

Without thinking, Chalee says, "Apple?" but there's no answer. That's right, Apple is gone, Apple had said something when Chalee was trying to put the look in the woman's eyes somewhere where she could find it when she needed it, and

Chalee had answered her, maybe not very nicely, and Apple had gone away. After she tripped on her shoelaces, she had looked at Chalee as though Chalee had just shot her.

"Oh, no," Chalee says. She suddenly felt chilled, and heavy with guilt. They hadn't eaten all day, and Apple had been hungry, and she, Chalee had promised . . .

She puts her drawing away, into the middle of the stack of paper so it won't get any wetter, and on the blank surface of the next page, she sees the look in Apple's eyes after she fell down. Without even knowing she's going to do it, she begins to slide the pencil over the page, beginning with the eyes, and then swooping up to the bird's nest of hair, fine and dry and broken, and below that the curve of the cheek. She stops, staring at all the mosquito bumps she's drawn, and then once again she bites down on the eraser, hard enough to make her teeth hurt, and manages to extrude a bit more. She wipes it on her sleeve, and then on the *inside* of her shirt because it's dryer there—a wet eraser makes a terrible, unfixable mess—and she banishes the bumps and gives Apple cheeks as smooth as a movie star's. The girl has, Chalee realizes as she draws them, beautiful lips when the lower one is in its natural place, and she gives special attention to the mouth, shaping it so it seems to make the paper beneath it bloom outward. Then she goes back to the eyes and removes some of the pain—not all of it because there's not enough eraser left, but anyway, if she took it *all* out it wouldn't be Apple anymore.

Five swoops of the pencil create the lines of the chin and the neck and the collar of the awful shirt. She stops, eyeing the shirt, and gives it a girly design of pale little flowers and adds diamond-cut buttons. She wants to write the girl's name, but she's not sure Apple will be able to read it, so in the lower right corner she pencils a small, shiny apple with a stem and a single leaf. Then she breathes out for what feels like the first time in hours.

The new drawing has taken just a few minutes. But when Chalee looks hard at the girl on the page, it's no one but Apple.

SHE PUTS HER NEW drawing safely in the middle of the stack, too, and slips the paper, careful not to wrinkle it or fold down the corners, into the torn backpack she dug out of a dumpster one lucky night and has carried ever since. Her back feels stiff when she gets up, and she realizes she's wet and cold. The drizzle creates circles of light around the streetlights like the one floating above Mrs. Claut's head.

For the first time since she saw the woman in the window, she surveys her surroundings. She's on a boulevard that's mostly stores, almost all of them full of things she'll never have, some of them with sparkly cotton to represent the snow she'll probably never see. She doesn't have a watch but her sense of time is keen, and it seems to her the stores have closed early. Most of the windows have gone dark.

There are, as always in Bangkok, people in the streets, many of them wearing Santa Claut hats that blink on and off. Some of them walk with the slow precision of too many drinks. From a store that's still open, a ribbon of music unfurls into the street, a Thai children's chorus.

Jinger Ben
Jinger Ben
Jinger aaadawaaayyyy

She's heard it every Christmas since they fled the village. She hates it.

She's hungry. *Apple* was hungry. Where's Apple?

It takes her a moment to remember that Apple went off

in the direction that was to her left when she'd been facing the window, so she goes that way, aware of the people in their blinky hats curving around her as though they might catch something, and for a moment she hopes she *does* have scabies and that it can jump onto them and make them scratch themselves until they bleed. The thought of scabies brings Apple to mind again, and she feels a curl of unease. The girl is sullen and maybe stupid and, let's face it, not very attractive, but she's young and alone and hungry, and there are people who look for girls like her. Chalee has had to deal with that, and Apple . . . Apple is too young.

"I'm a bad friend," she says aloud, and two passersby stare at her.

Two long blocks, no Apple. On a brightly lit cross street a *farang* entertainment district pours out a steady stream of middle-aged men accompanied by younger women, like Santa and Mrs. Claut. The girls cling to the men's arms as though they're afraid that the men will break the line and swim away, as Chalee's fish had. All the women are smiling, but there are a lot of Thai smiles, and these are masks that seem to cool the night even further. There are so many people that Chalee would have to push her way through if people hadn't noticed her and given her room.

No Apple.

Once she's past the entertainment district the crowds thin again, the lights are spaced farther apart, and *sois*, little streets that could lead anywhere in Bangkok, open up right and left. Apple could be on any of them. She'd said something about going back to the shelter, Chalee remembers. Some of these *sois* would take her in that direction, down toward the Klong Toey slums near the river where the former street child named Boo administers a small, hot shelter, a building crammed with throwaway children, boys on one floor, girls on another, and Boo and his wife and baby on the third, although now some girls have to sleep up there, too.

For a brief moment a few months back, Chalee had thought she might get adopted, after she and Dok had found a sick, feverish girl named Treasure in an alley and brought her to the shelter. Treasure was fifty-fifty, half *farang*, and beautiful, and a policeman and his wife wanted to take her in, but Treasure was terrified of men and insisted that she would only go for a trial period if Chalee came with her. Chalee had done everything she could think of to make them want her, too. She'd washed dishes and polished tables that were already polished, and smiled all the time, but in the end they had taken only Treasure, and Chalee was back in the shelter. She's thirteen now. She knows the window has closed. People want children, not teenagers.

And then Dok was taken out on trial by a fat man and his thin, sharp-looking wife. Dok didn't know that the two of them had argued before they took him, didn't know that the woman had said Dok looked like a rat and she wouldn't have him in her house, didn't know that the fat man had promised that if it didn't work out, they could just bring him back, like, he'd said, "One of those dresses you're always returning."

But Dok is still gone. Apple, with her mumpish cheeks, might be Chalee's only friend.

And Chalee had been so busy drawing she'd sent Apple away.

There's a sudden knot of people in front of her, a snarl in the flow of the foot traffic, and she hears shouting, some of it angry, and then three *farang* men push their way through, arms linked in defiance of the narrowness of the sidewalk, red faced and drunk, shouting "Happy Christmas Eve, assholes, happy Christmas Eve." One of them winks at her as they pass and says to his friend, "Too young and too dirty."

"Merry Christmas anyway, honey," his friend calls back. "Merry Christmas."

Chalee says, "Merry Christmas." Then she says it three or four times, just getting it right, since she hasn't said it for a year, and when she thinks she has it down she says to the next person who comes by, a *farang* woman with coppery hair who's wearing tight shorts, "Merry Christmas," and the woman smiles and said, "Merry Christmas yourself, cutie."

"Cutie," Chalee says experimentally. "Cutie." Then she says, "Merry Christmas, cutie." She tries it out on the next man she sees, but the way he looks at her makes her decide to retire her new word. It's just "Merry Christmas" from then on.

SHE'S GONE FOURTEEN OR fifteen *sois* now. The sidewalks are getting emptier and darker, and Chalee is getting hungrier and more frightened about Apple. Her eyes are gritty with exhaustion; the two of them had been awakened and moved along by the police every time they fell asleep the previous night, and they were wandering wide-eyed and yawning when the sun rose. They ate *tom yam* soup around nine, using half of the money in Chalee's pocket, but that's all they've had since the previous night.

Why had she been so mean to Apple? She realizes, with a little start, that it's not *only* Apple. She snapped a few times at Dok, too, when she was drawing and he wanted to talk to her about it. One time when he'd been praising her she'd said, "Don't like it until it's *finished*," and Dok had left the room, banging the door behind him. She'd even ignored Boo once, too busy trying to get some stupid, meaningless detail right.

But even as she feels the flush of shame heat her face, the

thought of drawing makes her slow and shrug off the backpack. Leaning against a storefront with a row of yellowish lights above it, she pulls out her stack of paper and fans through it until she comes to the two drawings.

There's Baby Noi, reaching toward the warmth of his mother's gaze. The look in her eyes and the tilt of her head make it seem as though you could go into that room and call her name and she wouldn't hear you. And the moon-curve flows through the two of them, connecting them like a bend in a river, exactly where it should be. This is something new, Chalee sees, something she'll have to think about.

She slips the picture back into the stack of paper and concentrates on the drawing of Apple. It's new in a different way, and she feels a tingle of excitement. It's Apple, yes, but Chalee has made her prettier. It's not just the smooth skin, it's the work she put into the mouth, the girl's strongest feature. She's never done this before, either. Up until now she's wanted her drawings to look like photographs. For a moment she thinks, *It's a lie*, but no. What she's drawn is probably the way Apple would like to look. Maybe, if she wants it enough, she'll actually look like this someday.

Two new things in one day. And she needs to find Apple.

She pushes the papers into the backpack, more carelessly this time, and takes off at a trot. A dark *soi* goes by and then one with a cluster of bars surrounded by *farang*, and she hears "Merry Christmas" again, and then there's a third *soi*, dark at her end but brighter at the other with the hard whitish glare of portable neon and the red glow of charcoal, and Chalee smells food. It's worth a look.

She's about a quarter of the way down the *soi* when someone shouts, a woman, and then there's a confused tangle of people that opens suddenly as the shouts scale up, and Apple bursts through, holding something in both fists and running full out. Some men laugh, not very pleasantly, and a few meters behind Apple a woman appears. She wears a white apron and she's shouting and waving a cleaver above her head, and she's coming after Apple as fast as she can.

She's heavy-built and not very fast, but Apple has short legs. There's no doubt that the woman will overtake her. Catching the light, the cleaver glints like broken glass.

When Apple is halfway to Chalee—Apple's eyes are wide and white in her dark face, and she obviously hasn't recognized her friend—Chalee sprints toward her. Apple falters and registers Chalee's face for the first time, and the missed steps bring the woman with the cleaver too close. Chalee produces her highest scream and rushes toward them, and at the moment the woman's outstretched hand lands on the shoulder of Apple's awful shirt, Chalee uses both hands to swing the backpack, heavy with paper and everything else she owns, over Apple's head and straight into the woman's face.

The shock of the impact travels up both of Chalee's arms and almost brings her down. She's taking a step back to keep from falling and trying to get the pack up to swing it again, but the woman with the cleaver goes down backward, stiff as a tree. Chalee tucks the pack under her arm and grabs Apple's hand, but something sticks her—the point of a wooden skewer with broiled meat on it, and Chalee sees four of them in each of Apple's hands—and Chalee snatches her hand back, waving it in the air to shake away the pain, and says, "Come *on.*"

She slows just enough to let Apple keep up. Looking back over her shoulder, she sees the woman with the cleaver beginning to sit up, her nose bleeding, her spirit clearly scattered from the blow. She's not even looking in their direction. Some of the men at the far end of the *soi* applaud.

"To the left," Chalee says when they reach the boulevard. Then she opens it up as much as she can, hearing Apple's steps grow fainter behind her, until she leans gasping against a building and waits for the little girl to catch up. The moment she does, Chalee is running again, pacing Apple this time, listening to the wheeze of her breath, punctuated by sniffles.

They take the next *soi*, which leads them to a cross-street, and they angle down that. They're in a neighborhood of apartment houses, some of them with Christmas lights blinking in their windows. One building is set back far enough from the road to sport some shrubbery, just a little higher than Chalee is tall. Shrubbery is the street child's friend, and Chalee grabs a fistful of Apple's shirt and yanks her into it, both of them ignoring the scratches they get as they push through the branches.

Once through the hedge they find themselves just outside a big window. The curtains are closed, but they're white curtains that let the light inside sift through, and the two of them, both panting, regard each other until Apple begins to laugh. Chalee joins in, her hand pressed over her mouth, until they've both gotten it under control.

Apple is still clutching the bouquets of skewered meat, and she glances at them and drops her eyes and licks her lips, suddenly shy. "I stole these for you," she whispers, extending her right hand. "I was going to take them back to you." She indicates her left hand with a tilt of her chin. "These are mine."

"Thank you, thank you, thank you." Chalee pries the skewers loose and sits on her haunches, letting the backpack fall to the ground. Apple kneels beside her. The smell of the cooling meat envelops both of them. When the skewers are clean, the girls sigh in unison.

Apple is studying the ground in front of her as though there's something very interesting lying there. Chalee sighs, opens her knapsack, paws through it, and says, "Here."

In the light of the night's second window, Apple lifts her eyes to the page in Chalee's hand and coughs up a little pop of breath, soft as a heartbeat. Her eyes widen, and the beautifully shaped mouth opens slightly, and for just a moment Chalee sees, in color and three dimensions, the face she drew. Apple starts to reach for the drawing but pulls her hand back as though she expects it to be slapped.

Chalee reaches out and takes Apple's hand and puts the drawing into it. "It's for you," she says. "I made it for you."

"You—" Apple swallows. She looks as stunned as the woman with the cleaver had. "You did?" She takes it between her fingertips, as though a breeze could tear it, and holds it close to her eyes, following the curve of the lines. "You'll *give* it to me?"

"Sure," Chalee says, batting away a slight tug of regret. She closes the backpack and slips her arms through the straps, rises to her feet, and offers Apple a hand. Apple shifts the drawing to her other hand, out of Chalee's reach, and grasps Chalee's outstretched hand, and a moment later, both girls are standing in a little litter of wooden skewers. Chalee puts her arm around Apple and hugs her close, gazing down at the straw-like hair, and smelling feet. "It was always for you," she lies. Then she says, "Merry Christmas," and after a moment's thought, she adds, "cutie."

Then she steps back and takes her friend's empty hand. Says, "Come on, let's go home."

THE CUBAN MARQUISE'S JEWELS

Teresa Dovalpage

 TERESA DOVALPAGE was born in Havana, Cuba, in 1966. She earned her BA in English literature and an MA in Spanish literature at the University of Havana, and her PhD in Latin American literature at the University of New Mexico. She currently lives in Taos, New Mexico, where she teaches Spanish at the University of New Mexico Taos and writes for *Taos News* and other publications. She is the author of eight novels, three short story collections, one novella, and two plays.

I

Padrino's home office was designed to cater to two different kinds of clients. A print of the Virgin of La Caridad del Cobre, Cuba's patron saint, welcomed those who came to consult him as a Santería priest. For those looking for a private investigator, diploma from the Police Academy attested to his career as a detective. Now retired from the police force, Padrino mostly took private cases.

The woman who had come all the way to the town of Regla to request his services was Cuban-American. Or, as she put it, she was a Cuban who, after having lived for three decades in the United States, considered herself "hyphenated." She looked more aged than old. Her heavy makeup covered the damages of sickness rather than the passing of time. Her speech was punctuated by a metallic cough. Her hair was shoulder-length and light brown, thick and shiny, with a synthetic feel to it. Padrino suspected that it was a wig.

"I realize that this sounds like a silly idea," the woman said. She sighed and added with a bitter laugh, "It's not like I have a lot of time left."

Her hands clutched her Gucci bag. Padrino noticed her nails, long and unnaturally curved. He wondered why somebody who was so close to the other side would spend so much energy on fake nails. But hey, she had come to hire him, not to be judged. She was royalty, or so she said—the last Marquise of Bello Monte, who had returned to Cuba in search of the family jewels she had left behind thirty years before.

"I know exactly where they are," she went on. "Look."

She showed Padrino a drawing that depicted the floor plant of the house where she had lived until 1983. She also handed him a list of items—three rings, a pair of diamonds earrings, two gold chains, and a platinum pin.

"Here is my bedroom, on the second floor." The Marquise pointed to a spot with her blood-red index nail. "I hid the jewels in this corner, on the wall, to the left of the fireplace. See the tilework? Once you take the third tile out, you'll find a metal box. That's where they are."

Padrino couldn't imagine anything more useless than a fireplace in Havana, where on December 20th the temperature reached eighty degrees.

"So you want me to talk to the current owners of the house, offer them two thousand dollars to look for the jewels, and promise them a thousand more if they get them all back to you," he said, still incredulous. "And you are paying me five hundred bucks to do the work. Is that right, Marquise?"

She smiled and nodded. "I've heard many good things about you," she said. "Even in Miami, people talk about the *santero* detective who—" The Marquise started coughing. She took a handkerchief out of her bag and the fragrance of Opium filled the office. She blew her nose delicately and said, "Ironies of life! If someone had told me thirty years ago that there would be private businesses in Cuba again, after all my family's properties had been confiscated, I wouldn't have believed it. Had they told me I would come back to ask someone like you for help, I would have laughed out loud."

She didn't laugh, though. She coughed violently for the

next minute. Padrino wondered if "someone like you" meant a former cop, a *Santería* practitioner, a mulatto, or all of the above.

"In any case, señora," he said when she recovered, "don't you think that it would be easier, and less expensive for you, to deal with these people directly?"

She shrugged. "Let's be clear about this: money is *not* an issue," she declared. "Three or four thousand dollars won't make me richer or poorer. That being said, I did try. I went to the house—quite a stressful experience. A young woman was there. When I attempted to tell her why I had come back, she slammed the door on me." The Marquise breathed in heavily and covered her mouth with one hand. Now her cough sounded forced. "That's why I decided to resort to you," she concluded.

"But you should be aware of the risks," Padrino said. "The jewels may not even be there. Someone might have found them already."

"I don't think so," she replied with a convinced look. "Nobody knows where I put them."

"Supposing you are right, the current owners could easily take the two thousand dollars and keep them *and* the jewels," Padrino said.

She shook her head with such force that her wig slipped a little forward. "These pieces aren't worth much. They only have sentimental value for me. Nobody would pay more than fifteen hundred for them, and I doubt there is a booming jewelry market in Cuba. These people will be better off dealing with you and me."

Padrino's brows bumped together in a scowl. "But wouldn't it be safer to wait until they bring you the jewels and then give them the entire amount?"

"*Señor*, remember that for these people I am an old *gusana*, a member of the bourgeoisie," she explained. "Why should they trust me? They'll need to break a wall and I know how difficult it is to find construction materials in Cuba. I want to give them proof of my good faith."

Padrino wasn't convinced but he relented. "If you say so."

She handed him $3500, all in fifty-dollar bills. When Padrino suggested she keep the last thousand, she refused.

"No, *you* keep it. I will call you in a couple of days to find out how things are."

Afterwards, they made small talk for a while. The Marquise told Padrino that this was her first time back. Everything looked different to her.

"I see Christmas has been reinstated," she said. "At the Meliá Habana Hotel there is a sign that reads FELIZ NAVIDAD Y PRÓSPERO 2013 next to a Che Guevara poster! There is also a huge Christmas tree. Back in seventies and eighties, people put their Christmas trees in the kitchen. Balthasar, Gaspar, and Melchior were accused of being CIA agents. Ha!"

Padrino gave a noncommittal nod. "Yes, things have changed," he said.

"The only thing that hasn't changed is the Christmas Eve dinner, I bet." She licked her lips. "Still black beans and rice, yucca with *mojo*, and roast pork for *Navidad*, eh?"

"Yes, that's pretty much it. And fried sweet plantains."

The Marquise left an hour later, but her perfume stayed. Padrino opened the windows, looked at the drawing again, and reread the description of the jewels. He felt something was fishy, but couldn't put his finger on it.

He could have turned her down, but you don't find five hundred bucks growing on trees. Christmas was getting close and he still needed to buy a pig. They were over three hundred dollars this year.

"Had they told me that I would come back to ask someone like you for help." Stuck-up bitch. If those people scammed her, too bad.

But what if *she* was the one trying to scam them? Padrino decided to go to a bank first and make sure the American dollars weren't counterfeit.

"One can't trust anybody anymore," he told his wife, Gabriela.

She agreed.

II

THE DOLLARS WERE LEGIT. After leaving the bank, Padrino drove in his VW Beetle to the address the Marquise had given him. It was in Miramar, an upscale area where diplomats and the Cuban elite lived. The large, two-story house was enclosed by a picket fence that was missing some boards. The gate led to a garden that had grown wild. A tarnished marble nymph stood next to a waterless fountain. The front porch was covered with dead leaves.

The house, like its former owner, had seen better days, Padrino thought as he rang the bell. No one answered. All the windows were closed. He couldn't see anything inside, but noticed the servants' quarters to the right of the main house. A separate path had been built to access them. He went around and knocked on a smaller house door.

An old woman opened. Her black skin contrasted with her white *Santería* dress. Her obsidian eyes sparked when she looked at Padrino, who was also wearing his *Santería* attire and the blue and white necklaces that identified him as a son of Yemayá. The woman's necklaces were white and red—she was a daughter of Changó, the African god of thunder, and he suspected she was a *mamalocha*, a priestess, as well.

"I knew you would come here," she said matter-of-factly. "People go to the main house, nobody answers, then they drop by mine. It never fails."

"I'm sorry," Padrino said. "I didn't intend to bother you."

"What do you want?"

Padrino hesitated. But the woman was a *santera* too. "I came with a message from the former owner of this property," he said.

"The Marquise, you mean?" the woman asked, surprised. "Why, is she back?"

"Yes."

"Come on in," she said. "I'm Emilia."

"Nice to meet you. I hope I didn't spook you."

Emilia laughed. "Nothing spooks me anymore, *mijo*."

It had been a long time since anybody had called Padrino *mijo*, my son. But then Emilia was well into her eighties.

"Sit down," she said. "Make yourself at home."

The living room was tiny and had no windows. Emilia left the door open. From his seat, Padrino could see the main house entrance.

"Now tell me, is that old lady still gallivanting?" Emilia asked. "She is no spring chicken. She is just a couple of years younger than I."

Padrino's mind flashed back to the Marquise. She hadn't seemed that old to him, but maybe she was. Out of Cuba, he had been told, people had ways to keep themselves looking young until they dropped dead.

"She was sick," he answered. "Coughing like crazy."

"She should have come to see me, no matter what," Emilia said, offended. "After all my family and I did for her!"

There was a pause. While Emilia fumed, Padrino noticed the picture of a young woman in a doctor's coat. The picture was hanging in the most prominent place of the living room, as if presiding over it.

"My daughter, Evelina," Emilia said proudly. "She is a surgeon."

"Does she live here with you?"

"Ah, *mijo*, no. She married an Italian and left with him."

"Ah."

"Evelina always wanted to leave." Emilia sighed. "It saddened me, but I figured better married to a foreigner than leaving on raft, you know. Now she has a practice in Naples. *Los Italianos* adore her!"

That was a problem that worried Padrino. So many young Cubans left the country, looking for better opportunities. But a few old ones were returning, like the Marquise. To recover their property. Was that right? But he didn't have much time to ponder the issue. Emilia's astute eyes bore on him.

"And what else's going on?" she asked.

Padrino proceeded with caution. He started off by saying that the Marquise wanted to see her old home again and had entrusted him with facilitating the visit. Did Emilia think the owners would agree? What kind of people were they?

"Florencio is a *pichidulce*," Emilia said. "A lady-killer, you know? Women are his only vice, he's always said. And by Changó that's true. Other than that, he is okay. Well, *more or less* okay."

"What does he do?"

"He is retired from the military."

"Is he married?" Padrino asked, remembering the young woman the Marquise had mentioned.

"No, but he has a girlfriend," Emilia snickered. "After he

kicked out his former wife, he brought in this chick, La Bandidita, but they haven't signed any papers, though they have lived together for over ten years now."

"The Little Bandit?" Padrino laughed. "That's not a nice name."

Emilia wrinkled her nose as if she were smelling trash. "She is not a nice girl. Well, she isn't a girl anymore either. But his ex-wife was better off, if you ask me. He cheated on her with every woman in the neighborhood."

She turned her eyes to her daughter's picture. Padrino smiled knowingly. Emilia shook her head.

"Don't get any ideas. When it comes to white folks, they love us as brothers but not as brothers-in-law, as the saying goes." She waged her finger reprovingly at the picture. "Eh, they might have had something when Evelina was very young, but I always told her she didn't have a chance with him. And I certainly didn't want him in my family. Uff!"

Padrino rubbed a hand over his chin. "Well, *doña*," he said after a while. "I believe I can trust you with a secret."

"I am a *mamalocha*," Emilia answered. "I don't gossip."

Padrino told her briefly about the Marquise's request. He omitted the location of the jewels and Emilia didn't seem interested in it.

"Do you know if there is anything true in that story?" he asked.

"Everything is true," Emilia said. "The Marquise hid her jewels before she left. My very own godfather, may Changó have him in the glory of his thunder, put a protection on them."

"What do you mean, a protection?"

This time Emilia wagged her finger at Padrino. "Come on. You *know* what kind of protection I'm talking about."

"A curse?"

"Yes, and you bet it was a strong one because my godfather worked with *Palo Mayombe*."

Palo Mayombe was considered by many as the dark side of *Santería*. Padrino didn't agree with that entirely, but he would be the first one to admit that it dealt with some dangerous forces.

"Was the Marquise a believer?" he asked.

Emilia raised an eyebrow. "Yep. She was so pale that you could see the veins under her skin, but she was very much into it."

She slapped her thighs with her hands. "*La cabrona*! I can't believe she's here and hasn't paid me a visit yet."

A pickup truck stopped in front of the main house. Padrino glanced at it, then turned to Emilia again.

"Don't you think that this Florencio guy might have already found the jewels?" he asked.

She paused for a moment, then said, "I know that he and his ex-wife turned the house upside down looking for them when they first moved here. She was an actor and had small roles in several telenovelas back in the eighties. She would have loved to get her hands on them. I don't think they found anything. But what do I know? If they did, they didn't tell anyone."

A young woman came out of the truck and opened the gate. She was curvy, with dyed blonde hair and big hips. The driver followed her. He was tall and lean, with a dark complexion. A handsome couple, Padrino thought. They both looked suspiciously at his VW Beetle, which was parked down the street.

"Is that them?" Padrino asked.

"The woman is La Bandidita," Emilia said with a sly wink. "The stud is her . . . best friend. Florencio is an old geezer.

Not as old as me, but you get the idea. Close to seventy. From the old guard."

The young man followed La Bandidita into the house. Four tires that seemed too big for the vehicle and an assortment of wood pieces were tied down in the pickup bed.

"Wait until Florencio is here to bring up the issue with him," Emilia told Padrino. "La Bandidita is likely to get the jewels and vanish into thin air."

She walked to the kitchen and began to make coffee.

"When will Florencio be back?" Padrino asked.

"In a day or two," Emilia answered as the water boiled. "Ah, these two wouldn't have *Navidad* without a Christmas pig. He went to Pinar del Río to get one."

When Padrino left, he could see through an open window that the young man was watching TV, shirtless and sprawled on a couch as if he were in his own house. La Bandidita had found another *pichidulce* to keep herself amused when the old one wasn't around. Padrino chuckled. He still didn't see clearly in the case, though. If the Marquise was a *Santería* believer, why hadn't she said anything when she visited him? He had been wearing his white clothes and necklaces. She could have made a comment, couldn't she? There was something amiss about all that.

He took another look at the house and decided to return the next day.

III

FLORENCIO'S LIVING ROOM WAS furnished with a sofa, two matching stuffed chairs, and a rocking chair. They were, Padrino guessed, contemporary of the Marquise. But there was a plasma TV in a modern entertainment center and a Christmas tree next to it. Florencio might have been an old-guard communist, but he had adapted to the new mores.

Tall and slightly stooped, Florencio was the ghost of an athlete. He was bald and weighed a good forty pounds more than he should have, but his muscles were still visible under the Nike T-shirt and his movements were quick and fluid. La Bandidita sat next to him on the sofa, while Padrino occupied the rocking chair in front of them. Looking closely at her, Padrino realized she wasn't that pretty. She had ample love handles. Her face was covered in pimple scars and her hair showed three inches of dark root growth. She kept quiet, listening to the men's conversation in attentive silence.

"I don't know what to think of it," Florencio said with a gleam of greed in his blue eyes. "I did hear about a 'treasure' hidden here, but people tell the same story of all the houses where the bourgeoisie used to live. It may be true, or it may not."

"You have nothing to lose," Padrino answered. "She didn't say you need to give her the money back if the jewels weren't here."

Florencio turned to La Bandidita. "Honey, go check on the pork chops, will you?"

She frowned, but got up meekly and walked to the kitchen swaying her hips. The smell of fried pork hung thickly in the air.

"How does this Marquise, or whatever she is, know that I am not going to pocket the money and give her nothing?" Florencio asked.

Padrino repeated what his client had said about the actual value of the jewels.

"She may be counting on your honesty," he added.

Florencio didn't answer. Padrino wished he could take a good look at the bedroom where the jewels were hidden, but the master suite was on the second floor. Besides, the Marquise hadn't asked him to do that. It might seem too intrusive. And Florencio hadn't committed to anything yet.

"Tell you what," Florencio said. "I'll look for the stuff. If it isn't here, I'll give you *half* of the money back. I'll keep the other half to compensate for the cost of repairing the wall. How does that sound?"

Padrino smiled. "Sounds fine, man."

La Bandidita came back. Her lips curled in a mocking grin when Padrino handed Florencio two thousand dollars and the drawing. He had left the list of jewels at home.

IN HIS OFFICE, PADRINO listened to the radio. Outside, the rain was pouring down. The trees bent low as the wind whipped around the house. Hurricane Lola was inching closer to the capital at fifteen miles per hour. A hurricane warning was in effect for the Havana and Pinar del Río provinces. It had been raining for the last two days. Padrino hadn't heard from Florencio or the Marquise, but most phones were not working.

An hour later, the rain turned into a light shower. The sky began to clear. Still, Padrino was surprised when a Soviet-era Lada stopped in front of the house and Florencio came out. He hurried to let him in.

"*Carajo*, I had to tear down the entire wall to find the stuff," Florencio grumbled. "It wasn't exactly where the map said, you know?"

"Really? The Marquise seemed quite sure of it."

"She's an old woman. Her memory is probably gone." Florencio offered Padrino a small package. "Here you go. I hope that makes her happy."

Padrino opened the package and saw a set of golden earrings with very big and very fake diamonds, a necklace with green stones that were a poor imitation of emeralds, and a silver ring with a pink stone. A cursory look was enough for him to realize that these were modern, cheap and probably made-in-China pieces. Florencio watched him, waiting for his reaction.

"Sorry, man," Padrino said as calmly as he could. "But you got the wrong stuff."

Florencio's face turned red. "What do you mean wrong?"

"The Marquise gave me a list of her jewels. It has nothing to do with this."

Padrino tried to give the package back to Florencio, who refused to take it.

"That old woman is crazy!" he yelled. "Didn't I tell you that the stuff wasn't where she said?"

"Well, I'll take what you brought and let her decide."

"So you aren't giving me the other thousand?"

"No. She needs to identify the jewels first."

Florencio clenched his jaw. "You should remember that what you are doing is illegal," he snapped. "Dealing with a *gusana*—working for her. I could denounce you."

"What you are doing is illegal too," Padrino replied. "The jewels don't belong to you. They are part of our national heritage because their legitimate owner left the country. And you just took two thousand bucks for them."

Florencio left in a huff. Padrino was happy he hadn't given him the rest of the money, which he planned to return to the Marquise. But still, he felt cheated.

"It was her fault!" he told Gabriela later. "I warned her not to give them the money first. That was such a stupid thing to do."

"Ah, *mi amor*, take it easy," she answered. "You did your job. Now we can buy our Christmas pig. I wish we could keep the other thousand and get a tree, a nativity scene and some cute ornaments, like everybody else."

"Don't even think about it," Padrino said.

LOLA CONTINUED GAINING STRENGTH. Winds reached eighty-five miles per hour. Waves crashed over the Malecón seawall. Power was cut off. It was impossible to go out for three days. Habaneros spent a wet Christmas that year.

As the storm wound down, Padrino kept waiting for the Marquise to call him, or to come and pick up the jewels. She would be mad, of course, when she saw them, but what could he have done differently? He had just followed her instructions. She had been too naïve.

Another day passed and she didn't show up. She had mentioned she was staying at the Meliá Habana Hotel, but aside from her title, Padrino didn't know anything about her. He cursed himself for not having asked her name at least.

Why hadn't she called?

On the 27th, Padrino drove to the hotel. A ten-foot Christmas tree shimmered in red, green, and gold. Next to it there was a Che Guevara poster dusted in fake snow. The clerk at the reception desk wore a red hat and an unfriendly attitude. No, he didn't know anything about a Marquise of Bello Monte. He stared at Padrino with a look of suspicion and added, "Besides, we can't give out the names of our guests. It's against our privacy policy."

Padrino could have used his contacts with the police to find out more but didn't want to get them involved if he could help it. Not that he had done anything *that* illegal, but he preferred to keep his business to himself. He decided to pay a visit to

Emilia instead. She would know the Marquise's name. He risked running into Florencio or La Bandidita, but the possibility didn't worry him.

He knows perfectly well that what he brought me was worthless. But what if—I don't know, what if the Marquise's story was faker than his made-in-China junk?

I V

THERE WERE THREE POLICE cars outside Florencio's house. A small crowd had congregated around the fence. When Padrino arrived, two cops were bringing out a body on a stretcher. A taxi waited across the street with the driver at the wheel. Padrino parked in the corner and made his way through the crowd.

"Poor Florencio," he heard an old man say. "May God take his soul, even if he didn't believe in God."

The sky blew open. The rain began to fall. It was a tropical downpour that in less than five minutes had dispersed the onlookers. The cruisers drove away. As Padrino hurried toward Emilia's house, he saw a woman who looked vaguely familiar get in the taxi. Was that the Marquise? He ran after her but the taxi was already speeding down the road.

Emilia opened the door right away as if she had been waiting for him. *"Ay, mijo!"* she exclaimed. "What a tragedy! Florencio wasn't a saint but he didn't deserve that."

"What happened?" Padrino asked.

"They killed him! I hadn't seen any of them since the day before Christmas, when we had that storm. Then I noticed the stench. It wouldn't go away so I finally went there, thinking that La Bandidita was too lazy to throw away her own trash.

The door was unlocked and Florencio was on the floor, butchered like a pig."

"What about his girlfriend?"

Emilia shrugged. "She is nowhere to be found. People are saying that she was the one who offed him."

Padrino felt a shiver down his spine. He left soon, with the Marquise's name written on a piece of paper. He was nervous, guilty, and out of sorts. He suspected his dealings with Florencio had had something to do with the man's death.

He returned to the Meliá Habana. A different, more obliging clerk assured him that no María Mercedes del Junco y Subirana was staying, or had stayed there recently.

"If she had, I would remember," she said, laughing. "That's a telenovela kind of name!"

The Marquise might have registered under a different name, but how would he know what it was? Padrino left, feeling like a fool. The whole situation made no sense to him.

THE HEAVY RAIN, a remnant from the storm, didn't stop until the following day. Padrino still hadn't heard from the Marquise. He kept thinking about the woman in the taxi.

Even if that had been her, Padrino couldn't see her killing Florencio. She was too sick for that. Or wasn't she?

What if she'd hired somebody? People would do anything for dollars and she seemed to have plenty of them. But why had she gotten him, Padrino, involved in the first place? And where was María Mercedes, in any case? Had she lied about the hotel too?

Gabriela, who didn't know about Florencio's death (Padrino liked to keep his family life as separate as possible from his work), continued lobbying for the Christmas tree.

"And think of all the other stuff we can get with a thousand bucks!" she said. "We haven't had a real Christmas in, like, forever."

"I've told you this money isn't ours," he argued. "When the Marquise finds out that she has been scammed, she'll want it back."

If she was still in Cuba, he thought. *If* she was a Marquise.

"That woman may not call you again," Gabriela insisted. "Wasn't she sick? She might have returned to Miami, for all we know."

"We don't know anything."

Padrino didn't consider himself a *pichidulce*. But his wife was much younger than he was. She had been born in the eighties, when all things Christmassy were banned. He could understand the attraction that the glittery ornaments held for her.

"If she doesn't contact me in a week, we'll use the money," he finally said.

"But today is the twenty-eighth," she replied. "In a week, it will be too late."

"Ah, people keep the trees up until January sixth, waiting for the Magi."

Gabriela smiled and kissed him.

That evening he caught her doing a ceremony to Oshún, the virgin of La Caridad. Gabriela had placed a toy Christmas tree on the living room altar and covered it with honey and cinnamon. Padrino shook his head but didn't say a thing.

V

THE NEXT DAY PADRINO changed his mind about contacting the police. If they discovered his involvement in the affair, he was going to be in trouble. He had better come clean. He decided to contact Lieutenant Marlene Martínez, a former student of his at the Police Academy. They had worked together on several cases, both in his private eye business and in her official assignments. She still called him "Comrade Instructor."

Marlene was now in charge of *Unidad* Thirteen, a police station in Centro Habana. Padrino went to her office, closed the door, and told her everything.

"The way things are, I feel responsible," he concluded. "I can't shake the thought that Florencio would still be alive if I hadn't given him the Marquise's money."

"You don't need to worry about that," Marlene replied. "The case is already closed."

"So soon?" Padrino exclaimed.

"Yes, Florencio was a decorated veteran. He had fought in the Sierra Maestra Mountains with Fidel. Imagine that! All hands were on deck for this case. But it turned out to be an easy one—Florencio's partner Zoila Perez, aka La Bandidita, killed him. Her fingerprints were on the knife used to stab him. Two people saw her leave their house in a pickup with a young man, her lover, on December twenty-fifth."

Padrino remembered La Bandidita's grin when he gave Florencio the thousand bucks. Emilia had been right. *That* made sense.

"Were they caught?" he asked.

"Unfortunately not," Marlene said, a note of disappointment in her voice. "They left that very night on a raft, probably for Miami."

"December twenty-fifth," Padrino repeated. "That's when the storm started."

"Yes, I don't think they got too far. No way they could have made it to Miami with the weather we had."

Padrino realized that three of the four people directly involved in the case might already be dead. *Is that the curse Emilia's godfather put on that stuff?*

"She might have killed Florencio to get the money you gave him," Marlene added pensively. "But there could have been other reasons. He was a revolutionary and probably opposed to her leaving. This, and the fact that she had a lover who fled with her, pretty much settled it."

It took Padrino a while to come to terms with Marlene's conclusion. Partly because his conscience kept nagging at him. But there was something else.

"I still would like to know if this young woman, La Bandidita, took the real jewels with her, since the ones that Florencio gave me were fakes," he said. "For that, I need your help."

"What can I do, Comrade Instructor?"

"I would like an authorization to visit Florencio's house."

"I'll go with you," she said. "This hidden treasure story has made me curious. It sounds like a telenovela!"

She laughed, but Padrino didn't find it amusing.

THOUGH THE CASE WAS out of her jurisdiction, it wasn't difficult for Marlene to get the corresponding permit. The house was going to be emptied soon and assigned to someone else, she told Padrino. There was no time to waste.

When they came in, the living room looked pretty much like it had the day of Padrino's first visit. But there was a big wine-colored spot on the floor, next to the sofa, where Florencio had lain bleeding to death.

"The coroner said he didn't die right away," Marlene said. "It seemed like he tried to get to the door, but couldn't."

Padrino looked for the stairs and took them two at a time.

He found the master suite, a huge room furnished with an Art Deco mahogany set—a dresser, a vanity, an armoire, and a king size bed. The fireplace was across from the bed, but the tile that marked the hiding spot wasn't there anymore. All the tilework, in fact, had been removed. The wall had been repainted afterwards, but he could still see the tiles' silhouette under the coat of paint. None of it had happened recently, though. The paint job was old and the walls were chipped in some places.

The dresser drawers were open and their content had been scattered on the floor. There were papers, medals, and a black and white photo of Florencio standing next to Fidel Castro. Padrino browsed through everything, still thinking about the jewels. Who had found them? And when?

He noticed a wedding album entitled *Nuestra Boda*, the kind that had been popular thirty years before. A yellowish invitation had slipped off its pages. Padrino opened it distractedly and saw the picture of a couple. "Compañero Florencio Laporte and Compañera Marisa Beltrán invite you to share in their joy at their wedding, which will take place at the Revolutionary Armed Forces Club on April 21, 1981, at 6 p.m."

The man was Florencio, beaming in his military uniform. Padrino kept looking at the woman. He recalled having seen her in several telenovelas in the eighties. Yes, Marisa Beltrán had played a farmer in *El naranjo del patio* and a student in *Hoy es siempre todavía*. But that wasn't all, was it? It took him a few minutes to realize that the dimple-faced girl who smiled next to the groom was a younger, healthier version of the Marquise of Bello Monte.

ARMED WITH A NAME, and accompanied by Marlene, it wasn't difficult for Padrino to find Marisa Beltrán's whereabouts. The clerk at the Meliá Habana reception desk suddenly turned deferential, his eyes shimmering like the Christmas tree.

"Yes, *compañera*, she was our guest until two days ago," he said to Marlene. "Señora Beltrán was in room one hundred twelve, but she had to be rushed to the hospital. She stopped breathing and the manager thought she was going to die here. Uff!"

"Which hospital is she in?" Padrino asked.

"Cira García, of course. The foreigners' hospital."

VI

CIRA GARCÍA CENTRAL CLINIC was in Miramar, not too far away from the Marquise's house. It catered to foreign businessmen, diplomats, and tourists. Padrino and Marlene were asked for their official identifications before they were allowed inside.

"It's good that you decided to come with me, *mija*," he told her. "With my *babalawo* attire and my obviously Cuban looks, they would have sent me away."

Marisa Beltrán's room was small but tidy and clean. A watercolor of the Havana Cathedral hung from the wall. On the bed, a woman rested under a white sheet drawn up to her chin. A few strands of gray hair covered her bald head, but Padrino identified her as the same person who had come to his house claiming to be a Marquise.

"Are you relatives of Señora Beltrán's?" a nurse asked.

She had come in so quietly that neither Marlene nor Padrino noticed her presence until she spoke.

"I am a friend," Padrino said.

"Is there any problem with her, *compañera?*" The nursed glanced at Marlene.

"Not at all," Marlene answered. "How is the patient doing?"

The nurse moved away from the bed. "Not too good," she whispered. "I just talked to her daughter, who is flying from Miami as soon as she can get a ticket. Señora Beltrán has lung cancer." She lowered her even voice more. "She is terminal."

"So that's what's going on with her," Padrino said.

"Well, that and a bad cold she got," the nurse answered. "She said that she went out in the rain during the storm. That didn't help."

"May we talk to her?"

The nurse looked at the charts. "Señora Beltrán was sedated around two hours ago," she said. "You may want to wait outside until she wakes up."

In the hall, Marlene shook Padrino's hand. "Sorry, Comrade Instructor, but I have to see enough disagreeable things every day at work," she told him. "I don't need any extras. When you find out what happened with the jewels, let me know, okay?"

She left. Padrino waited for an hour on a plush, comfy armchair. The clinic reminded him of a hotel. The foreign accents and non-Cuban outfits of Venezuelan and Spanish patients and their companions reinforced the similarity. Doctors and nurses hurried around with an efficient air. Some eyed his white clothes and *Santería* necklaces with distrust or open hostility.

The nurse returned with a tray of food. When she came out of Marisa's room, she told Padrino that Señora Beltrán wanted to see him. "But don't stay too long. She is very weak."

Padrino came in. Marisa sat straight on the bed and had put on her wig.

"That's—a surprise," she said feebly. "I never expected to see you again."

"Well, I had something to give you," Padrino answered. "We made a deal, remember?"

He placed a small package on her nightstand. She didn't even look at it.

"Don't you want to open it?" he asked.

With another shrug, she took the packet apart. The sight of its content didn't seem to surprise or bother her.

"Some crap," she whispered, putting it away.

Padrino handed her an envelope. "Here you have the other thousand."

Again, she didn't make a move to take it. "Why did you bring it back?" she asked. "You could have kept all that."

Padrino took a chair and sat close to the bed. "I know," he said. "But I wanted to know why you did this."

"Did what?"

"Pretended to be a Marquise. Asked me to deliver the money to your ex-husband. What was this charade for, Marisa?"

She looked alarmed at first. Then, noticing that Padrino's tone was soft, almost pleading, she collected herself.

"So you know," she said.

"I know part of it. What Emilia told me and—"

"Emilia! I wish I had seen her. But I couldn't risk—how is she doing?"

"Very well. She's a strong woman."

"She will bury all of us." Marisa smiled sadly. "She didn't like Florencio and me very much when we first moved there. Later she warmed up to me a bit. Sometimes I wish I had listened to her. 'Don't ever try to find the Marquise's jewels,' she told me when we started nosing around. 'There is *Santería* work protecting them. Don't play with fire.'"

"And you did?"

Marisa lowered her head. Her wig tipped to the left side. "Florencio and I found them," she admitted. "I wore them for a while, discreetly, but we sold most of them in the late eighties, during the gold fever, remember? When the government opened *La Casa del Oro*. With what we got from them, we bought a TV set, a washing machine, and clothes for him, our daughter and me. He only kept two or three, the prettiest ones. I bet La Bandidita took them, as she did everything else."

A coughing fit ensued. Padrino waited until it stopped. Marisa's breathing became heavier.

"He was crazy for her, totally *empapayado*," she said bitterly. "He had had many others before, but they came and went. I didn't care. With this one, it was different. I knew it since the first night he didn't return home. I realized he had found another *papaya* and its pull was stronger than mine."

"When was that?"

"Ten years ago. Katiuska, our daughter, was fifteen. La Bandidita was just a few years older. Kathy didn't take it too hard, but I was humiliated. I had loved Florencio so much."

Her eyes were full of tears.

"In 1993 I signed a contract with a Venezuelan producer to star in a telenovela," she went on. "At first I feared Florencio wouldn't let me take Katiuska out of Cuba, but La Bandidita convinced him. She didn't want us around. That was during the Special Period, and he also knew there was no future for our daughter here.

"When my work in Caracas ended we moved to Miami and began a new life. Katiuska went to college. Now she calls herself Kathy." Marisa laughed. "But I couldn't get any roles—I was too old for the industry. I became a hairdresser and opened my very own salon, La Marquesita. But I never forgot—I couldn't, anyway. Florencio and Kathy kept in contact by phone and letters. He was a good father. Or at least he tried to be. I kept waiting for La Bandidita to leave him. I am sure she cheated on him as he had cheated on me. What goes around, comes around."

Padrino nodded silently.

"A few weeks ago, out of the blue, he told Kathy that *la otra* wanted to leave Cuba. Someone had promised to take her to Miami on a raft for three thousand dollars and she was trying to make him come up with the money. He was furious."

Marisa stopped and fought to breathe. Her gasping turned to a choking sound. "Do you want me to call the nurse?" Padrino asked.

"No, no. This will pass. I know I'm talking too much, but now I want to tell you everything. It feels as if I were confessing my sins to a priest." She smiled. "Only you are a different kind of priest, a *Santería* one." Her voice faltered but she continued, "The idea occurred to me later that day. I couldn't send the money to La Bandidita. I couldn't go to their house, throw it on the floor and say 'Here, you guys fight over it.' But I remember the Marquise. I thought that I could come back, pretending to be her, and make sure that La Bandidita knew about the money. I'd make it the exact amount she needed to get out of Cuba. I had heard good things about you so I chose you to be my intermediary, so to speak."

"But why did you divide the money into two parts, when you knew damn well that the jewels weren't there anymore?" Padrino asked. "Why did you create a condition that was impossible to meet?"

"Ah, that was the artistic touch." Her pupils dilated a bit. "I am an actor, remember? Just to thicken the plot. Plus I wanted them to go around like headless chickens trying to match every item on the list."

Padrino decided not to mention that he hadn't given Florencio the list. While Marisa struggled to catch her breath, he guessed that La Bandidita must have gotten the remaining one thousand dollars somewhere else.

"I knew Florencio wouldn't resist the temptation to scam an old *gusana*," she said. "I suspected that he and La Bandidita would fight over the money, and that was what I wanted. I also hoped she would end up with it and leave him. But never in my wildest dreams did I expect that she would kill him and flee."

"Ah, you know that too."

"Yes, I kept going to my house, circling it—waiting for the movie to end. I wanted to be in the last scene, you know, when the villain is crushed and the heroine triumphs. I thought I would see him defeated, but I didn't think I would see him *dead*."

Her eyes were unfocused. Her words became slurred. "The Marquise must be happy now."

Marisa started coughing again and didn't stop for several minutes. When she finally did, her lips were covered in blood. She slipped off the bed. Padrino managed to catch her before she hit the floor. Her body was a dead weight in his hands.

"Nurse, nurse!"

VII

PADRINO WALKED AROUND HIS backyard, making sure the pig was done the right way. He was roasting it in a fire made with guava wood so the meat would absorb its sweet, slightly pungent smell. A curling column of blue smoke rose in the air.

In the living room, Gabriela was putting the last touches on the Christmas tree. It might be a little late for it on December 30th, but she didn't care. The tree was tall—the biggest one they had found at the dollar shop. She had gotten ornaments, too, and a made-in-Italy nativity scene. That was the first time there was such a display at Padrino's home.

Gabriela surveyed it and smiled to herself. Yes, it was the nicest Christmas tree in the neighborhood. It was also the only one, in the town of Regla and perhaps in the entire island, that wasn't crowned by an angel or a star, but a small statuette of *La Virgen de la Caridad*.

A MOTHER'S CURSE

Mette Ivie Harrison

METTE IVIE HARRISON

is the author of numerous books for young adults. She holds a PhD in German literature from Princeton University and is a nationally ranked triathlete. A member of the Church of Jesus Christ of Latter-Day Saints, she lives in Utah with her husband and five children. She has written three novels in the Linda Wallheim series, which features a Mormon bishop's wife who turns ward detective: *The Bishop's Wife*, her crime fiction debut; *His Right Hand*; and *For Time and All Eternities*.

I was out shopping at Men's Warehouse with Samuel for clothes he'd need for his Mormon mission when my husband, Kurt, called me. "Did you close the garage door and lock up the house when you left?" he asked without any greeting.

I was surprised enough that it took me a second to answer. "I think so, yes."

"I need you to be sure. If you're not sure, I'm going to go over right now and lock it up myself."

"Kurt, what's going on?" I asked.

"Someone's targeting homes in the neighborhood, going in through garage doors and back doors that aren't locked. They're taking Christmas presents, even wrapped ones, and any other big ticket items like TVs and laptops. They've hit three homes in the ward in the last night."

A chill ran through me, and it quickly turned to something else—anger. Who would do such a thing at Christmastime? It seemed the Grinch Who Stole Christmas come to life.

"Who's been robbed?" I asked.

"Swedins and Hansens," said Kurt. "I can't remember the third. Oh, it was the Gibbys."

The Gibbys were a newlywed couple, barely back from their honeymoon. They were adorable to watch in church together, often breaking the physics rule that said two things could not occupy the same space at the same time. And now they had had their new home broken into. I sometimes wondered why they had purchased a house so early in their marriage. They both worked, but they were just out of college and I couldn't help but think that all the square footage was going to waste. And really, who wanted the stress of a mortgage in those years when you ought to be carefree?

"The police are taking statements right now, going around asking if anyone saw anything, any unusual cars, or people lurking in bushes, I suppose."

Kurt's idea of investigating burglaries amused me briefly. Then again, he was an accountant. As well as a Mormon bishop, of course.

"Well, I didn't see anything," I said.

"Good, then you can keep out of it," said Kurt. And that was his opinion of me being involved in police investigations.

"Do we need to ask for donations to cover the losses?" I didn't want to think that anyone's Christmas was ruined. I remembered my first Christmas when Kurt and I were married. There had been one lone present under the tree for each of us because we were so poor. It was a wonderful Christmas, even so. Then again, we hadn't been shaken in our security in our home.

"I'd have already done it if I didn't know that the insurance companies involved had already promised to expedite the payments so they arrive before Christmas."

"Is there anything else we can do?" I asked, imagining baking up a batch of homemade wheat bread when I got home from shopping. The bill at the end of this adventure was going to put me into a mood to pound some bread dough, that was certain.

"I'm thinking about a prayer vigil," said Kurt. "And a reminder to priesthood holders that they have the power to bless their homes against Satan's incursions in any form, if they haven't done it already."

Well, I wasn't sure that would stop burglars, but it might bring people some peace, at least temporarily.

"Is it just our neighborhood or is it other neighborhoods in the same area?" I asked.

"I don't know. I haven't talked directly to the police, only to the Stake President. He called me and I called the families involved, the Relief Society President, the Elders and High Priest Group Leader, and then you."

That put me in my place, didn't it? Bishop's wife, in fourth place in terms of importance in the ward hierarchy. I was lucky to be there, in fact. I had no power. Everyone else in the ward had a neat chart of their authority over others. But the bishop's wife was only in charge of her own children.

"Linda? You didn't answer my question about locking up," Kurt said. "Do I need to go over? They tend to hit homes in the middle of the day, not at night. They seem to be watching when people come and go."

Then was it already too late?

I had a sudden flash of memory of me turning the lock on the front door. "I locked the front," I said. "And I closed the garage door. I don't know about the back, though. I didn't check."

"All right, I'll go back and double check it myself. You and Samuel keep shopping."

I hung up, then turned back to Samuel, looking at the six suits he was choosing among. Two black, two gray, one blue pinstriped and one brown.

"One black, one gray," I said, as I'd said to all my other sons. The black one would do for formal occasions, any funerals he had to go to while on a mission (God forbid), any weddings, or temple visits he managed to get to. The gray was lightweight enough to last through summer in Boston, which was where Samuel had been called to serve. His official mission call had arrived in the mail three weeks ago.

Two years from now, when he got home, both of these suits would go in the garbage can. Or to Goodwill. Samuel would never want to see them again. Wearing one of two suits every day for two years could do that to you. He would be allowed to wear something more casual on P-days—preparation days—and then only as long as he wasn't visiting investigators or the mission president.

"But which gray?" asked Samuel. He didn't try to argue for the blue or the brown, though either were acceptable colors according to the list of rules we'd been sent along with his mission call. And yes, there was an extensive list of rules about what was acceptable to wear, complete with online depictions of appropriate tie width, belt buckle size, and a list of dos and don'ts—you could wear a sweater under a suitcoat if you were cold, but never a hoodie. Jewelry was strictly forbidden, as were tattoos and backpacks.

"I think they're both fine," I said. "It's up to you."

Samuel had come out as gay to the whole family last summer, a big deal in Mormonism. He had been open about his sexuality in every step of the process of getting ready for his mission, honest with everyone from his college ward bishop to his college stake president. He'd even tried to find a place to add it on the mission papers, though it wasn't like there was a place to check on the form for being "gay." The church didn't even call it that. It was "same sex attraction," and they insisted it was just a temporary problem that would be solved in the resurrection, like being blind or having a missing limb—in his afterlife Samuel would be "restored" to heterosexuality, according to the Mormon church. I wasn't sure what I personally believed about sex in the afterlife, but I didn't think Samuel needed to be fixed in any way. He was the best of my sons, even if that wasn't something I told them openly.

The clerk who was helping us asked question after question to find us the right shirts: did Samuel want tags in the collar corners to keep them sharp, how heavy a fabric did he want, what color white shirt—apparently there were different shades of white to be considered—and what button shape, what cuff length, should the cuff be suitable for cuff links (no), on and on until I almost wished Kurt would call me and tell me we'd been robbed so I had an excuse to go home.

I'd done this with three sons already (Adam, Kenneth, and Zachary but not Joseph) and I think the shopping got more annoying every year. The first time, it hadn't seemed like there were that many choices. Or maybe Adam just made them himself and didn't look to me for advice every time. But Samuel had zero interest in fashion and shrugged and accepted the clerk's advice.

After shirts, it was ties. Samuel picked out ten from a stack and I had to double check to be sure he hadn't chosen two identical ones. They were all varying shades of red. We had them all packed up in tissue paper, then carted to the front where everything else was waiting. Shoes were next. And socks. The shoes were the first time that Samuel showed real interest. He went for the ones with the highest platform he could find. I wondered if Samuel had a complex about his height. He was nearly six foot, but it was true that he was the smallest of my sons, by about half an inch. They were all just about clones of Kurt when it came to their bone structure.

The bill, when we finally managed to make it to the register, was over two thousand dollars. I got out a credit card to pay for it, but Samuel waved me away.

"I've got it, Mom," he said.

"You're supposed to be saving that for the rest of your mission," I said. There would be a $400 bill for each of the twenty-four months he'd be gone, although truthfully Kurt and I had often stepped in to pay our sons' mission bills in the past.

"I can cover all of it," said Samuel proudly. "What do you think I've been doing with all that money I saved from summer jobs since I was eight?" He had always been a saver.

"If you're sure," I said, and held my card out for another moment.

"I want all the blessings, Mom," said Samuel. "I earned them, every one." His eyes were shining, and I admit, mine were a little misty, too.

I worried that he thought that making sacrifices like this would mean the mission would go more easily for him. I knew that wasn't going to be the case in Boston. I hoped he would get companions who didn't bully him for being gay, but that was about the extent of my hope. I doubted those conversions would come easily—if they happened at all. I was steeling myself for the most difficult missionary experience I'd ever seen. Samuel was a strong kid, maybe the strongest of all my sons, and if any of them could deal with a hard mission, it was him. But I would be praying for him every step of the way.

Between the two of us, we managed to get everything into the car in one load. The suits weren't finished yet. They'd taken measurements and would get them properly tailored in the next week. We weren't leaving much time to spare because Samuel had only eight days before he was expected to report to the MTC (Missionary Training Center) in Provo.

We drove home and when I opened the garage door, Kurt's car was still there.

I helped Samuel bring in all his things. We trooped upstairs, and that was when we realized what was wrong.

The missionary suitcases we'd purchased two days ago were

gone. They'd been at the foot of Samuel's bed when we left this morning, waiting for his clothes to go inside of them. He could take two suitcases' worth of things with him for two years, and he had to be ready at a few hours' notice to leave any apartment he was in and move to another one the mission president assigned him to.

We checked in the closet and under the bed.

"Maybe Dad came and got them?" Samuel said.

"Why would he do that?"

"If he thought we should get some different ones," Samuel said.

"He came with us and said those were the best ones," I reminded him. Kurt had been annoyingly picky about it, and had insisted he knew better than either of us. After all, he had been on a mission and we hadn't.

"Maybe he found a sale or something," Samuel said. "And he had to take them back to get the better price."

I went downstairs and checked the back door. Sure enough, it was unlocked. I thought I could make out footprints through the snow in the backyard, but I didn't go out and follow them. Instead, I closed the door and locked it tight, then closed the blinds as if that would protect us somehow.

After retreating back upstairs to Samuel's room, I got out my phone and texted Kurt: *Suitcases are gone. Did you take them?*

In a few minutes, Kurt texted me back: *Found them gone when I arrived. Also, back door open. Saw strange van pulling out of our street. Must have been parked nearby. Didn't notice when I passed. Got license plate and called police.*

Then why wasn't he at home, waiting for them?

Where are you now? I texted back.

I followed the van.

Kurt, my Kurt, the bishop, had gone chasing after criminals in a van?

Stay there so you can talk to the police, Kurt texted. *Can you find the receipt for the suitcases? We don't have a photo, do we?*

We didn't have a photo as far as I knew, but to my surprise, when I mentioned the question to Samuel, he pulled out his phone and showed me one he'd posted on Facebook.

"Where's Dad?" Samuel asked.

"He's out trying to follow the van with the people who stole your stuff."

"Dad?" said Samuel.

"I know," I said.

"Isn't that kind of dangerous?"

"I'm sure he won't do anything stupid. He's a grown up," I said. With responsibilities, I thought.

The uniformed police arrived a few minutes later. They seemed rather bored, to be honest. They had Samuel send them his photo and they took my receipt. Then they told us to wait for the detective who was on the case.

We were waiting when I got another text from Kurt: *Coming home. Don't worry about me. I'm fine.*

It was thirty minutes before he came through the front door, breathing heavily and his hair sticking up all over.

"What happened?" I asked. He wasn't carrying Samuel's suitcases with him, so he hadn't confronted the burglars—or had he?

"It's a long story," he said, pushing the front door closed behind him and slumping down right there on the tile of the foyer.

"Kurt, do you need something? Did they hurt you?" I asked.

He shook his head, then put it in his hands.

"Dad?" said Samuel, coming in and kneeling beside Kurt. "Do you want to pray with me?"

"Yes, I do. Would you say the prayer?" asked Kurt.

I knelt down beside them while Samuel spoke the words. It was a simple prayer, "Our Heavenly Father, please bless the people who stole my suitcases that they will know what is right. And please bless Dad so that he will be able to get better. Bless us all to forgive and to become more like Thy Son. Amen."

Kurt managed to get up after that, and moved slowly toward the kitchen. "No police yet?" he asked.

"The uniforms came, but we haven't talked to the detective yet," I said.

Kurt nodded and sat at the bar in the kitchen.

I got out the remains of the peanut butter cookies I'd made yesterday when Samuel asked. He'd eaten almost all of them himself, but I'd saved two for a treat for myself today. It showed how much I truly loved Kurt for me to offer them to him.

Kurt chewed the cookie thoughtfully. "I found where they live," he said. "It's the ward right next to ours."

"Seriously? We have thieves living in the neighborhood?" I asked nervously.

Kurt sighed. "They're parents," he said. "They have eleven children and they have two on missions right now. One will be leaving in the next couple of weeks. Just after Samuel, actually."

I stared at him. "They took Samuel's suitcases and all the other stuff?" I remembered meeting a mother of eleven at a Stake Relief Society night.

"It was their van on our street, and I saw Samuel's suitcases inside," he said. "The husband was driving it. I don't know if the wife has any idea what he's doing, or any of the children."

I sat with that for a long moment, trying to digest the idea that a father of eleven children was funding his children's missions by stealing Christmas presents from his neighbors. What kind of a messed up world did we live in?

"Did you talk to him?" I asked.

"I knocked on the door. As soon as he answered it, I recognized him from stake meetings. He's in his ward's High Priest Group leadership. He teaches Seminary, in fact, at the high school. He has one son on a mission and another preparing to go out."

I knew instantly who Kurt meant—I even knew his name, though I didn't say it out loud. I could see Samuel swallow an exclamation. He knew the man, too.

"What did you say to him?" I asked. Had Kurt confronted him about the thefts?

"I asked him if I could donate to his son's mission fund. I wanted to write a check for a couple hundred, but I was afraid he wouldn't take it. Instead, I held out all the cash I had, which was about sixty bucks."

"Did he take it?" Samuel asked.

Kurt shook his head sadly. "He said they didn't need any help and he was just fine managing on his own. He said that the Lord would send blessings to the faithful who waited on Him."

"And you didn't point out that maybe you were the blessing God was sending to him?"

Kurt chewed on more cookie and didn't answer. When he was finished with the first cookie, he picked up the next one. "Pride," he muttered.

"It makes no sense. Stealing from people because you won't accept any help?"

"I couldn't get him to talk enough to explain it to me. Maybe it makes sense to him," said Kurt.

"He's not on school break or anything, is he?" I asked, wondering how he had the time to sneak in and out of houses while he was supposed to be teaching.

"I suspect if we asked the police, we'd find out they all happened over his lunch break. Or his preparation period," said Kurt. "After all, it's not like he had to stake us out for days to learn our day-to-day habits. He knows us all pretty well, even if he doesn't live in the same ward."

It was creepy, thinking about a man who went to church in our same building, who was supposed to be a friend and ally, using the information he knew about us to do something like this.

"So do we give the detective his name?" asked Samuel.

It was an excellent question. I looked at Kurt.

"I've always thought I believed in telling the truth no matter what," he said. "But in this case, I don't know."

"If he's this confused, he may be headed for some kind of psychotic break. It might be helpful for him to have some kind of intervention," I suggested.

"An intervention, yes. But an arrest by the police for breaking into the homes of his neighbors and fellow Mormons? He'd lose his job and he might lose a lot more than that."

He could be excommunicated. His wife could well divorce him. And what about his eleven children? Would they be any better off? I could see why Kurt felt it was a moral dilemma.

"You could talk to the Stake President," said Samuel. "Maybe he could go privately to the man and make him give everything back."

"That doesn't absolve him of the crime, though," said Kurt. "The police will still want to prosecute him." He shook his head. "Look, I don't want to talk about it anymore. You two can talk to the detective, but only about the lost suitcases. Don't say anything about what happened to me yet." He went upstairs and I assumed he was going to our bedroom. To sleep? To pray?

The detective, Morales, came and took our statements. He was short and bald, but had a precise way of speaking that reminded me of my high school English teacher.

"Do you have any leads?" I asked, trying to see if he knew anything about the man in the van.

"I'm sorry, I can't tell you about that," he said, closing up his notebook and rising.

"Have you retrieved anything from any of the other thefts?" I asked.

"No, we haven't. You said you have homeowner's insurance that will cover the losses?"

"Yes," I said. And we were well enough off that we could buy new suitcases for Samuel immediately without having to wait to be reimbursed for the loss. We had that much plenty, even at Christmastime.

"Well, then, you'll hear from me again if I have more information later," Morales said.

I watched him drive away and noticed that he turned in the direction of the house Kurt had chased the van to. Did the police know what was going on, after all?

I told Samuel I couldn't bear to do any more shopping today, but promised we'd go out tomorrow and get him the same suitcases all over again. Then I went upstairs to talk to Kurt. He was lying flat on the bed, his hands folded together over his abdomen. His eyes were open, but he was still as death.

"What are you going to do?" I asked.

"I haven't decided yet," Kurt said.

"Maybe we could talk to his wife, get her to take some money."

"And make her deal with his anger if he finds out?" Kurt said. "No, I don't think so."

"We could talk to their bishop and make sure he knows about the situation," I suggested. It was the kind of strategy I would expect Kurt to pursue. Going through the proper channels and all that.

"I'll try that, but I don't know if it will change anything in terms of his pride," said Kurt with a sigh.

I tried snuggling up against him, molding my body to his. I wanted him to feel that he wasn't alone in this.

Kurt eventually fell asleep, which seemed like a good thing, considering how little sleep he got these days, between work and bishoping and parenting.

I snuck out of the room and went back downstairs. Samuel was working on a new batch of peanut butter cookies. "Well, I did something," he said.

"What?" I asked.

"I called up the store and asked them to send my suit to him, the son who's heading off on a mission."

"Do you think it will fit?" I asked. I didn't know the kid well enough to guess at his height and weight.

"He and I are almost exactly the same size. I told them to send it there and if anyone called, to say that it was an accidental duplicate and they couldn't take it back because it had already been altered."

That seemed rather clever of Samuel. "Well, he'll have a suit, then." The shirts and ties and shoes and socks were a different matter. But the suits were the most expensive part. "Your father and I are happy to buy you a new suit, of course. But you were so proud to have bought that suit with your own money."

"AND THAT'S WHAT WAS wrong with it," Samuel said. "Dad said that the man who took our things was too proud to take charity from him. It was pride that led him to do this, and it was stupid. I don't need to be proud of paying for my own suit. That's a way of feeling like I'm better than other people and it's not a good thing at all. I should be humbled, especially as a missionary. If I go into this thinking I'm better than the people I'm called to serve, I'm not going to reach them. They need to know that I'm the same as they are, that we're all sinners looking for redemption, or I won't succeed." He thought for a minute, then held up a finger. "I shouldn't even put it like that. It's not me succeeding. It's God who succeeds through me, if I can just get out of the way enough to let Him."

I hugged him and wondered how I was ever going to do without him. "I'm going to miss you more than you can imagine," I said. "I want you to know that."

He pulled away, uncomfortable. "Mom, I'm not dying," he said.

No, he wasn't. I knew that. But our family as it had been was dying. I had to figure out what would come out of the change in my role as mother of a herd of boys. They didn't need me anymore. Now it seemed like I needed them, just as they were ready to leave me and get on with their lives without me.

"They're lucky to have you, everyone in Boston. If they don't figure that out, I'm going to be very angry with them," I said.

The timer went off and Samuel got the first batch of peanut butter cookies out of the oven. "And you'll what? Send them burnt cookies?"

"No. I'll send them some of my Chinese food," I said with a grin. I did many things well in the kitchen. Chinese food wasn't one of them. Every few months, I thought I'd try a new recipe and see if I could get it right. It was supposed to be easy. Everyone could cook some vegetables and meat with some rice. Except for me.

"Please, Mom, don't make Chinese food," said Samuel, his hands up in a mock plea.

"I think I'll make some right now."

"Can't we just get some takeout?" Samuel asked.

"No. But maybe you can convince your father to actually take us out to a Chinese restaurant."

It was as good an excuse as any to spend a few last, precious hours with Samuel before he left. Once he did, we'd be allowed only weekly emails and two phone calls a year, on Christmas and Mother's Day.

In my mind, I cursed Samuel that he might one day have a son he loved as much as I loved him, and that he might have to say goodbye when his son left for a mission the way I had to say goodbye. I had no idea how that would happen, given Samuel's sexuality and the church's position on same-sex marriage, but it was the traditional mother's curse, and I wanted to give Samuel everything all the other boys had gotten from me, so I gave him that, too.

"SILENT NIGHT"

The Darkest of Holiday Noir

THERE'S ONLY ONE FATHER
CHRISTMAS, RIGHT?

Colin Cotterill

COLIN COTTERILL is the author of twelve books in the critically acclaimed Dr. Siri Paiboun series, which is set in Laos in the late 1970s, after the Communist takeover, and which feature a septuagenarian coroner-detective, Dr. Siri, and an offbeat entourage of misfit associates who help him solve crimes. The books include *Coroner's Lunch*, *Thirty-Three Teeth*, *Disco for the Departed*, *Anarchy and Old Dogs*, *Curse of the Pogo Stick*, *The Merry Misogynist*, *Love Songs from a Shallow Grave*, *Slash and Burn*, *The Woman Who Wouldn't Die*, *Six and a Half Deadly Sins*, *I Shot the Buddha*, and *The Rat Catchers' Olympics*. He is also the author of the Jimm Juree series, set in Thailand: *Killed at the Whim of a Hat*; *Granddad, There's a Head on the Beach;* and *The Axe Factor*. His fiction has won a Dilys Award and a CWA Dagger in the Library. Colin Cotterill is also a professional cartoonist and has been involved with several humanitarian and non-profit organizations in Australia and Southeast Asia. He lives in Chumphon, Thailand, with his wife and five deranged dogs.

Act One

The website of the British Embassy in Bangkok offers a good deal of useful information for travelers to Thailand. For example, there are two paragraphs giving cultural and practical advice on what to wear and not to wear in the tropics. But nowhere in these two paragraphs would one find mention of a Santa Suit. And perhaps it was as a result of this oversight that several hundred Thai bystanders witnessed Santa riding his Honda Dream motorcycle through the streets of Lang Suan on December 25th. He was certainly not traveling incognito. He waved as he passed and called out "Merry Christmas" and engaged in a good deal of "Ho"ing. Admittedly, his bright red tunic was cotton rather than wool and his black boots had holes drilled in them to let in air, but beneath a full sun in thirty-two humid degrees Centigrade, that was an extremely damp Santa.

He'd left the Tesco Mega Store car park at five minutes past midday and ridden along the parking lane on the wrong side of the Asia Highway all the way into the town. Lang Suan was one of those forgettable places you passed on your way to Malaysia. Not even Lonely Planet could think of anything to say about it. It was all un-matching shop fronts and untidy parking and southern lethargy. Santa had circumnavigated the fresh market, ridden three times around the messy traffic island and parked in front of the Felicitations Gold Emporium. The armed guard came to the door to greet him and was in the process of taking a cell phone selfie with Father Christmas when that cheeky Santa reached into the guard's holster, took out the gun and released the safety catch. In broken Thai he instructed the counter staff to load all of the jewelry from the display cabinet into his sack. They laughed. But to show he wasn't just being mischievous, he emptied a round into the clock above the counter. Thence he had everyone's attention. He scooped the cash from the register and even stopped to kiss the cheek of a smiling young lady customer who sat bemused on a stool. The few people who passed on the muggy street assumed it was an advertising stunt. Santa climbed back on his motorcycle, waved for a few more cell phone photos then zoomed off.

Eye witnesses saw him return to Tesco, park his Honda Dream and run inside. After responding to the Gold Emporium alarm, the Lang Suan police force had little trouble retracing Santa's steps. They turned up at Tesco at twelve forty-five to find the old fellow asleep in the store room that had been allocated to Santa as a dressing room. He was drowsy and disoriented and had no idea why he was being dragged out to a waiting police van. They didn't even give him time to put on his hat or belt up his trousers. There were those standing in his wake who admitted the man gave off a fragrance of alcohol. That was undoubtedly true as Rodger, aka Santa Claus, was a drunkard.

Boom, the store manager, accompanied Santa to police headquarters. He was particularly irked. Santa had been his idea: that is to say, a living breathing Santa was his *concept* for the festive season. For four years an electronic Father Christmas had stood guard in the doorway. His head bobbed on a spring in time to the endless loop of Christmas carols. And for no particular reason in that predominately Buddhist province, decorative lights and shortbread and small plastic trees sold extremely well over the month of December. Anything with a picture of Santa on the packet was procured off the shelf before New Year. The Thais loved an excuse to party, and Tesco pumped up the adrenaline for any festival on the calendar. Jingle Bells had rocked the aisles from mid October.

So Boom had decided to go the whole hog and hire a live Santa. Rodger was his first choice. He was a customer; an expatriate living in Lang Suan. English. In Thailand for ten years and able to speak one Thai word for each of those years. Had been married to a Thai woman who ran off with her ex-husband. Received a small pension from England. Spent almost all of it on booze. Sixty-something. White beard. Red nose. Huge gut. In Boom's mind it was as if Santa had moved to Lang Suan and was hanging around for eleven months waiting for the role he'd been created for. Rodger *was* Santa. So why would he hold up a gold shop in broad daylight?

It was two-thirty before the police could find an interpreter. Rodger still had no idea why he was there. He was thirsty but all they'd give him at the police station was Pepsi. What good was Pepsi without rum? He was still drowsy. The heat always knocked him out in the afternoon. The police station had no A/C and he'd gestured that he'd like to sit under one of the fans. The desk sergeant moved him immediately to maximize the breeze. The officer was exceedingly hospitable. He bowed and nodded and smiled a good deal. He'd asked Rodger to sign a piece of paper but there was nothing on it. At first Rodger supposed they'd fill in his confession later for whatever he'd done, but then he realized he'd been asked for his autograph. For most of the year he was a slob but here at Christmas he was a celebrity. He called for a second sheet of paper and signed "Father Christmas" for everyone there.

"You take gold?"

A masculine woman in a pink shirt and black slacks was

standing in the doorway. She held an enormous handbag. Her hair was as solid as a helmet.

"Oh, good," said Rodger. "You speak English."

"No, thank you," said the woman.

She walked into the office and sat opposite him.

"Why am I here?" Rodger asked.

"Yes. You take gold."

It seemed like some American Express mantra. It made no sense to Rodger at all.

"What have I done?" he asked.

A senior policeman came into the office followed by a photographer who started to take pictures of Rodger without asking permission. The officer spoke to the interpreter who replied with authority as if she'd already interviewed the suspect. He nodded at Rodger and asked a question.

"You put the gold?" said the woman.

"What gold?" said Rodger.

The woman laughed and translated a much longer sentence than "What gold?" The officer looked at Rodger and seemed to snarl. The translator translated.

"We know you. Everybody know you. Everybody see. Why you do this thing? No sense. No good. Stupid thing. Is where this gold?"

Rodger looked at her.

"What?" he said.

"Don't make game me," said the woman. "We police. We power you to speak. Understand?"

Rodger didn't. He tried to sidestep the translation. Used his ten Thai words in various order but could make no more sense than the interpreter.

"I want to call my lawyer," he said.

"Liar? I not liar. You liar," said the woman.

He wanted to punch her. He wanted a drink. The only lawyer he knew was the scumbag who'd handled his divorce. There was no way Rodger would phone him. The only friends he had were fellow drunks and they'd all be sleeping off their lunchtime beers. He was trapped and clueless. The officer asked another question through the interpreter.

"Where you motorcycle key?"

"I don't have a motorcycle," he said.

"Yes," said the woman.

"Yes what?"

"You have."

"No, I don't. I can't drive a motorcycle. I never learned. I've always been terrified of the things. I used to have this recurring nightmare when I was young that I'd drive a motorcycle at speed into a wall, my brains splattered across the brickwork. And I like a drink now and then. In fact I'd like one now. Drinkers can't drive motorcycles. We fall off and cause unlimited damage to ourselves. I have a truck. It doesn't matter how drunk you are if you have a truck."

He knew she'd have no idea what he'd said but it was his only recourse for revenge. She stared at him in silence for a while.

"Where you motorcycle key?" she said.

"No have motorcycle," he said; three words that happened to be in his Thai repertoire.

"No have motorcycle?" repeated the officer in Thai. He produced the gold shop security guard's cell phone from a plastic bag and keyed in the photo application. He held it up to Rodger's face. There, in crisp sunny colour was Santa Claus driving off on his motorcycle with a full sack of loot over his shoulder.

"That does look remarkably like me," said Rodger.

Act Two

"SO WHAT I DID was this . . ." said Gary.

The Aussie was seated in the front seat of the VIP bus beside a pudgy college student who'd been foolish enough to try out her English on him. Six hours on a bus with a foreigner; an English student's dream. But after half-a-dozen sentences she'd exhausted her repertoire and reverted to the Thai smile and nods. She had no idea what her seatmate was saying; didn't even recognize it as English, but that was cool. Gary didn't want a dialogue. He needed to vent. And May, the would-be teacher from Roi Et, was the perfect foil. In front of them the driver lunged his fat bus down the highway like a battering ram, forcing all the minions to part before him. He was high on something, but Gary recognized the glazed look of a man focused on completing his task rather than an idiot bent on self-destruction. Gary knew all those looks. In the underworld in Sydney's Kings Cross he'd learned to recognize the addictions. Your life often depended on getting them right.

"So, what I did was this," he said to the girl. "I got in conversation with the pom. That means Englishman in Australian if you want to know. Remember it. Could be useful. I knew he was a drunk first time I laid eyes on him. But he was a bloody fine Father Christmas if you don't mind your kids getting fumbled and having whisky fumes breathed all over them. He really looked the part. On his break he showed me his changing room. There was a cot in there he'd sleep on through his lunch hour. There was a window open to the offloading yard. So, yesterday, what do I do? I go to Tesco and I take him a little gift, just to help him make it to the afternoon, you know? It was in an extra large Amazon Coffee cup but it had a little tipple inside. Everyone thought he was drinking coffee. *Tipple*, that's another word you'll probably need to get through life. I watched him sip it between kiddies. I'd added a little sedative to make sure he wouldn't remember too much. He was asleep as soon as he reached his room at twelve. I followed him in. I had my own costume. They rent them out in Bangkok. I'd put it in a big Tesco bag and wheeled it in to the supermarket on one of their carts. Security checks you on the way out but never on the way in."

May had nodded off but it was of no mind.

"I dressed up like him, fake beard, stuffed a couple of cushions up my shirt, went to my motorcycle and made sure everyone saw me on my way into town. Must have been a couple of hundred witnesses. I filled up my sack with goodies from the gold shop and, twenty minutes later I was back at Tesco. Neat, right? Santa was still asleep. I took off my costume and left it in his room. The police would have assumed it was his spare uniform. Once I was out of the costume I looked nothing like Santa. I mean, look at me; skinny as a cheroot. I climbed out his window with my backpack full of plunder, went back to my motorcycle and I was off. And before you knew it I was on the highway on my way south. I went as far as Chaiya, parked the motorcycle with a bunch of others and became a common backpacker catching a VIP bus to Nakhorn Sri Thammarat. And here I am. And that's how you had the good fortune to meet me. See that, May? The perfect crime. Everyone in Lang Suan knows it was Santa who robbed the gold shop. There's only one Father Christmas, right? By the time they release him, if they ever do, I'll be long gone."

May was snoring now. Gary watched the road ahead, a long straight highway that probably killed more drivers from boredom than from recklessness. Apart from the kilometer markers and an occasional truck full of coconut monkeys there was nothing to entertain him so he decided to tell May about his cause.

"May, I've been very selfish in my life," he said. "I've cheated. I've stolen. I've hurt people. Yes, May, between you and me, I've committed acts of violence. Some men might even be dead because of me. I don't know for sure. I didn't stick around to find out. There's only one thing I'm proud of. Only one act in a lifetime of dishonesty that I can say was completely unselfish. I sponsored a penniless child here in Thailand. That's why I'm here, May. I got the idea from a Jack Nicholson movie called *About Schmidt*. You see that? Jack supported a child in Africa and it changed his life. I'm very fond of Jack. So I found this underprivileged boy called Tho Id Dte through this agency and funded him through school. His family are poor fisher folk. His sister's got MS. They live in a bloody hut. And, as if the cards weren't already stacked against him, the family's Muslim. See? He had nothing going for him. But because of me, Tho knuckled down to study and got good grades. He can *be* somebody because of me. He wasn't interested in girls. I don't think he's a poof or anything like that. Just serious, you know? Maybe I can get you two together. I doubt you've got a boyfriend. But that, May, since you asked, is why I'm going to Nakhorn Sri Thammarat. Took me a month to learn how to say the name of the place. That's where they live. They're not expecting me. I want to surprise them. Now you're wondering about the connection between sponsoring Tho and me robbing the gold shop. Am I right?"

May's cheek was against the window. Her drool snaked down the glass. The bus slowed as the traffic was funneled into one lane to avoid road works.

"I thought so. Well, here's the plan. I come to Thailand and look around for a quick heist in a place where the cops aren't too bright. In the countryside they're not used to investigating this sort of thing. No lateral thinking. What you see is what you see. Old Santa there sort of dropped on my lap. But it was a nice little caper. Like a Christmas present, you might say. I reckon I've got about fifty grand's worth of gold up there in the overhead rack. Maybe more. I reckon that's enough to send Tho to university and pay his sister's medical bills. Might even be enough to build a concrete house and buy a new boat with plenty left over for yours truly. This is the way you Thais do it, right? You live a life of sin then to make amends, you *tum boon*. Think that's how you pronounce it. You make a huge bloody donation or do a spectacular act of kindness and it cancels out the bad shit. I've been studying it, you see? This is my *tum boon*. Clean slate. Clean conscience. Gary the ex-villain philanthropist. I might even settle down here. Get myself a pretty wife and a pair of dogs. Grow mangoes. Drink with the neighbors. Could even go visit old Rodger in jail once a year. See, May? I've got it all worked out."

Act Three

AT THE TREE LINE, twenty meters from the highway, the boys waited. No amount of wiping their palms on their shorts would dry them. Ayan, the eldest of the three, had already wet himself. He it was who held the cell phone. He it was who'd send the infidels to their hell. Earlier, when the road was clear, the others had dragged the *Road Maintenance in Progress* barrier into the fast lane so the traffic would slow down as it passed their position. The bomb was in a trash can beside the road. Patience was killing them slowly but the man had told them to wait for a fancy bus full of tourists. There'd be Thais on board; the driver, the ticket boy, perhaps a few passengers. But in a war you couldn't pick and choose your victims. Their cell was comprised of young Muslim radicals from fishing communities along the coast north of Nakhon Sri Thammarat. They'd been entrusted with this mission to prove their worth to the fathers of the revolution. They had no right to question the orders.

They'd been there almost an hour when the gaudy VIP double-decker approached the barrier and slowed down. The driver bullied his way into the slow lane and dropped into second gear. The bus was full. The boys nodded and Ayan took a deep breath before pressing the final number that would activate the detonation device. The explosion ripped through the VIP bus like a blazing comet. Nobody could have survived it. A wall of air knocked the boys back into the grass their ears buzzing. Os, the youngest, was shocked at the devastation of the blast. He looked up to see an inferno that had started out as a brightly painted bus. Cooked meat that had once been passengers.

"We did it," he said. "Let's get out of here."

He and Ayan started to crawl on their bellies through the bushes. The third boy didn't budge.

"Hey, move your ass," said Ayan, but their friend lay face down on the grass. Os crawled back to him.

"What are you . . . ? Tho? Tho?"

He reached the body and could see that half of his friend's face was gone, hit by flying debris from the explosion. Tho Id Dte was on his way to meet the seventy-two virgins. It would be his first taste of romance.

MARTIN

Ed Lin

ED LIN is a journalist by training and an all-around stand-up kinda guy. He's the author of several books: two crime novels set in Taipei, Taiwan, *Ghost Month* and *Incensed; Waylaid*, his literary debut; and his Robert Chow crime series, set in 1970s Manhattan Chinatown: *This Is a Bust, Snakes Can't Run*, and *One Red Bastard*. Lin, who is of Taiwanese and Chinese descent, is the first author to win three Asian American Literary Awards. Lin lives in New York with his wife, actress Cindy Cheung.

We were heading to Martin's because he was in bad shape. He and his fiancée, Diana, had split up for what he said was for good. What an awful time for something like that, during the shit week between Christmas and New Year's.

I almost ate it by stepping in a giant pool of ice water on a corner. New York City was turning into a giant melting slushy with all the flavor sucked out. But I had to push on. The guys were depending on me.

I finally made it to the apartment and found that Sesh and Dougie had beaten me. Martin was sitting on the floor inside a curled-up blanket at the base of the floor lamp. Chipotle wrappers and Red Bull cans lined the nest, which cradled all the remote controls and phone accessories.

"I brought the headsets," I panted with pride, holding up my never-used gym bag. Considering the weather, I believed that my accomplishment was worth at least a pat on the back or equivalent form of appreciation. The guys left me hanging, though.

The four of us had grown up together in Jersey, but the other three seemed to forget about me unless they needed something. In this case, they wanted my Bluetooth headsets to play Call of Duty on Martin's Christmas present, a PlayStation 4.

Martin held out his hand to me and shook his head. "I'm so sorry, man," he said. "Someone should have gotten word to you that the PlayStation is gone."

"That's all right," I said. I put the bag on the floor and

hid it behind my legs. I was sweaty from running over and I looked for a place to sit and catch my breath a little. I'm a big guy, the biggest one in the group. Even so, there would have been plenty of room for me on the couch if Sesh and Dougie slid over, but they didn't. I dropped into the reclining chair. It made a fart sound and Sesh laughed like a mean dog.

"Nice one," he said. Sesh was never trying to hurt your feelings, but he didn't care if he did. He was a Wall Street guy. I guess you could say he was the most successful among us.

Dougie was definitely the smartest. He was in a PhD program at NYU for the human interface in computing. His housing was free, but he never had any money.

Martin was on the management track at the Apple Store and had also been on track to be the first of us to marry. He and Diana had met in college. She was so beautiful I could never understand why they had arguments. I would've given in to her every time no matter what. I always gave in.

I lived in an apartment that my parents owned on the Upper East Side. They now lived in China for tax-related reasons and were providing me a monthly allowance until I figured out what I really wanted to do. My father said maybe my weight would have to come down. For Christmas they had mailed me a juicer, straight from the Chinese factory.

I could begin my diet tonight. A large pizza with all the toppings was sitting on the coffee table. That meant two slices per guy. I knew I had the discipline to eat just one. I worked my way off the reclining chair and slid my first and last slice onto a doubled paper plate.

It was only after my third bite, after half the slice was gone, that I thought to ask, "Martin, where's your PS4? Was it stolen?"

Martin said, "Diana took it because she paid for it."

Dougie spoke up. "It was your present!" His voice hadn't changed since he was fifteen. "It should have protected status as a gift, even during a breakup."

"Oh, well," said Martin. "She's coming back for the flatscreen, the K-cup machine and the lamp, and I need all those more than the PS4."

Sesh surveyed the room. "Let's break all her shit," he said.

"No," said Martin.

Dougie reached in for his second slice and shut the box. A small card fluttered to the ground.

Sesh grabbed it. "What the hell is this?" he asked. "It says, 'What was the worst thing you ever did?'"

Martin took the card. "It's from a game called 'Sharing' that our couples therapist gave us. Was supposed to help us 'share' more of our lives together."

"What *was* the worst thing you ever did?" Sesh asked.

Martin sighed and stood up. He ambled to the open kitchen counter, washed his hands with dish soap and shouted over the splashing water. "When I was a kid, I wanted one of those California license plates for my bike. I liked how blue they were. We kept eating this one cereal to try to pull a California plate. Then I saw that the girl across the street had one, so I stole it off her bike." Martin shut off the faucet and shook his hands three times over the sink. "I saw her crying when she found out it was gone. I felt so bad I left her anonymous Christmas presents for years until she moved away." Martin returned to his nest, sat down and slapped his knees with a sense of finality.

Dougie fixed his glasses and said, "That's actually very touching."

"Sesh," Martin called, "what was the worst thing you ever did?"

"Jesus," he said. "So little to choose from. Well, actually, something I did in college." Sesh leaned back in his seat, folded one leg over the other and happily bounced his foot. "I was nominated to join this honor society because my grades were so good. One of the requirements for eligibility was that I had to do a community project. I chose to raise two hundred bucks for a local food bank. I stood outside the student dining hall every day for a week like a chump, trying to get people to donate. I only collected about fifty bucks." Sesh grabbed his foot to still it. "I couldn't stand the thought of groveling for another few weeks to scrape up the money, so I went to the ATM, took out a hundred and fifty bucks from what I had saved from my campus job, and put that into the pot."

Sesh put his foot down, leaned over and grabbed his second slice of pizza.

"Wait, I don't get it," said Martin. "That was your own money that you put in?"

"Yeah," said Sesh.

"What's so wrong about that?"

"I shouldn't have raised money for that food bank in the first place! If you give someone something for free, they don't learn how to work for it."

"A lot of the people who use food banks have lost their jobs or homes," said Dougie. "They have kids to feed."

"Let 'em starve a little! Look at good old jolly Saint Nick right here," he said, pointing at me. "Sorry, don't mean to single you out, but if you went hungry for a few days, I don't think too many people would say that that was a bad thing."

My face went hot and I licked my lips. *You'll see tonight, Sesh*, I thought. *You'll see me skip my second slice.*

"Let hungry people starve?" said Dougie. "That's so charitable of you this time of year, Sesh."

"I won't be swayed by plastic holiday nostalgia," said Sesh. "The truth is, when you try to comfort people in distress, you make 'em weaker. Let 'em find their own way. They'll be better off in the long run."

Dougie's knees danced excitedly. "Well, if that's the case, then why are we here comforting Martin?"

Sesh clutched his pizza slice and narrowed his eyes. "Martin is our friend," he said evenly. "He's not some jackass statistic in the street. What's wrong with you?"

I felt moved to speak up. Maybe I could say something to make them pity me, or at least recognize the pain I'd suffered. "The worst thing I ever did was kill a bunch of tropical fish," I blurted out. "In the saltwater tank at the dry cleaner's."

Martin tilted his head. "I thought they got rid of that tank because it was too expensive."

"Uh-uh, no," I said. "The power cord was paired up with the TV cable. I climbed onto the dumpster one Mischief Night and cut it with garden shears. Everything in the tank died."

"That's sick," said Martin.

"But I—I felt terrible about it," I stammered. "I knew what I'd done was so wrong. I couldn't go to the aquarium after that. I still have trouble eating fish." I had already lost everybody, though.

Martin said, "Wasn't the dry cleaner run by those hairy people?"

Sesh was done with his second slice and sucked his fingers. "Yeah, it was!" he declared. "Daughter was hot, though. She was in my gym class. I asked her once if she was adopted. She got all offended and I was like, 'I'm paying you a compliment and you're giving me attitude?'"

Martin laughed for the first time that night and pulled

out his second slice. He left the box open, and the last slice, which would have been my second, sat there, pointing at me, accusing me of being unable to resist it. But I would. I would.

Dougie broke his silence by saying, "Guys, I think I killed someone. No. I know I did."

"Get the fuck out of here," said Sesh.

"For real," said Dougie.

"What happened?" asked Martin.

"You know that pedestrian bridge over Wyckoff Road?"

"Yeah, we used to drop rocks on cars from it."

Dougie sprung from the couch and seemed torn about which way to pace. "Well, one night I couldn't sleep. I went out there. It must have been two in the morning, but some cars were still going by. I picked up this rock." He held up an imaginary M&M between his thumb and index finger. "I swear it was the smallest one in the world. It was just a pebble. I saw a pair of headlights and I didn't even throw it. I just kinda flicked it. I heard the windshield shatter. I saw the camper swerve and hit a tree. It sounded like a can being crushed."

Sesh snapped his fingers and pointed at Dougie. "I remember that accident. A piece of the bridge fell and broke the windshield. It wasn't a rock."

"It was me," said Dougie. "I killed that guy. I've never told anybody. I've never even really thought about it." His mouth trembled as his eyes opened wide with revelation. "I have to call the cops and confess."

"Hold on a sec, dumbass!" called Sesh. "It's all over. Statute of limitations has run out."

"Actually," said Martin, "there is no statute on murder."

Dougie burst into tears upon hearing the word and grabbed his phone.

"I'm calling the cops on myself right now," he said. Sesh grabbed the phone and threw it to the floor. He and Martin pulled Dougie down to the couch as he continued to wail. I saw how worried they were for him, how much they cared about him, how badly they felt for him.

I stood up and picked up the entire pizza box. I began to eat my second slice. I wasn't hungry. I just needed something to fill the emptiness.

The other guys only called me when they needed something, and sometimes they forgot I was there.

Dougie had forgotten that I was with him that night on the bridge. It was true, he had picked up the smallest rock in the world. But I had picked up a chunk of stone that had broken off the bridge. I heaved it down at the exact second he threw his pebble, aiming right for the driver's face.

As I chewed through the cold, sad toppings and congealed cheese, I looked over at the three of them, a trio of best friends. I thought about what Dougie had said, and I wished so badly that I could feel as awful about killing someone and have my best friends hold me.

QUEEN OF THE HILL

Stuart Neville

STUART NEVILLE is the author of seven novels: *Ratlines*, shortlisted for the CWA Ian Fleming Steel Dagger for Best Thriller; *Collusion*, a finalist for the *Los Angeles Times* Book Prize; *Stolen Souls*, which *The Guardian* said "confirms him as the king of Belfast noir"; *So Say the Fallen*, a *Boston Globe* Best Crime Novel of the Year; *The Final Silence*, nominated for the Edgar Award for Best Novel; *Those We Left Behind*, a *New York Times* and *Boston Globe* Best Crime Novel of the Year; and *The Ghosts of Belfast*, winner of the *Los Angeles Times* Book Prize and a finalist for the Macavity Award, the Barry Award, and the Anthony Award for Best First Novel. He lives in Belfast.

Cam the Hun set off from his flat on Victoria Street with fear in his heart and heat in his loins. He pulled his coat tight around him. There'd be no snow for Christmas, but it might manage a frost.

Not that he cared much about Christmas this year. If he did this awful thing, if he could actually go through with it, he intended on drinking every last drop of alcohol in the flat. He'd drink until he passed out and drink some more when he woke up. With any luck he'd stay under right through to Boxing Day.

Davy Pollock told Cam the Hun he could come back to Orangefield. The banishment would be lifted, he could return and see his mother, so long as he did as Davy asked. But Cam the Hun knew he wouldn't be able to face her if he did the job, not on Christmas, no matter how badly he wanted to spend the day at her bedside. He'd been put out of the estate seven years ago for "running with the taigs," as Davy put it. Still and all, Davy didn't mind coming to Cam the Hun when he needed supplies from the other side. When Es and blow were thin on the ground in Armagh, just like any other town, the unbridgeable divide between Loyalist and Republican narrowed pretty quickly. Cam the Hun had his uses. He had that much to be grateful for.

He crossed toward Barrack Street, the Mall on his right, the old prison on his left. Christmas lights sprawled across the front of the gaol, ridiculous baubles on such a grim, desperate building. The Church of Ireland cathedral loomed up ahead, glowing at the top of the hill, lit up like a stage set. He couldn't see the Queen's house from here, but it stood just beneath the cathedral. It was an old Georgian place, three storeys, and would've cost a fortune before the property crash.

She didn't pay a penny for it. The Queen of the Hill won her palace in a game of cards.

Anne Mahon and her then-boyfriend had rented a flat on the top floor from Paddy Dolan, a lawyer who laundered cash for the IRA through property investment. She was pregnant, ready to pop at any moment, when Dolan and the boyfriend started a drunken game of poker. When the boyfriend was down to his last ten-pound note, he boasted of Anne's skill, said she could beat any man in the country. Dolan challenged her to a game. She refused, but Dolan wouldn't let it be. He said if she didn't play him, he'd put her and her fuckwit boyfriend out on the street that very night, pregnant or not.

Her water broke just as she laid out the hand that won the house, and Paddy Dolan's shoes were ruined. Not that it mattered in the end. The cops found him at the bottom of Newry Canal, tied to the driver's seat of his 5-Series BMW, nine days after he handed over the deeds. The boyfriend lasted a week longer. A bullet in the gut did for him, but the 'Ra let Anne keep the house. They said they wouldn't evict a young woman with newborn twins. The talk around town was a Sinn Féin councillor was sweet on her and smoothed things over with the balaclava boys.

Anne Mahon knew how to use men in that way. That's what made her Queen of the Hill. Once she got her claws into you, that was that. You were clean fucked.

Like Cam the Hun.

He kept his head down as he passed the shaven-headed men smoking outside the pub on Barrack Street. They knew who he was, knew he ran with the other sort, and glared as he walked by. One of them wore a Santa hat with a Red Hand of Ulster badge pinned to the brim.

As Cam the Hun began the climb up Scotch Street, the warmth in his groin grew with the terror in his stomach. The two sensations butted against each other somewhere beneath his navel. It was almost a year since he'd last seen her. That long night had left him drained and walking like John Wayne. She'd made him earn it, though. Two likely lads had been dealing right on her doorstep, and he'd sorted them out for her.

Back then he'd have done anything for a taste of the Queen, but as she took the last of him, his fingers tangled in her dyed crimson hair, he noticed the blood congealing on his swollen knuckles. The image of the two boys' broken faces swamped his mind, and he swore right then he'd never touch her again. She was poison. Like the goods she distributed from her fortress on the hill, too much would kill you, but there was no such thing as enough.

He walked to the far side of the library on Market Street. Metal fencing portioned off a path up the steep slope. The council was wasting more money renovating the town centre, leaving the area between the library and the closed-down cinema covered in rubble. Christmas Eve revellers puffed on cigarettes outside the theatre, girls draped with tinsel, young men shivering in their shirtsleeves. The sight of them caused dark thoughts to pass behind Cam the Hun's eyes. He seized on the resentment, brought it close to his heart. He'd need all the anger and hate he could muster.

He'd phoned the Queen that afternoon and told her it had been too long. He needed her.

"Tonight," she'd said. "Christmas party at my place."

The house came into view as Cam the Hun climbed the

slope past the library. Last house on the terrace to his left, facing the theatre across the square, the cathedral towering over it all. Her palace, her fortress. The fear slammed into his belly, and he stopped dead.

Could he do it? He'd done worse things in his life. She was a cancer in Armagh, feeding off the misery she sowed with her powders and potions. The world would be no poorer without her. She'd offloaded her twin sons on their grandmother and rarely saw them. No one depended on her but the dealers she owned, and they'd have Davy Pollock to turn to when she was gone. No, the air in this town could only be sweeter for her passing. The logic of it was insurmountable. Cam the Hun could and would do this thing.

But he loved her.

The sudden weight of it forced the air from his lungs. He knew it was a foolish notion, a symptom of his weakness and her power over him. But the knowledge went no further than his head. His heart and loins knew different.

One or two of the smokers outside the theatre noticed him, this slight figure with his coat wrapped tight around him. If he stood rooted to the spot much longer, they would remember him. When they heard the news the next day, they would recall his face. Cam the Hun thought of the ten grand the job would pay and started walking.

For a moment he considered veering right, into the theatre bar, shouldering his way through the crowd, and ordering a pint of Stella and a shot of Black Bush. Instead, he thought of his debts. And there'd be some left over to pay for a home help for his mother, even if it was only for a month or two. He headed left, toward the Queen's house.

His chest strained as he neared the top of the hill, his breath misting around him. He gripped the railing by her door and willed his heart to slow. Jesus, he needed to get more exercise. That would be his New Year's resolution. Get healthy. He rang the doorbell.

The muffled rumble of Black Sabbath's "Supernaut" came from inside. Cam the Hun listened for movement in the hall. When none came, he hit the doorbell twice more. He watched a shadow move against the ceiling through the glass above the front door. Something obscured the point of light at the peephole. He heard a bar move aside and three locks snap open. Warm air ferried the sweet tang of cannabis and perfume out into the night.

"Campbell Hunter," she said. "It's been a while."

She still wore her hair dyed crimson red with a black streak at her left temple. A black corset top revealed a trail from her deep cleavage, along her flat stomach, to the smooth skin above her low-cut jeans. Part of the raven tattoo was just visible above the button fly. He remembered the silken feel against his lips, the scent of her, the firmness of her body. She could afford the best work; the surgeons left little sign of her childbearing, save for the scar that cut the raven in two.

"A year," Cam the Hun said. "Too long."

She stepped back, and he crossed her threshold knowing it would be the last time. She locked the steel-backed door and lowered the bar into place. Neither bullet nor battering ram could break through. He followed her to the living room. Ozzy Osbourne wailed over Tony Iommi's guitar. A black artificial Christmas tree stood in the corner, small skulls, crows and inverted crosses as ornaments among the red tinsel. Men and women lay about on cushions and blankets, their lids drooping over distant eyes. Spoons and foil wraps, needles and rolled-up money, papers and tobaccos, crumbs of resins and wafts of powder.

"Good party," Cam the Hun said, his voice raised above the music.

"You know me," she said as she took a bottle of Gordon's gin and two glasses from the sideboard. "I'm the hostess with mostest. Come on."

As she brushed past him, sparks leaping between their bodies, Cam the Hun caught her perfume through the room's mingled aromas. A white-hot bolt crackled from his brain down to his groin. She headed to the stairs in the hall, stopped, turned on her heel, showed him the maddening undulations of her figure. "Well?" she asked. "What are you waiting for?"

Cam the Hun forced one foot in front of the other and followed her up the stairs. The rhythm of her hips held him spellbound, and he tripped. She looked back over her naked shoulder and smiled down at him. He returned the smile as he thanked God the knife in his coat pocket had a folding blade. He found his feet and stayed behind her as she climbed the second flight to her bedroom on the top floor.

The décor hadn't changed in a year, blacks and reds, silks and satins. Suspended sheets of shimmering fabric formed a canopy over the wrought-iron bedstead. A huge mound of pillows in all shapes and sizes lay at one end. He wondered if she still had the cuffs, or the—

Cam the Hun stamped on that thought. He had to keep his mind behind his eyes and between his ears, not let it creep down to where it could do him no good.

"Take your coat off," she said. She set the glasses on the dressing table and poured three fingers of neat gin into each.

He hung his coat on her bedpost, careful not to let the knife clang against the iron. She handed him a glass. He sat on the edge of the bed and took a sip. He tried not to cough at the stinging juniper taste. He failed.

Somewhere beneath the gin's cloying odour and the soft sweetness of her perfume, he caught the hint of another smell. Something lower, meaner, like ripe meat. The alcohol reached his belly. He swallowed again to keep it there.

The Queen of the Hill smiled her crooked smile and sat in the chair facing him. She hooked one leg over its arm, her jeans hinting at secrets he already knew. She took a mouthful of gin, washed it around her teeth, and hissed as it went down.

"I'm glad you called," she said.

"Are you?"

"Of course," she said. She winked and let a finger trace the shape of her left breast. "And not just for that."

Cam the Hun tried to quell the stirring in his trousers by studying the black painted floorboards. "Oh?" he said.

"There's trouble coming," she said. "I'll need your help."

He allowed himself a glance at her. "What kind of trouble?"

"The Davy Pollock kind."

His stomach lurched. He took a deeper swig of gin, forced it down. His eyes burned.

"He's been spreading talk about me," she said. "Says he wants me out of the way. Says he wants my business. Says he'll pay good money to anyone who'll do it for him."

"Is that right?" Cam the Hun said.

"That's right." She let her leg drop from the arm of the chair, her heel like a gunshot on the floor, and sat forward. "But he's got no takers. No one on that side of town wants the fight. They know I've too many friends."

He managed a laugh. "Who'd be that stupid?"

"Exactly," she said.

He drained the glass and coughed. His eyes streamed, and when he sniffed back the scorching tears, he got that ripe meat smell again. His stomach wanted to expel the gin, but he willed it to be quiet.

"So, what do you want me to do?" he asked.

She swallowed the last of her gin and said, "Him."

He dropped his glass. It didn't shatter, but rolled across the floor to stop at her feet. "What?"

"I want you to do him," she said.

He could only blink and open his mouth.

"It'll be all right," she said. "I've cleared it with everyone that matters. His own side have wanted shot of him for years. Davy Pollock is a piece of shit. He steals from his own neighbours, threatens old ladies and children, talks like he's the big man when everyone knows he's an arsewipe. You'd be doing this town a favour."

Cam the Hun shook his head. "I can't," he said.

"Course you can." She smiled at him. "Besides, there's fifteen grand in it for you. And you can go back to Orangefield to see your mother. Picture it. You could have Christmas dinner with your ma tomorrow."

"But I'd have to—"

"Tonight," she said. "That's right."

"But how?"

"How? Sure, everyone knows Cam the Hun's handy with a knife." She drew a line across her throat with her finger. "Just like that. You won't even have to go looking for him. I know where he's resting his pretty wee head right this minute."

"No," he said.

She placed her glass on the floor next to his and rose to her feet, her hands gliding over her thighs, along her body, and up to her hair. Her heels click-clacked on the floorboards as she crossed to him. "Consider it my Christmas present," she said.

He went to stand, but she put a hand on his shoulder.

"But first I'm going to give you yours," she purred. "Do you want it?"

"God," he said.

The Queen of the Hill unlaced her corset top and let it fall away.

"Jesus," he said.

She pulled him to her breasts, let him take in her warmth. He kissed her there while she toyed with his hair. A minute stretched out to eternity before she pushed him back with a gentle hand on his chest. His right mind shrieked in protest as she straddled him, grinding against his body as she got into position, a knee either side of his waist. She leaned forward.

"Close your eyes," she said.

"No," he said, the word dying in his throat before it found his vocal cords.

"Shush," she said. She wiped her hand across his eyelids, sealed out the dim light. Her weight shifted and pillows tumbled around him. Her breasts pressed against his chest, her breath warmed his cheek. Lips met his, an open mouth cold and dry, coarse stubble, a tongue like ripe meat.

Cam the Hun opened one eye and saw a milky white globe an inch from his own, a thick, dark brow above it, pale skin blotched with red.

He screamed.

The Queen of the Hill laughed and pushed Davy Pollock's severed head down, rubbing the dead flesh and stubble against Cam the Hun's face.

Cam the Hun screamed again and threw his arms upward. The heel of his hand connected with her jaw. She tumbled backwards and spilled onto the floor. The head bounced twice and rolled to a halt at her side. She hooted and cackled as she sprawled there, her legs kicking.

He squealed until his voice broke. He wiped his mouth and cheeks with his hands and sleeves until the chill of dead flesh was replaced by raw burning. He rolled on his side and vomited, the gin and foulness soaking her black satin sheets. He retched until his stomach felt like it had turned itself inside-out.

All the time, her laughter tore at him, ripping his sanity away shred by shred.

"Shut up," he wanted to shout, but it came out a thin whine.

"Shut up." He managed a weak croak this time. He reached for his coat, fumbled for the pocket, found the knife. He tried to stand, couldn't, tried again. He grabbed the iron bedpost with his left hand for balance. The blade snapped open in his right.

Her laughter stopped, leaving only the rushing in his ears. She looked up at him, grinning, a trickle of blood running to her chin.

"What are you?" he asked.

She giggled.

"What are you?" A tear rolled down his cheek, leaving a hot trail behind it.

"I'm the Queen of the Hill." Her tongue flicked out, smeared the blood across her lips. "I'm the goddess. I'm the death of you and any man who crosses me."

"No," he said, "not me." He raised the knife and stepped toward her.

She reached for Davy Pollock's head, grabbed it by the hair.

Cam the Hun took another step and opened his mouth to roar. He held the knife high, ready to bring it down on her exposed heart.

He saw it coming, but it was too late. Davy Pollock's cranium shattered Cam the Hun's nose, and he fell into feathery darkness.

He awoke choking on his own blood and bile. He coughed and spat. A deep, searing pain radiated from beneath his eyes to encompass the entire world. The Queen of the Hill cradled his head in her lap. He went to speak, but could only gargle and sputter.

"Shush, now," she said.

He tried to raise himself up, pushing with the last of his strength. She clucked and gathered him to her bosom. He stained her breasts red.

"We could've been good together, you and me," she said.

His mouth opened and closed, but the words couldn't force their way past the coppery warm liquid. He wanted to weep, but the pain blocked his tears.

"You could've been my king," she said. She rocked him and kissed his forehead. "This could've been our palace on the hill. But that's all gone. Now there's only this."

She brought the knife into his vision, the blade so bright and pretty. "Close your eyes," she said.

He did as he was told. Her fingers were warm and soft as she loosened his collar and pulled the fabric away from his throat.

The cathedral bells rang out. He counted the chimes, just like he'd done as a child, listening to his mother's old clock as he waited for Santa Claus. Twelve and it would be Christmas.

It didn't hurt for long.

BLUE MEMORIES
START CALLING
Tod Goldberg

TOD GOLDBERG is the author of over a dozen books, including *The House of Secrets*, which he co-authored with Brad Meltzer; *Gangsterland*, which was a finalist for the Hammett Prize; and *Living Dead Girl*, a finalist for the *Los Angeles Times Book Prize*. His nonfiction, journalism, and criticism has appeared widely, including in the *Los Angeles Times*, *Wall Street Journal*, *Los Angeles Review of Books*, and, recently, *Best American Essays*. Tod is also the cohost, along with Julia Pistell and Rider Strong, of *Literary Disco*, one of the greatest podcasts in the history of sound. He lives in Indio, CA, and directs the Low Residency MFA in Creative Writing & Writing for the Performing Arts at the University of California, Riverside.

They disappeared during the coldest winter on record. There was no special episode of *Dateline*. No jogger stumbled on a human skull. Instead, it was Scotch Thompson's bird dog Roxanne who came running down Yeach Mountain, three days before Christmas, with a human hand in her mouth. And just like that, James Klein and his family were found.

"Damndest thing I ever seen," Lyle, my deputy, said. "All of them stacked up like Lincoln logs. Like they were put down all gentle. Terrible, terrible thing." We were sitting in the front seat of my cruiser sipping coffee, both of us too old to be picking at the bones of an entire family, but resigned to doing it anyway. "You think it was someone from out of town, Morris?"

"Hard to say," I said. "It's been so damn long, you know, it could have been anybody."

James Klein, his wife, Missy, and their twin sons, Andy and Tyler, fell off the earth sometime before November 12, 1998. Fred Lipton came over that day to borrow back his wrench set but all he found was an empty house and a very hungry cat.

"You think it was some kinda drug thing, don't you?" Lyle said but I didn't respond. "You always thought Klein was involved in something illegal, I know, but I thought they were good people."

"I don't know what I think anymore, Lyle," I said. A team of forensic specialists from the capital was coming down the side of the mountain and I spotted Miller Descent out in front, his hands filled with plastic evidence bags. I'd worked with Miller before and knew this wasn't a good sign. What

Roxanne the collie had stumbled onto was a shallow grave filled with four bodies, along with many of their limbs. The twins, Andy and Tyler, were missing their feet. James and Missy were without hands.

Miller motioned me out of the cruiser. "Lotta shit up there," he said. Miller was a tall man, his face sharp and angular, with long green eyes. He had a look about him that said he couldn't be shocked anymore; that the world was too sour of a place for him. "Like some kinda damned ritual took place. Animal bones are mixed up in that grave, I think. Need to get an anthropologist up here to be sure, which is gonna be hard with the holidays, but it looks like dog bones mostly. Maybe a cat or two. Snow pack kept those bodies pretty fresh."

"Jesus," I said. "What's the Medical Examiner say?"

Miller screwed his face up into a knot, his nose almost even with his eyes. "Can I be honest with you, Sheriff Drew?"

"Sure, Miller."

"Your ME about threw up when she saw all them bodies," he said. "You know, I was in Vietnam so this doesn't mean so much to me. I've seen things that'll make your skin *run*, but she just, well, I think she was a little bothered by the whole thing. You might want to have them bodies cut up by some more patient people upstate."

"I'll keep that in mind," I said.

Miller smiled then and scratched at something on his neck. "Anyway," he said. "You still playing softball in that beer league?"

I never knew how to handle Miller Descent. He could be holding a human head in one hand and a Coors in the other and it wouldn't faze him.

"Not this year," I said.

"Too bad," he said and then he shuffled his way back up Yeach.

I DIDN'T GET HOME that night until well past 10 o'clock. I brewed myself a pot of coffee and sat at the kitchen table looking over notes I'd written when the Kleins first disappeared, plus the new photos shot up on the mountain. Since my second wife, Margaret, died, I'd taken to staying up late at night; I'd read or watch TV or go over old cases, anything to keep me from crawling into that lonely bed. The holidays, I barely slept. I'd sit in the kitchen, remembering the smell of pork roast, the kind with raisins and cranberries, that Margaret used to cook on Christmas Eve. Or I'd think about how we used to wake up early on Christmas morning and unwrap presents, Margaret always getting me things I didn't know I wanted—one year, that was a kite, and every day after work for six months, I'd come home and fly it, like I was six. Or how she cried at the Christmas cards I made for her, every year. I used to carve them out of wood, so it would take me a few months to do it, but I found it relaxing, and it was better than getting her a sweater or something she'd leave behind on a plane. She'd see the plank of wood and she'd just tilt her head back and start sobbing, wiping at her eyes with the back of her hand, always ruining her makeup. "This is so silly," she'd say, "I'm a grown woman."

But that night, my trouble was not with the memory of a woman who I loved for the last thirty years of my life, or my first wife, Katherine, whose own death at twenty-four still haunted me, but for a family I had barely known.

The Kleins moved into Granite City during the fall of 1995. James Klein was a pharmacist, so when he and his wife purchased Dickey Fine's Rexall Drug Store downtown, everyone figured it was going to be a good match. Dickey had gotten old, and going to him for a prescription was often more dangerous than just fighting whatever ailment you had on faith and good humor.

James and Missy were in the store together most days. James wore a starched white lab coat even though it wasn't really required. It inspired confidence in the people, I think, to get their drugs from someone who looked like a doctor. Missy always looked radiant standing behind the counter smiling and chatting up the townspeople and, when skiing season started, the tourists who'd come in for directions or cold medicine.

All that to say I never trusted them. I'd known the family only casually, but I knew them well enough to know that they were hiding something. James sported a diploma from Harvard and Missy looked like the type of woman who was best suited for clambakes at Pebble Beach. They were not small town people—they drove a gold Lexus and a convertible Jaguar—and Granite City is a small town. I never had cause to investigate the Kleins, never even pulled them over for speeding, but I aimed to at some point just so that I could look James in the eye when I had the upper hand, when my authority might cause his veneer to smudge. That chance didn't come.

I picked up a photo from the gravesite and there was James Klein's face staring up at me. Miller was right: the bodies had been well preserved by the snow pack. The skin on James's face was tight and tugged at the bones. His eyes had vanished over the course of the year and a half—eaten by bugs or simply by the act of decay—but I could still picture the way they narrowed whenever he saw me.

His body had been lain face up, his arms flung to either side of him. He was draped on top of his wife, his hands chopped from his arms, wearing his now drab gray lab coat. Shards of bone jutted from underneath his sleeves, and I thought that whoever had done this to him had taken great pains to make him suffer.

For a long time I stared at James Klein and wondered what it would be like to know that you were about to die. Andy and Tyler, the twins, must have understood all too well that their time on Earth was ending before it ever had a chance to begin. They were only twelve.

I stood up, stretched my arms above my head, and paced in the kitchen while I tried to gather my thoughts. After the family had initially disappeared, I'd searched their home with Deputy Nixon and Deputy Person. We hadn't found any forced entry or signs of a struggle, but we did find bundles of cash hidden in nearly every crevice of the house. All told, there was close to half a million dollars stashed in shoeboxes, suitcases and file cabinets. The money was tested for trace residues of cocaine, heroin, and marijuana but came up empty.

For almost three months, we searched for the Klein family. In time, though, winter dropped in full force and even James Klein's own mother and father returned to their hometown. I told them not to worry, that we would find their son and his wife and their twin grandsons, but I knew that they were dead. I knew because there was $500,000 sitting in my office unclaimed, and no man alive would leave that money on purpose. And so, as the months drifted away and my thoughts of the Klein family withered and died in my mind, I figured that one day when I was retired someone would find them somewhere.

"Hell," I said, sitting back down at the kitchen table. My eyes fixed on a pair of pale blue Nikes, unattached to legs, pointing out from the bottom of the grave. I wanted to just sit there and cry for those boys but I knew it wouldn't do any of us any good.

I GOT TO THE medical examiner's office late that next morning, figuring I didn't need to see her slicing and dicing. But it turned out I was right on time. The ME, a young kid named Lizzie DiGiangreco, had been working in Granite City for just over a year. Her father, Dr. Louis DiGiangreco, had been ME in Granite City for a lifetime and had practically trained Lizzie from birth. She went to medical school back east and then moved home after her father died at sixty-four from heart failure. I was one of Louis's pallbearers and I remember watching Lizzie stiffen at the site of her father in his open casket. I knew then that her profession had not been a pleasant choice for her, but that she was duty bound.

Lizzie greeted me with a handshake just outside the door to her lab.

"Glad you could make it, Sheriff," Lizzie said, only half sarcastically.

"Miller said you were a little queasy up on Yeach," I said. "I can get someone else to do this, if you want."

Lizzie made a clicking sound in her throat, a tendency of her father's when he'd been about to be very angry, and then exhaled deeply. "I don't like to see kids like that," she said. "Maybe Miller is used to it, but I'm not."

"Understandable," I said and then followed her into the lab.

The four bodies were covered with black plastic blankets and lined up across the length of the room. Lizzie's assistant— what they call a diener—an old black man named Hawkins, was busy gathering up the tools they would need for the procedure. I'd watched a lot of autopsies in my thirty-five years as Sheriff in Granite City, but it never got any easier. Hawkins had been Lizzie's father's assistant, so he knew what I'd need to make it through the next few hours.

"There's a tub of Vicks behind you in that cabinet, Sheriff," Hawkins said. "These folks ain't gonna smell so fresh."

Lizzie glared at Hawkins, but she knew that he didn't mean any harm. Hawkins could probably perform an autopsy just as well as she could, and Lord knows he never went to medical school.

Hawkins pulled back the first blanket and there was James Klein's naked, handless body.

"Where'd you put the hands, Hawkins?" Lizzie asked.

"I got 'em in the jar by the back sink," he said. "You want them now?"

"No," she said. "But make sure not to cross them up with Mrs. Klein's."

Hawkins nodded in confirmation and I was struck by how, for these two people, this was a day in the office. For Lizzie, maybe, seeing those children would be different. But for Hawkins, they would be nothing but cargo, something to load onto a table and then something to haul back to the refrigerator.

Lizzie sliced James Klein with a Y incision, starting from his shoulder, across his chest, around his navel, and down through the pelvis using a scalpel. The room filled with a smell like raw lamb.

For the next two hours, Lizzie spoke quietly and clinically into a tape recorder, noting the condition of James Klein's vital organs as she examined and weighed them. I had to leave the room only twice: when Hawkins sifted through the intestines and when Lizzie and Hawkins peeled back James Klein's scalp and removed his brain.

After they'd removed all of James Klein's vital organs, his

corpse sat opened on the examining table: his trunk resembled the hull of a ship under construction. Both Lizzie and Hawkins were covered in blood and tissue.

"Well," Hawkins said to me, "he's dead all right."

"Why don't you go get a cup of coffee, Hawkins," Lizzie said. "The Sheriff and I need to go over a few things before we sew up."

Hawkins licked at his lips then and I saw that his hands were shaking a bit. "I don't know what it is," he said, "but doing these things damn near starves me! You want something, Doc?"

"No, Hawkins," she said and when he was gone, she started back up. "Off the record, because I'll need to look at the tox screens and some of the neuro X-rays, but I'd say the cause of death for Mr. Klein was suffocation plus blood loss from his hands being chopped off."

"Suffocation?"

"Look here," Lizzie said, pointing at James Klein's lungs. "He had severe hemorrhaging, probably caused by inhaling so much dirt, and there's bruising along the back of his neck. See that?"

There was a dark purple bruise along the base of James Klein's neck, but what was odd was the shape of the bruise. It was a pattern of small squares.

"What do you make of those marks?"

"Probably the bottom of a work boot or hiking boot," Lizzie said. "Like someone was standing on his neck, pushing his face into the dirt, while they cut off his hands."

"Using his head for leverage," I said, not as a question, and not really to Lizzie, but to myself. Said it because I had to hear myself say it.

Lizzie nodded and I saw that she was looking over my shoulder at the bodies of the two boys. "Yeah," she said finally, her gaze averted back to James Klein, "that's probably what happened."

"All right," I said. "How long will it take you to finish the rest of these up?"

Lizzie exhaled so that her bangs fluttered in the air for a moment. "About two hours for each of them."

"Okay," I said. "The families are flying in this afternoon. Can you get me something preliminary on paper tonight?"

"I'll try," Lizzie said and then both of us were silent for a minute.

"I miss your dad," I said, because at that moment I really did. We'd been good friends for many years and when he died I knew that the old school in Granite City was getting close to recess time. "He was a good man, Lizzie. I'm sure proud of the way you've stuck around here and I know he would be, too."

Before Lizzie could reply, Hawkins walked in with a slice of fruitcake in his teeth and two cups of coffee. As I walked out, Hawkins and Lizzie started dumping James Klein's internal organs back into his body in no particular order.

JUST AFTER NOON, A helicopter containing James Klein's mother and father, plus Missy Klein's mother, a Mrs. Pellet, landed on the football field at Granite City High School. Lyle and I were there waiting for it.

"I'm real sorry about this," I said to Mrs. Klein when I shook her hand.

"You said you'd find him," she said.

Before I could answer Mrs. Klein, before I could tell her that we'd found him just as I knew we would, her husband placed a hand on her shoulder and directed her away from me.

"This is a hard time for her," he said and then he too was gone, squiring his wife into the back of a rented Aerostar we'd brought for them. Mr. Klein wore a hound's tooth sport coat that hung off his shoulders like a dead vine and a pair of expensive sunglasses that day. I knew that behind those tinted glasses were the eyes of a man without hope. I'd seen that look on the face of every man who'd lost a son.

Lyle helped Missy's mother off the helicopter and I could tell that, like Mr. Klein, she was face to face with the dead end of life. She was older than I'd remembered her from the months she'd spent in town, but I guess waiting for bad news would do that to you.

We drove the three of them to the Best Western on Central, none of us speaking until we arrived there. The lobby was filled with a dozen gingerbread houses, each sponsored by different businesses in town: The Pizza Cookery. B. Barker & Sons, Accountants. The Paulson Mortuary and Home of Peace & Tranquility. Even Shake's Bar had a house, which tilted ever so slightly to the left. Somewhere, Neil Diamond was singing "Rudolph the Red Nosed Reindeer" over tinny speakers.

"When do we get to see them?" Mr. Klein asked. We were waiting for the elevator to take the Kleins and Mrs. Pellet up to their rooms.

"Tomorrow, I'd guess," I said. "Or after the holiday."

"We'll want to bury them in Connecticut," Mr. Klein said and Missy's mother, Mrs. Pellet, nodded in agreement. "Tomorrow is the last day of Hanukkah. I'd like to spend it with my son."

"The medical examiner still needs to finish getting some information though."

"For what?" Mr. Klein said. He reached over and pressed the elevator button twice, even though it was already lit. "So that we can be told my son suffered? I don't need to know anymore to understand that he's gone. That all of them are gone."

"It's a murder investigation," I said. We'd told both families that their loved ones had been found, though not the condition of their bodies. Foul play, we'd told them, was suspected. "There are procedures that must be followed. I'm sorry if you have to stay here one minute longer than you want to, but this is my job and I'm planning on doing it."

"Sheriff Drew," Mr. Klein said, "do you have any children?"

"I don't."

"I know my son wasn't a good person," Mr. Klein said. "My wife and I have reconciled that much. He was a drug addict and probably a pretty good one, if you want to know. He was also a gifted liar. I am sure he made enemies in many parts of the world or else why would he come to a place like this?" Mr. Klein swallowed and it seemed then that he'd come to some fine point in his mind, as if he'd figured out a troubling problem that had always been just within reach. "So, you see Sheriff, I don't need to know who did what. I don't need that kind of element in my life. I'd prefer to think that my son was the decent person he pretended to be."

"I'll keep that in mind," I said.

"Sheriff," Mrs. Pellet said, her voice soft and tired, "I just want to bring my baby home. Whoever killed her, if anyone did, is gone. If you haven't found who did this yet, you never will."

"She's right, you know," Lyle said as we walked back to the van. "They're both right, sort of. We went through every lead we had on this case over a year ago, Morris."

"But there's all kinds of new technology, Lyle," I said. "There's a national database of violent crimes, advances in science. DNA. We can try, can't we?"

Lyle reached into his pocket and pulled out a pack of Lucky Strikes and lit one. I'd known Lyle for half my life and he'd always been someone I could depend on. He wasn't what you might call book smart, but he knew things instinctively like no one I'd ever known, before or since. "Tell you what," he said, smoke drifting out of his nose in smooth wisps of gray. "I get cable just like you. I see all those forensic shows on Discovery and I think they're fantastic. I'm glad the cops in LA are solving crimes from the 1950s using Space Shuttle technology. But you know what, Morris? *This ain't LA.*"

He was right, of course, which made it all the more difficult to take.

I was sitting at the counter of Lolly's Diner eating meatloaf and reading the autopsies of the Klein family when Miller Descent walked in and sat down next to me. It was near nine o'clock.

"Lyle said you might be here," Miller said.

"Just reading about that family," I said, holding up the autopsy report. "And trying to swallow some food. Can hardly do either."

"We've got Bonnie's family staying with us for Christmas," Miller said, "so I've been eating my mother-in-law's food all week. You never had so much nutmeg in your life." Miller chuckled and then paused. "I wanna ask you something, Sheriff," he said cautiously, "and I don't want to offend you in any way by asking it."

"That's a tough order now." Lolly came by then to re-fill my coffee cup and Miller asked if he could have a slice of apple pie. "Well," I said when Lolly left, "spit it out."

"Do you think maybe you should turn this case over to someone else?" Miller said.

"That doesn't sound like a question, Miller," I said. "It sounds like a request."

"Assistant DA upstate saw some of the crime scene pictures," Miller said. There was a sheepish quality about him then that I wasn't used to, and I realized that this wasn't something he was enjoying. "I probably shouldn't have shown him a damn thing, but you know how favors work around up there, right, Sheriff?"

"I guess."

"Well, he thinks this is something the Brawton police, maybe the Homicide unit they got out there should get involved with, or at least maybe a more . . ." Miller trailed off when Lolly dropped his pie off. "Hell," he said. "You know what I'm trying to say here, right? Talk to the family, let them know it's an option."

What he was trying to say was that there was some glamour to this case: *A wealthy young family found murdered in the ski hamlet down state. $500,000 sitting in an evidence room gathering dust.* And glamour means an assistant DA upstate becomes DA, or Mayor, or worse—a congressman.

I also think Miller was trying to say that I didn't have a chance in hell of finding a killer and that maybe I should let the blame fall on somebody upstairs.

"Yeah," I said. "I understand."

Miller sat there and ate his slice of pie in silence after that, never once asking to see the autopsy file wedged between us. Eventually, Lolly went over to the six-foot tall artificial Christmas tree she kept by the front door and unplugged it, clicked off the battery-powered menorah over by the cash register, started to sweep up the strands of silver and gold tinsel that had fallen onto the floor.

"All right then," Miller said, standing to leave, his plate cleaned.

"You know," I said, "there's nutmeg in apple pie, too."

"Yeah," Miller said, zipping up his down jacket, "I figured that out."

"Don't you want to know how they died, Miller?"

Miller stuffed his hands into his pockets and sort of bowed, biting his bottom lip until it looked painful, and then shook his head. "This is what I know about these things," Miller said. "There ain't a cause or an effect once they've started to rot and such. They're dead and they're not coming back. If they were meant to still be alive, if God wanted them here right now, then God dammit, they'd be here. Time's up, that's all."

"You're wrong," I said, suddenly angry with Miller, angry with the DA who wanted a big city detective to run this case, angry with my wife Margaret for dying three years ago and leaving me alone. "There is cause and effect, Miller. People don't just punch in and punch out. Kids died up there, Miller. *Kids*. You can't apply your mumbo jumbo to them. No one deserves that. You know what? You're wrong, Miller. This isn't about rotting bodies and old bones. You can't just toss a blanket over every body you see and pretend that they aren't *someone*. Do you know that, Miller? Do you know?"

Miller frowned at me. "Acute hemorrhaging of the lungs, an occulation of the blood vessels around the eyes and face, suggesting suffocation. General failure of the major organs due to severe blood loss and the ensuing shock," Miller said. The words tumbled out of his mouth like he was reading from a textbook. "Wounds consistent with a number of drug related murders in a hundred different towns that aren't Granite City. I'm sorry, Sheriff," he said. "I really am." He put out his hand, but I didn't take it, so he shrugged, put it back in his pocket and started to toward the door. "Have a Merry Christmas, Morris. Take the day off. It would do you some good."

I watched Miller climb into his car, a beat up El Camino

that had a bright green wreath on its front grill, and drive off. I knew then that I didn't want to end up like Miller Descent: a hard man unable to shake the horrors from his mind. I also knew that I was halfway there and closing the gap. So, with an envelope filled with the pictures of a dissected family in my hand, I left Lolly's Diner and headed home, where I knew what I had to do, and where I knew I would not sleep.

IT WAS COLD AND overcast the next morning, Yeach Mountain lost behind a thicket of low, gray clouds. A light mist of rain fell as I drove through downtown Granite City toward the station. The streets, slick with moisture, refracted the glow from the strings of golden bulbs that were hung on the light posts each year by the Soroptimists and 4-H. I saw my dead wife Margaret duck into the yarn store on Porter, saw her coming from Biddle's Flowers with a bundle of poinsettias, watched her make a call from the phone booth out front of the library, let her cross in front of me on 9th Street, a ream of wrapping paper tucked under her arm. You live in a town long enough, the past, the present, it all occupies the same space.

But when I walked into the station, all I saw were Mr. and Mrs. Klein and Mrs. Pellet sitting in the lobby. And I thought, seeing Mr. Klein in his black slacks and yellow v-neck sweater, everything about him out of place in my station, that maybe my time in Granite City was coming to a close; that I couldn't bear to see despair in people's faces anymore. That, most of all, I couldn't keep on thinking about the daily rituals that still call to people even in their times of need: the soft pleat ironed down Mrs. Klein's pant leg, the way Mrs. Pellet had put on a nice dress and gold earrings.

"Been waiting long?" I asked.

"No," Mr. Klein said. His voice was low and I decided that he probably wasn't long for this place either. "Didn't get much in the way of rest last night."

"I've got the autopsies for your son's family," I said. "You can read 'em if you want to."

Mrs. Klein let out a short sob and squeezed her husband's arm. Mr. Klein kissed her on the forehead and patted her hand. "Did he suffer, Sheriff?" Mrs. Klein asked.

"No," I said. "No, it looks like he died peacefully."

"What about my Missy?" Mrs. Pellet asked. "And the kids; what about the kids?"

"The same," I said. "I think they got lost in the woods is all. A real tragedy." A look of relief passed over their faces, and though I believe they each knew that their children and grandchildren had died terribly, that in fact they'd been butchered, I had helped them in some way. Had eased something in them for at least a moment.

Lyle walked out then and tapped me on the shoulder. "Dr. DiGiangreco called for you," he said. "Needs you to call her right away."

I told the families to wait for just a little bit longer and I'd get the bodies of their loved ones released. Lyle followed me back to my office.

"What the hell's going on out there?" Lyle said. "I thought I heard you tell them their kids died peacefully."

"I did," I said.

"Morris," Lyle said, "their damn hands and feet were cut off!"

"I know that," I said.

"Lizzie said some DA called her," Lyle said. "You aware of that?"

I opened the door to my office and let Lyle stand in the hall. "You talk to your kids lately, Lyle?"

"You know, Morris, when I can," Lyle said. "Why?"

"How about you take today off and drive down and see your daughter," I said. "Shoot, take the whole week off. Fly out to California and see your son. When was the last time you spent the holidays with your kids?"

Lyle squinted his eyes at me and rolled his tongue against his cheek. "Whatever this is, Morris," he said, "I hope you know what you're doing."

LIZZIE ANSWERED ON THE first ring. "They're all wrapped up and ready to go," she said.

"How do they look?" I asked.

I heard Lizzie sigh on the other end of the line. "I had to use fishing line to sew the boys' feet back on, Hawkins had some thirty-five pound test that worked great," she said. "It should hold for a long time."

"I appreciate this Lizzie," I said. "More than you'll ever know."

"What do you want me to do about this DA who keeps calling?"

"Tell him to call me if he has any questions," I said. "The family hasn't asked for anything and it's not his case."

"You've got all the paperwork there?" Lizzie asked.

"Right in front of me," I said. "I'll sign off on it and get you a copy."

"Would my dad have done this?" Lizzie asked.

"I don't know," I said. "I don't know if you should have."

"Hawkins said that if there was a problem he'd take the blame," Lizzie said. "Said that's how it's always worked here in Granite City. 'Let the shit roll downhill,' were his exact words."

I thought then that my recollections of Lizzie's father had grown opaque in my mind—my memories colored more for what I wished were always true than what actually was. We'd worked together for a long time and time spares no one.

"Tell Hawkins I won't forget this," I said.

"Sheriff," Lizzie said, "can I ask you a question?"

"Sure."

"Why'd you stay here all these years?"

AFTER WE HUNG UP, I pulled out a piece of letterhead and scratched out a three-sentence letter of resignation. I held it in my hands and ran my fingers over every word, every period. I'd been the Sheriff of Granite City for thirty-five years and I'd never broken the law. I always did the legitimate thing, like telling men who beat their wives that they were going to hell when I didn't even believe in God, and then letting them go on back home because the law back then said we couldn't hold them. Like knocking on poor Gina Morrow's door at 3 o'clock in the morning to tell her that her husband had been stabbed to death in a bar fight over another woman.

I'd followed the letter of the law, no matter my opinion of it. What good did it do? Couldn't I have lied to Gina Morrow and told her that her husband had been stabbed to death trying to protect an innocent woman's honor? Couldn't I have dragged some of those no-good wife beaters out behind the station and pounded them into submission?

And yet, there I was with my letter of resignation in my hand and an autopsy report on my desk. Inside both documents were lies. Inside the autopsy report, Dr. Lizzie DiGiangreco, whose dead father I had carried to his grave, stated that all four members of the Klein family had died of exposure and acute hypothermia. She further stated that all members of the family were fully intact—that all hands and feet were connected. An accidental death, no note of foul play.

In my official report, typed the night previous on my old Olivetti, I stated that it was my belief that the Klein family had succumbed during the night of November 11, 1998. The almanac noted November 11, 1998, as being the coldest day of the month during what became the coldest winter in record. Over a foot of snow fell that night.

Case closed.

Snow fell in Granite City the night I quit, too. It was Christmas Eve, and though the roads were slippery and runny, I called Lyle and asked him to meet me at Shake's Bar. We sat for a long time in a small booth sipping beer and eating stale nuts, an old Johnny Mathis Christmas song bleating out of the tape player Zep, the bartender, pulled out on special occasions. That next day I'd recommend to the Mayor that Lyle be named interim Sheriff, a post he would eventually keep for three years until he died from emphysema.

"You know what, Morris," Lyle said, "I've been thinking a lot about just closing up shop and moving to Hawaii. You know I was stationed out there, right?"

"Yeah," I said.

"In those days, I raised a lot of hell," Lyle said. He had a faraway look in his eyes and I thought maybe inside his head he was on liberty in Maui. "I don't regret it, though. We all had to sow our oats at some point. Make bad decisions and then just close those chapters and move on."

"I never really did that," I said. "I've loved two women in my life, Lyle, and both of them are dead now. From day one, I've tried to do right. What has it gotten me?"

"Respect."

"They gonna put that on my tombstone? *Here rests a guy people respected.*"

"That wouldn't be so bad, when you think about it." Lyle took a final pull from his beer, then coughed wetly. "You did right by everyone, Morris," he said. "By everyone." He slid out of the booth then, tugged on a knit cap and gloves. "I called my kids, like you said. Daughter told me I was about five years too late."

"Keep calling," I said.

"Yeah, well," Lyle said. "The thing of it is, Morris, nights like this? You know, it's arbitrary. Holidays? What are we celebrating? I don't believe in God and finding those kids up there on Yeach, that didn't make it any better, you know? I mean, what are we celebrating?"

"That we made it through," I said.

Lyle considered that for a moment. "I shouldn't have to be told to call my kids. I shouldn't even have been at work today." He shook his head. "My dad was a cop. And you know what he did on Christmas Eve?"

"No."

"Nothing. He did nothing at all. He was just my dad. I don't know how that got lost on me."

"Go home, Lyle," I said. "You're drunk." Which wasn't true.

"I will," he said. "I thought I'd just take a drive through the streets. Make sure no one's stuck in the snow. You could positively die from the cold out there tonight."

Lyle smiled through his pursed lips and I knew that he had seen my report, had seen Lizzie's autopsy report, and that he didn't care. That he knew I'd made a judgment call not based on the nuts and bolts of the law, but on how people feel inside, on the mechanics of the human heart.

"I'll come with you," I said.

BO SAU (VENGEANCE)

Henry Chang

HENRY CHANG was born and raised in New York's Chinatown, where he still lives. He is a graduate of CCNY and the author of five novels featuring Chinatown born and raised Detective Jack Yu: *Chinatown Beat, Year of the Dog, Red Jade, Death Money,* and *Lucky.*

Dinner Before Noon

In late February, weeks past the Chinese New Year cel-ebrations, the Chinatown mornings at last returned to normal. Gone was the four-deep crush of the crowds clam-oring to buy chicken, *for yook* roast pig and duck. Missing were the flower vendors on every street corner, barking out offers of the gladiolas and carnations. There wasn't an empty seat to be had in the Chinatown coffee shops then. Even early in the morning, the streets had been crowded with Chinese. Then the white tourists arrived in busloads—just as the area's office workers broke for lunch—and the whole neighborhood seemed like it would burst with traffic, noise and bustle.

Now the quiet mornings had returned. It was comforting, like the solitude of his overnight shift. Michael Mak was slurping his thousand-year egg congee, dunking a fried *jow gwai* cruller into the hot soupy rice mix. He was at a lone seat at the back table of Big Chang's *fai sik* fast food restaurant. It was almost noontime, which for him was a late dinnertime, nearly four hours after the overnight security shift at Con-fucius Towers. The freezing morning wind had whipped up his appetite.

He'd sat with his back to the wall, as usual, and was reading the sports section from the free newspaper he'd grabbed from the sidewalk box at Mott and Canal.

There was a rush of cold wind and he looked up to see a crew of Chinese laborers enter Big Chang's. For them, this was lunchtime and they took the large round table in the middle of the floor.

Mak returned to his newspaper and cruller, occasionally sneaking a look at the group as they placed their orders with the red-vested waiter. The quick-eats restaurant started filling up, the lunchtime crowd driven indoors by the February freeze.

He kept his head down, pretending to read the newspaper, when he heard one of the men use the phrase *jook sing*, the derogatory term for the American-born Chinese—empty piece of bamboo.

Michael Mak himself was *jook sing* but was capable of speaking functional Cantonese and Toishanese, the main Chinatown dialects. He knew that native-born Chinese held the American-born in contempt, citing their ignorance of the great celestial traditions. He took no offense at the talk.

Mak folded the newspaper, then raised a lazy glance at the men, a cup of tea at his lips. The laborers continued their chatter. They were oblivious to him, but he focused on one of them. It was a face he hadn't seen in twenty years and now it was causing his blood to rise. The man was Tsi Mun, a former Chinatown gang member who, like Michael Mak, was in his forties now.

Mak lifted the newspaper so as to obscure his face. Tsi Mun was an old enemy with whom he had a longtime score to settle.

Twenty years before this congee morning, Tsi Mun had been a member of the Black Dragons street gang, a motley crew of Hong Kong hotheads and Chinatown discards.

Tsi Mun was better known by his Cantonese street name, *Doe Jai*—Knife Boy. He had a reputation for being good with a blade.

One hot summer night, Doe Jai had bugged out and, in a fit of inexplicable rage, stabbed Mak's cousin, *Leng Jai*—Pretty

Boy—so nicknamed because he was a good-looking flashy dresser, popular with the Chinatown girls.

Pretty Boy survived eight hours on the operating table, and that was just the first of his surgeries. They had opened him up and stitched him back and the jagged scars left a roadmap across his torso and back. Pretty Boy was never the same after the attack. He had all kinds of problems and was always in pain. The surgeons removed part of his bladder and he couldn't even piss like a normal person.

Pretty Boy wasn't so popular after that.

A few years later he committed suicide.

Despite Michael Mak's attempts to locate him, Doe Jai was nowhere to be found. He had disappeared from Chinatown.

Mak's family and relatives relocated to Seattle Chinatown soon after, but Michael stayed behind and took over the rent-controlled family apartment in the tenement walkup on Bayard. For the first few years, Mak kept a lookout for Doe Jai, but over time the idea of revenge diminished, distant but not forgotten.

Now HIS TARGET SAT at the middle table, only fifteen feet away. Mak quietly clenched his fist, brought it under the table, trying to stay calm, trying to ignore the drumbeat in his chest.

A half-dozen plates of rice arrived at the big table. The men tore into the assortment of *saam bo faahn* dishes, their waiter ladling out steamy bowls of chicken feet soup.

Mak put his head down, appearing to read the table menu. He listened for the sound of Doe Jai's voice. His face was expressionless as he cast a last glance their way, leaving a dollar tip under his teacup.

He kept his back to the laborers, who were still gulping down their meals as he made his way out of Big Chang's.

Outside Mak crossed the street diagonally and went into the May Wah coffee shop, where he bought a *nai cha* tea. Opening his newspaper at the window counter, he watched the door of Big Chang's.

He knew it'd take at least another fifteen minutes for the men to finish their meal. He blew the steam off the rim of the cardboard cup as he scanned the street and considered the twenty years.

After almost half an hour, the construction crew came out of Big Chang's. With full bellies, they sauntered across Mott toward Bayard, back to work.

Mak followed at a distance, his breath white in the frigid air. They came to a worksite on Pell, where they were repairing the exterior of a walkup tenement belonging to the Chin clan. There was a scaffolding setup and a dumpster on the street.

Mak knew the work gangs didn't quit until six P.M., their crew bosses wringing the last ounce of sweat from the men before calling it a day. He watched Doe Jai go into the building as the men began to load the dumpster. He checked his watch. It was 1 P.M.

As he walked home, feeling tired, he resolved to take only a short nap behind the drawn afternoon shades of his dark tenement bedroom. Then he'd return to Pell.

His nap was a fitful series of violent snapshots and when Mak finally awoke he felt groggy and nervous. When he got to Pell Street the gray afternoon was drifting into darkness and the work crew had turned on the light bulbs under the scaffolding.

It had gotten colder, but Mak was toasting inside his down-filled jacket, his head covered by the black Mets cap he'd tilted down over his eyes. He went along the street and found a spot under Wah Kee's awning, near enough to the dollar mini-car stop for him to be mistaken for a passenger awaiting the cheap ride.

School children came down the street with their book bags and old folks mobbed the LeeLee Bakery for the discounted late-day pastries.

Mak kept his eyes on the construction site.

AT 6 P.M. THE work crew packed up their tools and left the tenement building. The men split up on the corner and Mak stayed a half-block behind Doe Jai and two others, following them down the long stretch of East Broadway until they passed beneath the Manhattan Bridge and turned off into Mechanics Alley.

There, under the shadow of the looming bridge, was a blue car parked halfway onto the sidewalk. The noise was deafening. The roar and screech of the subway trains careening across the bridge assaulted his ears. In the rare intervals when there were no trains, the sound of traffic, five stories or so above, remained constant. It all made for a steady violent rumble, its rhythms broken only by the thuds and clangs of heavy trucks as they banged their way over the East River to Brooklyn or back.

One of the laborers continued on as Doe Jai and the other man got into the car.

Mak stepped back away from the corner as the car came out of the alley and turned uptown. He wrote its plate number across his palm, wondering if Doe Jai regularly left the car there.

Walking back along Division Street, he realized he had five hours before the midnight shift and decided to pay a visit to one of the gambling basements on Bayard. At rush hour and dinnertime the gambling joints were usually empty.

Inside Number Seven, the basement was brightly lit with a mahjong game underway at the back of the long room. Otherwise, there were only a few of the association's cronies hanging around, making lowball bets just to keep the action going.

It was cold and for the true night crawlers the evening was very young.

Mak saw the old man he was looking for, hunched over a card table near the back, where they kept pots of coffee and tea. He was reading a Chinese newspaper, occasionally looking up at the players at the mahjong table.

This man, Jum Sook, was known to be a former boxer for the clan association. He'd been a *Hung Kwun*—a Red Pole enforcer—in the hierarchy. Retired now, his responsibilities to the clan consisted of managing the house supply of brandy, tea, cigarettes and coffee.

The cagey old man had recommended Mak for the overnight security guard position at Confucius Towers, where the clan owned a number of apartments. Knowing Mak spoke English well, Jum Sook had made him the clan's link to the building manager's office where he was always to have his eye out for shady subleases. Mak had been on the job over four years and had helped thwart several rental scams.

Jum Sook gave Mak a small grin and allowed him to sit at the card table.

Mak told the story of Doe Jai's assault and Pretty Boy's suicide. Afterward the old man said quietly in Chinese, "You have no reason to kill anyone. The victim was weak at heart and could not find the courage to face his future."

Mak explained that he felt an injustice had been committed, one that required vengeance.

Jum Sook shook his head sadly, then made a crude sketch with Chinese notations in the margins of his newspaper. The drawing looked a little like a screwdriver. The old man wrote *six inches* in Chinese next to it. Further down along the margin he wrote the phrase *where the eye meets the nose*.

He never said another word. He just kept writing on the newspaper, directing Mak's attention to the scrawl of Chinese characters. In silence, Mak read more phrases that sounded in his mind vaguely like a poem—*an eye for an eye* and *he shall hate what he sees*. Finally, Jum Sook drew a cartoon face with a drooling crooked mouth and a blind eye.

Jum Sook stood up and rolled the newspaper into a tube, wrapping his fists around it. The old Red Pole enforcer held it at eye level and suddenly thrust a short jab, twisting his wrist at the end of it, striking like a Shaolin kung fu arrow fist.

A few players entered the basement and Jum Sook stuck the rolled paper into his back pocket. He started to refill a teapot even as Michael Mak left the cool musty basement.

The Shift

MAK WENT IN THROUGH the porter's trash door, avoiding the front lobby's bank of black and white surveillance monitors. The security guards were at their half-sized lockers in a basement room next to the building engineer's office. The staff consisted of five guards and a supervisor. Michael Mak did the overnight, with the other guards splitting Mak's shift on his nights off.

He punched in at the time clock by the door. There were several boxes in a corner that the afternoon shift had signed for. He checked the log. Luck Yee Dental Offices accounted for two of the boxes that the day shift would then have to turn over to the receptionist. Mak knew that Luck Yee was one of the several offices that secretly disarmed their alarms, annoyed that the system frequently went off at night in response to electrical spikes, thunderstorms and blackouts.

Few guards wanted the night shift, but it suited Mak. It was the one shift with no one looking over your shoulder. He just answered to a bank of surveillance monitors, a log book and a schedule of patrols controlled by a computer. There were no asshole supervisors or building managers like there were during the day. There were no deliveries to handle and no building inspectors or fire drills on the graveyard shift.

The overnight was boring and lonely, but there was no bullshit.

At 4 A.M. Mak activated the electronic Patrol Scan wand, pocketed the security set of master keys and proceeded to conduct his building patrol, top floor down to the basement. The patrol layout was structured around fifty coded elec-tronic chips positioned strategically along the corridors and stairwells of the high-rise building. The chips' locations were downloaded into the wand with a beep-tone each time the guard made contact, recording the time as well. The electronic patrol system was supposed to keep the guards focused on a diligent patrol round, ensuring that they walked the length of the corridors and checked the stairwells and didn't nap in any of the porter's supply rooms. A computer-generated weekly review of the patrols rated the guards' performances. The day supervisor posted the results and admonished or commended individual guards.

Mak actually liked the patrol routine. He always hit the chips in a timely fashion. The building patrol took an average of thirty-eight minutes and he scored consistently high accuracy.

The patrol gave him a chance to stretch his legs, to get away from the security podium at the front lobby. He took the elevator to the top floor and walked down the corridor, twenty-five steps each way, touching the chips on the stairwell doors. He followed the pattern on the next landing and made his way down, the silence broken only by his footsteps and the beep of the wand.

WITHIN THIRTY-FOUR MINUTES HE'D arrived at the ground floor of Confucius Towers and continued the patrol round, checking the doors of all the street-level storefront businesses and the basement exits that the porters and engineers used.

On the way back up he returned to the Luck Yee Dental Offices, using the master key to get in. He went to the supply closet, grabbed a handful of latex gloves and took a small bottle from the shelf.

Mak was done before thirty-seven minutes had expired. He wrapped up the patrol, tapping the wand against the last electronic chip in the locker room. He logged the wand back in, placed it in its charger and returned to the front lobby.

It was 4:39 A.M.

As usual, no one was around.

AT 6:30 A.M. MAK took his break and went down to the lockers. In the building engineer's tool dump area, he found a rusty screwdriver that was about the right length. He placed it into a plastic sandwich bag and put the bag in his coat.

He used the master key set to open the security supply closet and removed a cardboard box containing several pairs of discarded handcuffs left behind by former guards. The handcuffs were worn down and dented but still usable for restraining perpetrators. He removed one pair, tested it with his key, then put it into another plastic bag and into his coat pocket.

From his own half-locker he removed his aluminum mini-thermos and sipped a hot cup of dark *bo lei* tea before residents would be leaving for work. The weak dawn light would stream through the lobby and rush hour would begin.

It was a new day. He wondered if the blue car would appear in Mechanics Alley.

Eight-fifteen and Mechanics Alley was empty. Mak went to the Vietnamese shop on the corner and bought a grilled pork *bahn mi* sandwich, wolfing it down while he waited.

A half-hour later there was still no sign of the car and he didn't feel like waiting any longer.

Maybe it was Doe Jai's day off.

Mak decided to return and check it out in the afternoon.

BACK IN HIS TENEMENT apartment, Mak put the screw-driver, latex gloves and the small bottle of anesthetic into a black zippered sack. He dropped the handcuffs into a rice bowl of cleaning fluid and drained two big shots of Remy before falling asleep in the shady morning light.

It was early afternoon when he awoke, feeling rested. Eager.

When he returned to the alley, the blue car was there and Mak strolled casually past to confirm the plate number.

There was no doubt.

He fought the urge to go by the construction site to sneak a look at Doe Jai, but he didn't want to risk getting noticed by any of the work crew.

Concentrate on the car, he told himself.

As he came back down Henry Street, a few people were frantically making their way to the subway in the piercing cold February air. It was Friday. He had the night off. The opportunity to strike was at hand.

He drifted over to the Duk Chen Seafood market. The Fukienese fish monger thought it strange that someone would buy just two *hai* crabs, but he could discern nothing from Mak's appearance.

Bait, the fish man figured.

Mak carried the bag of crabs back toward Bayard, stopping at Mon Kee's for takeout lo mein noodles. Noodles would be easy to digest, he thought, and would sustain him into the night.

He knew that Friday was payday for the construction crews, and they usually stayed together for the crew boss's free Chinatown dinner and for drinks and gambling after.

Things would run late, maybe ten or even eleven o'clock, Mak figured. The freezing weather would mean fewer people out on the streets.

All good, Mak thought, as he turned for home to prepare the tools he'd need for the job.

MAK PLACED THE BAG of *hai* crabs into the kitchen sink. He put on a pair of the latex gloves and started eating his lo mein. He could hear the crabs scuttling and scratching around inside the brown paper bag.

He took the handcuffs out of the rice bowl and put them on top of the takeout napkins, letting the cleaning fluid soak into them.

The crabs scratching, poking around.

He got an old face towel and wiped down the handcuffs, tossing everything into the black zipper sack.

Chewing down the noodles, he took a black woolen cap from his closet. It was a ski mask that could be rolled into a seaman's cap and worn that way. They sold them for two dollars on Canal Street at the first hint of winter. All he had to do was pull the eyeholes down. There was a bigger mouth hole also, but he wasn't planning on having a conversation with Doe Jai.

He finished off the noodles, then took from the bottom of his closet an object that resembled a black hand-held radio but was actually a stun gun. He'd purchased it by mail order from the Enforcement Brigade America catalog before the guns were declared illegal in New York.

It came with a leather holster and a charger. For home defense purposes, like it said in the catalog.

HE OPENED THE BROWN paper bag, turned it upside down and shook the two crabs into the kitchen sink. As he juiced up the stun gun, the crabs danced around the drain hole, their agitated pincers up high.

Mak jabbed the gun at the first crab and it attacked immediately, clamping onto the gun's electric prong. The jolt blew the crab back across the sink, but one claw remained fused to the metal prong. The severed claw turned lurid red. Mak tapped it against the side of the sink and it fell off, leaving a thin trail of smoke.

The second crab, sensing electricity from above, backed away waving its ragged claws.

Mak thrust the gun tip at its mouth. The crab flipped up into the air and landed on its hard shell in the sink, joints arched backwards. Two crabs fully cooked. Mak stared for a moment, then turned off the gun and placed it into the black sack.

He cleared the crab carcasses from the sink and set the clock radio alarm to 5 P.M. Staying off the alcohol, he lay in bed, imagining how he would do it. It occurred to him that it might be best to leave the handcuffs on. That way if anything went wrong, he wouldn't wind up wrestling in the gutter.

Still, it would probably be best if he removed the cuffs. One less piece of evidence. Mak thought he'd take Doe Jai's wallet as well. That would stall the identification process. While the brain bled.

When the alarm went off, it was dark outside. Another Chinatown night was beginning.

Patrol

WEARING THE LATEX GLOVES, he approached Pell Street carrying the zippered bag like a knapsack. It was just before 6 P.M. and he waited until the work crew came out and went toward Mott. Doe Jai was among them as they trooped into Wong Kee's Famous Pork Chop King.

Mak figured he'd give them a couple of hours, plenty of time to patrol the streets around Mechanics Alley and see what things looked like.

Along East Broadway the foot traffic was thinning out as the evening turned black and ominous. He found a spot near where Market Street became Division. A place where he could observe from a distance anyone walking from the far Mott Street end. If Doe Jai wasn't alone when he entered the alley, the attack would have to be postponed. Mak had twenty years of patience and was prepared to abort the mission today if necessary.

Above him the subway trains shrieked.

The street lamps were spaced far apart. A few were broken and the rest threw a sickly yellow glow over the tenements.

Allen Street led north to Canal. He'd want to circle away from the alley in that direction. The sidewalks would be lined with stacked garbage bags from the restaurants, awaiting morning pick up. When he was done, he'd shove his tools into one of the bags and no one would be the wiser.

He planned to use one of the payphones along Canal Street.

His patrol led him past the dark car twice. He had to decide which stone bridge column to hide behind. One that provided a clear view of the car. There he'd roll down the ski mask and be good to go, everything ready.

Several men came down East Broadway, but none of them resembled Doe Jai. It was early.

A LITTLE AFTER TEN, two men came down East Broadway from Mott. As they got closer, Mak could make out that one of them was Doe Jai, carrying a tool bag.

Mak backed away from the corner, retreating to his spot at the rear of the alley, where barbed wire fencing joined the graffiti-tagged stone column. From his view a few steps behind the car, he saw the two men part ways at the opening to the alley. He took several deep boxer's breaths and unzipped the black sack.

Doe Jai came down the alley throwing a look over his shoulder. He coughed and spat out a clot of phlegm. He passed the front of the car, opened the trunk and dropped the tool bag in. Doe Jai slammed the trunk shut, but all Mak could hear was the thunder of the subway above.

Mak rolled down his ski mask and drew the stun gun from the sack. A blue spark jumped between the prongs when he juiced it up.

Doe Jai had his key in the driver's side door when Mak made his move. The door popped open. Mak barreled into

him. Doe Jai managed to yell, "*Dew!* . . . Fuck!" but his cry
was drowned out.

He threw his arms up and Mak jabbed him with the stun
gun where his jacket rose. The charge jolted Doe Jai across the
hood of the car like he'd been slammed by a hundred-pound
sack of rice.

His head racing, Mak shoved the man face-down between
the car and the building. He put a knee between Doe Jai's
shoulder blades, pulled the limp arms back and snapped on
the handcuffs. He could see Doe Jai was struggling to even
catch a breath and gave him another jolt.

His body jerked spasmodically as Mak poured the drug
from Luck Yee's onto the rag. He cupped the rag over Doe
Jai's mouth and nose and held it in place until after the bridge
noises subsided. Doe Jai still twitched against the hold of
the handcuffs, even as Mak pocketed the stun gun and took the
screwdriver from his bag. He rolled Doe Jai over and saw his
slack, open mouth and half-closed eyes. He was still fighting
against the blackness clouding his mind.

Mak remembered his cousin Pretty Boy's jagged scar tor-
ment, his humiliation, his sorrow and pain.

He positioned the screwdriver tip on Doe Jai's face *where
the nose meets the eye.*

Fuck you, was Mak's last thought as he readied the jab
thrust.

He could feel the vibration from the subways above. The
sharpened screwdriver tip shoved easily through orb, liga-
ment, muscle and nerve. Doe Jai's mouth jerked open in a
silent scream as the steel shank penetrated tissue, carving out
damage to the lobe, with Mak's hand fishtailing as he pushed
into the man's brain.

Mak imagined how one side of Doe Jai's face would sag,

the muscles weakened, leaving him to drool frequently. He'd have memory loss and speech impairment. Doe Jai, Knife Boy, would become a slurring, gooey idiot, seeing from one eye the horror he'd become, unable to understand what befell him.

The righteousness of the Tao. The way of all things.

He took Doe Jai's thin wallet, removed the handcuffs and left him lying there beside the car. He left the alley riding a wave of adrenalin. North on Allen, Mak dumped the rag, the little bottle, the handcuffs and the screwdriver in one of the dozens of black garbage bags lining the curb.

It was all he could do to keep from breaking into a run, to start screaming at the moonless black night.

When he got to Canal he veered left toward the bustling heart of Chinatown. He found a sidewalk payphone near the park at Forsyth. The 911 operator directed his call to the Chinatown precinct.

What is your emergency?

There's a man bleeding on the ground in Mechanics Alley, under the Manhattan Bridge. He knew they'd start tracking his call.

Yes, sir, can you tell me where you're calling from? Your name, sir?

Could be a white man. He looked hurt bad.

What's wrong with him? Sir?

In Mechanics Alley, near Market Street.

Market Street, right, and what's wrong with him?

He's laying there in the alley, next to a blue car. Looks like he's dying.

Mak was imagining the wail of sirens as he hung up. He crossed Canal, made his way to Bayard.

BACK INSIDE HIS APARTMENT, Mak poured himself a glass of Remy and cracked open the window. The cold night air was invigorating, the brutal gusts somehow keeping him in touch with all that had happened.

Mak pulled out the contents of Doe Jai's wallet. He took a sip of the Remy before sifting through the assorted cards. The brandy was to calm him, not to knock him out. It was to help balance the *yang* of his hate. He'd planned to stay awake this night anyway, like it was just another overnight shift.

He splayed the cards on the cheap folding tray in the kitchen space.

The skinny wallet gave up a twenty dollar prepaid telephone calling card and creased flyer advertising in Chinese for *leng siu jeer*—sweet and pretty young ladies. There was a pocket calendar from the Global China Bank and a Visa credit card issued by First Abacus Trust. Stuck to the credit card was an old Lotto ticket. Knife Boy's luck just took a turn for the worse, thought Mak. The last item he touched was the driver's license.

The New York State Driver License featured a color photo of Doe Jai. The date of birth was about right, making him forty-four. *Say say*, which sounded like *double-death* in Chinese. The address was down Madison Street, on the far side of Chinatown that used to be Black Dragon's territory.

It was Doe Jai, all right, even though the photo looked like an old one.

But it was him, definitely.

Did Doe Jai—Tsi Mun—really think it was going to be that easy? Just let the years run by and everyone would forget the stabbing? It was arrogance and carelessness on Doe Jai's part, Mak figured. He hadn't even bothered to somehow change his face. How hard would it have been to grow a mustache, a beard or shave his head? Something, *anything*.

Fuck him, Mak concluded, taking another hit of the Remy.

He turned on his old color TV and kept the volume low, just enough to have some movement and noise in the lonely apartment.

He put away the cards and the wallet and sat in front of the open window. Occasionally he heard sirens from the distant darkness. Waiting for daybreak, he finished what was left of the bottle of Remy. He wondered what kind of flowers to bring to Pretty Boy's tombstone when the *Ching Ming* grave sweeping season rolled around again.

THE NEXT DAY HE bought a *Daily News* and a *New York Post* from MayLee's newsstand and searched for news while he sat at Big Chang's back table waiting for the congee to cool. There was nothing in the *Post*, but in the *Daily News* he found a short paragraph in the Crime File section. It was titled "Manhattan Man Knifed in Robbery" and came after "Park Ave. Hit and Run" and "Pilot Busted in Belting of JFK Customs Agent":

> *A man was attacked during an apparent robbery yesterday evening on a Chinatown street under the Manhattan Bridge. The victim, whose name was not released, was stabbed in the eye by an unknown assailant, police said. There have been no arrests. Anyone with information is asked to call Crime Stoppers at (800)-555-TIPS.*

MAK READ THE PARAGRAPH three times. Back to the wall, he blew at the steam rising from his bowl of congee and dunked in the *jow gwai* cruller. The sun had broken through the clouds and washed over the red formica tables. He had a few hours before he had to be back at work and could enjoy the afternoon.

RED CHRISTMAS

James R. Benn

 **JAMES R. BENN** is the author of the Billy Boyle World War II mysteries: *Billy Boyle, The First Wave, Blood Alone, Evil for Evil, Rag and Bone, A Mortal Terror, Death's Door, A Blind Goddess, The Rest Is Silence, The White Ghost, Blue Madonna,* and *The Devouring.* The debut, *Billy Boyle,* was named one of five top mysteries of 2006 by Book Sense and was a Dilys Award nominee. *A Blind Goddess* was long-listed for the IMPAC Dublin Literary Award, and *The Rest Is Silence* was a Barry Award nominee. A librarian for many years, Benn divides his time between Florida and Connecticut with his wife, Deborah Mandel.

December 24, 1953
Blue Rock, Ohio

Ethan Shard shuffled through the fresh white snow. Barely an inch, and the temperature already above freezing as the late afternoon sun broke through the fleeing clouds. People were bundled up, thick scarves around their necks, gloves and mittens warming their hands.

They had no idea.

The shimmer of snow gave Blue Rock a look of new-found purity, like a penitent woman wearing her white veil over a low-cut dress. The whole town was nothing more than a few stores, a diner, and a cluster of houses surrounded by farmland on the banks of the Muskingum River. Brightly colored lights decorated streetlamps, inviting shoppers to stop at the Ben Franklin five and dime for last minute gifts.

Shard stomped his boots free of snow on the sidewalk in front of the diner. Time for a homecoming, such as it was.

"Coffee," he said, taking a stool at the counter, near the cash register and the rack of candy bars. He was the only customer. A solitary pine—needles already littering the floor—stood in the corner, draped in tinsel and gaudy ornaments.

"On the house, pal," the counterman said, pouring Shard a mug. "I'm closing early, so the grill's shut down. On account of it's Christmas Eve."

"No problem. Hey, is Sully around?"

"Naw. I bought the place from him a coupla years ago. He's up in Ashtabula now. You from around here?"

"I was," Shard said. "He told me to see him when I got out of the army, said he'd give me a job. I used to work weekends here when I was in high school."

"Sorry, buddy, I run the place myself, not that I have a lot to show for it. Blue Rock ain't exactly a boom town, but you must already know that. You were in the war? Korea?" As if Shard might not have heard of it.

"Yeah," Shard said. "Just got out." It wasn't a job he'd come looking for; he had plenty of back pay.

"Must feel good to be home. You got family here?"

Shard shook his head, sipping at the coffee. Hearing the question out loud, he wondered why he'd come at all. After the army released him from the hospital, he'd made for Ohio without much thought, looking for familiarity, the illusion of a home to return to. "Not anymore." They were all in the ground.

"You got no place to go?" The counterman looked like he was ready to offer sympathy, or worse yet, charity.

"I can go anywhere I want," Shard said, knowing charity offered on Christmas Eve might sour by morning. His eyes wandered, taking in the pies in a glass case, the soda foundation, candies by the register, the refrigerator stocked with everything from hot dogs to cheese and eggs. Maybe to this guy it didn't mean much, but to Shard it was heaven.

"Suit yourself," the counterman said, topping off Shard's coffee before turning to clean the grill. Shard added sugar, watching the crystals fall like thick snow, his mind's eye filling with the swirling Siberian storms that had coated their compound last winter. Hands around the warm cup, he shivered as the memories returned, unbidden and relentless, as vivid as that day one year ago.

December 24, 1952
POW Camp 11, North Korea

ETHAN SHARD WOKE FROM his dream, gasping for breath. Schuman had visited him again. Schuman had been dead for two years.

To the day.

Shard nudged Skitter awake, motioning toward the rice paper door of their hut. They rose, hunching against the sloping roof, their heads bowed. Shard stepped over the prone bodies of his hut mates as they groaned and cursed quietly beneath plumes of frosted breath.

Skitter danced across the twelve-foot room, his feet finding the small bare spaces between bodies, avoiding the straw mats that marked the boundary of each man's tiny territory. He was small, quick, and wiry enough to move easily through the dark and cramped chamber. He slid the rickety wooden frame open, drawing it shut behind them before the men inside could summon up a complaint about the sharp blast of cold, bleak, biting wind.

Skitter followed Shard without hesitation, a habit born out of greed and avarice, cemented in terror, horror, and survival. They walked the snow-packed path along the wire, toward the high ground, the crumbling cliff face, and the garbage dump.

The men stared at what was left of the refuse pile. After being picked clean by guards and prisoners, then scavenged by civilians who trudged up the hill from the village below, there wasn't much.

"Hardly the Ginza, Skitter," Shard said.

"This whole damn country ain't worth shit," Skitter said, squatting on his haunches and intently watching one of the villagers scrounging for firewood. A young woman, obvious even at this distance. Skitter's eyes lapped her up, not out of lust, but in hopes of keeping the memory of lust alive. Shard sat next to him, lifting his head to the sky, willing the clouds to part and grace his face with winter sunshine. "Now Japan, that was something else. We were kings there, remember?"

"Yeah," said Shard. "I remember." It was what he said every time, reliving their heyday as black market operators, stealing the army blind, getting rich off Uncle Sam. Memories and talk were all the living had left. They spoke their lines like actors, giving it all they had, wondering if the play would ever end.

"What's wrong?" Skitter asked, sensing Shard's unease.

"I dreamed about Schuman last night," Shard said, watching the woman plod back to her hooch. "Remember him?"

"Sure. Died that first winter, didn't he?" Skitter said.

"Yep. Christmas Eve. Exactly two years ago."

"Weird," Skitter said, standing and beating his arms against his torso. "What'd he have to say?"

"I couldn't understand him, his voice was muffled. Can't figure out why he'd be in my dreams," Shard said, rising and dusting off the snow that stuck to his blue quilted POW jacket. He couldn't bring himself to mention the blood, the bright crimson gash on Schuman's cheek from where the Red Chinese guard had struck him before he was hauled away. "Can't stop thinking about him now."

"Dreams are bullshit," Skitter said, staying close to Shard. It was automatic, like taking a piss in the morning. Get up, see what Shard is doing. Keep in his shadow. It had worked so far. "So why we out here, anyway?"

"There's a new guy, transferred in from another camp. He knew Coop."

"Coop?" Skitter said. "Jeez, I haven't thought about him for a long time. Poor guy."

"Yeah, he deserved better," Shard said, walking along the cliff edge.

"Don't we all," Skitter said, working to keep up with Shard's long strides. Back in Japan, Skitter had wanted to be the boss, the brains of their black market operation. But here, deep in North Korea, Skitter had always known his chances would be better in Shard's shadow. "How'd this guy find you?"

"Asked around when he was brought in," Shard said, picking up the pace as he turned up his collar against the cold. "He knew Coop was missing in action and hoped he was here."

Coop was a sergeant who'd stayed with his men, discarding his chevrons to disguise his rank and help maintain discipline against the divide and conquer tactics of their captors.

"That's a long shot," Skitter said. "Hey, what's the hurry?"

"We got a job to do," Shard said. "Hauling supplies into the officers' camp. Let's go." He headed to a line of trucks by the camp gate. The officers' compound was surrounded by barbed wire six feet high. To protect the common soldiers of the working class from the corrupt ruling class officers, according to the political lectures the Reds insisted they attend. A lot of guys liked that. If you had to be a POW, at least you only had to worry about the Commies bossing you around, not your own brass as well. Communication between enlisted men and officers was punishable by execution.

Shard gave a nod to Horseface as he slipped him four cigarettes, the going rate for a spot on the supply gang. Horseface, a senior guard, was named for his equine looks; big ears, a long nose, and eyes set far apart.

"So we see Coop's buddy after this?" Skitter said as he shouldered a sack of soybeans.

"No," Shard said. "He's here. A lieutenant with the Fifth Marines."

"Jesus Christ," Skitter said, walking through the gate under the scrutiny of guards, their bayonets fixed.

POW officers were housed in a series of dilapidated farmhouses, not much more than mud huts with straw roofs, surrounded by wire. Skitter and Shard carried in burlap bags of soybeans, kidney beans, turnips, sorghum, a sack of onions, and one case of canned meat.

An officer in Marine fatigues checked off the items on a list as guards watched for any forbidden communication. When the last of the supplies were in, Horseface ordered the other guards out. He took one of the tins of meat, put it in his pocket, and left.

"We have three minutes," the officer said. "I'm Lieutenant John Cooper. You're the guys who knew Freddie?"

"Yeah," Shard said. "Me and Skitter were in his company."

"You mean Coop?" Skitter said. "Never got his first name. You related?"

"Yeah," he said. "He's my cousin. I heard he was taken prisoner, but he's listed as MIA. You were in another camp with him?"

"I was half-dead with dysentery," Shard said. "I never saw him. Skitter did."

"How was he?" Lieutenant Cooper asked.

"Not too bad, considering," Skitter said. "He and Sergeant Kelso had gotten in among the enlisted prisoners, and were trying to organize things. Someone must have spilled the beans. First they came for Kelso and took him away. Then they shot Coop."

"You sure?" Cooper asked. "I heard he was alive at some place called the Mining Camp."

"He was there all right," Skitter said. "But that's where they killed him. Sorry."

"Shit," Cooper muttered, the light of hope gone from his face. "Do you think this Kelso guy talked?"

"No," Shard said. Skitter shook his head in agreement. They'd never seen Kelso again. "Not Kelso."

"Any idea who did?"

"Coulda been anyone," Skitter said. "Guys in his barracks must have known. Hard to say." He looked around nervously, waiting for Horseface to come in and beat them for fraternizing.

"You both knew, right?" Cooper said.

"Hey, watch who you're accusing," Skitter said. "Coop was our pal. And Shard was delirious when it happened."

"Sorry. You're certain?" Cooper asked, a hint of desperation in his hooded eyes.

"Saw the body myself," Skitter said, walking to the half-open door and peeking outside. "We should go."

"Sorry, Lieutenant," Shard said, his eyes lingering on the supplies stacked on the shelves.

Soup. A memory of soup came back to him. He'd been sick in that camp when he heard of Coop's being shot for the crime of hiding his stripes. Skitter had brought him soup, with onions.

Horseface hurried them out of the enclosure. There was another job.

"I always wondered who betrayed Coop," Shard said, as they climbed into the empty truck.

"It's hard to get upset about someone who's been gone almost three years. Coop missed a lot of suffering," Skitter said.

"True," Shard said. "But he also missed everything good that could happen, after the war. Home and family."

Skitter didn't answer. Things so distant and unattainable were unworthy of comment. If it couldn't keep him alive today, it had no value. He knew what happened to guys who forgot that. They drifted into apathy. *Give-up-itis,* the POWs called it.

Their vehicle stopped in front of the camp warehouse where the Chinese stored their supplies. Horseface pointed to another truck, larger and stacked with food, then to the open warehouse.

"No stealing," Horseface warned with a wagging finger. Shard spread his hands and grimaced, as if offended by the warning. Horseface laughed, a good sign.

Shard and Skitter finished with the heavy crates and began moving sacks of rice and flour, stacking them on pallets. When they couldn't be seen by the guards, Shard searched for something to steal.

"No," Skitter said. "You heard Horseface."

"Horseface was only acting tough. He might pat us down, but he's not going to make a big deal out of it. He selected us, so it would make him look bad if we got caught." Shard took his time, checking the stores of food. Under the rice sacks he found heavy burlap bags filled with cabbages. He worked a finger into the thin material and pulled, exposing the vegetables. Shard took off his blue cap, ripped leaves off, and stuffed them inside the hat.

"We need greens," Shard explained. "Cabbage has vitamins." Skitter reached up and tucked an errant cabbage leaf under Shard's cap, shaking his head at the chance his friend was taking.

They finished unloading and found Horseface and the other guards laughing and smoking, paying them no attention. Horseface told a joke, or so it seemed by the tone of his voice. As Horseface grinned and drew on his cigarette, a look of stunned horror spread across his face. Comrade Yuan rounded the corner, followed by two other senior comrades. Political officers.

Horseface dropped his butt at the same time he raised his voice at the other guards, berating them for smoking on duty. They stood to attention as Yuan drew closer. Horseface advanced on Shard, yelling incoherently. He swung his rifle butt, determined to show Comrade Yuan he was on top of the lazy recruits and even lazier prisoners. The rifle caught Shard on the shoulder, sending him tumbling to the ground. Shard's cap flew off, revealing the hidden stash of bright green cabbage.

Shard instinctively curled up as boots and rifle butts crashed into his torso. He heard Skitter begging Horseface to stop, but all else was lost in a torrent of high-pitched yells, Horseface screaming his lungs out, hoping his fury would distract Comrade Yuan from his lack of diligence. A prisoner could be shot for stealing food. A guard could end up in the front ranks of a human wave attack for letting him get away with it.

Yuan's voice broke through the melee, and the blows stopped immediately. "Stand, Prisoner Shard!"

"Yes, Comrade Yuan," Shard said, wincing as he spoke.

"You are stealing the people's food."

"Capitalism is theft, isn't that what you taught us?" Shard asked, remembering a phrase from the indoctrination classes. "I was brought up a capitalist. It's a hard habit to shake."

"At least you were paying attention," Yuan said, stepping closer and studying Shard's face. Then he backed up, perhaps uncomfortable at having to stare up at the tall American. "But tell me, why steal a few cabbage leaves? Is that worth a life?"

"I apologize, Comrade Yuan," Shard said, hating himself for the bow he gave. "I failed to control myself." Shard figured it was worth a try. Maybe Yuan would be in a merciful mood.

"I do not sense sincerity," Yuan said with an irritated sigh. He spoke to the guards and they grabbed Shard by the arms. "Now you will be shot."

Shard twisted his arms as the guards held him tight. He felt fear in the pit of his stomach, and relief at the back of his mind. He didn't know which was more frightening.

"Comrade Yuan, please wait," Skitter said, as Yuan unbuckled his holster.

"What?" Yuan snapped. Skitter was one of the leading progressives, a valued prisoner who eagerly participated in political classes and showed interest in the Marxist line. If anyone else had interrupted an execution, it would have meant two corpses.

"You asked for prisoners to come forward and confess," Skitter said, his eyes darting from Yuan to Shard, then back to Yuan's hand on his pistol. "About the germ warfare. I'm ready. I helped load the planes in Japan."

"Good," Yuan said, extending his arm, aiming the pistol at Shard's forehead.

"But Shard is my friend. He's misguided, that's all. Please, spare him, Comrade Yuan."

"You will make the recording? A full confession?" Yuan kept the pistol trained on Shard.

"Yes."

"Good. Tomorrow, then," Yuan said, holstering his pistol. "Or you will both be shot."

Yuan turned on his heel, barking orders to the guards. They began to beat Shard, on Yuan's instruction or on general principles, it was hard to tell. Shard felt himself go unconscious as he hit the ground. A minute, or an hour, later Skitter was helping him get up.

"What'd you do?" Shard said, wincing as Skitter helped him walk.

"I made a deal," Skitter said. "I'm going to confess, about germ warfare. Yuan's been after someone to do it."

"But there's no germ warfare, it's all Red propaganda."

"That's exactly why I can do it," Skitter said. "Everyone knows its bullshit. So why not?"

"Because it's aiding the enemy," Shard said, doing his best not to hobble as they made their way back to their hut. "What the hell do you know about germ warfare anyway?"

"Well, we were right next to an airbase," Skitter said. "Close enough."

"I shouldn't complain," Shard said. "Thanks for saving my life."

"Works both ways. I owe you," Skitter said, helping Shard to sit on the log bench outside their hut.

Minutes later, four guards marched double-time out of the administration building, rifles at the ready. Shard watched their approach carefully, calculating at a certain point that they were not coming for him, but heading for the officers' enclosure.

In ten minutes they returned with Lieutenant John Cooper, prodding him with bayonets toward the admin building. He looked at Shard as they passed, accusation burning in his eyes.

"Christ," Shard swore. "He has to think I betrayed him so Yuan would let me go."

"It had to be Horseface," Skitter said, as they watched the guards shove Cooper. "Cooper'll figure it out. Maybe he doesn't even know what happened."

"News travels fast," Shard said, standing and groaning. The

story of Shard, his cabbage leaves, and near execution probably went through the camp in minutes.

"Horseface might've reported that Cooper tried to bribe him, to get back in Yuan's good graces," Skitter said. "It would have been a good move."

Yuan descended the steps of the admin building. They were close enough to see Cooper struggle in the grip of the guards.

Saw the guards lean away as Yuan drew his pistol and fired.

Cooper's head snapped back and his body slumped, then crumpled as the guards let go. A blossom of bright red blood fed the snow, the crimson color fading to pink as it soaked into the soft whiteness.

"Shit," Skitter said. "One more for the list."

The list of the dead. At first, they'd memorized the names of the dead, chanting them under their breath as they marched. After fifty, it was impossible to remember all of them, so Shard and Collier started a secret list, using whatever scraps of paper they could scrounge. The Chinese didn't want to admit how many POWs had died in their care, so it was a forbidden activity. Only Shard and Collier knew where the list was hidden. It was their mission to bring the list out when they were freed, to bear witness to what the North Koreans and Chinese had done.

"You sure the list's safe?" Skitter said, pulling at Shard's sleeve. There had been two lists. The duplicate was discovered by the Chinese three months ago. The reprisals had been ferocious.

"We're fine," Shard said, shaking off Skitter's grip. "I'm going to take a walk. See you in a few."

"Sure. I'll see if I can find out anything about Horseface. Be good to know if more trouble's brewing." Shard didn't answer.

He was too stunned by the execution. An hour ago, it could have been his blood and brains in the snow.

He limped toward the garbage pit, thinking about what he knew and what he guessed. He caught a glance of Skitter moving fast, making a circuit around the administration building, head down and hands bunched in his pockets, a shadow darting from one dark corner to another.

Shard feared Cooper would join Schuman in his dreams tonight. He sought a distraction, anything to stop the mad swirl in his brain. He walked to the kitchen. No guards at the door. Maybe all the commotion had disrupted things. Worth a look. It was locked between mealtimes, the penalty for breaking and entering, death.

But the door was open, inviting. No guards in sight. He took a step inside, ready to retreat, bribe, grovel, whatever he had to do, the lure of food too great to resist. He stood in the hallway leading into the main kitchen, the cooks intent on their tasks. He laid his hand on the pantry latch and pressed, quietly and slowly, holding it tight as he pushed the door open.

He froze.

Horseface was on the floor, straddled by a chunky Korean girl, her back to Shard. She was naked from the waist down, Horseface's pants down around his ankles. She moved languidly, her long black hair caressing Horseface in undulating silence. Shard edged back, one hand reaching for a can of tinned pork as the other pulled the door shut without a sound. He waited for a moment, listening for any sign he'd been heard. Then he left, the can in his pocket and the image of the girl's buttocks burned into his mind.

Later, Shard and Skitter sat hunched in their hut. Skitter had come back saying he'd seen Horseface getting a tongue-lashing from Yuan. He claimed that gave credence to his notion of Horseface fingering Cooper for attempting to bribe a guard. But Shard had seen Horseface, and it wasn't Yuan who'd been lashing him.

Shard spoke after the silence had become too heavy. "Someone's gotta pay."

"Sure," Skitter said. "But it ain't gonna happen. It's not like the last war where we won and put people on trial."

Shard didn't reply. He inhaled deeply, drawing the cold air into his lungs. The faint aroma of fried fish rose in his nostrils.

Then, he understood what Schuman had been trying to tell him.

The truth came at him hard, and he retreated into another deep silence, until Skitter roused him to search for firewood. The guards let them wander as far as they wanted; after all, there was nowhere to run.

"How'd we ever make it that first winter?" Shard said, as they picked up branches and twigs. "No boots, rags for shoes, never enough to eat."

"You taking a trip down memory lane today, Shard?" Skitter said, hefting his load of branches. "More ghosts?"

"Ghosts are just bad memories," Shard said. "The bad things burned into our minds."

"I try not to think about it," Skitter said, uneasy with talk of things past.

"Does that work?"

"No. Not really."

"You got boots that winter, didn't you?" Shard said, his eyes watching Skitter, taking his measure.

"Yeah. Traded a pocketknife to a guard."

"You were lucky he didn't turn you in."

"It was Cho, remember him? Crookedest Commie you'd ever want to meet."

"Yeah, Cho. He'd trade anything, not that we had much," Shard said. "How'd you get that knife anyway?"

"Traded up for it. Started out with hard candies in the first Red Cross parcel we got. Christmas, remember? Then got some cigarettes, and the guy who had smuggled the pocketknife in was dying for a smoke, so he traded. I showed it to Cho and he wanted it right away. I knew he wouldn't snitch, since that way he'd get a pat on the head but no jackknife. He came through with the boots and a couple pair of socks, remember? I gave you a pair."

"Best Christmas of my life," Shard said. All POWs had been stripped of their combat boots, many of them marching barefoot in snow and ice. Finally, Shard had been given a pair of worn out North Korean sneakers. With the wool socks, he had an edge, enough to avoid frostbite.

"You took a chance to get those boots," Shard said, holding his bundle of firewood under one arm as they walked. "Cho could have turned you in; what do you think they would have done to a prisoner with a weapon?"

"Aw hell, it was only a little pocketknife," Skitter said. "The real risk was getting frostbite."

"Yeah," Shard agreed. Frostbite was a death sentence. "Who did you trade with for the knife?"

"Uh, Schuman. John Schuman," Skitter said, after a moment's thought. "Hey, the guy you dreamed about. Funny, huh? I almost forgot his name."

They walked in silence back to their hut, memories of that terrible winter swirling in Shard's mind like remnants of a nightmare, a vision that remains even as you tell yourself you're fully awake.

After dumping the firewood at their hut, Skitter made for the recreation hall and class with Comrade Yuan while Shard waited for the afternoon meal. Rice balls with millet for the reactionaries, while the progressives ate rice with vegetables off real plates in the rec hall. A lot of guys attended the sessions for the extra food, but many got kicked out. You had to show interest in the class struggle, be willing to criticize yourself, your buddies, your country, over and over again until Yuan was satisfied. But he never stayed satisfied. That was the problem with giving in; the demands never ended, there was always another bit of your soul to surrender.

"Look," Shard said, as he met up with Skitter after class. "I went into the admin building while you were critiquing the ruling class and asked about hot water for baths. They threw me out, but not before I got these off an orderly's desk." He opened his pocket, showing Skitter a pack of Chinese cigarettes. Skitter told Shard he took too many risks, and that the big news was that the Chinese were looking for volunteers to refuse repatriation when the war ended. They wanted some American soldiers to make Red China their home, to counter-balance the thousands of North Koreans and Chinese who were likely to decline repatriation. No one had raised their hand.

They walked through the crowd of progressives leaving class. They had a fullness to their faces from the extra midday rations. Shard got whatever fullness he had from thievery and trading, while half-starved POWs suffered with gaunt, sunken cheeks, night blindness, and swollen gums.

It began to snow. They made it to their hut as heavy flakes fresh from Siberia draped the compound.

"Hey, O'Hara, you're back," Shard said. O'Hara was one of the prisoners from the original group.

"Been to the Yalu River, unloading barges at night," O'Hara said.

"Feed you okay?" Shard asked.

"Yeah, we ate pretty much what the soldiers got. Rice with beans and some kinda greens. Wasn't bad." O'Hara shrugged. "Not as good as what the birdies get, though. Skitter, you're looking well."

"I don't mind listening to the Reds," Skitter snapped. "And I don't mind eating their food. Small price to pay."

"If you say so," O'Hara said. Skitter glanced at Shard, eager to leave, even with the snow.

"Hey O'Hara," Shard said, as if he'd just thought of it, "weren't you and Schuman buddies?"

"Yeah. We were together since basic."

"Me and Skitter were talking about him and his jackknife," Shard said. Skitter shuffled his feet in the enclosed space, staring at the floor. "Skitter traded with him about then, didn't you?"

"Yeah," Skitter said.

"I told him a million times, he was taking a chance keeping that jackknife," O'Hara said.

"That's what he traded with me," Skitter said, looking to Shard.

"Naw," O'Hara said. "His granddaddy gave him that knife. He'd never have traded it. But the damn Chinks found it. Threw him in the hole for that little knife. Lasted three days before he froze."

"No, really, I traded with him," Skitter said. "I gave him stuff from my Red Cross parcel. Food. A pocketknife doesn't do you much good if you starve to death, does it?"

"You still got it?" O'Hara asked.

"I traded it on to Cho. For boots."

"They shipped Cho out last spring. Bastard always was good for a trade," O'Hara said.

"Yeah. My feet were in bad shape," Skitter said. Shard knew

how much his feet had hurt on that first march after they'd been captured. He'd watched men with black, frostbitten feet wrapped in rags, limping through the snow as tears froze on their cheeks. Saw them fall and welcome death.

Shard recalled the last time Skitter told the story of the jackknife. Before, he said he'd traded cigarettes for the knife. Now it was food. Shard felt sick, the certainty of betrayal like a rock in his gut.

"Let's go see Marty and Hughes," Shard said. "They'll want to trade for these cigarettes."

"You could trade with anybody," Skitter said. "Why them?"

"Because they're new," Shard said, tossing a wave to O'Hara, who'd grown silent. "They haven't had time to shake the nicotine habit, so I'll get the most from them."

"Yeah, makes sense. And the sooner you ditch those Chinese cigarettes the better." Skitter shoved his hands in his pockets and hunched his shoulders against the cold, shuffling through the freshly fallen snow. In one of the huts, men sang half-hearted Christmas carols. "I'll Be Home for Christmas," with the mocking refrain, *If only in my dreams.* "Why are we making the grand tour today, anyway?"

"It's like that story, Schuman had to be the ghost of Christmas past," Shard said, watching as glints of sunlight broke through the rapidly moving clouds. "You know, *A Christmas Carol?* Hell, he died on Christmas Eve, and I saw his ghost. And Cooper, he has to be the ghost of Christmas present, since he died today. Right?" He watched Skitter out of the corner of his eye, catching the frightened look on his face, there and gone.

"You're crazy," Skitter said, shaking his head.

"Could be. Can't even remember the whole story. How about you?"

"I don't know," Skitter said. "Some little crippled kid died, I think. Drop the ghost stuff, okay?"

Shard ignored his plea, watching a group of prisoners light a fire outside their hut. They had two rats ready to roast. Catching, gutting, and cooking a rat, without benefit of a knife, was a valued skill in Camp Eleven. Country guys were the best at it, and this hut was lucky enough to house three backwoods boys and a cook from Brooklyn.

They found Marty and Hughes sitting outside the next hut.

"Hey guys," Marty said, raising a hand in greeting. Shard and Skitter took a seat on a log. Marty was thickset, with dark wiry hair and the scarred hands of a mechanic. Hughes was younger, thinner, and wary. He nodded a greeting and went back to staring off in the distance.

"Thought you boys might want to trade," Shard said, after they'd settled into the silence for a while. "Chinese cigarettes, a dozen."

"Wouldn't mind," Marty said. Hughes nodded his assent. "What're you askin'?"

They settled on a packet of crackers and a cube of cheese from a recent Red Cross parcel. Shard passed them the cigarettes, the pack decorated with a pagoda and Chinese characters.

"Don't hang onto that pack," Shard said.

"Sure," Marty said. He gave one cigarette to Hughes, took one himself, and struck a match. He put the pack away inside his tanker's overalls as he drew on the cigarette with a denied smoker's delight.

"Not a lot of tankers in here," Shard said. "You ever notice that, Skitter?"

"Guess so," Skitter said, shrugging.

"Occupational hazard," Marty said. "If a tank is hit, the

whole crew gets it. If they bail out, there's a ton of small arms fire going on. Hell to pay if you gotta run."

"How'd you get captured?" Shard said.

"We hit a mine. Blew a tread clean off. Me and Hughes got out to check the damage, and artillery starts dropping all around us. We dove into a ditch, and the next thing we know a round hits our tank dead center. The Chinese swarmed all over us."

"You were lucky," Skitter said. "Sort of."

Hughes nodded. Luck was a relative thing. Here he was, smoking with his buddy on Christmas Eve, while his pals decayed on some forgotten hillside.

"We knew a couple of guys back when we were first captured," Shard said. "They were from a Pershing tank. Remember them, Skitter?"

"Yeah, I think so. Don't remember their names."

"Miller," Shard said, "and Lefkowicz. You guys know them?"

"When was this?" Marty asked.

"Back in 'fifty, late September," Shard said.

"Never heard of 'em," Marty said, blowing smoke. "Hell, Hughes was still in high school back then." Hughes closed his eyes, a distant smile crossing his face.

"When the North Koreans interrogated them, they claimed they were from a disabled Sherman. Why'd they do that, I wonder?" Shard said, as if he didn't have a clue.

"The M26 Pershings were new to Korea back then," Marty said. "The Reds wanted the dope on 'em real bad. Armor thickness, gun velocity, all that technical stuff. When we first got Pershings, the brass told us to avoid capture at all costs. Easy to say sittin' on your ass in Tokyo."

"What happened to them guys?"

"The camp commander took them one day," Shard said.

"Maybe someone talked, told him they were from a Pershing. Never saw them again."

"Guys shoulda kept their mouths shut," Marty said. "How many GIs knew about them?"

"Everyone in our section," Skitter said. Shard nodded his agreement. A dozen of them. Some had been sick, too weak to do anything, others killed shortly after by the North Koreans, making it unlikely they were informers. They were the only two left.

"Miller and Lefkowicz," Hughes repeated. "They on that list of yours?"

"Yeah."

"How many names?"

"Four hundred plus," Shard said.

"That's one dangerous list," Marty said.

Skitter and Shard left after a while, stopping to watch the rat feast in progress. Men were peeling off tiny shreds of meat and licking fat off their fingers.

"You add Cooper to the list yet?" Skitter asked, his voice nonchalant as he blew warm air on his fingers.

"Not yet," Shard said. He moved closer to the fire, watching one guy toss rat bones into the flames. The fire danced higher, charring the carcass until there was nothing left but the lingering smell of rat.

"We need to talk," Shard said to Skitter. "Where no one can listen."

"What's wrong with right here?" Skitter said. They were back on the log outside their hut. The wood was shiny and cold, worn down by months of sitting, watching, and waiting. Moonlight cast long shadows across the camp like a searchlight.

"I don't want someone hearing us. Come with me," Shard said, standing and waiting for Skitter.

"Jeez, Shard," Skitter said. "Is this another ghost story?"

"Yeah. It's about the ghost of Christmas future. Let's head to the rec hall."

"We're not supposed to be in there alone," Skitter said, jogging to catch up with Shard. "And stop with the ghosts."

"You're one of Yuan's prize progressives," Shard said. "He won't mind."

"Yeah, well I didn't spend all that time listening to Yuan to blow it at the last minute," Skitter said, checking the area for guards. He hugged himself against the cold, his legs jittering in place as Shard opened the door. The sound of Christmas carols, sung low and quiet, drifted across the frozen ground.

"Sit down," was all Shard said, hard, between clenched teeth. He moved to a table near the window. He motioned for Skitter to take the chair across from him.

"Shard, I'm fed up with this," Skitter said, slumping in his seat. His eyes took in the darkened room, searching for a reason as to why they were there, as red silken banners hanging from the rafters rippled in the draft.

"I know," Shard said, the words like a sigh from deep within.

"You know what?" Skitter said, leaning forward, his voice barely a whisper.

"I know it all, Skitter. I know what you've done."

"What?" Skitter spread his arms and laughed. "What have I done?" His eyes darted back and forth, and Shard felt a childhood memory wash over him. When Pa accused him of some misdeed, he'd played it the same way. Buying time, trying to figure out what his old man knew, his mind racing to make sure he didn't reveal anything Pa hadn't found out about.

But this was North Korea, not an Ohio farm. It wasn't broken windows or skipped chores.

"Schuman, Kelso, Coop, Miller, and Lefkowicz. You betrayed them to keep yourself alive," Shard said. "And today, Cooper."

"No."

"I know," Shard said, nodding solemnly. "You kept me alive to watch out for you, to make sure you were protected."

"Shard, this is your buddy Skitter you're talking to. What's come over you, pal?"

"We aren't buddies, Skitter," Shard said, slamming his palm down on the table. "We're criminals. We stole from the army and made a lot of money selling to gangsters. You were crooked in Japan and I was a fool to think you'd be different here. Miller and Lefkowicz, the two tankers. Far as I recall, you and me were the only ones who knew about them to survive."

"What is this, an inquisition?" Skitter spread his hands in supplication. His fingers trembled, and he quickly stuffed them into his pockets. A sigh's worth of condensation filled the cold air between them.

"Kelso and Cooper, they were your big catch. You told the Reds about Kelso. Then you saw Coop was there too and turned him in."

"Shard," Skitter said. "How can you believe that?"

"You got extra rations for us," Shard said. "You needed me alive so I'd watch your back. Like today. You didn't want me killed, so you snitched on Cooper and promised a germ warfare confession. What was your reward for that?"

"I only offered the confession to save you," Skitter said, panic entering his voice. "That's all I did, I swear."

"You came back smelling of fried fish," Shard said, leaning

into Skitter's face and sniffing the air. "You're an informer, a rat, and they feed you for it."

"No," Skitter said, his eyes wide with disbelief, unable to take in his best friend turning on him. "I saved your life. Dysentery would have killed you. You needed those extra rations, you needed to live!"

"Yes," Shard said. "Yes. God forgive me, I did. I can still feel that soup filling my belly. The taste of betrayal. Onion soup."

They faced each other across the moonlit table, neither man moving.

"Shard, we're a team," Skitter said, his voice almost breaking.

"What about Schuman? You told Yuan about the jackknife, didn't you? For a pair of boots. What did that have to do with us being a team?"

"I gave you a pair of socks," Skitter whispered, his head bowed. He was acting like a child, his voice a whine, as if socks answered all questions.

"Coop and Kelso dead," Shard said. "Miller and Lefty tortured and killed. Schuman. Cooper shot today. What else, Skitter? What else have you done?"

"You can't tell anyone, Shard, please," Skitter said, folding his trembling hands as if in prayer.

Now it was out in the open; the blood on Skitter's hands.

"I haven't told anybody, Skitter." That seemed to calm him. Skitter looked up at Shard, eyes gleaming with tears.

"I've been so afraid," Skitter said, the words tumbling out. "Yuan hounds me every day, and I worry about the guys finding out. I'm dead either way if I screw up."

"Hounds you for what?" Shard said.

"The list, he knows there's another list," Skitter said. Shard didn't have to ask how he knew. "What are you going to do? You're not going to rat me out, are you?"

"No," Shard said, shaking his head. "But there's something you have to do."

"What?"

"You have to refuse repatriation. You're a progressive, you'll do well. It won't be a prison camp, they'll treat you like royalty. If you don't agree, I tell the whole camp what you've done." Shard laid his hands on the table. He wished Skitter had taken a different path, but he hadn't, and here they were, Shard playing the ghost of Skitter's Christmas future.

"No. No," Skitter cried. "They'll tear me to pieces."

"Exactly." The hardness was back in Shard's voice.

"I can't go to Red China. What would my folks think? They're decent people. Please tell me you don't mean it."

"I do."

"Why me? Why not you? You took the soup, didn't you? You knew!" Skitter stood, his body quivering, his mouth twisted.

"I figured things out," Shard said. "Too late. There's a line, Skitter. I don't pretend to know where it is, but you crossed it."

"I kept us both alive," Skitter said.

"And I'll remember the price other men paid for the rest of my life," Shard said. They sat in silence, alone in the cold moonlight.

Shard rose and walked to a desk, bringing back paper and pencil. "If you want to write to your folks, go ahead. I'll take it to them myself. Write their address out and I'll hand-deliver it." He set the paper and pencil in front of Skitter and placed a hand on his shoulder. Gave a reassuring squeeze.

"You won't say anything to my folks about the other stuff?" He wiped his sleeve against his nose, cleaning away tears and snot. Shard knew Skitter. He was quick to agree, but he'd try to find a way out later, to skitter out of trouble. The list would be his ace in the hole. The final betrayal that could get him out of this jam.

"I promise, not a word to anyone," Shard said, meaning it.

"Okay." Skitter wrote out his parent's names and address in Lewiston, Michigan, then stopped, his hand hovering over the page. "I don't know what to say to them."

"Tell them you're sorry," Shard whispered, his hand resting on Skitter's shoulder. "How very sorry you are."

Skitter craned his neck back and smiled at Shard. He took a deep breath, and began to write, lead scratching against coarse paper.

Shard watched from behind, the slanting rays of moonlight casting his long shadow over the table. Skitter bent to the task, a schoolchild facing a tough assignment. As he wrote, Shard murmured *good, good*, nodding in rhythm to the soothing words, patting him on the shoulder.

He lifted his hand from Skitter's shoulder and swung it across his throat. He dug his right elbow into the shoulder and pushed against the back of Skitter's head with his right palm. He grabbed his right arm with his left hand, as he'd been trained, and with one sharp push, Skitter's neck broke.

The pencil still in his hand.

Gently resting Skitter's head on the table, he patted his hair. All that remained was to be sure there was no retribution for the death of a prized progressive.

He took the sheet of paper and carefully folded and re-folded it until he could tear off the address and salutation in a neat straight line. He took it and left the remainder on the table.

I am so sorry.

Hoisting Skitter's body onto the table and climbing up, he grabbed the nearest red banner. He twisted the silk fabric until it was tight, then knotted it in several places. He tied it around Skitter's neck, holding up the body as high as he could.

He let go. Skitter's feet, still in the boots he had traded for Schuman's life, rested on the tabletop. Shard moved the table away, leaving Skitter dangling two feet above the floor.

I am so sorry.

Outside, several huts had chimed in on the same carol, the words drifting over Shard like new-fallen snow.

> *God rest ye merry, gentlemen*
> *Let nothing you dismay*
> *Remember, Christ, our Saviour*
> *Was born on Christmas day*
> *To save us all from Satan's power*
> *When we were gone astray*
> *O tidings of comfort and joy,*
> *Comfort and joy*
> *O tidings of comfort and joy*

It brought Shard no comfort. Joy wasn't even in the cards.

Blue Rock

HIS COFFEE HAD GONE cold. The counterman was busy cleaning the stainless steel fixtures, whistling to himself, ignoring Shard. It was time to go. He had five hundred miles between him and Lewiston, in Michigan's northern woods. He saw no reason to linger in Blue Rock.

"Merry Christmas," Shard said, leaving a dime tip on the counter.

"Merry Christmas," the counterman echoed as he rubbed down the refrigerator door.

Shard glanced back, then out the window. The afternoon light was already fading, the cheery colored lights in the street struggling against the approaching grayness. No one was looking.

He did a double snatch. Two Hershey bars disappeared into his coat pocket, nestled against the worn paper with Skitter's note, written out last Christmas Eve. Outside, he gave Blue Rock one last look.

I am so sorry, he said, watching the words turn into plumes of frosty breath and vanish into the air.

They always came back.

"I SAW MOMMY KISSING SANTA CLAUS"

And Other Holiday Secrets

WHEN THE TIME CAME

Lene Kaaberbøl & Agnete Friis

LENE KAABERBØL and AGNETE FRIIS are the Danish duo behind the Nina Borg series. Kaaberbøl has been a professional writer since the age of fifteen, with more than two million books sold worldwide. She has been nominated for the Hans Christian Andersen Medal and is the author of the historical mystery *Doctor Death*. Friis is a journalist by training, and is the author of the stand-alone literary thriller *What My Body Remembers*. Kaaberbøl and Friis's first collaboration, *The Boy in the Suitcase*, was a *New York Times* and *USA Today* bestseller, has been translated into 30 languages, and has sold half a million copies worldwide. The book introduces Danish Red Cross nurse Nina Borg, a compulsive do-gooder who aids undocumented immigrants in Copenhagen. There are three further Nina Borg novels: *Invisible Murder*, *Death of a Nightingale*, and *The Considerate Killer*.

Ørestad, Copenhagen

"**S**hit."

Taghi felt the tires on the junker Opel Flexivan sliding and losing traction in the icy mud. If he drove any closer to the entrance they might get completely stuck on their way out. The marble sinks were heavy as hell, and right now a wet, heavy snow was barreling out of the black evening sky, forming small streams in the newly dug earth in front of the building. The walkway around the building lacked flagstones. Nothing at all, in fact, had been finished. The whole place had been abandoned, left as a gigantic mud puddle, slushy and sloppy, and they were forced to park out on the street.

Taghi backed up, swearing in both Danish and Farsi. It would be backbreaking work lugging all the stuff that far, but there was nothing he could do about it now. He wasn't going to risk getting bogged down with all that shit out here in the middle of nowhere. No goddamn way.

They hopped out on the street and stood for a moment, hugging themselves in the icy wind. The building looked like every other place out here. Glass and steel. He'd never understood who would want to live in such a place. True, there was a view of some sort of water if you were up high enough, but otherwise . . . Taghi sneezed and looked around. The other brand-new glass palaces were lit up as if an energy crisis had never existed, but there was no life behind the windows. Maybe nobody wanted to live this way after all, when it came right down to it, and it would for sure be a long time before anyone moved into this particular building. The workers had been sent home several weeks ago. Something to do with a bankruptcy. Taghi didn't know much about it, but he had been by a few times in the past week to check it out. They could pick up some good stuff here.

At the corner of the enormous glass façade, pipes and cables stuck up out of the ground like strange, lifeless disfigurements. A stack of sheetrock lay to the side, the top sheets presumably ruined by now; the middle ones might be okay but they were a waste of time. They were after the marble sinks in the ten apartments. Three men, three hours' work, and a short drive out to Beni's construction site in Valby. It was exactly what he needed, Beni had said.

The front door stood open a crack.

When they had been by earlier that day it was locked, and Taghi sensed Farshad and Djo Djo exchanging glances when he carefully shouldered the door open and stepped into the bitter cold hallway.

"Let's go, ladies."

Taghi's voice rattled off the unfinished cement walls, and he regretted wearing hard-heeled boots. Every single step rang upward through the stairway, fading into weak echoes that vibrated under the large, clear skylights, the steel beams, and the tiles dusty from all the construction. He fished his flashlight out of his pocket and let it play over the steps.

Had he heard something?

Djo Djo stumbled over a few half-empty paint cans, and Farshad laughed at him, a loud, ringing sound. Djo Djo grumbled and hopped around on one leg, the paint cans clattering around on the dark tiles. Those two jackasses. Annoyed, Taghi bit his lip and decided the ground-floor apartment to the right was a good place to start. For some reason he had gone totally paranoid. Wanted out of here, quick. He felt a prickling under his skin.

"Shut up, you two. It's not that goddamn funny."

Farshad stifled another giggle, but at least they didn't speak until they reached the half-open apartment door, and now there was that sound again. A muffled, drawn-out moaning that rose and fell in the empty pitch-dark surrounding them.

Taghi stiffened. "What the hell is that?"

Djo Djo's whisper broke, his voice on the edge of failing him. "What if it's some kind of ghost?"

The muffled moaning was weaker again. They stood listening until it died out, and now the only sound was Djo Djo's nervous feet on the dusty tiles.

"We're out of here, right, Taghi?" Farshad had already stepped back, he was gripping Djo Djo's arm. "We can always come back tomorrow."

Taghi didn't answer, he was gazing at the darkness in the doorway while he considered the situation. The truth was that he felt exactly the same way as Farshad. He wanted to get out. He felt sticky underneath the down jacket Laleh had found for him in some bargain bin at their local mall. He heard a faint scraping sound and possibly a sigh from inside the apartment. Uncertainty was creeping in, but he was the oldest, after all, and he had to decide what they should do.

"It's not a ghost," he said, in a voice as strong and steady as he could make it.

The others hesitated behind him when he pushed the door open and entered the apartment, the beam from the flashlight bouncing in front of him like a disco ball out of whack. There was an open-plan living room and kitchen, bathed in a pale orange light from the plate-glass window facing the canal. Taghi knew instinctively that this wasn't where to look. It was too open, no place to hide. An empty space at the opposite end of the living room led into what must be the guest bathroom.

If there had been any doors in the apartment they were gone now. Maybe someone else had gotten here before them, Taghi thought. Something dark was moving in there, rocking back and forth on the floor still covered by clear plastic from the painters. He heard Farshad gasping behind him. He had followed, while Djo Djo hung back at the newly plastered island in the kitchen.

Taghi pointed the beam of light directly at the black shadow, and before the figure even turned its head toward him, he knew he'd been right.

It was a woman.

She crouched next to the crapper, her skirt hanging sloppily around her hips and thin legs and her arms arched like taut bows around the toilet bowl. Like someone throwing up, Taghi thought. But he knew what the woman was doing. First it was as if she didn't know they were there, not really, anyway. But when he stepped closer she turned her head, and her eyes, completely naked and black, met his.

THEY HAD BEEN SO close. So close that she could see the bridge, see the long rows of lights leading to Sweden. After the nightmarish days on the open deck of the ship, after months of overcrowded rooms that smelled of fear, with nervous men who always wanted more money than agreed upon, with uncertainty and despair about her belly that kept growing and growing . . . after all that, only one thing was left: get over the bridge. When she got there she was supposed to call Jacob, and he would come and take care of everything, the rest of her life, he had promised, with her and the baby . . . She felt an overwhelming yearning in her gut, almost as fierce as the contractions, and her lips formed the words he had taught her to say, the magic words that would open the gate so she could be with Jacob forever: *Jag söker asyl*—I seek asylum. But don't say it before she got to Sweden, he had said. And whatever happened, she must not be discovered before she was inside Sweden, otherwise the gate to her life with Jacob would close. If she wasn't sent back—a terrible, horrifying thought—she would end up in some sort of refugee camp, someplace he couldn't get to her, couldn't be with her. It would be like prison, he said, and it could be for several years.

That was why Chaltu had set her jaw and kept quiet about the jolts of pain shooting through her body. She had tried, *tried*, but eventually she couldn't hold it back. The sounds were coming out no matter what, just like the baby. And then it happened, the one terrible thing she couldn't let happen. Her water broke, came rushing from between her legs and out over the seat beneath her.

The driver stopped the car. This is no good, he said. He cursed about the seat that was wet now, but even worse was how she couldn't sit upright and keep quiet when the contractions came. They would be stopped, and he wasn't going to prison because of her, he said.

She screamed and wailed and begged, and they had to drag her out of the car by force. She even tried to run after them, but of course that was hopeless. The driver floored it and a shower of slushy gray snow sprayed up in her face, and then the car was gone.

I will die, Chaltu thought. The baby will kill me and neither of us will ever see Jacob. She punched her stomach with both hands, blows of helpless rage, and she had to bite her cheek not to say out loud the curse that was on her lips. I must not curse my own child, she thought. God will punish me for that. Holy Virgin, what have I done? But she knew well enough.

Her sin was love. Love for Jacob, a love that had no future in Adis Ababa, but maybe in Sweden, where he had lived since he was seven and was now studying, in Blekinge College, to become an agronomist.

She kept walking without knowing where she was going. First she thought she might be able to find the bridge again and cross it on foot, but she quickly lost all sense of direction. What kind of a city was this? There were no people, none at all. It was almost as if the buildings owned the city and the streets, as if they had decided that they didn't want their careful order disturbed by the mess and movement of anything living.

A strange singing tone stopped her. For a moment she wondered if she were hearing angel voices because she was so close to death. But then a light popped out, an entire snake of lights, and she saw that it was a train, even though it zipped through the air above her, on a track supported by concrete pillars. There was water underneath the track, long shiny-black sheets of water reflecting the lights. Why couldn't the train run on the ground? Chaltu wondered. It was as if someone had erected a bridge just to remind her of the one she couldn't get across.

There were people on that train, she noticed. They were being carried through the dead city and they looked warm and cozy and cheerful in the belly of the train snake.

The wet snow was denser now, and the wind drove it into her face so she could no longer feel her skin. When she noticed the building still under construction, with the fence knocked down and the empty, dark windows, she realized it might be a place she could stay without being discovered. No one could be living there.

And it was dark and quiet in there too, but there were so many windows. She thought the whole world must be able to see her. And it was almost as cold as outside. There were no blankets, no furniture, nothing soft whatsoever. Some of the inside doors were missing. The wind whistled through the main hallway, and the wet snow slid quietly down the enormous panes of glass.

A violent contraction came—it felt as if God Himself had grabbed her with His giant hand and squeezed until she was close to breaking apart.

"Stop," she whispered desperately. "Stop." If only it would hold off again. If the contractions would stop; if the baby would just stay in there and leave her alone—then maybe she could cross the right bridge to the right country instead of dying in the wrong one.

She crouched down on the tile floor beside a toilet bowl because she felt least visible there. But the sounds from inside kept coming, and what good did it do to hide?

Here there is no one, she told herself. The building is empty, it is unfinished. No one can hear you now. But suddenly there *was* someone. She hadn't even heard him come in. She just opened her eyes and there he was. Her heart took a long, hovering leap and ended up stuck in her throat.

He was just a silhouette in the dark, a darker outline, and the glare from the flashlight blinded her even more. A moment earlier she had thought she would die either from the cold or from her baby. Now another possibility had shown up.

"Leave me alone," she said, but of course he didn't understand her.

The man said something, and she realized he wasn't the only one there.

"Don't kill me," she said.

And he didn't. To her amazement he took off his coat and put it around her shoulders.

His name was Taghi. She understood that much from his words and gestures, even though they had almost no common language. And he was trying to help her. This was so strange that she could barely comprehend it. His hands were friendly, his tone of voice reassuring. And he said one word she understood.

"Doctor," he said in English. "We will get you to a doctor."

"No," she answered, the word scaring her. "No doctor."

"It is okay," he said, slowly and clearly. "It is a secret doctor. Okay? You understand? Secret doctor okay."

She couldn't answer. The next contraction hit her, and she was only vaguely aware that he brought out a cell phone and called the okay secret doctor.

NINA WAS STARING AT the vending machine when the telephone rang. For a measly five kroner you could choose between coffee with cream, coffee with sugar, coffee with cream and sugar, bouillon, pungently sweet lemon tea, and cocoa. Unsweetened and uncreamed coffee had once been an option, but that particular function had been on the blink since the mid '90s, if those who had been here even longer than her were to be believed.

It's Morten, she thought, without taking the phone from her white coat. And he'll be pissed at me again.

She was tired. She had been on duty since seven that morning, and the Danish Red Cross Center at Furesø, commonly known as the Coalhouse Camp, was every bit as ravaged by December flu as the rest of Copenhagen, with various traumas and symptoms of depression thrown in, plus an epidemic of false croup among the youngest children in Block A.

Despite all that, she could have been home by now. If she

had left at four, after the evening nurse delayed by the snow-storm had finally shown up, she could have been sitting right now in their apartment in Østerbro with a cup of real coffee and a few of the slightly deformed Christmas cookies Anton had baked in the SFO, his youth center. Why hadn't she? Instead of hanging out on a tattered, tobacco-stained sofa in the Block A lounge, listening through the walls to Liljana's thin cough, her professional ear focused. How obstructed was the child's respiratory tract? How much strength was there behind each cough? Should she be suctioned again, and when *was* the last time her temperature had been taken?

The sick-staff excuse was about as worn out as the sofa—Morten wasn't buying it any longer.

"Damnit, Nina. She's *your* mother!" he had snapped the last time she had called home to say she'd be late. He was supposed to be going to some sort of do with his coworkers, and if she wasn't there it would be the second night in a row that Nina's mother would be alone with the kids.

The phone began to repeat its cheery little electronic theme. Reluctantly, Nina grabbed it out of her coat's pocket.

It wasn't Morten. It was an extremely frantic voice she didn't recognize until he said his name.

"It's Taghi. You have to help. There's a woman, and she's . . . she's about to have a baby."

Even then it took her some time, because it had been three years since Taghi had been a resident of the Coalhouse Camp, and there had been so many others since then.

"Take her to the hospital," she said, even though she knew that wasn't an option. Not when he was calling her.

"No," he replied. "She's from Africa. She won't go to the hospital. You have to help."

I'm not a doctor or a midwife. The words were in her mind,

but she didn't speak them. Her exhaustion was already gone. Adrenaline shot into her bloodstream, she was clear-headed and energetic. Morten will have a fit, she thought. But this would be so much easier than trying to explain to him why she couldn't handle spending another night alone with her own mother after the kids went to sleep.

She set the plastic cup of lukewarm coffee with cream down on the scratched table. "What's the address?" she asked.

TAGHI GLANCED AT HIS watch. Wasn't it about time she got here? He was out of his league here, he wanted so badly to hand over this woman and baby and the contractions and birth to someone trained for it. He was a man, damn it. He shouldn't even be here.

He heard a sharp metallic click, and suddenly the whole apartment was bathed in a piercing white glare from the halogen spotlights set into the ceiling.

The woman crouching on the floor grabbed desperately for his arm. Taghi heard Djo Djo and Farshad swearing softly outside in the kitchen area. An instant later they had both crammed themselves into the small bathroom alongside Taghi and were hugging the only wall that would shield them from being in full view from the street outside.

Someone else was in the building, in the stairwell outside, and Taghi immediately assumed it was the police, and thought that the residency permit he'd worked so hard for was about to go up in smoke right now, right here, in this godforsaken barren wasteland of a place. Someone had turned on the building's electricity and the harshly lit apartment made him feel like a fish in a very small aquarium. The bathroom was the only place to hide. He caught Djo Djo's eye and held his index finger to his lips, warning him to stay silent.

The footsteps outside rapped sharply against the tiles. Whoever they were, they weren't afraid of being heard. They walked past the door to the apartment and stopped farther down the lobby. At least two of them, Taghi thought, maybe more.

The dark-skinned foreigner on the floor fidgeted and held both hands over her eyes, as if to protect herself from the whole world. Another contraction was on its way. Her backbone formed a round, taut arch underneath her summer jacket, Taghi noticed; soon she would be moaning again. Soon they would be discovered.

If they nailed him for theft they would send him back to Iran, or at the very least back to the refugee center. To the knotted-up feeling of not knowing where he would be the next day or the rest of his life. The letters from his lawyer, from the state. The stiff white sheets of paper folded perfectly with knife-sharp edges. How would he take care of Laleh and Noushin then?

Taghi caught the woman's eye when the next contraction overtook her and she moved to get back on her knees. As if she was trying to flee from the source of the pain. He stopped her halfway and pulled her head against his chest while shushing her, the way you would shush a young child.

Now the men outside were arguing. It was impossible for him to hear what it was all about, but one of them yelled that the other was an asshole. Then their voices were muffled by the creak of an elevator door, which slid shut and swallowed the rest of the argument.

Quiet. "Shit."

Djo Djo was the first to stand up; he slapped the light off in the kitchen area. The snow outside swirled in the cloudy yellow spotlights illuminating the building's façade. Taghi rose and moved to the window facing the street. Farshad came to stand beside him.

"Why don't we just get out of here?"

Farshad looked warily over his shoulder at the bathroom door. He was more afraid of the woman than the men, Taghi thought. Farshad was nineteen and Djo Djo eighteen. Childbirth was obviously not in their comfort zone.

Taghi's pulse was pounding in his temples.

"Okay, you called that woman," said Farshad. "Time to split. Me and him, we're out of here for sure." He gave a jerk of his head in the direction of Djo Djo.

"And leave her here alone? *Na baba*. You've got to be kidding." Taghi pointed out to the van. "We're taking her with us."

A metro train whistled past on the tracks above the black canal. No conductor—it was some kind of new technology they had installed when the metro was built. It was all automated. The light from the windows of the empty cars reflected in the water.

He supposed the shadow came first, hurtling past the window, but it was the sound that Taghi reacted to. A hollow, wet thud, like the sound of a very large steak being slapped down hard on a cutting board.

The man had landed on the stack of wet sheetrock less than a yard from the window. He was most definitely dead. Taghi didn't need to go outside to check. He was lying on his belly, with his neck twisted back and to one side, so that they could see his forehead and his eyes. Or rather, eye. The part of his face that was resting against the sheetrock had been crushed so completely that it was just a pulped mess. His one identifiable eye was staring at Taghi, Farshad, and Djo Djo with a strangely irritated expression.

"Fuck! Fuck, fuck. What the fuck do they think they're doing?" Farshad's voice broke, shrill and pitched too high in the dark behind them, and Taghi knew right then that Farshad was a bigger problem than the woman in the bathroom.

Her eyes were wide, but she had stopped talking. He couldn't even hear her breathe. He felt the shock himself, like a strap tightening around his chest. Despite this he managed to reach out and clap his hand over Farshad's mouth.

"*Khar.* Shut up, you big idiot," he spat.

Farshad thrashed around like a drowning man under Taghi's right arm. Now they heard quick steps on the stairs. The front door opened and slid shut with a quiet click. A moment later a pair of headlights swept over the glass façade. The car took off and the sound died behind the thick triple-glazed windows.

Taghi slowly removed his hand from Farshad's mouth. He wasn't sure that Farshad was completely calm yet, but at least he wasn't shrieking like an old hag anymore. In the bathroom the woman had begun to groan again. It sounded like she was calling out for someone. She no longer had the strength to crouch, she was rolling on the floor, trying to curl up as the contractions grew stronger. Her lips formed a fluid and nearly silent stream of words, and her long, slim hands clutched at thin air, then grabbed a corner of his sweat-soaked T-shirt.

"Jacob?"

Taghi rubbed a hand across his eyes. He needed to think.

Djo Djo had stepped right up to the window to get a better look at the corpse.

"What the hell we do now, Taghi? He's fucking *dead*. The police will come. They'll be all over the place and they . . ." Djo Djo spoke slowly, searching for his words, as if the reality of the situation first struck him as he talked about it. "Maybe they'll think we did it. Then we're fucked. They'll throw us out, they'll kill us."

Taghi had been thinking the same thing.

Their fingerprints were everywhere. Farshad's gloves dangled from his pants pockets. One in each pocket. Djo Djo hadn't even brought any. All they had planned on doing was liberating a couple of fucking sinks. That's not something they'll nail you for—not seriously, anyway.

The woman had another contraction. They came every few minutes now. She was pulling him down, as if all she really wanted was someone she could drown with. She was crying.

"You have to find something to cover him up with."

Djo Djo glared silently at Taghi. Then he grabbed Farshad's shoulder and dragged him toward the door. Farshad stumbled, found his feet again, and trudged off behind Djo Djo, who was as agile as a cat in the dark.

A second later, Taghi saw the two brothers standing outside the window, struggling with the green tarp from the van. The wind grabbed the tarp, making it look like a dark, flapping sail against the multitude of brightly lit windows on the other side of the canal.

The woman on the floor loosened her grip on Taghi a bit, and as he straightened up he noticed a thin figure walking their way, leaning into the wind, hands over her face to shield herself from the big wet flakes.

She had arrived.

NINA ZIPPED HER DOWN jacket all the way up to her nose before getting out of the car.

Brave new world. The streetlights' reflections shimmered in the black water of the canals, and the elevated railway looked like something out of a sci-fi film. Trees and bushes didn't belong in this vision of the future, the general impression was that organic life forms were unwelcome here. How in the world did an African woman about to give birth end up here? BRAHGE LIVING, a big sign said, illuminated by a powerful floodlight. 24 EXCLUSIVE CONDOMINIUMS—FOR SALE NOW! The colorful, optimistic drawing of the finished development formed a sharp contrast to the muddied mess of construction and the toppled wire fence.

Brahge, she thought to herself, hitching up her shoulder bag. He was that guy who went broke. One of the most publicized bankruptcies in recent times, because Torsten Brahge had been regarded as one of the best and brightest, having just won some big business award a few weeks earlier. Investor megabucks were in danger of evaporating. She had seen the man's slightly chubby, Armani-clad figure on the front page and in several self-pitying television interviews, though she couldn't remember what he had said. She didn't have a lot of time for wealthy people moaning about the financial crisis and the real estate collapse.

A battered-looking van was parked beside the fence, and she caught sight of two young men grappling with a green tarp just outside the building. Life in the desert, she thought, and lifted her arm in a stiff, frozen wave.

"Is Taghi here?" she yelled.

Both of them stared at her as if she were some monster that had crawled out of the canal. But one of them nodded.

"Yes," he said. "Are you the doctor lady?"

"Nurse," she corrected.

He shrugged one shoulder, *whatever*. "He's inside. Ground floor to the right. You'd better hurry."

She found them in the apartment's tiny guest bathroom, the woman on her knees in front of Taghi, clinging to him with both hands. The quiet hope Nina had been nourishing that it might be false labor and a touch of hysterics immediately disappeared. The woman's coat and skirt were soaked with amniotic fluid. *If there are any complications,* Nina decided, *she's off to a hospital whether she likes it or not.*

At that moment the woman's eyes flew open, and she looked straight at Nina.

"Hi," Nina said in English, in her most reassuringly professional voice. "My name is Nina, and I'm here to help you. I'm a nurse."

"Doctor," the woman gasped. "Secret okay doctor."

"Just say yes," Taghi said. "I don't think she understands much English. Her name is Chaltu." Taghi didn't look so hot himself, Nina observed. Anxious, nervous, but that wasn't so surprising, either. She had a good idea what he was doing here. Or anyway, what he would have been doing had a woman giving birth not gotten in the way.

He tried to stand up, but Chaltu kept clinging to him. "No go," she said. "Jacob no go."

"Sometimes she calls me Jacob," Taghi said. "Don't ask me why."

Nina touched Chaltu's arm. Her fingers were bloodless and gray, her skin icy cold. She let go of Taghi with one hand and swatted at Nina, who was trying to see how far she had dilated. "Chaltu," Nina ventured. "I must look. Look to see if baby is coming."

"No baby," Chaltu groaned. "No baby here. In Sweden. *Jag söker asyl.*" And she pressed her legs together so hard that her thigh muscles quivered.

Jesus, Nina said to herself, and took measure of the woman's desperation. If it was possible to delay a childbirth by will alone, this would turn into a very long night.

"We have to get her someplace where we can keep warm," Nina said. "Is that your van?"

Taghi looked toward the window facing the parking lot, and Nina followed his eyes. She saw the two young men outside, pulling a blue nylon rope through the green tarp's grommets. A violent gust of wind rammed them. One of them slipped in the mud and lost his grip on the tarp. It flew up, flapping like a bird trying to fly away. Underneath was a dead man.

It took her only a few seconds to recognize him. The Armani suit had had a terrible day, and the man inside a worse one. There was no doubt, however, that it was the head of Brahge Living lying there, very much dead.

The two young men got the tarp under control and tied it down, and the well-dressed corpse disappeared from sight. But it was too late. Nina had seen him. And Taghi knew it.

They stared at each other over Chaltu's head.

"We didn't do it," Taghi said. "The guy just went flying past us and—wham!"

Nina nodded. She also stuck her hand in her pocket and began pressing numbers on her cell phone blindly, not bringing it out. But he noticed. He tore away from Chaltu, who screamed in a burst of fright, and suddenly he had a knife in his hand. The blade was barely two inches long. A pocket-knife, Nina thought, no murder weapon, and he didn't hold it as she imagined a murderer would. It looked more as if he were about to sharpen a stick to roast something over a fire.

All the same. He had a knife.

"Give me your phone," he said. "Now!"

She thought about what was at stake for him if the police came. Everything he stood to lose. She gave him the phone.

Chaltu looked back and forth between them with eyes that could hold no further terror. Taghi plopped Nina's Nokia into the toilet. Then he brought out his own cell phone and punched a few numbers. Through the window she watched one of the young men let go of the tarp and put his hand to his ear. Taghi began to speak, fast and in Farsi. Nina didn't understand a word. Yet for the first time she felt a jolt of fear.

FUCKING MORONS.

Taghi could barely control his anger. He felt it, warm and throbbing just under his skin. No one had better touch him. No one. Especially not those two idiots standing there fidgeting by the door. Just covering up a body with a green tarp—you would have thought it was a pretty simple job. It wasn't like he was asking them to perform brain surgery.

They stood there staring at Taghi and the doctor lady and the woman on the floor. Farshad squirmed around like a three-year-old in need of a pee. His eyes shifted uneasily between the doctor lady and Taghi, as if he was trying to figure out what Taghi was thinking. Taghi knew he ought to say something, but he didn't know what. Plus, he didn't want to even talk to that idiot. Not right now. They had a problem. The African wouldn't go to the police, of course. The doctor lady, on the other hand . . .

Would a Danish woman, a Danish nurse, be able to drive away from here and forget everything about the squashed corpse on the sheetrock outside? Could he let her go?

His thoughts were broken by Farshad, who again spoke way too fast and way too loudly. "Shouldn't we . . ." He hesitated and flashed another look at the women in the tiny bathroom. "Shouldn't we kill her, Taghi? Isn't that what we should do?"

Taghi caught Farshad with a whipping blow across the back of the neck. He didn't want to talk to him, mostly he wanted to hit him again, harder. Farshad's astonished expression stopped him, and instead he spoke slowly and clearly.

"No, we are not going to kill her. *Ajab olaqi hasti to.* You are as stupid as a fucking donkey." Taghi's low, tense voice quivered. "Keep your mouth shut while I think."

Farshad, clearly hurt, stared at him, then he bowed his head.

"Taghi." The doctor lady's voice sounded like a gunshot in the tense silence. "You're all going to have to help me hold her. She won't do anything."

Taghi gaped at her. She couldn't be serious. Did she think they looked like a bunch of midwives? He was about to say something, but he stopped. One glance at the sinewy little figure beside the African woman convinced him that there was no room for discussion at the moment.

The doctor lady had made a pallet for the woman consisting of Taghi's down jacket and Djo Djo's fleece. On top of that she had arranged a layer of clean white towels from the shoulder bag she'd brought along.

"Sit so you can support her head, and then shut up. Apparently you're Jacob at the moment, and it works a lot better if you're not yelling at your cousin."

Taghi trudged back into the bathroom, and slid to the floor without another word. He raised the woman's head and shoulders so she could rest against his thighs. He dared a quick glance at Djo Djo, who was still standing in the kitchen area, his expression an absurd mixture of terror and amusement. A brief, nervous laugh escaped him.

The eyes of the doctor lady gleamed fierily in the dark. "You two can make yourselves useful and go see if there's any hot water in the pipes."

Djo Djo and Farshad got going too. Taghi heard them

swearing beneath their breath at the kitchen sink. There was water, but it was cold. The African woman hunched over and pushed so hard he could see the small veins in her temples standing out in the weak light from the streetlamp. He put a hand on her forehead and sent a quick prayer off to heaven. For her, for the baby, and for the three of them—Djo Djo, Farshad, and himself.

He turned again and looked at the doctor woman. Nina.

Her face blazed with a pale, persistent concentration.

"It's coming," she said, glancing up at him with something resembling a weak smile.

"I know."

The African woman opened her eyes and looked directly at him as the next contraction hit. And he thought about what it must be like—to give birth here, among strangers, among men.

Down between the woman's legs, the doctor lady reached out with both hands and made a quick turning motion, and Taghi heard the wet sound of the baby slipping out onto the white towels.

It was a boy, and he was already screaming.

"BLESSED VIRGIN, MARY FULL of grace, free me from this pain, Gaeta, Gaeta, Lord have mercy upon me, may all your saints protect me, and I will honor you . . . *honor* you . . ." Chaltu had to pause for a moment because God's fist squeezed the air out of her, but she continued the litany in her head and time disappeared for her; it was the priests' mass she heard, she thought she could smell the incense and feel the pressure, not from labor but from the crowd, all trying to catch a glimpse of the procession, the long parade of holy men clad in white costumes trimmed in red and gold. "*Hoye, hoye,*" the children sang, swaying and clapping their hands, and farther forward she could see the Demera, the holy bonfire waiting to be lit. The Meskel festival had arrived in Addis Ababa, and she was a part of it, swaying in rhythm to it, and she felt uplifted, she felt like she could float above the crowds and see over them instead of standing there among backs and thighs and shoulders and legs.

"Chaltu, push. Go on now, push!"

Hoye, hoye . . . be joyful, for today the true cross is found, praise God Almighty for today all sins are forgiven . . . and Jacob's eyes gleamed at her, his hands supported her so she didn't stumble despite all the people around her pushing and shoving. In that moment it made no difference that she hardly knew him, that he was only home for a visit, that he wasn't the one she was supposed to marry. She loved him, loved the open look in his eye, his rounded upper lip, the way his earlobe attached to his neck. Loved him, and wanted to make love to him. It was as if the holy Eleni herself smiled upon them and promised them that their love would be clean and unsinful. *Hoye, hoye.* Today life will conquer death.

But why did it hurt so badly? She no longer understood this pain, no longer remembered the baby, instead she called for Jacob, again and again, but he faded away from her, as did the priests, the singing and clapping children, and the bonfire, the flames of which were supposed to show her the way to salvation.

God's hand crushed her, she could neither think nor scream. She could just barely sense that she was surrounded by strangers, and that the arm she was clinging to wasn't Jacob's.

"Look, Chaltu. It's a boy. You have a son."

They laid a tiny, wet creature, a baby bird, on her stomach.

Could it really be hers? She knew she should hold it, but her arms felt cold and heavy as stone.

It took several minutes before she realized that the baby had been born, and that she was still alive. A miracle, it was, and she only slowly began to believe it. For the first time in many days she felt something other than pain and fear. She raised her heavy arm and curled it around the baby-bird child. Breathed in its odor. Began to understand. *Hoye, hoye,* little one. We are here, both of us. We are alive.

NINA REGARDED TAGHI'S TENSED-UP face. She sensed that the truce was over. The umbilical cord had been cut and tied off. The placenta lay intact and secure in the plastic basin she'd brought along from the clinic. The little boy whimpered in Chaltu's arms, pale against her dark skin. And Nina's reign had ended with the birth. Now they were back to the corpse and everything death brought with it.

Farshad said something or other, his voice catching nervously. Taghi answered him, negatively Nina thought, but she wasn't sure. How terrifying it was that they could discuss what to do with her without her understanding a word. Taghi had said that they didn't kill Brahge, and she couldn't really believe he was a cold-blooded murderer. They aren't evil, she told herself, and tried not to think how absolutely normal, unevil people could do horrible things if they were pushed far enough. "Why don't you just leave?" she said. "You can take Chaltu and the baby with you, and I'll wait until you're long gone before I call the police."

"Yeah, right," Djo Djo said, and scratched himself quickly and a bit too roughly on the cheek.

Taghi said something sharply, obviously an order. Djo Djo protested, and Farshad started to titter nervously, maybe at what Djo Djo had said. But finally the brothers left the apartment. Nina saw them through the window, lifting the tarp-wrapped body and carrying it over to the van.

All of a sudden they were rushing frantically. They pitched the body in the van, threw themselves into the front seats, and roared off. Seconds later Nina could see why. On the other side of the canal, on Ørestads Boulevard, a police car was approaching slowly, its blue lights flashing.

EGGERS STOPPED THE PATROL car.

"There's a building with balconies," he said. "And that van didn't waste any time driving off."

Janus shrugged. "We'd better check it out, I suppose." He had his regular black shoes on, not his winter boots. The radio hadn't mentioned anything about snow when he left the suburbs that morning at a quarter past seven.

Eggers called in the address. "We're going in," he told the shift supervisor. "But it looks peaceful enough."

Janus sighed, opened the car door, and lowered his nice, black, totally inadequate shoes into the muddy slush. "Does anyone even live here?" he asked. The place was all mud, with construction-site trash everywhere, FOR SALE signs in most of the windows.

"At least there's light," Eggers growled. "Come on. Let's get it over with."

The street door was open, a bit unusual nowadays. Eggers knocked on the door of one of the ground-floor apartments. After quite a while, a thin dark-haired woman opened the door. She stared at them with an intensity that made Janus uneasy.

"Yes?"

Eggers told her who they were and showed his ID. "We

had a report from a passenger on the metro who saw someone fall from a balcony in this area. Have you noticed anything unusual?"

A whimpering came from within the apartment. It sounded like a baby.

"Just a moment," she said, and closed the door in their faces.

Eggers and Janus glanced at each other.

"She looks a little tense," Eggers muttered.

Then the door opened again, and this time she held a very small baby in her arms. "Sorry," she said. "We just got home from the hospital and it's all a bit new to him."

The baby made a low murmuring sound, and Janus instinctively smiled. Lord. Such a tiny little human. No wonder his mother wasn't too pleased about the disturbance. She was looking at the baby, not at them, and even Eggers was thawing out a bit, Janus noticed. There was something to this mother-and-child thing.

"Like I said, we just want to know, have you noticed anything?"

"Nothing," she said. "It couldn't have been here."

"There was a van over here a little bit ago," Eggers said.

"Yes," she replied. "It was the plumber. There's something wrong with the heat, and now we have the baby . . . we have to get it fixed."

"Sure, of course. Well. Have a nice evening." The woman nodded and closed the door.

"I bet that plumber was after a little undeclared income," Eggers said.

"Yeah. But it's not our business right now."

They walked back to the car. The snow felt even wetter and heavier now. Janus wished he'd at least brought along an extra pair of socks.

TAGHI WAS ELATED WHEN the police left. It was as if he'd forgotten all about threatening her with a knife a minute ago.

"*It was the plumber . . .*" he said, in a strange falsetto mimicking her voice. "Fuck, you were good! They totally bought it."

It took a moment for Nina to answer. "Get out, Taghi," she said. "Don't think for one second that I did it for you."

He came down like a punctured balloon. "I'm sorry," he said. "I got a little crazy, I think."

"Just leave. And don't call me again." She remembered her cell phone and got him to fish it out of the toilet bowl.

"It doesn't work anymore," he said.

"No. But I'm not leaving it for anyone to find."

ALL THE WAY ACROSS the bridge Chaltu sat with her eyes closed, praying, as if she didn't dare hope she could make it without divine intervention. Nina let her off at the University Medical Center in Malmø and tried to make it clear to her that she should wait until Nina had left before saying the only three Swedish words she knew. Chaltu nodded.

"Okay, secret doctor," she said.

Nina looked at her watch. *11:03.* With a little luck her mother would already be in bed when she got home.

THE SNOW TURNED SLOWLY into rain. The gray slush around the building in Ørestaden was melting into the mud. The blood of Torsten Brahge mixed with the rain seeping into the sheetrock, which eventually grew so pulpy that not even Beni in Valby would be able to find a use for it.

HAIRPIN HOLIDAY

A 1920s BOMBAY MYSTERY

Sujata Massey

SUJATA MASSEY was born in England to parents from India and Germany, was raised mostly in St. Paul, Minnesota, and lives in Baltimore, Maryland. She was a features reporter for the *Baltimore Evening Sun* before becoming a full-time novelist. Her novels have won the Agatha and Macavity awards and been finalists for the Edgar, Anthony, and Mary Higgins Clark prizes. Visit her website at sujatamassey.com.

Perveen Mistry strode along the Bombay's famed Esplanade, catching sight of the red-suited, life-sized Father Christmas figure in the glass front of the Army-Navy Store. MERRY CHRISTMAS AND HAPPY NEW YEAR 1921! was emblazoned on a green banner held in his stiff hands. His bright blue glass eyes seemed to regard her reproachfully, as if he knew she was not a true celebrant.

When she was six, Perveen had confused the Army-Navy Father Christmas with Zarathustra, the prophet of her family's faith. Both men had such beautiful white beards; it was an easy mistake. Perveen's mother had set her straight, and when she'd wept with disappointment, bought her the hobbyhorse in the window. And because they were Parsis rather than Christians, she could play with her new toy immediately, rather than wait till December 25.

Bombay was a city of almost eight million, and Europeans numbered less than ten thousand; yet the rulers' hold was clear. Perveen had grown up thinking that having a big department store with lavish Christmas displays was a mark of the city's sophistication. But now, having listened to Gandhiji and Madame Cama and other independence activists, she didn't feel the same—although she would never begrudge children their pleasure at the sight of a local Indian tree festooned with colored balls and tinsel.

Perveen sidestepped two young children marveling at the piles of soap flakes that had been mounded to look like snow. The window showed a wintry world very different from 85-degree Bombay. She had shifted back into the reality of being Bombay's first woman solicitor, who had just missed an important appointment.

Her client, Henry Sopher, wouldn't like to know this. His hotel, Paradise Gardens, had suffered a string of minor legal troubles over the last several months, and the upcoming League of Realists booking had him in a tizzy. Mr. Sopher had been represented for the previous eight years by her father, Jamshedji Mistry, one of the most prominent solicitors in Bombay. But since Perveen had joined Mistry Law as a partner, she had taken on Mr. Sopher's concerns.

And the last thing she wanted was for him to complain to her father.

Henry Sopher had asked Perveen to meet Helene LeVasseur, the Parisian founder of the Realists, and her assistant, Vidya Blackwood, at Victoria Terminus to escort them to Paradise Gardens. But the women leading the internationally renowned philosophy league hadn't come on the Bombay Mail. The head porter for the platform informed Perveen two European widows had stepped off an express that came in fifteen minutes earlier. They had hired two porters and set off on foot.

From the station, Perveen hurried off toward Garden Street. The women had certainly showed spunk and curiosity to walk to their hotel, but she prayed nothing would befall them. The newspapers had reported that during the two Realists' time in New Delhi, there was an unsuccessful robbery attempt on their hotel room. And in Madras, where Madame Helene had also been lecturing, there was some kind of riot. They sounded like trouble.

"Their notoriety presents a slight risk," Henry Sopher had confided to her the previous week. "And the Realists' lecture will go head-to-head with the Asiatic Society's holiday party.

But the Realist ladies are paying full price for my most expensive suite—and they've got admirers coming from outside the city who are booking rooms, too."

Perveen had recommended that Mr. Sopher hire plainclothes detectives to shadow the ladies and off-duty constables to monitor the ballroom during the lecture. She'd also agreed to meet their train, escort them to the hotel, and stay overnight in a room near theirs to attend to any delicate situations. It sounded simple and practical; but in the year she'd worked for her father, she realized that clients' demands often turned out to be different than anticipated.

Perveen's heart rate slowed as she turned onto Garden Street and caught sight the big white hotel on the corner. It was a beauty. The Paradise Gardens Hotel had been built in 1900, ten years after Watson's Hotel, a 130-room hotel whose claim to fame was its external cast iron frame and equally rigid rule disallowing Indians and dogs. Mr. Sopher, a Baghdadi Jew, thought differently. His hotel was open to any person able to pay the tariff of five rupees per night—although he prohibited dogs. The only animals were the parrots and monkeys sculpted into the lintels running across the top of the hotel's veranda.

Perveen didn't mind spending a night away from her parents and brother. She pictured herself nestled in a sea of pillows in a fancy room, ordering tea and crumpets from room service and, if all went well with the evening's event, maybe even champagne.

When Perveen drew close enough to see the guests enjoying late morning breakfast on the veranda, she saw two ladies in white saris in conversation with Mr. Sopher, who was twisting his hands in an anxious manner. That was why the porter had thought them to be widows—white was the mourning color for Hindus. But these ladies weren't Hindus.

Madame Helene, who was fifty, looked both stout and strong, reminding Perveen of the washerwomen and cooks she'd seen in England. Her pompadour of thick black hair was mixed with white, and her skin was lightly tanned, making her turquoise blue eyes stand out as boldly as the Father Christmas mannequin's. A pretty young woman who looked barely over eighteen was standing at Madame's side. Her large brown eyes and golden-brown skin looked Anglo-Indian, so Perveen guessed this was Vidya Blackwood, the secretary who'd handled all correspondence from their headquarters in Pondicherry, a South Indian district still under French rule. She wore her dark brown hair cut in a chin-length shingle, a style that was popular in England but was still rare in India.

As Perveen bounded up the steps to the veranda, Mr. Sopher frowned at her, clearly a reproach for her late arrival.

"Good afternoon, Madame LeVasseur and Miss Blackwood!" Perveen said, panting from exertion of her rapid walk. "I'm awfully sorry I missed you at the station. I heard you'd set off on foot, so I've been behind you all the way."

"It was a simple matter indeed to walk ten minutes with the assistance of our brothers," Madame Helene said in an accent as smooth as a French cheese.

"We were fine, except that the porters got a bit of a splash. Somebody threw out dirty water from an overhead window." Vidya had an odd accent; neither English nor Indian. "Madame is so good at stepping out of the way; she's always missing accidents."

Madame Helene said, "Mademoiselle, I'm afraid I don't know your name?"

Perveen held out her hand. "I'm Perveen Mistry, Mr. Sopher's solicitor. He sent me to fetch you from Victoria Terminus. But I understand you arrived on a different train."

"We saw an opportunity, and wished to save time. But why would you send a solicitor on such trivial duty?" Madame looked askance at Mr. Sopher.

Perveen didn't want Mr. Sopher to reveal his security concerns, so she spoke quickly. "I'm interested in the well-being of any female professionals visiting Bombay. I'll be staying in the room next door, should you wish assistance before or after your lecture."

Madame arched an eyebrow as she regarded Perveen. "I didn't know girls could be lawyers."

"I studied at Oxford," Perveen said, feeling the defensiveness rise in her, as it did with almost every discussion of her identity. Her father had earned the admirable nickname of "King of Contracts," while she was spoken of as "Bombay's First Girl Lawyer." "Madame, I didn't know you liked to wear saris."

"We are wearing khadi, homespun cloth woven on village looms, not European mills. It is the symbol of our sympathy with the Mahatma Gandhi," she said with a beatific smile. Her eyes ran over the pale blue chiffon sari that Perveen wore. She must have recognized the chiffon as French.

"Madame, may we begin the registration?" Mr. Sopher asked. "Now is also a time to place valuables in the hotel safe."

Madame Helene wrinkled her nose. "We don't think much of safes; they can be opened and my treasure examined. But would you please tell me the dining hours, and when the dhobi arrives to collect laundry?"

As Mr. Sopher recited the information, Perveen yearned to ask what treasure she spoke of. It wouldn't be wise to bring this up on the veranda, where a number of tea-drinkers were stationed. Instead, she offered to help Vidya Blackwood and the hotel's bellmen bring the luggage upstairs while Madame checked in.

Room 100 was large and elegant, with matching four-poster beds dressed in crisp white linen. Filmy curtains draped four tall windows overlooking the hotel's courtyard garden.

Turning to Vidya, Perveen said, "I heard you suffered a burglary attempt last week. What happened?"

Vidya's long-lashed eyes fluttered as she spoke. "In the dark, I awoke to hear someone moving about the room. I screamed, and the evil intruder fled."

Perveen thought about the treasure Madame had mentioned. "What do you think the thief wanted?"

"Most likely the Book of Truth. The manuscript is our only volume, so we are careful to carry it wherever we go."

Madame Helene appeared at the door, and Perveen wondered if the special book was inside her large crocodile purse or perhaps tucked up underneath the white sari.

Madame looked around slowly, and then went to the window where Perveen stood. "You must also feel the strong energy field coming from the east."

"I notice the proximity to the garden. Shall I ask Mr. Sopher if you could shift to a higher floor?" Perveen asked.

Madame shook her head. "As Vidya said, we will be careful with our good book. That book is as much hers as mine. She fixed my English grammatical mistakes."

"Fixing grammar is nothing like writing a four-hundred-page book." Vidya demurred. "There are so many insightful thoughts in the Book of Truth! When Madame reads a random passage, it is always a marvel, because someone in our audience declares the message was intended chiefly for them."

"I sense a need, and I find the correct line," Madame said, as if sensing Perveen's puzzlement.

"Is that what people call clairvoyance?" Perveen asked, recalling a letter in the newspaper protesting Madame's appearance.

Madame Helene shrugged. "I leave the occult to others. In my opinion, it's merely heightened awareness. Now, we must rest before going to tea. Some Bombay Realists wish to meet us before the lecture."

Perveen decamped to the hallway and found two large men in suits sitting on a pair of dainty chairs set near the suite's doorway. These were Messrs Rowe and Singh, the plain-clothes detectives hired by the hotel. Mr. Rowe was slightly built and had a clean-shaven, weather-beaten face—likely an ex-military man. Mr. Singh wore a well-wrapped violet turban and had a Sikh's long, well-groomed beard. Rowe chatted brightly while Singh remained silent, his hooded eyes seeming to judge her own trustworthiness.

"This floor is an easy climb for a thief. Could one of you keep vigil in the courtyard below?" Perveen asked after explaining her concern about the women's insistence on keeping the Book of Truth.

"Absolutely not!" Mr. Rowe harrumphed. "We were hired to guard the hallway entrance and the ladies only."

"But it's a possible entry point into the room." Perveen looked beseechingly at Mr. Singh.

"It is more effective for the two of us to work together," he said. "Perhaps more labor was needed?"

"All right, then," Perveen said, realizing the two wouldn't budge. "Please tell me if the ladies leave their room. I'm staying in 102."

Perveen's room was a quarter of the suite's size, but had neatly made twin beds, a modern bathroom and a veranda overlooking the city. She took a relaxing bath in the long porcelain tub and rested for an hour. Then Mr. Singh was knocking at her door, alerting her that the ladies had gone downstairs.

Perveen draped herself in a fresh pink silk sari and sped downstairs, where Mr. Sopher greeted her.

"I'm glad you are following. Madame and her secretary are on the veranda along with some members of the Bombay Realists' Lodge. Before you join them, could we speak privately?"

She was slightly alarmed by his tone. "What has happened?"

Inside the management office, he handed her a paper. "During check-in, Madame LeVasseur surprised me with this business proposition. She offered to give me fifty-five percent of ticket sales if I'd comp the cost of her suite."

Perveen was puzzled. "Why would she offer so much?"

"She learned the Bombay Realists' Lodge would pay her room expense. She wishes to save them money."

"How much is the suite?"

"Nine rupees per night." He paused. "And our office has already sold two hundred rupees' worth of tickets."

"This sounds very profitable for you; but it makes no sense for her." Perveen read aloud from paper written in an elegant looping script. "'Monsieur Henri Sopher provides a secure, ventilated room for Madames Helene LeVasseur and Vidya Blackwood for one night, free of cost.'" She pointed a finger at the word. "I'm wary of the term 'secure.' If anything's taken from the room, she could have a case against you for breach of contract. And she could sue you personally because she used your name, not the hotel's."

"But Paradise Gardens Hotel is utterly safe and—"

Perveen looked at the bottom of the paper and gasped. "Mr. Sopher, you already signed the paper! How could you, when you're paying me to advise you first?"

"I wished to be accommodating, since she'd had a difficult walk to the hotel, no thanks to you. But everything should be fine from now on, with the detectives and off-duty constables coming to stand in the ballroom."

Perveen couldn't shake the unease she'd felt since the moment she'd looked into Madame's cold blue eyes. "Could you assign some of the hotel watchmen to stand underneath the suite's windows from now through their departure?"

"That would necessitate taking two men from duty at the front of hotel. Robbing Peter to pay Paul," he added grumpily.

"Are you turning Christian, Mr. Sopher?"

"It is only a saying!" he said with a frown. "I am as committed to my faith as you are to yours. In the very room where that Realist will speak, I recently hosted a Hanukkah party for our congregation's children."

"You might run out of the funds for good deeds if your hotel is slapped with a lawsuit," Perveen pointed out. "A man's fortune is only a hairpin's breadth away from loss. You'll rest easier if you know precautions are in place."

"You talk of rest? With all those bright lights going up, I won't sleep a wink."

Perveen followed his gaze across the hall to the smaller banquet room, where white-uniformed employees were stringing lights across the entrance. A waiter carried in a tray that was loaded with bright orange Indian jelebis and pink and green laddu sweets, followed by another worker bearing a massive fruit-and-cream trifle. But the most fascinating character was in the rear, a young Indian man wearing an obviously stuffed red costume. He was struggling to fix a false white beard on his face. At Perveen's amused look, he cast his eyes downward, as if embarrassed.

"Whose party is that?" Perveen asked.

"The Asiatic Society's holiday party."

She laughed. "I thought they were a group of stuffy old men who loved history books."

"Hush, they are all coming with their children and grand-children. Every year, Saint Nick comes to read a story and gives bags of sweets." He sighed heavily. "This morning, the fat Irish pianist who always plays Saint Nick fell ill, so our new boy on the front desk is replacing him. Lucky he's Christian, because none of my Hindu or Muslim staff would do it."

"That was fortunate."

"I hope he succeeds. He won't be playing the piano." Mr. Sopher looked doubtfully at the young man, who'd gotten the beard straight and was now helping a bearer hang lights. "They are setting up late because of the extra work preparing the ballroom for the Realists."

"Everything will be fine. Just put some guards in the courtyard, and I'll worry about the rest." Perveen went out to the veranda, where Madame Helene and Vidya were holding court with two local people. The ladies' white saris appeared freshly ironed, and Madame had a bouquet of hibiscus and tuberose in her hands, Vidya a pink hibiscus behind her ear. Bombay's finest pigeons roosted along the edge of the roof, keeping an eye on the tea table, which was loaded with crisp samosas, sausage rolls, tea sandwiches, and a guava tart.

Mr. Akshay Prasad, president of the Bombay Realists' Lodge, was a rotund man with a forceful personality. After introducing himself and the Bombay lodge's publicity director, Mrs. Nargis Boatwalla, he clapped his hands together in excitement. "So glad you are with us, Miss Mistry. We are anticipating a won-derful lecture this evening. Two hundred seats were sold and one hundred standing room places are almost filled!"

"Good for you. And will you address a particular topic tonight, Madame?"

"Should I?" Madame Helene's thinly plucked brows drew together.

Perveen wondered if she'd been too bold. "It's hardly necessary. But I wonder what the Realists hope to achieve in 1921."

"I do hope—" Abruptly, Madame Helene leapt up and away from the table. As she did so, a fat green-and-white bird dropping landed where she'd been sitting.

"Terribly sorry, madam. These birds in Bombay have no mercy!" A waiter rushed forward to remove the offending chair, and another brought a new seat for the Frenchwoman.

"That was remarkable," Perveen said. "Madame Helene, how did you know the dropping was coming? You weren't even looking overhead."

"I smelled that dropping as the bird began to make it," Madame said. "I have a very sensitive nose."

Her blunt words seemed to have made the Indians at the table look slightly sick. Perveen watched Mr. Prasad push his plate of half-eaten cakes away, and his companion, Mrs. Boatwalla, took a long sip of tea.

"Madame is extra-sensory," Vidya said. "She senses very small things, whether they are motions, emotions, or even changes in the air, as this was."

"I can tell something about you, Miss Mistry."

"Oh?" Perveen asked nervously. God forbid she had guessed that Perveen was dead set on protecting Mr. Sopher from troubles she might cause.

"I have a sense, from the pattern of your eyes, that you desire some food. Please do take a seat and have something."

"But—" Perveen hesitated, knowing she should refuse, but not really wanting to. She'd never seen a prettier guava tart. "Thank you."

The food was as delicious as it looked. Perveen relaxed

as she ate, and Mrs. Boatwalla, the publicity lady, began discussing the various newspapers that wished to cover the lecture. "I only allowed the three most important. *The Times*, the *Chronicle*, and the *Samachar*."

"I hope they will be more accurate than the papers were in Delhi and Madras," Madame Helene said.

"What really happened in those places, then?" asked Prasad. He leaned forward, inadvertently nudging his tea cup.

Swiftly, Madame righted the cup and said, "In Delhi, Vidya scared off someone, no doubt a Theosophist, who wanted our book. The press proclaimed it was a publicity stunt. In Madras, there was a supposed riot, but it was simply a case of the crowd arguing amongst itself after an audience member said the Book of Truth is a fraud."

Theosophists were the older and better-known group of mystical and occult-inspired philosophers. They were led by another European woman, Annie Besant, who had taken up the cause of Indian freedom. Perveen could understand why the Theosophists might take offense at Madame Levasseur's actions and dress.

"How can people have the audacity to discuss the content of your unpublished book?" Mr. Prasad said, shaking his head.

"When I read aloud, people make notes. They admire the principles so much that they want to repeat it. But how can I control what they choose to write?" Madame raised her hands as if exasperated. "Bof!"

"Some people were selling unauthorized pamphlets on Realism right outside Bombay University!" said Mrs. Boatwalla. "I wanted a copy, but they were scared off by constables before I could get it."

"Given the troubles, perhaps we should stop all Theosophists from entering," said Mr. Singh, the plainclothes detective. Perveen had almost forgotten he and Mr. Rowe were quietly standing guard behind them.

"Anyone holding a ticket has a right to enter," Perveen explained. "Also, discriminating against some lecture goers would create bad publicity for the hotel."

"I agree with Mademoiselle Mistry," Madame said. "I am—how do you say?—*optimiste*. I believe the audience will be seekers of truth, not enemies."

Mr. Rowe bent down and put his mouth to Madame's ear. "If the situation becomes too difficult, give me a signal and I'll carry you off to safety."

"But please don't lay hands on Madame!" Vidya Blackwood said anxiously. "There is a force field of energy around her. It is so strong, it could damage your health."

"I strive to be mannerly, but I'm hired to protect," Mr. Rowe snapped.

"We never requested detective service," Madame cut in. "We believe in trust and sharing."

"Madame, your safety and welfare are the hotel's concerns," Perveen soothed. "Although I'm certain there's nothing to worry about."

AFTER TEA, MADAME HELENE and Vidya visited with a few more Realists who'd arrived at the hotel. Perveen went into the ballroom filled with cane chairs. She selected a second row aisle seat and turned her chair so she could watch the audience stream in.

Most ticket holders appeared to be Indian scholars, students, and activists. Some might be Theosophists, judging from snatches of conversation about "the pretender" or "charlatan truth." After the seats were all filled—as well as the aisles—she noticed several Indian and European men standing in the back holding small notebooks. They were either journalists or entrepreneurs working on black market Realist pamphlets. She was tempted to confront them, but Madame wasn't her client.

At the sudden sound of applause, she turned around to the front. The lecture was on. Mr. Prasad and Mrs. Boatwalla had come out to introduce the guests of honor. Mrs. Boatwalla draped Madame with a jasmine garland and Vidya with marigolds.

"Some say that truth comes above all religions," said Madame, whose voice seemed to soar over the now-hushed room. "But the notion I'll discuss tonight is that truth rests within each religion, which means we are more unified than it seems."

There was a murmur of approval throughout the room.

"For this reason, we cannot say Christians born overseas should rule at the top of the country. But we cannot say Hindus have complete power; nor the Mohammedans. When Indians and Europeans sit down together and speak of shared dreams, they are coming into truth."

Perveen couldn't believe what she'd just heard. Madame had stated that she didn't believe overseas Christians should rule India. Indian freedom fighters had been jailed for making such statements in public.

The quiet broke. Conversation rumbled and questioning hands shot up all over the room.

"Do the Realists support a political party?" called a man with a Gujarati accent.

"Certainly not. Politics are individual as one's faith," Madame Helene answered.

A teenage girl wearing a school uniform shouted, "Madame, what is your answer to ignorant prejudice?"

"I have answered that in the Book of Truth." Smiling,

Madame opened the book on her podium. "I shall find the right passage for you."

"Don't you know it by heart?" a man with a British accent sniped. Was he one of the men in the back? Perveen turned, but the crowd was so thick she couldn't see.

"Please be patient," Madame said, and Perveen noticed her hands trembled as she turned pages. Despite the strength of her words, she might be tense.

"Those are stolen ideas!" thundered an Irish-sounding voice from the center of the room.

Irish. Perveen thought about the pianist who'd cancelled playing Saint Nicholas. Was he here on a secret mission?

Just then, the room went black.

Electrical load shedding was common throughout the day and evening. Hotels, schools and wealthy householders had private generators to remedy the problem. Everyone should have known to be patient. However, the audience broke into shouting and screaming. Three hundred people began pushing each other in an attempt to get out to the main hall. Despite knowing the room's layout, Perveen was swept up by feelings of entrapment and claustrophobia.

Amidst the clamor, she heard Henry Sopher shouting, "Stay calm! Stay calm! The lights will return!"

Perveen remembered Mr. Rowe was seated in the heart of the audience, and Mr. Singh was in another corner. She was the closest one of the team to the Book of Truth. She would have to defend it.

Perveen wove her way through the crush of bodies. Within a few steps, she bumped up against the stage. She clambered up, trying to recall the placement of the podium. She touched its smooth wood and reached out.

In the next instant, her right hand was jabbed with

something long and sharp. She couldn't stop her scream. It felt as if a knife had slashed through her. Perveen drew back her wounded hand, pressing it with her left as she attempted to stifle the hurt.

The lights flashed on again and Perveen stared at Vidya, who was holding a long, bloody hair pin in her left hand. At her side was Madame Helene, who had the Book of Truth clutched to her massive bosom.

"Miss Mistry! My goodness, it's you!" Vidya's voice broke.

"I was only trying to make sure the book was secure," Perveen muttered. Black spots were appearing before her eyes, and she feared that she might faint against the small crowd of onlookers who'd gathered.

"The book is fine. I kept it safe," said Madame, who frowned at her while keeping the book clutched to her bosom.

"My apologies—I'm so very sorry about the lights. There is overload, with the party across the hall." Mr. Sopher had arrived, out of breath. "You've been attacked, Miss Mistry! Where is the culprit?"

"There isn't one. I was only trying to save the book." Perveen stammered, feeling utterly hapless. And the way Madame was looking at her, it seemed her statement was being doubted.

"Yes, I was the one who stuck her. I didn't know. It was an accident." Miss Blackwood gave pleading look to Madame Helene.

"It's all right," Perveen said, but she felt the sweets she'd had at tea rising up from her stomach. As she fought to keep from spewing, the black spots grew larger, and she began falling forward—only to be expertly caught in Madame's hands.

"Excuse me," she whispered as the lady set her on her feet. She'd been mercifully spared from vomiting, but she still felt weak.

Mr. Sopher wrapped his handkerchief around Perveen's bloody hand and began leading her out to the hallway. The room went black again, and a throng of annoyed lecture goers trudged out alongside them. The Asiatic Society partygoers had clustered in the grand hall because their room had also gone dark. Prakash, the Indian Father Christmas, was out in the hall, ordering a flunky to fix the fairy lights.

Firoze Dastur, a Parsi physician, emerged from the masses. "You're Jamshedji Mistry's daughter, aren't you? May I help?"

"That's most kind. I've a number of things to do," Mr. Sopher said, dashing off.

"Don't tell my pappa about this. He might never let me stay away from home again," Perveen said. There were far too many people looking at her—even the tiny Father Christmas who was standing alongside Vidya.

"I shall not break confidentiality," Dr. Dastur said in a kindly tone. "But do tell me who caused you what looks a most vicious injury?"

"I believe it was Miss Blackwood's hairpin." When he looked uncomprehending, she said, "Miss Blackwood is the secretary of the famous Realist, Madame Helene, who was speaking tonight."

"The Anglo-Indian girl wearing rags?" he queried.

"Not rags, it's homespun," she chided him. "She and Madame dress that way to show their unity with India."

"Funny for an Anglo-Indian to want the British out. And the girl's hair is cut like a boy's! Why would she have pins in it?"

"She had a flower in her hair," Perveen said, remembering. "The pin was sharp, but at least it didn't go into my wrist."

"Take some water. Are you convinced that Miss Blackwood did it accidentally?" The doctor sounded skeptical.

"Of course. She was only trying to keep the book safe."

As Perveen said the words, she felt suddenly unsure. But she could not risk suggesting anything, because her goal was to keep Mr. Sopher's hotel free from scandal. So she drank the water and let Dr. Dastur tend to her.

Dr. Dastur said the puncture was deep and would take time to heal. He bandaged the hand with cotton and gave her two Bayer tablets.

Perveen was desperate to know how the events below had continued—but she imagined her presence, with a wrapped hand, might cause questions from journalists. It was a relief when a waiter came up an hour later to say there hadn't been further trouble. The lecture had gone on, just as the Asiatic Society's Christmas party had. Now people were heading out, and Mr. Sopher wished to know if she was hungry. Dr. Dastur had recommended consommé, but she thought differently. Perveen ordered the grilled lamb chop with mint chutney, rice with barberries and peas, a mince tart with cream, and a champagne split.

After the waiter had gone downstairs to give the order, Perveen ventured into the hallway and saw the two detectives had returned to their chairs. "They're in for the night," Mr. Rowe said with a yawn.

"I'll just ask if they need anything." Perveen knocked on the door with her good hand.

The door cracked open, and Vidya looked out. "You again? What now?"

Perveen felt affronted. After all, the girl had stabbed her hand. "I wanted to hear how the lecture went."

Vidya spoke after a long pause. "Once the people calmed, it went very well. If you wish to know more, ask Madame tomorrow."

The door was closed in her face. Perveen returned to her

room and dinner. The food was delicious, but it was hard to relax. Vidya's description of the calm crowd was surprising. There had been several critical voices in the audience: British voices, who probably considered Madame a betrayer. And why had the lights gone out? Was it really a matter of load-shedding, or was it an act of sabotage, perhaps to permit someone to grab the book?

At last she was too weary to think about the awful events of the evening, and drifted off to the sound of mating cats outside on the streets.

THE NEXT MORNING, SHE opened her eyes at the sound of knocking at the door. The clock on her bedside table read seven-fifteen.

Perveen climbed out of bed, feeling the stiff soreness in her right hand as she pulled her pink silk dressing gown over the cotton caftan she'd slept in. It took some effort to unchain and unlock the door with her left hand. Vidya Blackwood was standing outside, not wearing the white sari from the day before, but a plain gray frock that ended a few inches above her narrow ankles. Her hair was covered by a blue cloche with a gray feather.

"Are you going somewhere?" Perveen asked, trying to smooth her own wild mane.

"We don't leave until midday." Vidya's voice dropped. "About last night. I came to say I'm sorry."

Perveen eyed her, thinking again about her suspicions. They were stronger than ever. "Let's go to the balcony to talk."

After Perveen closed the French doors behind them, the two settled on the room's balcony overlooking Garden Street.

Vidya apologized again.

"I won't accept your excuse." As Vidya stiffened, Perveen added, "I don't believe it was your hairpin. Nor your hand."

"It was!" Vidya protested, but her voice sounded uncertain.

"Please give me the hatpin you're using in your cloche."

Using her right hand, Vidya adjusted her hat and withdrew a cheap black hatpin. It was small and blunt; quite different from the miniature stiletto that had injured Perveen.

"This isn't sharp enough to do any damage. I believe the brass hairpin yesterday belonged to Madame Helene. Using her superior awareness, she sensed me coming toward her in the darkness, and she stabbed me."

"You've no reason to speak ill of Madame—"

"You're right handed, and that pin was in your left when the lights came up. She must have passed it to you, and you quickly assumed the blame. Why was that?"

In a small voice, Vidya said, "Madame can't be faulted. The Book of Truth is very special."

"Why do you work for Madame?"

Vidya looked down. "My mother's a Hindu born in Pondicherry. My father's a soldier from Liverpool. They could hardly ever find a bungalow to rent or anyone to play with us children. My parents sent me off with Madame three years ago because they wanted me to have a grand life."

"But is serving Madame truly a grand experience?"

Vidya looked earnestly at her. "Realists don't follow one religion, and you saw how we are all races. It's a new society. It's the best place to be."

There was a loud sound of opening doors. On the porch next to theirs, Mr. Singh and Mr. Rowe had appeared, waving their hands like characters in a comedy film. Mr. Rowe shouted, "There you are! We've been knocking on the door!"

"We never heard—"

The detective didn't let her finish. "You both are needed on the other side. There's been a theft!"

They hurried to the ladies' suite, where Madame Helene stood stock-still in a purple velvet wrapper. Tears streamed down her face. Looking straight at Vidya, she said, "Where were you? The Book of Truth has been stolen!"

"Where had you placed the book for safekeeping?" Mr. Rowe asked, his face red with emotion.

"On the nightstand between our beds," Vidya interjected. "Last night at eleven, I read one passage aloud to help prepare us for sleep. I think it was there in the morning, but I don't remember looking."

"How could a thief have come inside when I was sleeping?" Madame sobbed. "You men were supposed to guard the doorway!"

"We were," snapped Mr. Singh. "Both of us stayed awake!"

Perveen went over to the room's bank of windows overlooking the courtyard. The windows were open, as they had been before. She called down to the idle-looking watchmen and asked if anyone had entered the courtyard during the night. They answered in the negative.

Perveen mulled over the situation. Either Rowe or Singh could have slipped into the room after Vidya had gone to visit her. No. They hadn't known Madame was still sleeping, and Vidya had been with Perveen just five minutes. More importantly, Madame had pressured Mr. Sopher to sign the agreement guaranteeing a secure room. Perveen's suspicion of a faked theft was probably the truth.

Perveen eyed the half-packed suitcases resting on racks. "I wonder if anything else was taken from you?"

In Madame's long look, Perveen could tell that the Realist understood her suspicion the book might just have been packed. Coolly, she said, "Vidya, would you mind unpacking both of the suitcases for Miss Mistry?"

When Mr. Sopher arrived, clothes were all over the floor, and the chief valuables—Madame's hatpins and jewelry, their cash, and Vidya's watch—were displayed on the beds.

"Someone has stolen my Book of Truth!" Madame Helene announced.

"I can't believe it," Mr. Sopher muttered. "Just can't believe."

"Such theft has always been my worry. This is why Miss Blackwood's letter requested a private suite with a secure lock."

"I gave you that, and I paid for security men and extra guards. I also offered you the safe. I'm sorry if you lost an item, but hotel policy is—"

"Stop!" Perveen interrupted her client, because apology could be seen as admitting fault. "Mr. Sopher, will you come to the hall for a moment?"

As they made their way toward the open doorway, Perveen noticed a young washerman with a clothing bundle tossed over his back. He stooped to pick up a cloth bundle lying next to the door. Tying this bundle into his larger one, he hurried off. Something about the way he moved was awkward. And it was strange the ladies would have put out laundry on the day they were scheduled to depart Bombay.

Perveen thought the man looked young, and his face was familiar. Then she realized who it was: Paul, the new employee who'd stood in for Saint Nicholas.

"Get that dhobi!" Perveen shrieked, rushing out to the hall—but he was gone.

"No shouting, it will wake others!" chided Mr. Sopher. "And why was that fellow so early? Ten o'clock is the usual timing."

Perveen had no time to explain. "Detectives, take the main staircase. Is that a service staircase at the end?"

"Yes, but it's for staff only—" Mr. Sopher protested.

Perveen was off before he could finish. She learned quickly why he didn't want her to go down the service stair. It was filthy, and several workers were sleeping on thin blankets on the landing, rubbing their eyes in confusion as the lady guest in a pink dressing gown flew past.

"Stop that thief!" Perveen yelled when she saw Paul trudging down the stairway. He looked up and then began running downstairs. If he reached the ground floor he would get away. Summoning all her strength, she made a wild leap to close the last eight feet between them.

Perveen fell on top of him. Paul screamed Hindi profanity as he wiggled out and made it through the door to freedom. But he'd left the bundle behind.

"Are you all right?" Mr. Sopher called as he came down the stairs.

"Yes. Let's see if it's still here." Using her good hand, Perveen unrolled the layers of white cloth. Holding up the large green book, she said, "Behold the Book of Truth."

The door at the top of the stairs opened to admit Madame Helene, Vidya, and the two plainsclothesmen.

"What a relief that your book is safe!" Mr. Sopher cried. "Miss Mistry has saved the day. How did you guess the dhobi took the book?"

"He's not a real dhobi—he's that newly hired fellow you believe is named Paul," Perveen said, watching Vidya and Madame Helene exchange worried glances. "Who provided his references?"

"He brought a letter from his old employer in Pondicherry."

"The home base of the Realists," Perveen said, watching Madame Helene's face fall. "I noticed Madame and Vidya standing near him the hallway during the events yesterday— perhaps to ensure his special service this morning."

"What rot!" sputtered Madame Helene. "Mademoiselle, please return my book. It's too powerful to be held by anyone but me or my dear Vidya."

Perveen raised her bandaged right hand. "Madame Helene, I believe you intentionally gave Mr. Sopher a false time of arrival, because you didn't want anyone from the hotel meeting you at Victoria Terminus."

"A mistake—"

"Not a mistake," Perveen shot back. "You wished to have some unobserved time in the city so you could meet with Paul and whoever else might be part and parcel of your scheme."

"What a silly thing to say!" Vidya bleated. "Let us just thank God that the book is safe."

"Which God do you mean?" Perveen said. "I thought Realists didn't worship a deity."

Madame Helene gave Perveen a powerful stare. "Give me my book."

"Not yet." Perveen slowly turned the pages that were a mixture of French and English phrases. All told, there were just twenty pages of writing, interspersed with many blanks. "There isn't much here," Perveen said, looking up at Madame.

"It's a work in progress," Madame retorted.

"Maybe so. But you fought to keep me from getting hold of it yesterday evening. You don't want anyone knowing that your infamous manuscript is just a shell."

Madame's hard face seemed to crumple, and Perveen realized her words were as wounding to Madame as the sharp hairpin had been to her.

"We never meant to mislead," Vidya said softly. "But Madame said this book has gotten bigger than truth itself, that we had to let go of it. And if Paul and I helped her, she'd pay us enough that we could make a real start together."

"What do you mean by that?" Perveen prodded.

"Paul and I hope to marry. If we do our best to help Madame, she will promote us, and also gift us enough money to rent our own flat."

"I can see why you'd help Madame, then," Perveen said. "It is her reasoning for the deception that is troubling. The idea of having a book stolen throws suspicion on your rivals, the Theosophists. And she might have intended to enrich herself by suing my client."

"I won't do that," Madame said wheedling tone. "We can tear up the agreement and let bygones be. Now we must prepare to travel to our next stop."

"Madame, you shall go alone," Vidya said fiercely. "I'm quitting! I must find Paul to tell him. This adventure has just been too much!"

The stairwell door opened. Two Bombay Police constables, plus one of the journalists she'd seen the night before, rushed through and surrounded the group.

Perveen addressed Madame Helene. "Mr. Sopher shall take his time deciding whether to press a suit against you for attempted fraud."

"Can I go?" Vidya pleaded.

"Why don't you tell your tale to the nice policemen? And then we'll speak to them," Perveen said. "In the meantime, Mr. Sopher and I will step aside for a brief chat."

"That French fraud planned to cheat me," Mr. Sopher said when they were sequestered. "But it never happened. Is that a case for the court?"

"No harm was done to you," Perveen said. "So it's rather unlikely. However, Vidya seems rather frightened since the constables arrived. She seems likely to make a full confession; she also doesn't know that *Times* reporter is writing down everything. Now, what about the lights going out yesterday? Is there any chance it was connected to the pretend robbery?"

"One of the maids saw that damned Irish pianist dash across from the ballroom into the Asiatic Society party. My guess is he turned off the lights in the Realists' lecture and pulled the electric cord across the hall."

"We'll have to hear what Paul has to say for himself, if he can be found," Perveen said.

Mr. Sopher's eyes gleamed. "Those Realists will suffer one thousand misfortunes after their misdeed appears in newspapers across India. And my hotel will look top-class to have foiled such schemers."

"I hope so." Perveen had a sudden inspiration. "In exchange for not pressing charges, you might ask Madame to cover the expense for the detectives and extra guards. It only seems fair."

"I'll do that," Mr. Sopher said, nodding with satisfaction. "However, I insist on footing the bill for my lawyer, who's worth her very weight in gold."

Reaching into his desk drawer, he pulled out a long box wrapped in gold foil.

Perveen felt embarrassed. "There's no need. You pay me enough!"

"You've a taste for Perrier-Jouet," Mr. Sopher said with a twinkle. "I know from the order you made last night, and it's what the King of Contracts ordered the last time we drank at the Royal Bombay Yacht Club. Take this home to your parents, and they'll be so chuffed they won't even notice the hole in your hand!"

"You're quite a detective!" Perveen accepted her holiday gift with thanks.

THE PRINCE (OF PEACE)

Gary Corby

GARY CORBY lives in Sydney, Australia, with his wife and two daughters. He blogs at A Dead Man Fell from the Sky, on all things ancient, Athenian, and mysterious. He is the author of six critically acclaimed mysteries set in 4th century BC Greece and feature Nicolaos, agent for the statesman Pericles and who, together with his clever priestess wife, Diotima, investigates murders in Classical Athens: *The Pericles Commission, The Ionia Sanction, Sacred Games, The Marathon Conspiracy, Death Ex Machina, The Singer from Memphis,* and *Death on Delos.*

"We must consider Christmas to be a necessary evil," said Niccolo Machiavelli. "For you are to consider that there is no surer sign of the degradation of the state than that its people disregard the rites of their religion."

Cesare Borgia laughed. "You will hear no argument from me, the son of a Pope," he said. He sprawled across a large, ornate chair of carved wood and plush velvet. In one hand he held a silver goblet of fine wine, in the other a festive pie of spiced meats. His entire manner was relaxed, even friendly.

Borgia paused to drain his cup. He placed it empty upon a gold table beside him. A servant instantly refilled it.

Borgia observed that Machiavelli's cup remained full.

"You do not drink, Signor Machiavelli. Does the wine not please you?"

"It does, my Lord Duke, but my habits have always been abstemious. It's my digestion, you understand."

"Then that explains why you are so thin."

Machiavelli was indeed thin, and tall, and dark, and his face was as ascetic as his reputation. Despite which this son of a modest lawyer had by the power of his pleasant conversation and his incisive mind risen to become secretary to the most powerful of Florence. He was their most valued ambassador, in which capacity he was here in the city of Cesena, at the court of Cesare Borgia.

"Yet your words do not entirely resonate with me," said Borgia. "The people certainly think Christmas is necessary, but why do you say that it is evil?"

"The inefficiency, my Lord, and the sloppy thinking that comes with merriment," Machiavelli said.

"This is a problem?" Borgia asked.

"Of course, my Lord," Machiavelli said. In Machiavelli's world, there was nothing more abhorrent than imprecise thinking.

"Then there is the difficulty of presents," Machiavelli went on. "How much to give, and to whom?"

"I do not understand," said Borgia.

"Consider the case of two members of a family, two brothers for example. What happens if one gives the other a present of great value, while the other gives a token of affection that might be sentimental but is of low value? Does not such an imbalance sow discord within the family union?"

"In my family, when we receive a gift, we tend to inspect it very carefully for hidden poisons," Borgia commented.

"Yes, my Lord, very wise." Machiavelli gave a slight bow from where he sat. He reflected that he had not perhaps chosen the best possible example with this man, who was widely believed to have murdered his own brother. Machiavelli hurried on, to smooth over the slight faux pas. "Then again, consider the case of a man who gives a present to his neighbor, but receives none in return. One of these two has miscalculated the strength of their relationship. One has valued it too highly, or the other too lightly. In either case, resentment is sure to linger, so that at some future time when neighborly accord is required, there will instead be an underlying discord that could have been entirely avoided, if only Christmas did not require the giving of presents."

Borgia rubbed his chin in thought. "There is something in what you say," he conceded. "I had never considered the matter in those terms."

"This issue of gifts is a puzzle to perplex even the greatest students of political thought," Machiavelli said. "I confess I have never mastered the problem."

"Perhaps you should give it some thought," suggested Borgia.

"I will, my Lord."

LATER, IN THE DARK, chilly early hours of the morning, Machiavelli went for a walk to think about the reasons for gift-giving—which were quite mysterious to him—and to consider his many problems concerning Borgia: of the necessity to maintain good relations with this most powerful man, while at the same time not giving him what he wanted.

For Machiavelli was on a mission of the greatest importance to Florence. Borgia had demanded of the free city of Florence that they appoint him commander of their militia, and the Florentines had immediately dispatched Machiavelli to deal with Borgia, with orders to make sure this never happened. The Florentines would not have Borgia at any price.

Machiavelli made his way through the slightly labyrinthine corridors of the *Rocca Malatestiana*, the great fortress of Cesena. The fortress was newly built and among the toughest in Italy, the main reason Borgia had set up his headquarters and home in Cesena rather than one of the more fashionable cities. Machiavelli's steps echoed in the near-empty passages. Guards saluted as he passed by.

The garden outside the fortress walls was quiet. Machiavelli had never been one for gardens, especially not in mid-winter. He passed through quickly to the city square beyond, the Piazza del Popolo, the piazza of the people.

A dim pre-dawn now arose to give some form to the shadows of the crisp December morning, and though there was a fine white covering of clean snow, there was none falling to cloud the vision. It promised to be a beautiful day, though Machiavelli observed that the nearby row of gallows and the headsman's block in the center of the square somewhat detracted from the festive spirit. Dark stains upon the chopping block looked ominously fresh, and several corpses were suspended from the gallows in various states of decay. Early risers passed by without looking up.

When Borgia had captured Cesena he had found the city to be in a terrible state, its officials incompetent and corrupt (a state can tolerate one or the other, but never both). Borgia had assigned his lieutenant Ramiro De Lorca to clear up the problem. De Lorca had proven even more cruel, vicious and in some ways more devious than his master. Corruption had disappeared almost overnight, as indeed had the corrupt, mostly to unmarked graves beyond the city walls. But De Lorca had not stopped with the criminals; unfortunately for the people of Cesena, De Lorca enjoyed his bloody work.

Machiavelli noticed a woman and her two children, boys of seven or eight, who stood beneath the body of a hanged man, recently dead. The woman had her arms around the boys, who wept into their hands. Machiavelli had no trouble guessing the relationship, but was inquisitive as to the cause of the disaster. This family was too well dressed to be beggars, not rich enough to be a threat to the state. The man had been an artisan, perhaps. What could he have done to earn his fate?

Machiavelli approached. He said, respectfully, "Madam, I grieve to see you in this state. May I ask, what brought this about?"

"He spoke out against all the arrests," the woman said, in misery. "He said it was unfair. That's all he did, sir. I swear to you."

"Ah." An honest man then, who could not keep his mouth shut. They were usually the first to go.

The woman's information was valuable to Machiavelli. It told him that De Lorca had begun a terror, but that it had not yet reached the stage where wealthy men were executed for their gold and mansions. But that would surely come. Machiavelli gave it six months before this city of Cesena would be ripe for rebellion. It was a fact that Florence could use.

"And your property?" Machiavelli asked, though he anticipated the answer.

"Confiscated," the woman said. "We must find succor, or we will starve. I have a sister in Ravenna, though how we will get there, penniless, I do not know."

"I do." Machiavelli felt he owed her for her information.

Machiavelli knew the family would need to depart as soon as possible. The sight of the father could only be distressing to the boys, and they certainly did not want to see what was to come, for the executed are normally left to hang as long as possible, as a reminder to others. The only good thing to be said of dead bodies in winter is that the cold tends to delay the inevitable. It would be a day or so before the miasma of degradation became overpowering.

Beside the Cathedral of Cesena was the Hospital of Saint Thomas. Like most hospitals, it was the stopping place for holy travelers on their way elsewhere.

Machiavelli led the woman and children to this place. It was in a poor state of repair, but the rushes that covered the floor were at least clean and fresh, which was a good thing, for it was the only place to sleep. In a distant room someone was cooking a stew, from the smell. The man in charge was a Franciscan, who was almost as gaunt as the poor people he tended. Machiavelli spoke to him.

"Brother, I feel sure that at some point there will be pilgrims passing through here on their way to Ravenna."

"It is quite common," the brother agreed.

"I should like you to select such a group with whom this orphaned family will be safe." Machiavelli presented the woman and her sons.

The brother looked doubtful.

"This for their expenses, and for your trouble." Machiavelli handed the brother a small bag of coins. The brother felt the weight, heard the jangle, and smiled.

"It shall be as you say. You are generous, sir."

The money was nothing to Machiavelli. He cared as little for avarice as he did for comfort. What he lived for was the cutting edge of deadly politics.

A GUARD APPROACHED MACHIAVELLI as he left the hospital. It wasn't one of Borgia's men, but a man dressed in the colors of the city.

"Sir, I believe you are the esteemed Ambassador of the Florentines, Signor Machiavelli?" the man asked, though it was obvious he already knew the answer.

"Indeed," Machiavelli said.

"Your presence is requested, Signor Machiavelli."

"By whom?" Machiavelli assumed his most haughty posture and looked down his nose at the soldier. The fellow's manner had been polite, but his words a little too presumptive for Machiavelli's taste.

"By his Excellency the Governor of Cesena, Ramiro De Lorca." The soldier sweated slightly.

"Please tell his Excellency that I will be with him as soon as practicable," Machiavelli said brusquely. He intended to make De Lorca wait an hour or two, to make a point, particularly since De Lorca was not the object of his mission.

The soldier swallowed, then said, "His Excellency commands your presence at once, my Lord Ambassador."

Now Machiavelli truly was taken aback. De Lorca was Borgia's creature. If Borgia had an issue with Machiavelli, he would have dealt with the Florentine directly. What then was this De Lorca playing at?

"In that case, I will allow you to lead me to your master," Machiavelli said.

THEY LED HIM TO the Rocchetta di Piazza—the little fortress in the piazza—a ludicrously ornate stronghold with its own loggia. It stood proud beyond its station. De Lorca had his offices in this little fortress, just as his master Borgia held the true fortress further away.

De Lorca was like most Spaniards: of dark complexion for a European, stocky, sporting a finely manicured beard, and unfailingly courteous.

He rose from behind his desk as Machiavelli entered the sumptuous office.

"I apologize for the abrupt invitation," De Lorca said before Machiavelli had a chance to complain of his treatment. "Unfortunately, it was necessary."

De Lorca led Machiavelli to a chair. Machiavelli noted that De Lorca had passed by two others of more cushioned design to offer Machiavelli a chair more to his liking with a straighter back. Someone had told him that Machiavelli disliked soft chairs. De Lorca may have been abrupt in his invitation, but he had taken the time to research his guest. Machiavelli was favorably impressed.

"May I begin by wishing you the joys of the season?" De

Lorca said. He gestured to a servant, who brought wine and the inevitable festive pie. Machiavelli hated festive pies.

"Thank you," Machiavelli said. "Your request was apparently quite urgent."

"It is, and of great delicacy," De Lorca said, sitting down opposite Machiavelli. He sounded sincere. "I would like to discuss with you the assassination of our mutual friend, Cesare Borgia."

Machiavelli blinked in shock. It was the only outward expression he allowed himself. Conspiracy was an everyday part of Italian politics, but one didn't normally discuss the details quite so openly until after the corpses were on the floor.

"Why are you telling me this?" he asked.

"For a very good reason, my dear Ambassador. The fact is that the position of Florence in this matter is of some interest. I am well aware that you are here to block Borgia's ambitions, not promote them. If there was any chance of Florence accepting Borgia, it would already have happened."

"Is Borgia aware of this?" Machiavelli asked.

"He is not stupid. He knows, but bides his time. Sooner or later he will lose patience. Before that happens, it is in your interests that he be removed."

De Lorca's words coincided with what Machiavelli himself thought.

"Borgia's removal is likely to upset His Holiness, Pope Alexander," De Lorca said.

Machiavelli reflected that was an understatement of epic proportions.

"His Holiness will respond," De Lorca said. "If I am to hold Cesena, I will require assistance."

"Ah, then I understand why we are speaking. You want support from Florence." Machiavelli raised an eyebrow.

"From Florence," De Lorca affirmed. "You wish to understand why I am doing this, of course."

"The question did cross my mind," Machiavelli said.

"Then let me say at once that I think you are a man much like me, Signor Machiavelli," said De Lorca.

"I cannot imagine what you mean," Machiavelli said, for he could not recall ever having hanged a man, nor caused a man to be beheaded, nor terrorized a city. Machiavelli found the thought of any similarity to De Lorca distasteful.

"I mean that you come from a family that has fallen on hard times," De Lorca explained. "Your father is a lawyer, is he not?"

"He practices law," Machiavelli acknowledged. He did not add that his father had never been admitted to the guild of lawyers. A crushing family debt, inherited from his grandfather, had put paid to that hope.

"And yet it is said that your family is descended from the past distant rulers of Tuscany," De Lorca said. "Your family was once great."

Machiavelli remained silent. It was not a subject he liked to discuss, and certainly not with strangers.

"Forgive me for touching on what must be painful to you," De Lorca continued. He sounded sincere. "I mention these things because my family too has fallen from a higher state. You are a man who has risen by his own abilities, Signor Machiavelli. So have I."

"I take your point," Machiavelli said.

"Then you will understand the driving ambition to restore a family's fortunes." De Lorca leaned forward in his seat. His voice became more urgent. "I will be honest with you. This is my one and only chance to make myself a prince. Here I am, at the behest of Cesare Borgia, Lord of Cesena. I find that I enjoy the power."

"Your words are of the greatest interest," Machiavelli said. "But I must ask—forgive me for such bluntness—what is to stop me from warning Borgia?"

"That would certainly be unfortunate," De Lorca said. "Two things prevent it. Firstly, it is not in Florence's interest. Secondly, if you warn Borgia, and my plot succeeds anyway, then your life will of course be the price you pay for your misjudgement."

It was the answer Machiavelli had expected. He would have said the same thing in De Lorca's position.

"Of course you may choose not to participate in the conspiracy, but in that case a studied silence would be your best stratagem," De Lorca said. "If you follow that path, then Florence will receive from me what it has failed to get from Borgia."

"And that is?" Machiavelli asked.

"A complete lack of interest in your city."

Machiavelli could not prevent a smile. He asked, "When do you plan to enact this plot?"

"Before the next dawn. I generally find the darker hours best for these things, don't you?"

"That quickly!"

"It is why I called you now. I am well aware of the fate of anyone who lets a conspiracy linger too long."

Machiavelli acknowledged the truth of that. "And the method?"

"I thought perhaps a gift," De Lorca said. "A bottle of wine. Poisoned, of course. White arsenic is the usual choice."

Machiavelli was shocked. "That's the oldest, most unimaginative trick there is," he scoffed. "Borgia would have to be a complete fool to be deceived by anything so transparent. Why, his own sister Lucrezia has used white arsenic in food to eliminate enemies."

"That's why the gift will be sent to *you*, my dear Ambassador," De Lorca said smoothly. "This is why I need your assistance. Borgia won't suspect a gift sent to you, Signor Machiavelli. Everyone likes you."

"Then the assistance you require from me—"

"Is to not drink the wine which will be sent to you when next you are in Borgia's presence. It's simple, is it not?" De Lorca chuckled. "Your abstemious habits are well known. No one will question your survival. Nor will anyone suspect your complicity, since the gift was to you. I will arrive—too late, alas—with news of a recently discovered plot against the Florentine Ambassador. Thus suspicion will attach to neither of us. Some suitable culprits will be found and executed before questions can be asked."

Machiavelli had to admire the simplicity of De Lorca's plan. He put his hands together, as if in prayer, and he thought hard. He had always prided himself on his ability to see through the machinations of men—of being a quick thinker—but this decision was more dangerous than most. He genuinely saw good reasons to support De Lorca, but also to support Borgia, and to stay right out of the coming crisis. Which of the three was best?

"You require my answer at once?" Machiavelli asked.

"It would be convenient for both of us," De Lorca said. "But I understand your difficulty. A few hours of grace is possible. Shall we say, until dusk? During that time, I would advise you not to have any private conversations with our mutual friend, nor send any messages. That would cause me to make an unfortunate assumption."

"Then you shall have my answer before the day is out," Machiavelli said.

DE LORCA HAD NOT bothered to say that Machiavelli would be watched closely. Both men took that for granted.

Machiavelli stepped out of De Lorca's offices. He wondered for a moment where he might go to think quietly. If he returned to the Rocca Malatestiana, where Borgia resided, then De Lorca might get the wrong idea. But the name suggested another solution. Machiavelli ambled, with what air of calmness he could muster, to the one place where he could be sure neither Borgia nor De Lorca would ever visit: the Biblioteca Malatestiana, the city library.

The Biblioteca was Cesena's greatest innovation. The former Lord Malatesta had created a library not for his court, not for the abbey that lay atop a distant hill, but a library owned directly by the people. It was a *public* library. Machiavelli thought this idea very interesting, but wondered what might happen if anyone could simply walk in and read the wisdom of the ancients.

It seemed that half the city had done precisely that. The library was crowded. There was row after row of long lecterns. Men stood at nearly all of them, the books they read chained to the posts so that no one could run off with the precious words. Despite which, half the readers were ignoring the books and talking together in loud voices. The librarian—a frazzled looking man—spent more time shushing the readers than he did supplying them with books.

The cacophony was awful. Machiavelli thought to himself that if this was the result of allowing the general public into a library, then rulers had nothing to fear from an educated populace.

Machiavelli abandoned his plan to think in a quiet library and instead went to the cathedral. Not that he was a man for prayer—he had seen too much of the world, and been in the company of too many powerful men, to think that prayer would do anyone any good—but within the dark building he could stop to sit and think, and no one would interrupt him.

Somewhere, a choir was singing. It was the middle of the day, so no torches had been lit, which paradoxically made the large space darker than it would have been at night. Machiavelli sat in an empty pew toward the middle, where it was darkest.

Machiavelli found himself in a most unusual position. He was aware of two conspiracies, hatched by two men, apparently friendly, but each plotting the other's downfall. The only man who knew both sides was Machiavelli.

De Lorca's schedule would see him strike first. If Machiavelli did nothing—and to do nothing was so very easy—then Cesare would be felled, and Florence's aim to avoid a Borgia alliance would be instantly achieved. Best of all, Florence would be held blameless. This would leave Cesena in the hands of De Lorca, whom Machiavelli judged to be not the stuff of princes. De Lorca would likely continue an unwisely cruel and sadistic reign in Cesena, which would eventually win him enough enemies to bring him down.

This all seemed very satisfactory, but so too was the other course of action.

Machiavelli could alert Cesare to his danger. Borgia would be grateful, and this would be leverage over the son of the Pope.

Florence could not lose. But Machiavelli could. If either conspiracy discovered that he had spoken with the other, his life would be measured in brief minutes. The thought chilled him. Such was the danger of any ambassador in any court, but those who dealt with the Borgias were in greater danger than most.

"May I offer you a gift?"

Machiavelli looked up, startled. A monk in a brown habit stood there, neither young, nor old, by his looks.

"I would not have interrupted, except that you appeared more contemplative than prayerful," the monk explained.

"That is the case," Machiavelli said politely, and wished the monk would go away.

"Then may I ask, upon what is it you contemplate?" the monk asked.

Machiavelli wondered what would happen if he told the monk that he was pondering which of two men to kill. Somehow it didn't seem quite the right answer for Christmastime.

"I was wondering," said Machiavelli, from where he sat, "how one chooses between evils."

The monk raised an eyebrow. "That is not the usual sort of thought for a church. But perhaps you are not the usual sort of man."

"Possibly not."

"There are some men whose brains are larger than their hearts," the monk said.

"Yes, I have often observed this among princes, and those who work for them," Machiavelli said. He knew himself to be such a man. "Especially when their wishes conflict."

"This is the subject of your contemplation?" the monk asked.

"Yes," Machiavelli said.

"Is there not another prince whose wishes must be considered?" asked the monk.

The question startled Machiavelli. He thought hard, but could not think of another prince who was a player in the coming crisis.

"I cannot think who you mean," he said.

"The Prince of Peace," said the monk.

That took Machiavelli aback.

"I'm afraid that when the affairs of princes are considered, that particular prince's concerns are not much valued," Machiavelli said drily.

"Perhaps an exception could be made in this case?" the monk suggested. "It is his birthday, after all."

"You make a fair point, sir," Machiavelli said politely, and he bowed from where he sat.

The monk turned to go.

"Wait," said Machiavelli. "Are you not going to deliver a homily on good versus evil?"

The monk turned back to him.

"No, Signor Machiavelli," he said. "A man of intellect such as yourself already knows all about that. I'm sure you could quote a hundred sermons from memory. The question is what you choose to do with the knowledge, don't you think?"

Machiavelli wondered how the monk knew his name, but perhaps he was more recognizable than he thought.

"Are you a member of this church?" Machiavelli asked. "I have not noticed you before."

"I belong to a somewhat larger diocese," the monk said blandly.

The monk pulled something from his pocket that was wrapped in greasy paper. He offered it to Machiavelli. "I forgot about my gift. Would you like a festive pie?"

"No, thank you," Machiavelli said.

"Between you and me, I don't like them either," the monk said in a conspiratorial tone. "But the old lady selling them at the door offered it to me, and it would not have done to refuse. I'm sure I'll find someone who would like it."

"There is a fatherless family in the hospital next door," Machiavelli suggested.

The monk raised an eyebrow. "Thank you for letting me know. You are not quite the selfish, compassionless man you think you are, Signor Machiavelli."

"If you could see what is inside my mind, brother, I doubt you would maintain that opinion," Machiavelli said.

The monk handed the pie to Machiavelli. "Perhaps you could take this to the poor family?"

Now the monk did leave, walking into the unlit corner of the nave, where he seemed to disappear into the darkness.

MACHIAVELLI PAUSED AT THE exit to buy two more pies. Then he went next door.

"These are for you," he said, slightly embarrassed, and laid the pies on the floor beside the widow. She sat on the ground, where she appeared to be tearing her dress to shreds while working with a needle and thread. She looked up at him and smiled.

"I cannot thank you enough, *signore*," the lady said. "You have been very good to us."

"What do you do there?" Machiavelli asked.

"I make gifts, *signore*, for my children."

The lady continued to sew the strips torn from the hem of her dress. Into these she stuffed her shorn hair.

"But you have so little with which to make them, and what funds you have surely must go to food and shelter."

"This is true, *signore*," the woman agreed. "It is why I make my gifts with what I have to hand." She held up her work. Two dolls. "They are not very good, are they? But of course, that's not the point."

"It isn't?" Machiavelli was perplexed. "Why did you not ask me for assistance, madam? Was I not clear that you were to call upon me for any sundry expenses?"

"But *signore*, the point is for *me* to do something nice for the ones I love." She smiled at him. "I have always thought gift-giving to be such a selfish exercise."

"Gifts are selfish?" Machiavelli said, surprised.

"Do you not find it so? After all, it's all about the pleasure one has in the giving."

"What one gets from the giving," Machiavelli half-repeated her words. It was the one possibility he had never considered. Here was something he could understand.

"Thank you, madam," Machiavelli said. "You have assisted me with two very difficult questions."

MACHIAVELLI RETURNED TO DE Lorca. He looked up, surprised to see Machiavelli return so soon.

"I agree to your proposal," Machiavelli said.

De Lorca smiled. "Enjoy your dinner," he replied.

BORGIA AND MACHIAVELLI DINED together that night, as had become their custom. It was Christmas Eve.

At the end of the dinner, two of the more prominent merchants of Cesena arrived at Borgia's palace with a gift for Machiavelli: a bottle of the fine local wine. "In hopes of future profitable trade with the wealthy city of Florence, home of the excellent Ambassador Machiavelli."

Machiavelli wondered how much these two had been paid to risk their lives so. He thanked them courteously, and the men departed.

Machiavelli held the bottle in his hands, looked up, and said, "Do you trust me, Cesare?"

"No," said Borgia at once. "I trust no one outside my family."

"Very wise," said Machiavelli.

"But if you are about to offer me some of that wine, I will gladly drink with you," Borgia said. "As long, of course, that you drink some first."

Machiavelli held out the bottle. A servant opened it, and poured two cups.

Machiavelli took a deep breath, and drained his wine to the bottom. He suddenly coughed and choked. But a hard knock on the back from a strong servant assisted, and Machiavelli, slightly red-faced—he wasn't used to drinking so quickly— placed his cup upside down upon an expensive table.

Borgia smiled, and drank.

De Lorca's spy in Borgia's court must have been a good one, for De Lorca marched in exactly on cue.

"Gentlemen! We have just received word of a terrible plot against the Ambassador . . ."

De Lorca trailed off, obviously expecting the thud of at least one body before he completed his sentence. But when Borgia failed to die, De Lorca could only say, "What happened?"

IT HAD BEEN THE simplest matter for Machiavelli to switch the bottle with one he had brought himself. By the time De Lorca had marched in, the poisoned bottle remained as evidence, and De Lorca's prescient arrival had betrayed his guilt.

It was early on Christmas Day. At any moment the bells would ring to call the faithful to celebrate. Machiavelli stood in the center of the piazza and was a happy man, if only because he was still alive.

The same could not be said of Ramiro De Lorca. The ex-Governor of Cesena was raised high upon a pole in the piazza so that his headless body was at the same height as his hanged victims. His head, which had so recently been separated from the rest of him, had on the orders of Cesare Borgia been left by the headsman upright upon the chopping block, set to stare at those who came to see.

Passersby on their way to church marveled at this sight and exclaimed to themselves that their fears were over, for that excellent noble man Borgia had saved them from the tyranny of De Lorca. Machiavelli smiled and was content for Borgia to receive the credit. It was all the better for his own plans.

A party of pilgrims emerged from the Hospital of St. Thomas. Among them was the lady he had assisted and her two sons. The brothers of the hospital had found them a safe escort to Ravenna. They were heading north this Christmas Day.

The widow as she passed looked at the headless body of De Lorca, and she didn't flinch. She said, "It is justice." She offered her hand. "Thank you for this gift, Signor Machiavelli."

"The pleasure was mine," he replied truthfully. He had always lived for the deadly cut-and-thrust of politics. This past day had been more deadly than most.

Machiavelli had extracted from Borgia the promise that Cesena would be ruled with leniency and justice. Indeed, Machiavelli had represented to Borgia the advantages of doing so. After the excessive savagery of De Lorca, all the true criminals were gone. At no cost to himself, Borgia could portray himself as a lenient prince. Borgia had readily agreed, thanked Machiavelli for saving his life, and asked what he might do in return. Machiavelli had had his answer ready. There would be no more demands from Borgia to command Florence. It was mission accomplished.

Cesare Borgia trudged over the snow toward him, on his way to pay observance at the cathedral, as behooved the son of a Pope.

"Good morning, Niccolo," he said, and covered a yawn. "My apologies, it's been a rather long night."

"The joy of Christmas will surely refresh us both," said Machiavelli diplomatically.

"Indeed," said Borgia. It was impossible to tell if he was being ironic. "I would offer you a gift, but . . ." Borgia shrugged.

"No," Machiavelli said. "Men like us don't indulge in such things."

"It's safer that way," Borgia agreed. After a pause he added, "I have a question."

"Please," said Machiavelli.

"You chose me over De Lorca, when from Florence's point of view, De Lorca would have been the more malleable prince of this province. Why?" Borgia seemed genuinely puzzled.

Machiavelli answered easily. "I received good advice to consider the third prince in this affair."

"A third prince?" Borgia asked.

"The Prince of Peace. De Lorca could never have been more than yet another petty ruler. But you, my dear Borgia, you have the ability to unite Italy, perhaps, and finally bring peace to our ravaged country."

Borgia laughed. "I do not think I should be mentioned in the same breath as that other prince."

"Perhaps."

"By the way, did you ever solve that puzzle?"

"What puzzle?" Machiavelli asked.

"Why people give gifts at Christmas?"

Machiavelli looked up at De Lorca's decapitated body. "Yes, it's all about what one receives from the giving."

At that moment, the bells in the nearby Cathedral rang out, a beautiful, clanging, insistent sound that filled their ears with the joyous announcement of the birth of the Christ child, one thousand five hundred and two years ago.

"Happy Christmas, Niccolo," said Borgia.

"Happy Christmas, Cesare."

CABARET AUX ASSASSINS

Cara Black

CARA BLACK is the author of seventeen books in the *New York Times* bestselling Aimée Leduc series: *Murder in the Marais, Murder in Belleville, Murder in the Sentier, Murder in the Bastille, Murder in Clichy, Murder in Montmartre, Murder on the Ile St-Louis, Murder in the Rue de Paradis, Murder in the Latin Quarter, Murder in the Palais Royal, Murder in Passy, Murder at the Lanterne Rouge, Murder Below Montparnasse, Murder in Pigalle, Murder on the Champ de Mars, Murder on the Quai,* and *Murder in Saint-Germain*. She lives in San Francisco with her husband and visits Paris frequently.

To Sherlock Holmes [Irene Adler] is always the *woman.*
I have seldom heard him mention her under any other name. In
his eyes she eclipses and predominates the whole of her sex . . .
There was but one woman to him, and that woman was the late
Irene Adler, of dubious and questionable memory.
—"A Scandal in Bohemia"

Nice, 1914

Eighteen-year-old Neige Adler's hooded dark-brown eyes narrowed behind her rimless spectacles as she paused in the shadows of the fringed areca palm. Her mother, barely in view, lay reclined on a wicker chaise, her eyes closed, her face sunken, her hands folded atop her chest, and Neige knew she'd come too late.

"I'm sorry. So sorry," said the hired nurse, taking Neige's arm and guiding her across the villa's sunporch. "Your mother didn't want you to know how ill she'd become. She passed away a half-hour ago, very peacefully."

A tear welled in the corner of Neige's eye. No matter their differences, Neige had loved her mother. And Irene Adler had reciprocated in her own eccentric fashion; those whirlwind weekends in the Swiss Alps, a bottle of perfume on Neige's sixteenth birthday, and the promise to take her daughter on an extended vacation, though that never did happen with Irene always rushing off for her next tour.

"*Merci,*" Neige whispered to the nurse, who left her alone in the room to grieve.

She approached the chaise, gently set down her portmanteau and crossed herself. Her mother looked tranquil at last.

Neige slumped down onto a wicker ottoman. In the distance, the peach-washed tobacco-tiled buildings of Nice sloped toward the turquoise Mediterranean. Hot air hovered in the cloudless Provençal sky. Outside her mother's villa window, small lemon-colored finches twittered on the balcony railing. The scent of orange wafted from the orchard below.

Growing up, Neige had seen little of her mother, an actress who once sang at La Scala before nodes had developed on her vocal cords. Irene then took up acting and had toured constantly. But she never performed at Piccadilly or Broadway, where the parents of Neige's schoolmates attended the theater. *My* théâtre public *love me on the Continent, my dear,* she'd always told Neige. Raised in a convent boarding school, Neige spent holidays with either Léonie, her mother's former housekeeper, or school friends. She knew nothing about her father, and had learned not to ask.

Yet her mother's last telegram had promised answers to those unspoken questions. Now Neige'd never fully understand where she came from.

Bereft and disappointed, Neige pinned a stray hair into her chignon and fanned at the stifling humidity. She was a true orphan now, though she'd always felt like one. Below the window, an awninged trolley bus trundled over the cobbled street fronting the villa.

The nurse returned. "About the funeral arrangements . . ." Neige began. She knew her mother would have left no instructions—god forbid she think so practically. Neige had always been the responsible one, ever since she was a child.

Before she could finish, the nurse handed her a carpetbag. "Your mother left this for you. She gave it to me last week, just in case . . . It was very important to her that you examine its contents."

Inside lay a tooled leather journal, a sagging album of photographs and a stack of frayed theater programs. As Neige unbound the journal, folded paper written in dark blue ink with her mother's concise dipped script spilled out. She picked it up, smoothed the thick sheets, and began to read.

My dearest daughter,

If you are reading this, I can no longer tell you the truth in person. So I must do my best in writing. Not my first choice, but considering what a coward I've been, perhaps it's for the best. I know you've always disapproved of my lifestyle, and I'm sure you won't like what you learn about my past as you read on, but then, we don't always get what we deserve in life, which I am unexpectedly grateful for. I know you want to know more about your father, but I must explain that in my own way, by telling you another story first.

Before you were born, and a few years after as well, I worked as an agent for the ministry in Paris.

Neige blinked, and her hand trembled lightly. Her mother had been a spy? How could such a secret have been kept from her?

But Irene Adler had always been a private woman. Like a set of Russian nesting dolls, one of her identities could be pulled apart only to find another beneath. Neige took a breath and continued to read.

You weren't even a gleam in your father's eye when all this began. I'd fallen on hard times after my opera career came to an abrupt end, and a bank collapse ruined my late husband's investments. I was stranded in Paris in the frigid, wet Parisian January of 1896, living in a tiny chambre de bonne *I could barely afford.*

Thankfully, certain ministry officials remembered that I'd once outwitted Sherlock Holmes, during our brief encounter in Bohemia.

Dr. Watson's accounts never mentioned my later involvement with the prominent detective. But Watson didn't like me—he was a jealous, crafty man. So simian! Most of the time, he set out to make himself look good. I never cared to find out more about Watson's odd friendship with Holmes.

Holmes himself, however, had often crossed my mind . . . I had been so impressed by his mental acuity. He was the only man, aside from my dear, departed Norton, whom I could never call a fool.

That bitterly cold night was our final performance of The Importance of Being Earnest *at the Théâtre Anglais. Just after New Year's Day, I'd auditioned and landed the role of Gwendolyn—all when Oscar Wilde was the talk of London. It was a limited-run engagement. Performing was such a stimulant—the gaslight reflecting off fellow actors' faces, the soft fluttering of my peacock-feather fan, the roar of laughter and applause from the audience. I knew it was my true calling. But more than occasionally, it failed to make ends meet.*

Holmes was in the audience that night, which I didn't realize until just before curtain call.

Neige paged through the album to find the faded theater program. There was her mother, hair swept up like a Gibson girl, in a bustle dress with a shimmering peacock-feather fan in hand. So young, vibrant. A striking beauty. Neige winced. She'd inherited her father's looks, whoever he'd been.

After our performance, a distinguished, gray-haired man in a black opera cape appeared at my dressing room door, bearing a gigantic bouquet of rare Canaan lilies.

"Madame Norton, please accept this modest offering and my compliments, past and present," he said. "Your performance was as pure and unsullied as lilies in the field."

The unmistakable deepness of the voice alerted me. But the man stood quite tall, taller than I remembered Holmes, and he had a much rounder figure. His wide face was that of a different man.

"Please do come in, Monsieur . . ." I trailed off, puzzled.

"Duc de Langans," he finished as he moved swiftly inside the door, belying his bulk, and raised a finger to his lips. His dark eyes glittered, and my chest pounded ahead of my realization: This was indeed Sherlock Holmes.

"I wonder if you would enlighten me . . . Duc." I smiled. "I find little comparison between myself and these hothouse flowers. A wild desert scrub, battling the wind and blossoming in rain, seems more apt."

"A wise man would agree." His gaze lingered. "Yet when could those of my sex be accused of wisdom?"

I beamed against my will. I did not remember Holmes, a man for whom logic and deduction ruled, possessing such charms. The air in the room was charged with an emotion I couldn't define.

I was so intrigued that I'd forgotten his outward appearance. The stagehand poked his head in, announcing, "Encore curtain call, Madame Norton, quickly please!" He glanced confusedly at the aged, portly gentleman sitting so close to me. When he left, I relented to a sudden, unexpected impulse and pulled Holmes—or rather, the Duc de Langans—close for an impassioned, though very brief, kiss.

Holmes pulled away, and I feared I had misstepped. But to my surprise, he whispered, "And here I'd thought you'd forgotten me." As he turned to leave, his gaze clouded, and I wondered for a moment whether he hadn't reappeared to gain reprisal for his earlier defeat.

The stagehand ran back into the room and tugged at my sleeve, pulling me out to accept my applause. What ran through my veins was a thrill I had not felt since my opera triumphs at La Scala. To my surprise, I cared not about the reasons Holmes wore such a disguise or his greater machinations, but the blaze of passion and intrigue that had re-entered my dull, work-sore life.

Visions of a late brasserie supper of moules-frites, *a belated New Year's champagne toast, danced in my mind. But when I returned from my final curtain call, Holmes had disappeared. I lingered, foolishly hopeful, as my fellow actors repaired to a bistro to celebrate our final performance. A soirée I could ill afford. More disappointed than I cared to admit, I picked up Holmes's bouquet from the dressing table, careful not to disturb the pots of powder scattered beside it.*

Outside the backstage entrance, no hansom cab was in sight; only the yellow glow of the gas lamps and wet, slippery cobblestones greeted me. Depressed, I pulled my cloak closer for the trudge to my room in hilly Montmartre. The journey promised to be especially long and arduous in the chill drizzle.

Why had Holmes appeared in disguise? Employing me as part of a ruse, perhaps, to exit the rear of the theater. I clutched the flowers, heavy and ostentatious, ready to throw them onto the trash heap . . . I didn't relish struggling with them on my upward trek through the steep streets to Montmartre.

Under the rue du Louvre gaslight, I bent to relace my boots. As I did so, a sparkling object fell from among the lily stems. It landed with a small clink on the pavement; upon closer inspection, I discovered it was a glass tube with a white paper rolled inside. I uncorked it and shook out the paper, which read in small, spidery black writing:

WAIT FOR ME AT PLACE GOUDEAU, S'IL TE PLAÎT.

How unlike Holmes to say please.

I knew this tree-filled place, *which fronted the old washing house—now an atelier for artists. It lay only a block from my apartment. Stuffing the piece of paper into my boot, I stood up and hurried toward Montmartre.*

Place Goudeau's dark-green domed Wallace fountain, with its four cast-iron maidens, trickled in the night. The flickering gaslight caught the veins of water icing the cobbles. Anxious, I found a dark doorway and huddled in my cloak against the cold. A skeletal tree canopied the deserted place.

From an open skylight in a sloping rooftop across the way drifted muffled sounds of laughter. A tall figure stole along the building. Then the Duc de Langans stood looming over me, silhouetted against the fretwork of black branches cutting across the starless sky.

"Why the secrecy, Holmes?" I asked, catching my breath.

"Bear with my pretense, Irene, for I have only a moment." He took in my bedraggled appearance, so different from that of the costumed performer in makeup accepting accolades just hours before. I turned away from him, flustered.

"I couldn't ask earlier, with so many prying ears nearby," he said. "I need information on Comte Charles Marie Ferdinand Walsin Esterhazy."

A simple intelligence job . . . that was what this was all about? My initial excitement from seeing Holmes crumbled.

"You say this name as if it should mean something to me," I said, my breath emerging in frustrated staccato bursts of frost.

"Perhaps you know him as Charles, Bijou's new paramour?"

Bijou was our revue's contortionist, a mere acquaintance of mine, much younger, and eager to make friends in all of society's echelons. I vaguely recalled that her latest beau was an officer.

"It's rumored Esterhazy has gambling debts," said Holmes. "Serious ones. Keep watch on him, Irene. Find out his habits at the Military ministry offices; secure invitations to his gambling dens. There is one above the printmaking shop and another behind closed doors at the Cabaret."

"Who's employing you, Holmes?"

"I cannot answer that, Irene. Please. Only you can be my eyes and ears. I won't ask any other favors."

Why did I feel I would come to regret this charade? "Tell me who it is I would be helping, Holmes," I persisted. "A rich client or King and Country?" Unbeknownst to Holmes, I had already offered my intelligence-gathering services to a relative in the French Ministry named Meslay, though he had never exercised it. A conflict of interest here could prove disastrous.

"Irene, I'm begging you to trust me."

He took my silence as a tacit agreement and palmed a wad of francs into my coat pocket. For a brief moment, he found my frigid hand, clutched it with his own warm one, and kissed it.

"I'll find you again soon," he said. And with a swirl of his cape, he was gone.

This involved much more than gambling, I was sure, or Holmes would've simply sent in a paid spy to do the work. I paused at the café below my building and purchased a small tin of coffee and a few lumps of coal, using a fraction of my payment from Holmes. The night and the long walk had chilled me to the bone. In my narrow Montmartre garret, I stuck the Canaan lilies in a chipped decanter on the table, lit a small fire, and banked the coals. I nestled against the bricked fire flute and kept toasty as I gazed out on the slate-gray Paris rooftop view from my window. This was the first time I'd burned charcoal since prices soared in the frigid 1896 winter. And, even in my fatigue, I relished my warm bed. After putting my apprehensions aside for the night, I slept.

Neige's knuckles whitened as she tightened her grip on the journal. Her mother, an agent for the infamous, reclusive Sherlock Holmes? What different lives they had led.

"This way, dear, rest yourself in the salon," said the nurse, taking Neige's hand. "I'll prepare your mother now."

Neige sat down on a cane backed chair to a welcome cup of tilleul, the tisane infusion of linden tree flowers and leaves. She thought of the nurse washing her mother, preparing the shroud. Tears rimmed her eyes. There was so much she hadn't known of this woman whose body lay beyond in the honey glow of the veranda. Searching for answers, she reopened the journal and turned the page.

As I drank my weak coffee the next morning, I fingered my parents' obituary. They'd perished in a Trenton blizzard some years before. My only tie to America was gone. Back on the boards again, my old washhouse Ma would have said about my career, had she still been alive. I thought back to my childhood on the New Jersey shore, so different from the Right Bank of Paris.

But that was a lifetime ago. No one's left in America for you, dear Neige. France, my adopted country, is your country.

I lodged in Montmartre when it was still a village ridging Paris. Not only was it a bohemian center of painters, anarchists, and writers, but the cobbled and packed earth streets made it cheap. Dirt cheap.

The tinny music of the barrel organ grinder floated down the street. His grinning half-wit son, seated on the cobbles, turned the crank. They often slept in the nearby viaduct. I tossed the boy a few centimes whenever I passed by, if I could afford it. I filled a pitcher with icy water and shivered as I washed my face in it.

Only when I returned to my room did I discover a previously overlooked envelope under my door. Inside was written:

FINALLY, A JOB FOR YOU . . . EXPECT ME IN THE MORNING. MESLAY.

Startled, I rubbed a cloth over the table, put my few belongings to rights and pinched my cheeks for color. Why was this happening now?

My first husband, Norton, had had a brother-in-law named Meslay, a young French Army officer who recruited him for the occasional mission. Only after Norton's tragic death under the wheels of a runaway carriage did I learn that he'd also assumed the unofficial role of Parisian emissary to King George—a pawn of two governments. We hadn't lived cheaply, and I had often wondered how his salary matched mine without a regular government position. But now, my fortunes had been reversed, with neither ministry nor world stage willing to keep a widow without means on their payroll.

I still had my looks; the waters in Baden-Baden, when I'd been able to afford them, were to thank for that. But I was approaching what the French politely refer to as a woman d'un certain âge. *A bleak future of genteel penury in coastal Saint-Malo teaching drama to vacationing English children loomed.*

Fearing this would be my last chance at the theater before such mundane prospects were enforced upon me, I'd called on my connections in the demimonde—perhaps those who had courted me in my fame would repay old favors.

This twilight world of courtesans, artists, dance halls, and café-cabarets offered sporadic employment, though this gave me time to audition for "proper" theater. If only The Importance of Being Earnest *had continued its tour, it would have supported me, I would gladly have given up everything else.*

Surprisingly, it turned out to be Meslay who offered me a chance at paying work. A mission had been promised many months ago, when I'd run into him in the Tuileries gardens, but I'd received no other word from him until now.

A loud knock sounded on the door.

I opened it to admit Meslay. His regal bearing and blue serge wool cape, masking his regimental uniform but not his glistening black boots, looked out of place in my cramped quarters. "Charmant," he said, glancing around my single-room garret and the ice on the window. "Pardonnez-moi. I meant to speak with you sooner, Irene."

"I appreciate your visit, Meslay. I realize we haven't been close since Norton's death." We had never been close, in fact, and Meslay owed me little, so I was grateful for even this consideration.

"My superiors have use for an American expatriate's services in Paris," he said, smoothing his tapered mustache. Meslay, who usually enjoyed conversational sparring and endless discussion in the Gallic tradition, seemed unusually direct this morning.

"And what exactly would these services entail?" I asked.

"Certain underpinnings in the Third Republic warrant scrutiny," said Meslay, his gaze on my wall of theater posters. "Ongoing surveillance, if you understand my meaning."

And here he was, speaking in riddles again. Realizing this would be a long meeting, I offered Meslay a glass of vin rouge, *which he accepted, despite the early hour.*

"I'm not sure which skills of mine you would have use for. I can translate rather well . . ."

"This involves your acquaintances in the demimonde," he interrupted.

So this was why he had turned to me. A man of his rank dealt with high-profile, very public government cases—not those in a world already half-submerged in crime.

"You float among barmen with more government friends than I have, and masters of gambling dens worth millions of francs. *You have an entrée where few can go, the casinos and bordellos, the smoky dens of the opium addicts. You could pay discreet visits in a way that a man's presence would trigger suspicion."*

Meslay made it sound exotic and lush, unaware that to survive this cold, unglamorous life, I had been pushed to my bounds, forced to project both submissiveness and allure. Women walked on tightropes in the cabarets. It was the only way we avoided the streets.

"Oui, Meslay, you could say I'm acquainted with this world," I said. "But I would still be in danger if the wrong person discovered I was spying."

"We'll make it worth your while," Meslay said, holding out a five-hundred-franc note. His eyebrows tented in supplication. "You are uniquely suited to this task."

Holmes had said much the same thing.

What exactly did Meslay want me to do? The note in his gloved hand could afford me so much. My costumes were pawned, our last hotel bill from rue de la Paix still unpaid and my maid, Léonie Guerard, gone to the workhouse after I'd been unable to afford her any longer. My conscience nagged at me as I recalled seeing her son begging in the street.

Now I could at last pay Léonie's overdue wages.

"What information would I be gathering, Meslay?" I asked.

He set down his half-drunk glass and smoothed his mustache. "Irene, I would propose that you weave a . . . web of sorts among your contacts in the music halls, theaters, and bordellos of Montmartre. Make new acquaintances, with particular attention to the concierges, maids, café habitués, and restaurant maître d's."

"That is more difficult than you make it out to be," I said. Theater crews were close-knit.

"A judicious scattering of these will help," he said, pulling a wad of ten-franc notes from his pocket.

He had a point, and I certainly hoped he was right.

I waited for the guillotine to drop—when would he tell me his objective? His distracted gaze followed the crinkled silver mist creeping over the hill on the right side of the window. Below us,

a wooden charcoal cart thumped over the cobbles as its seller cried,
"Charbons!"

"I must know what I am looking for, or I can't build the right
network."

He shrugged. "D'accord. We're interested in the habits of a
certain French officer. An associate of Captain Dreyfus."

Alfred Dreyfus, the only Jewish officer on the French General
Staff in 1894, had been accused of selling French military secrets
to the Germans. He was court-martialed behind closed doors, con-
victed in a unanimous verdict, and sentenced to life imprisonment
on Devil's Island in French Guyana. He was branded a traitor.
And, worse in the eyes of the French, a Jewish traitor.

"And what do you suspect this man of being party to? Black-
mail?"

"Possibly, but more along the lines of bribery," said Meslay. "He's
an officer, and his name is Charles Esterhazy,."

I carefully controlled my expression, despite my shock at hearing
the name a second time.

"Anything you can learn of him—his vices, peccadilloes—would
be of use to me. I hope that is sufficient information to get you
started. I must go. Let's say I will know you are ready to meet again
when," he said, picking up the empty wine bottle, "this bottle sits
on your window ledge."

"We shouldn't meet here. Your visits could draw attention," I
said, thinking of the inquisitive concierge to whom I owed a week's
back rent. "We can meet in the evening at the Bouillon de Pères."
The Pigalle soup canteen run by the good fathers to save wayward
souls, situated between Restaurant de la Bohème and Club Boum-
Boum in Place Pigalle. "Père Angelo can be trusted with messages
in case one of us fails to come."

"Ah, a dead-letter drop," said Meslay.

We arranged our next meeting, after which he ducked his head under the slanting timbered roof and left. I watched his long-strided gait as he turned onto slick rue Lepic. He didn't turn back, though I'm sure he knew my eyes were on him from the window.

I hoped finding information about Captain Dreyfus's associate wouldn't prove too difficult. I debated my options: Grease the palm of painters' models in Montmartre ateliers over a bottle of absinthe? Enlist the aid of Rose la Rouge, streetwalker and occasional cabaret singer? Ask the pianist who entertained in his infamous Sentier brothel to keep his eyes out? All that would take too much time for the tidbits I'd glean, if any. Trustworthiness was another consideration. Better to bribe the devil I knew, the crooked-nosed bouncer at the Cabaret aux Assassins, to inform me of officers' visits.

Though it further racked me with guilt, I also enlisted Léonie's services. Due to the importance of the mission, Meslay was able to procure her a position cleaning ministry offices and assisting the concierge, who had a bad leg and approached retirement. So my former housekeeper, now posing as a cleaning lady, could keep a close eye on Esterhazy and the military officials surrounding him.

I was then headed off to rehearsal—the perfect opportunity for me to speak with Bijou, the contortionist. As I glanced up at the round metal tabac sign above the dark wood shop at the foot of rue Tholozé, my mind wandered back to Holmes, and I wondered if he and Meslay could possibly be working for the same side. If they weren't, I was in a rather precarious position.

Doing what Holmes had asked of me would also prove helpful to Meslay. But how could I get Bijou, barely an acquaintance, to invite me to one of the gambling dens? I couldn't even think of anyone I knew in Bijou's confidence.

The brick-red moulin visible atop the building loomed in the distance, its sails having long ceased to turn. I climbed the wide *stairs, directed by the crowned, dark-green gaslights dividing the staircase. Every few steps, grilled landings to tall apartments and shops branched off from its spine.*

I still had no inkling of a plan by the time I reached Le Chat Noir. I would simply have to improvise. I forged my way backstage past clowns, ventriloquists and belly dancers toward Bijou, who was limbering up for her contortion act. She lifted one ruffle-clad leg straight up in front of her face and wrapped her ankle behind her neck. After another vigorous stretch in which she stood with one foot on the floor and the other on her nose over an arched back, she collapsed into a full split.

"Fantastique," I said, clapping. "Bijou, you must be triple-jointed."

She grinned. Her gap-toothed smile was infectious.

I walked over to her dressing room table, unadorned except for a bottle of expensive scent. I picked it up and held it to the light, admiring its glittering blue.

"Where did this come from?" I asked.

"Ask my new boyfriend," she said, her muscular arms supporting her as her feet rose in the air. "He's a grand mec, a real aristocrat, not that you'd know it in the bedroom." She rolled down to the ground and sighed. "I'm mad about him, Irene."

Her rose-flushed cheeks attested to that. "What's he like, Bijou?" I hoped she might view me as a confidante, despite our age difference.

"I'm usually so guarded with men, but for the first time, I don't have to be." Her eyes glimmered. "Our circumstances don't even matter when we're together. Have you ever known that kind of love, Irene?"

"Only once, Bijou."

And that love, my dear Neige, involves a Royal seal of secrecy and has gone with me to my grave.

Bijou loosened her dark-brown topknot, shook out her curls, and retied them.

"So your grand mec *enjoys the good life, does he?" I asked, hoping she might let something helpful slip.*

"He does like the tables," she said.

"Ah. Poker or baccarat?"

She laughed. "Both, of course."

"I'm partial to chemin de fer." I confessed. "Believe it or not, I helped many a friend at the Grand Casino. We broke the bank of the Monte Carlo once. A Moldavian prince bought me chips at the start of the night. And I kept on winning. Piles and piles of chips. When I collected my winnings, I treated all the waiters to champagne."

"But you're down on your luck now, eh, américaine?"

"Perhaps, but when I feel lucky, nothing gets in my way."

Chill emanated from the damp stone walls of the cabaret. The smell of greasepaint and fug of bodies weren't hidden by the cheap rosewater the cancan girls liberally applied.

"I feel like I might hit a lucky streak soon, in fact," I said, applying powder in front of the mercury glass mirror that ran the length of the small dressing room. "Why don't you introduce me, Bijou?"

"You'd like to play?" Bijou arched an eyebrow, then looked me over. "Eh, américaine . . . *he might go for that. He's got friends who'd like you."*

Le Chat Noir's curtains opened onto a whistler in a black and white Pierrot costume, his face painted white with artificial tears; his tune rivaled those of the birds. Strains from an accordion wheezed in the background as Bijou and Fréderique, the revue's other contortionist, performed.

Then came my skit, a parody of the English; Anglo-French

relations had been rocky since the Battle of Waterloo. I pantomimed Napoléon calling Britain "a nation of shopkeepers." For the entertainment of the stuffy bureaucrat, I would pick the nearest portly gentleman in the crowd, sit on his lap and get him to eat peanuts out of my hand. It was a crowd favorite.

To my disappointment, there was no apparent trace of Bijou's comte *in the audience.*

And the next day, there was no sign of Bijou, either, which I discovered after trudging through the icy streets of Pigalle just to speak with her. Frustrated, I decided to check in with my informant, hoping to loosen his tongue with more francs.

"Ça va, Anton?" I asked the doorman at the Cabaret aux Assassins, joining him under the fan-shaped awning of glass and iron.

"Pas mal, but the world looks heavy on your shoulders," said Anton.

"Nothing some news wouldn't lighten," I said quietly. Several bearded men speaking in a foreign tongue emerged from the cabaret door, nearly slipping on the wet cobblestones. Anton motioned to me to wait.

Good, so he did have information. I needed a lead, or at least the promise of one.

To my surprise, the men refused Anton's offer to hail them a hansom. I watched them trundle down the steep winding street.

"So, those 'assassins' prefer to walk?" I eyed the rain dancing on the cobbles.

Anton grinned, and his crooked nose shone in the lamplight. "Just Prussians and Austro-Hungarians with full bellies, wanting to work off their meal," he said. "They were inquisitive, though, as they'd been waiting for a friend. A Hungarian officer—a count, they said."

My ears perked up "And this man didn't show up?" I asked, hugging myself against the chill as the rain beat down.

"This Hungarian is also a commissioned French officer. No love lost there, I'd say, from their conversation."

Intrigued, I probed further. "You speak Hungarian?"

"My mother came from Budapest," he said. "But I don't share that with many." This didn't surprise me, as France's attitude toward Eastern European immigrants had worsened of late.

"Did they mention a name?" I said.

He tugged at his beard. "Yes, it was Ferdinand Walsin. The man they were looking for actually did arrive earlier tonight, but paid me well not to mention it to them. I'm surprised they didn't find him inside—I didn't see him leave."

Charles Marie Ferdinand Walsin Esterhazy . . . What luck!

"Are you sure he couldn't have left?"

"Don't have eyes in the back of my head when I take my dinner, do I?"

"But I thought all doormen had another set," I said, winking.

Anton laughed, but said nothing more. I had to take a gamble.

"Anton, does this happen often? Men entering the cabaret and not coming back out?"

He looked away, silent. I pushed a wad of francs into his hand and asked, "Where do they go?"

"I've heard whispers of a gambling ring," he said, in a low voice.

"Higher stakes than the one above the print shop in Place Clichy?"

"Police closed that down last month. This one only opened a year ago, but already many an inheritance has been traded in the basement as dawn rises over Montmartre."

I wondered how much Esterhazy had already gambled away in that year. I wished I could glean more now, but barging in would raise suspicion, and the night's performance had exhausted me.

"If this Walsin shows up again, no matter what time, send a runner to find me or leave a note with my concierge."

I then turned and tramped home in the sleet, but soon noticed a stocky, side-whiskered man following me, starting from the Bateau Lavoir, an old washhouse. Fear invaded my senses, and I quickened my pace.

He kept close behind as I passed the small park and took a winding path up the winding cobbled streets.

When I finally escaped from his view around a corner, I ducked into the local alimentaire. *My pursuer waited outside, eyeing the window. I could see his large form through the letters painted on the shop window, wavering to and fro.*

After selecting a hub of cheese, I paid the amount owed on my credit and scribbled a quick note to the propriétaire, *who bagged my purchase, rubbed his hands on his stained apron, and gave a quick nod to the rear of the shop. And a wink.*

I scooted past the tubs of brined fish, freshly slaughtered rabbit haunches on ice, and leaning flour sacks. Behind rue Lepic, the narrow cobbled street lay ice-sheathed, and icicles hung from handcarts.

Relieved to see the narrow street deserted, I battled the slick ground to my oval courtyard on the adjoining street. After paying off my many debts, there wasn't enough left to find alternative lodging. So I appreciated my luck in having a warm garret, with a location unknown to my stalker.

Madame Lusard, my concierge, a wire-haired battle-axe of a woman, thrust a letter into my cold hands. She pulled her shawl tight around her, opened the door of her loge, and returned to a purring cat in front of her glowing grate. My excitement crested as I mounted the groove-worn stairs of the building, feeling the embossed vellum envelope. Surely evidence of a wealthy sender.

Inside, I struggled out of my wet cloak, leaving puddles on the rough wood floor. After sticking scraps of newspaper into the crevices at the edges of the window to block the drafts, I pulled on my only dry pair of leggings and lit the candle. The small room warmed up quickly, thanks to Madame Lusard's fire below. Even though I'd run out of charcoal, the brick radiated heat, which kept me comfortable and dried my clothing in a matter of hours. I was grateful not to be among those who slept in the chill damp and caught pneumonia every winter.

As soon as my hands were dry, I opened the thick envelope to find an upcoming audition announcement at the Théâtre Anglais.

Not forgotten . . . How wonderful! For a secondary role in a George Bernard Shaw drawing-room farce. I knew most of the first act, and could learn the rest in a day. Joy filled me. A serious role, and someone had thought to send word my way!

I sat down with my back against the warm brick, a glass of wine in one hand, the audition announcement in the other. It was then I noticed the bottle on the window ledge. It was flipped around, the label facing me. This was supposed to be my *signal to* him, *but he'd entered my garret and undertaken the signal himself. My stomach knotted in unease. What little I'd discovered thus far made me an unworthy informant, and the idea of trudging back out in the bitter cold filled me with dread.*

I drained my glass, found my still-damp clothing and the small stone I kept warmed by the brick. For night journeys, I kept the stone in my muff, and its warmth kept my fingers nimble.

Meslay might have arranged this meeting, but I would use it to discover the purpose of my inquiries—or wash my hands of our arrangement, I decided. I was so determined to make sense of this mess that the joy at my upcoming audition had withered.

I noticed Meslay, who had replaced his dashing uniform with a drab overcoat, spooning soup at a long table at the Bouillon de Pères. The windows, nearly opaque with steam, gave off a faint glow and fairylike appearance to the seedy Place Pigalle outside. Père Angelo greeted me with a warm handshake and an empty bowl. I stood in line with the clochards, *fatigued ladies of the night, and assorted hungry of Montmartre. Fragrant and hot, the onion soup with a layer of thick melted cheese promised to fully coat my insides. This time I dropped a few bills in the donation can, relieved to finally be able to thank the fathers for their help.*

"Why did you go into my room?" I asked, taking the seat across from Meslay.

"And a good evening to you, too, Irene," he said, sipping his table wine laced with water.

"No more secrets. I need to know why you've hired me," I said. "Or count me out."

He frowned. "And what have you done to earn your pay thus far?"

"I've learned some, but I don't know what I'm looking for."

He glanced at our table companions: an old woman who'd nodded off and a clochard *attacking his onion soup with vigor. "Just tell me everything you've learned. My superiors and I will rate what is essential."*

I hesitated. Meslay wouldn't be a good contact to alienate. And had already paid me for this job. I recounted what I had learned about the gambling ring at the Cabaret aux Assassins, and Ester-hazy's appearance. I neglected to mention Bijou, whom I felt the odd instinct to protect, or my own invitation to the baccarat den.

Meslay's expression changed to one of anger, and his knuckles whitened as his grip strangled his spoon. "I believe you're leaving something out, Irene."

Fear rose in my throat as I remembered the man tailing me. Had Meslay had me followed . . . watched?

"This contortionist in your revue," he said, "you've spent some time with her. And it fits with rumors that Esterhazy's found himself a new lover in the dance halls."

My panicked expression was all the proof he needed.

"I need you to make contact with Esterhazy through the girl," he said, his voice lowered.

My annoyance at being tailed by my own employer bubbled into fury. "Her name is Bijou. And I'm sorry, Meslay, but I've given you plenty of answers for what you've paid me. Unless I know what I'm working toward, please consider my services at an end."

"Irene, the less you know—"

"The less I can find out for you," I finished for him. "My word and discretion are to be trusted. Norton should have told you that."

From Meslay's downward gaze, I believed my late husband had. "Very well. We suspect Esterhazy of selling secrets."

"Who do you mean by 'we'? And to whom would he have sold them?"

"A contingent of the French ministry believes that Dreyfus is innocent, and that Esterhazy is the one who sold military secrets to Germany. What we don't know is whether the Balkan plan is already in the hands of Kaiser Wilhelm."

"What's the importance of this Balkan plan?"

"If the Germans have the Balkan plan, they'll know all of our defense strategies. We can still change the plan and implement new strategies, though they will be much weaker, before the upcoming peace negotiations in Vienna. But we must know."

"And how am I supposed to learn Esterhazy's greatest secret?"

"We know that he keeps a tally of his winnings, his losses, and his betrayals—though those are in code. He's joked to his colleagues about his 'bank of secrets.'"

"And Captain Dreyfus?" I asked. "Will the military exonerate him then?"

Meslay's eyes flashed. "I can only speak for my section. Esterhazy would suffer a court-martial," he said. "But I need your help in furnishing proof of whether the plan was compromised. I've even

*heard that the Crown is looking into this—unofficially, of course—
with their own spy, Sherlock Holmes."*

So Holmes worked for England, then, and I for France.

"Does that mean he's adversarial to your ministry?"

*"Tiens." Meslay crumbled up the soft inside of his baguette,
rolling the pieces into small white beads. "It means England's
for England and France for France in keeping the Kaiser at bay.
Napoléon was right about our neighbors across the river . . .
Selfish!"*

*But wasn't France selfish, as well? Perhaps it was considered
self-preservation, since our home and hearth bordered Germany.*

*Meslay and I arranged another meeting in two days. As he
left, my heart weighed heavy with conflict. Holmes and I were
competing once again. I resented that he had attempted to use our
history to manipulate me into assisting his own King and Country,
the very same monarchy that had used my late husband.*

*Fortified by the soup and ready for action, I headed toward
Le Chat Noir to find Bijou. Time for me to sharpen my acting
skills.*

*"Haven't seen or heard from Bijou in days," said Vartan, our
wire-thin backstage manager. "As far as I'm concerned, there's no
need for her to come back. She's always getting luxury tickets and
crawling back for her job when they expire. Know what I mean?"*

*I doubted this harsh characterization of Bijou, but nodded
nonetheless.*

"She borrowed one of my costumes. Know where she lives?"

"Doubt she's there. Probably off with her louse of a grand mec."

*Vartan certainly had an axe to grind. I guessed he was jealous
of Esterhazy.*

*"Still," I said, "I could at least ask whoever's there where she's
gone. Making a living is hard enough without buying new costumes."*

He shrugged. "Fine. Rue Androuet. Her mother's the concierge of the corner building. Can't miss it."

I set off straight to the corner he mentioned and knocked on the loge *door. No answer. Down a passageway was the building's dim courtyard, where a woman was hunched over the communal water spigot. She saw me and straightened up, then took halting steps toward me with a bucket in one arm. In the darkness, she appeared old and racked by slight shakes of palsy. "Oui?" she said, squinting at me and wiping her other reddened hand on her none-too-clean apron.*

"Bonsoir, Madame. You must be Bijou's mother—"

"Older sister," she interrupted.

"Ah, of course, please forgive me. The light here is nonexistent, and I was told Bijou's mother was the concierge."

But Bijou's sister could have been her mother, she looked so haggard and worn. Aged before her time, perhaps, by too many children? Too much work at the washhouse, I could tell from her painfully chapped hands.

"Neither's here. My mother's gone to Lille, and Bijou hasn't lived here in years."

I suspected she was lying—about Bijou, anyway. She must have been used to the wrong sort of person asking after her sister, a popular figure in the cabarets. Before I could press her further, I noticed the portly man in the bowler hat who'd been following me the other night. He was paused in front of the boulangerie *window opposite, checking his gold pocket watch, which glinted in the gaslight.*

A baby's cries floated from inside the loge, *and Bijou's sister hurried ahead. I tried to keep pace with her, but gave up as she trundled inside the* loge's *heavy door without so much as a good-bye.*

The bowler-hatted man was approaching the door, though he hadn't recognized me yet.

I only had a few seconds . . . Where could I go?

I slipped back into the courtyard, where the door to the down-stairs cellar lay ajar. I stepped inside and pulled it shut, figuring I'd wait until he left, then come out. But as I reached the bottom of the steep damp limestone steps, I noticed a faint glow up ahead. This was no dead-end cellar, but a tunnel.

Montmartre was full of limestone quarries, webbed by tunnels and large empty pockets like a cut of Swiss cheese.

On the damp wall, crude lettering indicated the street names and gas main locations. The smell of damp mold and refuse grew stronger as I walked.

At last, I found another stairwell leading out, depositing me on a street just a few minutes from my own home. Dejected, I hiked up narrow Montmartre stairs. My visit to Bijou's home had been fruitless.

As I approached my building, I noticed someone standing in the shadows. I tensed, wishing I had a weapon or anything I could use to defend myself.

To my relief, Léonie jumped out and rushed over to greet me with a hug. She pulled me upstairs before anyone could see us, even my concierge, who was asleep with her head down on the small front desk.

Once we were safely upstairs, Léonie handed me a bag. "I got these for you, Madame Irene."

I opened the bag to find a stack of papers. "What are they?"

"Remember the concierge with the gamey leg . . . the one who's indisposed sometimes? Well, yesterday, her leg was quite swollen up, and hurting badly, so it was my job to light the fires, clean the big reception rooms, and fetch the contents from the wastebaskets. As I was fixing to throw the waste into the furnace, she screamed, 'Non, non!' She said she needed it put in the back room, giving some daft excuse, and I just nodded and went along with it. That

was when I found out she doesn't throw away the papers from the wastebaskets—she saves them."

"So these are old letters?"

"Yes, and memos and lists, too! I pocketed as many papers with Esterhazy's name on it as I could before she checked on me."

"Marvelous work, Léonie!"

"These are all jumbled, as I had no time to sort them, but I'm hoping they'll help."

I recognized the blue bordereau of a few of the letters, exclusive to the military offices. "You're a miracle-worker, Léonie!"

Her grin reached her sparkling eyes, and I regretted how little my life included her. As I saw her off, I slipped a thick wad of franc notes into her hands and told her to stay home for a while with her son.

I pored excitedly through the papers, carefully setting aside and arranging the military correspondence. One memo listed six officers who had been granted the highest level of access to classified military documents. I recognized two names on the list: Esterhazy and Dreyfus. I smoothed out the crumpled blue bordereau, struck by the angular writing. Another in the same hand had only a few words, and several scratched out. The ink had run into an indentation, which I realized had been imprinted from the pen's pressure on a previous page. I took a charcoal sliver from the fireplace grate and rubbed it across the indentations, turning my fingers sooty. I could make out "Balkan defense line" and a name that resembled "von Schwartzkoppen," the well-known German military attaché. But no signature at the bottom! Merde.

While this was proof enough for me, a court-martial would certainly dismiss it as evidence. Dreyfus was imprisoned on Devil's Island, and the military seemed largely satisfied with that resolution.

A knock sounded on my door, startling me.

"J'arrive!" I yelled, quickly shuffling the papers together, prying up the floorboard by the fireplace and stuffing them in alongside my last few pieces of jewelry.

I paused before turning the knob, remembering the man who'd been following me.

"Who's there?" I called.

An envelope slid under the door.

When I finally peeked out, there was only a deserted hallway. The messenger had gone.

The nurse had lit a lamp and pulled the curtains closed. "Still reading, Mademoiselle Neige?"

She'd been so immersed she hadn't noticed the lengthening twilight. She nodded without looking up.

SORRY I MISSED YOU EARLIER! COME TO THE BASE-
MENT OF THE CABARET AUX ASSASSINS TONIGHT
FOR A GAME OF CHEMIN DE FER. — BIJOU

Finally, here was the gambling invitation I had angled for. But doubt was setting in that this risk would provide what Holmes and Meslay had anticipated: proof that Esterhazy's gambling problem was as serious as rumored, and that he was desperate enough to threaten the very security of his country.

But a promise is a promise, my Neige, so I locked away my mis-givings, donned an outfit accentuated with black taffeta, fiddled my hair into a vague semblance of a chignon, and trudged to the Cabaret aux Assassins.

Every seat in the cabaret was taken. Accordion strains, effusive conversation, and the tinkling of glasses filled the air. As I walked, several patrons, all a bit worse for the wear from drink, took note of my outfit and asked me to join them. Ignoring their offers, I walked past the heavy velvet curtain hung to prevent drafts from entering the door to the basement. The man behind the counter, discreetly standing guard, walked over to me.

"I'm meeting Bijou," I said.

"Ah, yes, so she mentioned, Miss Adler," he said, pulling the curtain aside. Stacked wine bottles greeted me as I moved down a narrow walkway to the basement stairwell.

A low hum of conversation drifted from behind a water-stained wooden door at the bottom. Taking a deep breath, I opened the door.

Amidst the thick cigar smoke, I could make out three men seated around an ornate oval table, glasses and cards in their hands. Piles of colored chips and a whisky decanter sat on the table.

I froze when I saw the Duc de Langan on the right, glad that the smoke obscured my expression. How had Holmes secured an invitation?

"Always ready for a new player." Bijou, fanning herself, leaned on Esterhazy's shoulder. Handsome and flushed, he sported a manicured red goatee and mustache. Bijou winked at me, then affected a bored look.

"Let our lady friend join us," said Esterhazy, smoothing the edge of his mustache.

I put on the slight, coquettish smile I had once worn at the tables in Monaco, and took the fourth and final seat at the table.

"Don't be foolish, Esterhazy," the man to my left began, slurring with drink. "Settle up, or . . ."

Judging by the stains and dribbles of food on his waistcoat, he had already had enough liquor for the night.

"Anything to keep you quiet, old man." Esterhazy pulled a chit from near the chips, scribbled on it and stuck it into the man's chest pocket.

My gaze lingered on the promissory note poking out from the

pocket. Aware that I was being watched, I looked up, accidentally locking eyes with Holmes.

The drunk had passed out, and a side-whiskered man came to lift him out of his chair and set him on a stool in the corner. I cringed as I realized the enforcer was the stocky man in the bowler hat who'd followed me the other night. His small, beady eyes terrified me. How had he come to be here?

"Bonsoir, Madame Norton."

I tilted my head toward him. "Who are you, Monsieur?"

"Emil Cavour," he said, doffing his hat and stroking his lamb-chop side-whiskers.

"Bijou says you bring good luck," said Esterhazy, patting the now-empty chair beside him. "Why don't you sit by me instead?" Bijou's expression fell as I complied and Cavour took my old seat.

The game commenced among Emil Cavour, the "Duc de Lan-gans," Esterhazy, and myself. Bijou had wedged herself between me and her lover, leaning against him. Holmes ignored me, intent on his part—he had always relished disguise—and the game. I wondered why he had bothered to enlist my help when he'd made his own way into this gambling ring.

Emil Cavour nodded to the waiter, who appeared at the table in seconds.

"Bring us some more whisky," said Cavour.

"Good idea," said Esterhazy. "I'll pay this time."

"How, sir?" asked the waiter suspiciously.

"A promissory note."

"Another one?" said the waiter.

Esterhazy scribbled on another napkin.

"Take this," he said, pressing the note into the waiter's hand.

I drank quickly, needing the courage. Holmes played the part of an older roué *with a fondness for cards to the hilt, twisting his mustache and groaning when he'd lost a hand. Esterhazy won the first round, and his confidence bloomed. My cash depleted, I refused the next hand, but he had me tap his cards for luck, and he won again. As he poured himself drink after drink, he squeezed my arm. Eventually he held onto it. "You are quite the lucky charm."*

He sickened me. He certainly exhibited all the signs of a compulsive gambler. Poor Bijou had become nearly as invisible as the room's wallpaper, a hideous mauve explosion of peonies with severe water damage.

Esterhazy pulled me close. He stank of liquor and cigars. "Don't say a word. Just stay lucky," he breathed into my ear.

Bijou glared at me, her fury palpable. Holmes continued to act as if I didn't exist.

Every bet Esterhazy made, every shove of the chips, every card he was dealt and played was accompanied by another drink of whisky. Cavour played cautiously, making modest bets. Within a short time, Esterhazy was losing to the Duc de Langans. His voice rose, he signed more promissory notes, and the Duc accepted them in a show of sangfroid.

I didn't know what Holmes was attempting to do, but he was certainly a talent at chemin de fer.

The tension in the room soon rose as Esterhazy, now quite heavily inebriated, took greater risks, going for higher stakes. His words began to slur; I ignored his drivel until I heard ". . . Schwartzkoppen . . ."

Emil Cavour folded his cards. "I think you've had enough, Esterhazy. Time to call it a night."

". . . all his fault . . ." Belch. ". . . damn defense plans."

And there, in his drunken stupor, Esterhazy had proven to me that he had penned the bordereau.

"Where's my luck gone?" His nicotine-stained fingers crept up my shoulders to my neck. He tried to kiss me, and would've succeeded if

Bijou hadn't slapped him away. Her eyes flashed at me in hatred. She grabbed the man she'd told me she loved.

"Enough. We're leaving. Call us a hansom cab."

The waiter stabbed out Esterhazy's smoldering cigar. "The comte's got to settle his account."

Bijou reached for her scarf and beaded evening bag I recognized from the theater. She draped the arm of the stumbling Esterhazy over her shoulder.

"He'll take care of it," said Bijou.

"Now, the owner says."

Bijou and Esterhazy pushed past him up the stairwell, and the corridor at the top swallowed up the shouting.

Holmes, or the Duc de Langans, smiled at Emil Cavour. "Your deal, Monsieur Cavour, or mine?"

I excused myself, saying I needed to powder my nose. I followed Bijou and Esterhazy, whose voices led me to the cabaret owner's office near the stairwell entrance upstairs—a small room behind a door I hadn't even noticed on my way down.

I could see the owner and waiter arguing with Esterhazy, the waiter clutching a handful of signed chits. When he and Bijou ran outside and the others chased them, I seized the opportunity and slipped into the candlelit office. It was a dark, wood-paneled cavern, piled high with ledgers and boxes. I found the latest accounts log open on a table next to a gas lamp, the chair adjacent to it still warm from the bar owner's derrière.

Esterhazy's drink and gambling sums, not only to the cabaret, but to other gambling parties, had been transcribed in detail. I gasped at his crippling debts. Definitely a sum large enough to sell his country's secrets.

As I suspected, his signature on the gambling log matched the handwriting on the bordereau, at least to my untrained eye.

"Who do you work for, Madame Norton?"

Emil Cavour stood in the doorframe.

"*I believe you already know that, Monsieur Cavour. I'm a stage actress.*"

"*Why, yes, of course, in the cabarets that are ever so popular with the working class and slumming aristos,*" *he sneered.* "*Lines form down Place Pigalle for your late-afternoon matinees.*"

"*Who are you, really? And what do you want?*" *I asked.*

He handed me an engraved visiting card: EMIL CAVOUR, OFFICE OF STATISTICS. "*Let's say I'm part of the greater good, as the military refer to themselves, safeguarding Mother France.*"

Intuition warned me to leave my brother-in-law's name unspoken.

"*We know about your liaison with a certain Bohemian crown prince, Madame Norton.*"

I closed the door, not wanting the entire building to hear about my past. What was this portly weasel after? Even if my affair had been known, I had the sole existing proof, a photograph that rested in a bank vault in Switzerland. "*I fail to see what that has to do with—*"

"*The Prussian ignominy of 1870 and the* communards *have torn the fabric of our society apart,*" *he interrupted.* "*Bijou first mentioned you to me. Told me to keep an eye on you.*"

So then, had Cavour used Bijou as a spy?

"*But why? We're on the same side, Cavour,*" *I said, hoping my vague reply wouldn't engender any questions.*

"*I will take you at your word, Madame Norton,*" *he said.* "*I count on your utmost cooperation. But a warning, if you think you have other plans. The evidence against Dreyfus must not be compromised. The military and all branches of government will go to any lengths to protect Esterhazy.*"

"*But why protect this drunken gambler?*"

"If one military man is attacked, we all stand with him. Count Esterhazy, a French officer, must be protected."

"But I don't understand; you didn't defend Dreyfus, an officer . . ."

"He's a Jew, Madame," he interrupted. "They defend their own kind."

"So that's what this is about?" My fists tightened in rage.

"Dreyfus was an outsider, of course; he sold secrets."

"But let's presume he didn't, and someone else from the officer pool did. It would disgrace your branch. 'Never admit a mistake, but blunder on.' Isn't that your military motto?"

Cavour's mouth tightened. His glance took in the open log of Esterhazy's gambling debts. "You'll leave this alone. There's too much for you to lose."

"Meaning what, exactly?"

"Your secret, Madame Norton. The world will know if you don't stop asking questions and stay away from Esterhazy."

"My secret is nothing to me. Esterhazy's endangering all of us just so he can continue losing a card game. Unlike either of you, I would make any sacrifice necessary to protect my country."

"Your country? You're not even from here," he spat. "You're a filthy club performer and have no right to insult me." A small glint caught my eye as he produced a knife.

"Get out!" I yelled, my hand grabbing the heavy ledger book to shield myself.

The door swung open. "I believe Madame Norton has requested your departure. Of course, I'm happy to assist, should you need help in that regard."

Cavour and I turned, staring into the face of Holmes, or the Duc de Langans. Cavour rushed at him with his knife, but in one swift, easy motion, Holmes caught Cavour's wrist, wrested it from his hand, and pinned him to the ground. He was impressively quick for a man in a padded costume.

"Cavour, should any injury or scandal befall Madame Norton or myself, my contacts will ensure that you spend the remainder of your days in a military prison."

Sensing that the promise of violence wasn't an idle one, Cavour glared at us as he got to his feet. Within moments, he vanished.

Holmes waited until his footsteps had cleared the hallway, then stepped inside. He pinched the candlewicks between his fingers, plunging the office into darkness, and walked over to the window.

"I could have handled that, Holmes," I said.

"And no doubt you would have done so very well, Irene. I, for one, have limitless respect for your capabilities. But you only know half the story," he said. He removed his cape and put it around my shoulders, then held out his hand. "May I accompany you on the walk home?"

"Cavour's gone," said Holmes, peering down from my garret window. "But his paid spy, the organ grinder, is the one watching you now."

I was saddened, but felt no anger. I couldn't begrudge the poor man for taking any job he could find in this cold.

Holmes approached me, then turned abruptly and sat down cross-legged with his back against the bricked-up chimney.

I pressed my face right up to the window to look out on a dark canvas of sky, pockmarked with stars. "All this bone-chilling weather, and it hasn't even snowed! I've never seen Paris with snow. Can you believe that, Holmes?"

"Neither have I, Irene," he said, his tone tinged with resignation.

I sat down and curled up next to him, resting my head on his shoulder. The heat of the chimney and his slow, steady breathing calmed me.

"I want to explain things to you, Irene, The problem is, you French and we English make strange bedfellows."

"You know I'm American, Holmes."

"But France is your adopted country."

We sat there in silence for many long minutes, until Holmes made up his mind to tell me what he knew. But I hadn't mentioned that beneath the very floorboards we sat on were the letters Léonie had brought from the ministry. And in my pocket, Esterhazy's promissory napkin for whisky and a page ripped from the ledger of the Cabaret aux Assassins. I was unsure that it was sufficient evidence.

"We can't afford another war. With Kaiser Wilhelm least of all," Holmes said. "The Royal Navy hasn't recovered from the last one. They've kept this secret for years."

"How does this involve Vienna?"

"So you know about the conference, too," Holmes sighed.

"Only rumors," I said, wishing I'd kept my mouth shut.

"Somehow the Balkan plan, which reveals our diminished fleet and less-than-sterling naval capabilities, is something the French know about and privately gloat over. Yet their navy is almost as decimated and couldn't withstand a German attack, meaning they would rely mightily on ours. The dastardly conundrum for all is that, if our military leaders shared secrets, a traitor in one government could bring down several."

So the British and French were both "selfish," as Meslay had put it, but for good reason.

"How would you know whether Esterhazy passed the Balkan plan on to the Germans?"

Holmes stretched out his long legs. "Not the most imaginative fellow. In code, he simply nicknamed it 'B.' But we don't have copies of his bordereaux; it seems the ministry concierge was the one passing his letters to the Germans, and destroyed all evidence of his betrayal."

I wanted to tell him that the letters he sought were within his reach. But, whether it was out of loyalty to Meslay or anger at the British for misusing poor Norton, I held back. I battled my attraction to Holmes, an equal and possibly more, knowing a real relationship between us was impossible.

"What difference does it make, Holmes, whether the English or the French find proof against Esterhazy? Dreyfus is in prison for life, and the Balkan plan has been compromised."

"I suppose you have proof of this?"

"If you'd like to continue chasing proof, then by all means, continue to do so, but war is brewing, and your government should already be planning for the worst."

He looked exhausted. "I think, Irene, that this chess game of European politics will soon have run its course for me. One day, I'm retiring to South Downs to tend to my bees."

Was I to believe him?

And then I noticed thick white flakes dancing outside. I ran to the window. Snow dusted the cobbles and rooftops like confectioner's sugar. A young boy ran in the street, shouting, "Neige, neige!" until his mother called him inside.

"Look, Holmes, our first Parisian snow!"

He came to join me at the window. He curved his arm around my waist.

"It seems I've grown accustomed to you beating me at the game, Irene," he said pulling me back toward the brick fireplace. "I may have even come to like it."

We took up where we'd left off backstage at the theater, but with no curtain calls to distract us this time. He spread my blanket and his cape on my bed, and in the darkness, with only the silent falling snowflakes as witness, you, my dearest Neige, were conceived. By two people who could never be together.

Before dawn, I crept through the garret, gathering the few things I owned and the letters. I turned the bottle on the windowsill. The only souvenir I took from Holmes was his cape, since it was a frigid morning and I'd left my coat in the gambling den. I paused at the door and pulled out one of the bordereaux. The cryptic message, with the letter "B" throughout, was written and signed by Esterhazy. I laid it on the table. While I owed nothing to the Crown, I wanted to be generous with Holmes, who had come to my rescue and won my affections. I know that if I hadn't left that very morning, I could never have torn myself away from your father. But we both presented a danger to the other.

I sent the promissory note, the page from the gambling ledger, and the rest of the letters by post to Léonie, trusting her to relay them to Meslay and inviting her to leave Paris and join me in a week. At the Gare de Lyon, I bought a one-way ticket south. And so, my dear Neige, you were born nine months later in Grasse, a small perfume-making village in the mountains.

As you grew up, I heard occasional news of the Dreyfus case, which was a cause célèbre for several more years. Esterhazy was court-martialed but never officially convicted, even when strong evidence against him came to light.

But Dreyfus was eventually exonerated, and now, after all this time, the French government wants to award me a medal for my small part in L'Affaire Dreyfus. So, my Neige, I hope you will go to Paris and accept this honor at the Conseil d'Etat on my behalf. This is the last request I'll ever make of you.

Well, perhaps there is another. Holmes knows nothing of you, his own daughter. I last heard that, true to his word, he eventually moved to South Downs and became a beekeeper. Armed with this story and, I hope, a greater tolerance of your mother, I leave it to you to decide whether to seek him out. Whatever your decision, my darling Neige, I know it will be the right one.

Your loving mother

NEIGE'S TEARS STAINED THE carpet. Several emotions overtook her: the sadness of not truly knowing her mother while she'd lived, the pain of this unknown sacrifice, and the newfound joy of knowing who her father was. When the nurse returned, she found the young woman shouldering her portmanteau. "May I help you find accommodation nearby?"

"No, thank you. I'm going to the station," Neige said. "If I hurry, I can catch the last train to Paris. I'll only be there a short while."

"And then, *mademoiselle*?"

"And then I'll fulfill my mother's last wish. I'll be catching the Channel ferry to England."

JANE AND THE
MIDNIGHT CLEAR

Stephanie Barron

STEPHANIE BARRON was born in Binghamton, New York, the last of six girls. She attended Princeton and Stanford Universities, where she studied history, before going on to work as an intelligence analyst at the CIA. She wrote her first book in 1992 and left the Agency a year later. Since then, she has written twenty-six books, including thirteen novels in the critically acclaimed Being a Jane Austen Mystery series, which features the great author as sleuth. Under the name Francine Mathews, she is the author of the Merry Folger Nantucket Mystery series: *Death in the Off-Season*, *Death in Rough Water*, *Death in a Mood Indigo*, *Death in a Cold Hard Light*, and *Death on Nantucket*. She lives and works in Denver, Colorado.

(Editor's note: This fragment of a Jane Austen mystery was recently discovered upon the editing of her thirteenth journal, Jane and the Waterloo Map. *It dates from more than a decade previous, to 1804 in Bath, around the period of* Jane and the Wandering Eye.*)*

Monday, 31 December 1804
Bath

"I shall not know how to go on, Miss Austen, once I have quitted Bath," Lady Desdemona Trowbridge observed as she achieved her grandmother's carriage, which had been standing already a quarter-hour before the Upper Assembly Rooms this evening. My young friend's countenance was tinged with exasperation and amusement. "Only think! There are places in England where balls do not end at the stroke of eleven!"

Many a girl of eighteen has been prey to a similar indignation after an Assembly in this tedious watering-place. I used to feel contempt myself when the Master of Ceremonies lifted his watch and the orchestra fell silent in mid-phrase. But Bath is a town of elderly invalids as well as people of Fashion. An early end to all amusement is sternly advised by our prosperous physicians.

And tonight, moreover, was New Year's Eve. All the Trowbridge party should be established before an excellent fire in Laura Place by the stroke of twelve.

The most venerable Trowbridge of all, Eugènie, Dowager Duchess of Wilborough, smiled indulgently at her granddaughter. Despite her seventy-odd years, Her Grace is neither tedious nor elderly, and entirely comprehended Mona's passionate desire to dance. The girl is but lately engaged to be married, and the curtailment of an evening in the company of her betrothed, the Earl of Swithin, must rank as a severe disappointment. Shivering beside me on the pavement, however, was Miss Wren—a spare, gray-haired and depressingly respectable lady who figures as Mona's companion. Miss Wren does not share the Dowager Duchess's benevolence. She regards her young charge as thoroughly spoilt and in constant need of restraint.

"I should hope, my dearest Mona," she said, "that your fund of quiet sense will always recommend the wisdom of an early hour. Many a delicate constitution has been destroyed by the ceaseless pursuit of pleasure."

"On New Year's Eve, Wren?" demanded Lord Swithin as he handed his beloved into the coach. He is a commanding figure, with guinea-gold hair and arresting blue eyes. "If I had my way, the music should never cease, and this sprite never stop dancing."

His reward was an ecstatic look from Lady Desdemona, who agreed only a fortnight ago to become the Earl's wife. The future that awaits Mona in Town is one of luxury and freedom, indulgence and affection, at the hands of the Season's most eligible *parti*.

Not to mention balls that rarely end before dawn.

It is unusual to harness a team in the steep streets of Bath, the custom being for sedan chairs, but the bitter cold and the advancing hour had persuaded Lord Harold Trowbridge, the Dowager's son and Mona's uncle, to summon the Duchess's coachman. He judged correctly that the ladies' flimsy evening wraps were unequal to the weather. The gentlemen of our party, however, should walk home. The Duchess settled her voluminous skirts—the fashion of a vanished age, when she was a notable French beauty—on the carriage's forward seat. Lady Desdemona squeezed in at her side. Miss Wren and I sat opposite, beside Lady Fane, one of the Dowager's guests and a notable member of Bath Society, whose acquaintance I had only just formed.

I had been invited to accompany the Trowbridge Set to the Upper Rooms, and return with them to the Dowager Duchess's establishment in Laura Place to see in the New Year. At Lord Harold's behest, I had scraped acquaintance with young Lady Desdemona some three weeks before. An unfortunate murder threw us much together and deepened our bond.* My regard for Lord Harold—Gentleman Rogue, Man About Town, and Government spy—is of longer duration, however. We met two years previous over another dead body, and have been firm friends ever since. There are few gentlemen, indeed, I regard with greater respect—and none with whom I should so readily trust my person.

My heart, of course, is another matter. The Rogue is everywhere known for a hardened rake.

I was permitted a parting glimpse of his silver head and dashing tricorn as our carriage rolled off, but was returned to an awareness of my companions by Lady Fane's elbow, which dug sharply into my corseted ribs. She had raised her quizzing glass and was staring avidly at Mona's throat. Her la'ship is a sharp, hectic woman much given over to gossip; her husband, Sir Ambrose Fane, is a Whig Member who is by way of being a Trowbridge cousin. This family connexion encourages his lady in every sort of impertinence.

"My dear girl," she exclaimed, "are those the Wilborough diamonds? I have not seen them this age!" The full moon was high and brilliant in the winter sky, and a shaft of light had found its way through the carriage window, picking out

---

* See *Jane and the Wandering Eye*, Bantam Books, 1998.

the quaint stones that encircled Mona's neck. The settings were old-fashioned and heavy, and the gems gleamed dully. "I had thought your mother to have hidden them away. How do they come to be in Bath, and not at Wilborough House?"

"You mistake, Amelia," the Dowager Duchess said. "The diamonds were never part of the family jewels. My husband presented them to me in his youth. He directed that they pass directly to Mona upon her betrothal—and so they have."

Lady Fane craned to study the gems more closely, but the Duchess's skirts defeated her. She dropped her quizzing glass and toyed with the chain, turning the polished lens in her gloved fingers. I thought for an instant she intended to question Eugènie further, but wisdom forestalled her. The Dowager Duchess was once an actress on the Paris Opera stage, and from her delicacy in speaking of the diamonds it seemed probable they had been given her before her marriage—when she was merely the late duke's mistress.

It did not do to talk of such things before Lady Desdemona. Tho' Mona may be Her Grace's granddaughter, and possessed of all the family secrets, she is as yet unmarried. A nod to Innocence must quell Lady Fane's desire for gossip; and the remainder of our journey passed in blessed silence.

WE HAD NOT BEEN arrived in Laura Place a quarter-hour, and Her Grace's footmen were busy about the supper tables, when the five gentlemen made their appearance. The Earl of Swithin; Sir Ambrose Fane; Lord Harold; his nephew Lord Kinsfell, Mona's elder brother and heir to the Duke of Wilborough; and Kinny's intimate friend Mr. Mortimer, a young gentleman lately sent down from Oxford for setting a bear on his Proctor. He is a fresh-faced youth of one-and-twenty, with a passion for cards and little conversation.

Instantly all was animation. Bonaparte's latest outrage was canvassed by Lord Harold and Sir Ambrose; Mr. Mortimer taxed Lord Kinsfell to hunt this winter with the Quorn; Lady Fane attempted to gain Lord Harold's notice, her jeweled fingers grasping his sleeve, as she asserted that Josephine should never be crowned Empress—the Consort was barren, and must be Divorced in time. Glasses of claret were passed before the roaring fire, and trays of lobster patties offered, and of a sudden, the Earl of Swithin tapped his crystal with a silver fork.

The elegant drawing room fell silent.

"It is a custom at the turning of the year to offer gifts of a humble order," Swithin observed. "—Talismans of happiness for the year to come. The Dark Man brings bread and greenery, gold coins and coal. I am neither dark nor humble—" at this, Desdemona laughed—"but I have a talisman to offer all the same. A bit of coal for you, my dearest Mona, a transmutation of carbon—a charm toward your future happiness."

He bowed, and drew a velvet box from within his coat.

Desdemona's easy looks were fled; all the uncertainty of youth was writ plainly on her countenance; she had not expected this, and was almost unequal to answering it. She extended a trembling hand.

Lady Fane drew a sharp breath as the box was opened, and a thousand fires seemed to leap before our eyes. Mona lifted Swithin's carbon—a simple necklet of graduated diamonds—from their velvet bed. Her mouth formed in a soundless O.*

"Should you like to wear it?" he asked.

---

* Diamonds were known to be formed of carbon as early as 1772, when Antoine Lavoisier, a French nobleman generally acknowledged as the father of modern chemistry, who was guillotined in 1794, established their chemical basis. – *Editor's note.*

"Above all things," she replied.

He went to her and gently unhooked the Wilborough gems, placing them carefully on the fireplace mantle behind him. Then he draped his own exquisite offering around Mona's neck and fixed the clasp. I saw her cheeks flush at the touch of his fingers at her nape; she looked, for an instant, as though she might swoon.

"Delightful," Miss Wren observed flatly. "A very pretty offering, to be sure. A trifle *showy* for a girl of your years, perhaps—"

Eugènie swept by and grasped her granddaughter's shoulders. "I wish you great joy, *ma chère*," she said. "Swithin! We must have champagne!"

Lord Harold was suddenly at my side. He drew me slightly away from the rest of the party under cover of the general excitement. We had not yet had a moment to converse in all the bustle of the evening. With a satiric glance at Lady Fane, his lordship enquired, "And what do you think of our friends, my dear?"

"It is a delightful grouping."

"You are polite to a fault, and suppress all judgment. Sir Ambrose is fatuous, his lady a Harpie; my nephew is weak, and his friend Mortimer a tedious influence. He lost half his father's fortune in an hour at the card tables this evening—or should have done, had I taken up his debts of honour. I shall burn his vowels, of course. One cannot dun a guest."

"But the Earl and your niece are paragons of happiness," I retorted. "At least *there* you must declare yourself satisfied."

"Certainly. They shall be either the ruin or the making of each other."

"I refuse to credit the former."

"You have not lived so long as I." He took a glass of

champagne from a passing footman and offered it to me. "It is nearly midnight, Jane. I could stand to bid this year farewell—could not you?"

I reflected that we had recently endured an inquiry into murder; that I had lost Madame Lefroy, my oldest friend; that my father was aging and my naval brothers exposed to all the vicious schemes of the French Monster. But the year had not been unalloyed with sweetness. There was this shrewd and intriguing silver-haired Rogue, for instance, who never failed to bring novelty into my life.

I raised my glass. "To happiness, my lord."

"Very well. You shall inspire me." He touched his crystal to mine. "To happiness, Jane."

Clear through the midnight came the sound of the Abbey's bells, tolling the hour and the death of the old year.

The Earl of Swithin raised his glass—but at that moment there was a loud and formal knock upon the front door. From the sound, someone was striking it with a heavy wooden stave.

"The Dark Man!" Mona cried, and tripped gaily off in the wake of Her Grace's butler.

The portals of the Dowager's home were thrown open, and there—lit by flaming torches on either side—stood a figure of caprice and foreboding: The Dark Man, emissary of the coming year. This particular fellow was not above twenty, I should judge: a lad from the poorer hovels by the river, decked out in borrowed finery, with a black beaver on his sooty curls and a high courage in his youthful face. His shoulders were squared and his gaze was brilliant, as he surveyed the privileged party in the entry before him.

"What business have you here, sirrah?" the butler demanded.

The lad stomped his heavy oak stave three times on the Dowager's marble. "I come to bear away the Old, and herald the New!" he cried. "Welcome me to your health and good fortune! Shun me at your loss and peril!"

The butler glanced around for his mistress, but being advanced in age and unsteady on her feet, Eugènie had not yet achieved the entry. Lord Harold gave a nod in his mother's stead. The butler bowed to the Dark Man, pressed a guinea into his palm, and fell back from the threshold.

All over Bath, I should judge, a similar scene was enacted in prosperous squares, before brilliantly-lit houses, filled with self-satisfied and comfortable folk. Our particular Dark Man swept into the Dowager Duchess of Wilborough's drawing room, and we hastened behind. He halted dramatically before the hearth.

"It is the custom on New Year's Eve for tidings of hope to enter the house," he declared. "Therefore I present you—" he turned to Lord Kinsfell—"with green branches of spruce to ensure health and long life. To you, ma'am," he said to Lady Fane, "I offer bread against hunger."

Her la'ship took the hard crust he offered her with a sneering look.

"To you, sir, I give base coin, that you might never be in want of gold," the Dark Man told Mr. Mortimer—who flushed deeply and thrust his hands in his pockets. Coppers rained at his feet.

"And to you, my lady," the Dark Man said, as he turned to the Dowager, "I offer coal—that you might never suffer from the chill North Wind, nor fear the cold of the grave."

This was a sombre ending enough; but Eugènie offered her best curtsey to the Dark Man. —One great performer, I surmised, acknowledging another.

He swept off his hat in a general salute. "And now I must carry away the ashes of the Old Year, so that no taint of past suffering might remain in this house!"

The Dowager's footman stood ready with a shovel. He thrust it deep into the embers beneath the firedogs. Then he offered the still-glowing ashes to the Dark Man, who seized the shovel's shaft and followed the footman from the room. We listened to their footsteps dwindle, toward the rear of the Dowager's house. The door to the kitchens would already be flung open, so that the Dark Man might toss the Old Year's ashes on the Dowager's rubbish heap, and depart by the mews.

But for those of us who remained in the drawing room, fresh amusement was already offered: a fiery bowl of Snapdragon. We took turns at snatching the brandied fruit from the flames' blue glow. Every manner of sweetmeats had been set out on the supper table, along with syllabub and cakes, and for full half an hour we moved about the room, content to converse and admire Lady Desdemona's glorious gift.

I was conscious, however, that chairmen willing to adventure to Green Park Buildings after one o'clock, on behalf of a clergyman's daughter, should be increasingly rare. I therefore made my adieux to Lord Harold and his mother, and set my face to the door.

"Swithin shall summon a chair for you, Miss Austen," Mona cried, "as he must also depart. Won't you, Swithin?"

But to my surprise, the Earl was fixed before the fire, his puzzled gaze on the empty mantle. "I beg your pardon, my dear," he said. "I was not attending."

"What is it?" Lord Harold demanded roughly. "Why do you look so, Swithin?"

"The jewels. *The Wilborough diamonds.* They are gone," he said.

FOR THE NEXT QUARTER-HOUR, each of us searched the carpets and cushions of the Dowager's drawing-room as thoroughly as it is possible for ten decorous people to do. The butler and footmen who had attended us that evening were summoned, and when questioned about the matter, expressed all their bewilderment. None had noted the presence of the Dowager's diamonds on the fireplace mantle. Only one of the servants had approached it, and that with an iron shovel already grasped in his hands. We each of us had observed him to draw out the embers, but not one could say whether the Wilborough diamonds were then still in their place on the mantel above. Our eyes had been fixed on the shovel and the Dark Man, who had stayed only long enough to take the ashes from the room.

"A conjuring trick," Lord Kinsfell muttered.

Desdemona's hands were at her neck, as tho' she feared her own gift might be torn from her at any moment. "It is too absurd," she said. "Who would steal Grandmère's diamonds?"

"Any man in need, and cool enough to brave it out," declared Mr. Mortimer. —Then, as tho' conscious of a solecism, he turned rapidly away and made a study of one of the portraits on the walls.

"With your permission, Your Grace, I shall examine John Footman's person," the butler said gravely, "and require him to turn over his clothes."

"It must be done, I suppose," Eugènie returned, "but I cannot like it. I am sure none in my employ had a part in the loss."

"You'd better watch, Harry," Sir Ambrose whispered to Lord Harold, "lest the butler be another in the conspiracy."

"I shall do so," his lordship replied clearly, "if you will consent to search my pockets, Fane, and let me turn out yours. We are none of us in this room immune from suspicion."

Sir Ambrose flushed darkly. His wife uttered a snort of contempt.

"Indeed," Swithin said gravely. "May I be the first to submit to scrutiny? I suggest all the gentlemen retire to one end of the room, and the ladies to the other. The Duchess's painted screen might be usefully employed."

And so it was done; and some thirty minutes later we reconvened, not one of us the wiser.

The Wilborough Diamonds had vanished into air.

IT WAS HALF-PAST TWO in the morning when at last a chair was summoned, and the Trowbridge family saw me wearily to the door. Lord Harold leaned close as he helped me into my seat and said, "When you have slept, Jane, and risen, send me a line. We have matters to discuss."

I nodded. I had been given furiously to think while I submitted to Miss Wren's search of my person, and subjected her to my own. She had approached her task with the brisk efficiency native to a former governess, betraying not the slightest qualm as she ran her fingers over the whalebone of my corset. We were social equals, after all—both aging females of respectable birth and dependent status, whose prospects should never equal those of the ladies surrounding us. I was less sanguine as I patted her bodice; I did not like to think of poor Miss Wren as a possible thief, a cuckoo in the Wilborough nest. Her slight figure could hardly disguise the bulk of the Dowager's jewels. But suspicion must be faced: Wren endured a position of subjection in Laura Place, and perhaps one of gnawing envy, that might make theft a mad impulse of the moment. Mona should leave her behind upon her marriage, and Wren's future means were slim. Perhaps the discarded necklace beckoned with the promise of security?

And what of Lady Fane? Her dress and air appeared prosperous enough, but what did any of us know of private circumstances? Her ladyship was acquainted with the history of the Wilborough diamonds and seemed irresistibly drawn to them. From the instant of espying the necklace around Mona's throat, she had been as one mesmerized. Had she determined even in the carriage to make the jewels her own?

Lady Desdemona, on the other hand, could have no reason to steal her own property—nor, indeed, could her grandmother. That both ladies submitted with grace to a search of their persons was testament to their good breeding.

On the gentleman's end of the drawing-room, I could not credit either Swithin or Lord Harold with coveting the Dowager's necklace. Lord Kinsfell, too, was a son of the house—heir to a dukedom that should throw mere diamonds into the shade. It was possible, I supposed, that debts of honour might pinch his purse—but if such were the case he should be more likely to appeal to his uncle Lord Harold for a loan, than he should be to steal his sister's inheritance. Of Sir Ambrose Fane, however, I could surmise nothing. He appeared a gentleman of Fashion; but such men were notoriously loath to settle so much as a tailor's bill. Fane might appear a prince, but in fact be a pauper. The same might be said of young Mr. Mortimer, late of Balliol. Lord Harold had suggested he was frequently dipped at cards. And Oxford youths were such creatures of impulse! But the Dowager's diamonds had not been discovered in Mr. Mortimer's pockets.

Indeed, they had been discovered nowhere. The linkboy raised his lantern, and the chair lurched as the Irish bearers lifted their poles. I inclined my head to Lady Desdemona as she bade me farewell. She seemed impossibly delicate between her affianced lover and the swirling skirts of her glorious grandmother—a sprite indeed, as Swithin had called her. His talisman blazed coldly at her neck in the waning moonlight, as tho' shards of ice were heaped there.

I narrowed my gaze as the chair moved off, and glanced over my shoulder for a last glimpse of the diamonds. Such brilliance! The modern cut and setting of the gems framed their beauty as the old Wilborough piece could not.

As the doors closed behind the Trowbridge party and the lights of Laura Place dwindled, I leaned forward and called to the chairman.

"Pray, sirrah, will you go round to the mews behind Laura Place, and tarry there a moment? I neglected to leave a token with the housekeeper."

He complied, and within seconds I had breached the service entrance to the Dowager's garden. The rubbish heap was apparent under the moonlight, the footman's shovel laid down beside it. I had only to lift the thing in my gloved hands and stir the ashes to find what I sought.

I wrapped the filthy Wilborough necklace in my best dress handkerchief, and carried it home in my reticule.

"JANE!" MY MOTHER HISSED from her position by the parlor window, "you will never guess who has come to pay us a call! You must change your gown at once and prepare to receive a duchess! Make haste, my dear—make haste!"

I carefully set aside my needlework and joined her at the window. "It is the Wilborough arms on the carriage."

"I do not know how to account for such an honour! The Dowager Duchess—condescending to Green Park Buildings!"

"I begged Lord Harold to bring her to me, when I wrote to him this morning."

"You *wrote* to him?" my mother gasped incredulously. "To Lord *Harold?* My dear, when am I to wish you joy? —Although

I cannot believe him deserving of you, and must advise your father against the engagement."

"There is no engagement," I told her patiently. "A note of thanks, merely, for my entertainment last evening."

Her face fell. "Then it was decidedly improper of you, Jane, and more than the tedious man deserved. Had you written to Lady *Desdemona*—"

She broke off as our maid hurried past in attendance upon the door.

"You must leave me, ma'am," I said. "His lordship is come on a private matter."

"Does he mean to ask for your hand *today*?" She looked all her bewilderment. "And your father not even at home!"

"Please, Mamma," I said gently. "I beg of you—"

"Very well." She sighed—at the waywardness of daughters, or her disappointment in a duchess, I could not tell; and hurried herself from the room.

THE DOWAGER DUCHESS swept upon me first, and accepted a chair, her aged face very small and porcelain-skinned beneath a monumental hat. Her son did not sit, but stood with one booted foot upon the brass fireplace surround. He appeared to be studying the flames; but I knew from the composure of his looks that he merely awaited an outcome he had foreseen long since.

"Your Grace is very kind to wait upon me here," I stammered. "I regret that the exertion was required."

"I ought to have paid this call long before," Eugènie said dismissively. "You have come so often to Laura Place."

I bowed my head, then reached for my needlework. Concealed within its folds were the Wilborough diamonds, cleansed of their ashes. "I did not think it right to disturb

Your Grace's peace, by presenting these in your drawing room."

She stared wordlessly at the necklace for an instant, her figure immobile. Then her eyes lifted to mine with the faintest smile. "A more brazen woman would demand to know how you came by these—and what moved you to repent of the theft."

"Miss Austen did not steal your diamonds," Lord Harold said tiredly.

I set them on the Dowager's lap. She put aside her fine Malacca cane and lifted them to the light in her gloved hands.

"It was foolish of me to subject my guests to such suspicion," she sighed, "and my servants, too. I regretted both as soon as I had time to think. This was the act of an instant, you understand--but an instant, as all of you trooped to the entry in search of the Dark Man, and I was left behind with my jewels. I dropped them in the embers of the fire, and made sure they were well covered with ash. When poor John Footman shoveled them out—"

"I can imagine it was painful to part with the late duke's gift," I suggested. "Desdemona has no need of your diamonds now; the Earl has given her a better necklet, in being a token of love. You hoped the loss of these gems would be ascribed to chance—the passage of an unknown street urchin through your house."

"But unfortunately, your meddlesome son and the keen-eyed Miss Austen were present," Lord Harold broke in. "And when you went to retrieve the diamonds from the rubbish heap this morning, you were disappointed."

"I? Retrieve this *abomination* of stones?" Eugènie's eyes flashed all her indignation. She set the Wilborough diamonds on the little table beside her. "I hoped they would be carted away by the dustmen. They have caused me nothing but sorrow, these forty years at least!"

Lord Harold carried the necklace into the full light of the window. I waited while he studied it.

"Paste, Mama," he said.

"Paste," she agreed.

"You sold the real stones years ago?" His narrow gaze was fixed upon her now like a hawk.

"Needs must, Harry."

"Gambling debts? —Or blackmail?"

The Dowager Duchess reared a little, her dignity foremost. "I do not think I shall answer that question. You were not used to be impertinent, Harry. You are too much my son."

"You could not allow Mona to learn the piece was trumpery," he suggested. "As she was bound to do, the first time she sent the diamonds out to be cleaned."

"And yet, my trustees required me to present them to her," the Dowager said. "I had no choice but to do so at her engagement, under the terms of your father's will."

"That must have been excessively provoking."

"I was *enragée*, I assure you."

Eugènie's beautifully gowned form was rigid in her chair. To suffer such a catechism in the presence of a mere acquaintance cannot have been comfortable. Every one of Lord Harold's words seemed a whip, and the barbed ends stung.

"These were *your* jewels, were they not?" I cried. "Given to you personally by the duke? You said they formed no part of the Wilborough estate. You had *every right* to exchange them for paste, years since, if you so chose. It was only the late duke's will that made the difficulty."

Eugènie leaned toward me gratefully. "How did you suspect

me, my dear Miss Austen?" she enquired. "What made you search in my rubbish pile?"

"Your performance was flawless," I assured her. "But you were the only person alone in the drawing-room when we all went to meet the Dark Man. In the end, however—I must credit the moonlight."

"Moonlight?" she repeated.

"On a midnight so clear, the Wilborough diamonds shone dull. The Swithin necklet flared gloriously! All that was required was to have seen them both, to apprehend the difference. One was paste, the other real."

"I wonder if Lady Fane knows," Eugènie mused. "I cannot like her little quizzing glass. And she is a ruthless gossip."

"She would never offer the house of Wilborough such an insult, as to voice her doubts," I replied. "Your Grace is unassailable."

Eugènie crowed with sudden laughter. "If only that were so! One may dress the Paris Opera girl in a duchess's clothes, Miss Austen, but one cannot change her essence. *That* is what my Harry is thinking. He knows I am paste tricked out as diamonds."

"I should never regard you with such contempt, ma'am," Lord Harold interjected. "I am, as you say—too much your son."

She held out her hand to him, charming as ever.

"You cannot know the desperation I felt—the ends to which I was driven—the secrecy to which all women are put, dependent upon men and powerless as we are—before I sold my jewels. Even the grandest of ladies, who believe they may summon every comfort, cannot escape their own lies! Mona will learn this with time—but who am I to enlighten her *now*? She is in love with Swithin; and happiness is fleeting."

"It is much the same with clergymen's daughters as with duchesses," I said. "I would not lessen an iota of Mona's joy, by telling her the truth."

A look of relief passed over the porcelain countenance, and Eugènie closed her eyes.

"It is time we took our leave."

Lord Harold bowed over my hand. With his other, he pressed the Wilborough diamonds—the Wilborough paste—into my palm. "Get rid of this for me, will you, Jane?"

IT WAS PERHAPS A day or two later that the curious notice appeared in the Bath *Chronicle*, regarding the recent theft in Laura Place:

> OUTRAGE COMMITTED UPON THE DOWAGER DUCHESS OF W—, WHOSE NEW YEAR'S EVE REVELS WERE PUT TO FLIGHT BY A TREACHEROUS DARK MAN, WHO ABSCONDED WITH THE FAMOUS W— DIAMONDS. NOTHING IS KNOWN OF THE MISCREANT, AND NO TRACE OF THE DIAMONDS IS FOUND. THE DUCHESS IS SAID TO BE PROSTRATE. PERHAPS THE IMPENDING NUPTIALS OF HER GRANDDAUGHTER AND THE EARL OF S— WILL CONSOLE HER. THE EARL HAS DIAMONDS TO SPARE.

SUPPER WITH MISS SHIVERS

Peter Lovesey

PETER LOVESEY submitted his first short story, "The Bathroom," to *Ellery Queen Mystery Magazine* in 1973 and had it rejected. After sober consideration, he didn't blow his brains out in despair and ultimately won the Ellery Queen Readers' Award for "The Crime of Miss Oyster Brown." He has written more than a hundred stories, including five collections, and would cheerfully make a living at it if they paid better. In the meantime, he has written more than thirty novels, including the Peter Diamond series, set in modern-day Bath, England, and the Sergeant Cribb mysteries, set in Victorian London. In 1995, he won the Golden Mysteries competition staged by the Mystery Writers of America to mark its fiftieth year. He won the Crime Writers Association Short Story Dagger in 2007 and was insufferably proud when his son Phil won the same honor in 2011. As a footnote to the Ellery Queen rejection, "The Bathroom" was eventually published by the magazine with a different title, and this year Peter was invited to contribute a story to the 75th anniversary issue.

The door was stuck. Something inside was stopping it from opening, and Fran was numb with cold. School had broken up for Christmas that afternoon—"Lord dismiss us with Thy blessing"—and the jubilant kids had given her a blinding headache. She'd wobbled on her bike through the London traffic, two carriers filled with books suspended from the handlebars. She'd endured exhaust fumes and maniac motorists, and now she couldn't get into her own flat. She cursed, let the bike rest against her hip and attacked the door with both hands.

"It was quite scary actually," she told Jim when he got in later. "I mean the door opened perfectly well when we left this morning. We could have been burgled. Or it could have been a body lying in the hall."

Jim, who worked as a systems analyst, didn't have the kind of imagination that expected bodies behind doors. "So what was it—the doormat?"

"Get knotted. It was a great bundle of Christmas cards wedged under the door. Look at them. I blame you for this, James Palmer."

"Me?"

Now that she was over the headache and warm again, she enjoyed poking gentle fun at Jim. "Putting our address book on your computer and running the envelopes through the printer. This is the result. We're going to be up to our eyeballs in cards. I don't know how many you sent, but we've heard from the plumber, the dentist, the television repairman and the people who moved us in, apart from family and friends.

You must have gone straight through the address book. I won't even ask how many stamps you used."

"What an idiot," Jim admitted. "I forgot to use the sorting function."

"I left some for you to open."

"I bet you've opened all the ones with checks inside," said Jim. "I'd rather eat first."

"I'm slightly mystified by one," said Fran. "Do you remember sending to someone called Miss Shivers?"

"No. I'll check if you like. Curious name."

"It means nothing to me, but she's invited us to a meal."

Fran handed him the card—one of those desolate, old-fashioned snow-scenes of someone dragging home a log. Inside, under the printed greetings, was the signature *E. Shivers (Miss)*, followed by *Please make my Christmas—come for supper 7pm next Sunday, 23rd*. In the corner was an address label.

"Never heard of her," said Jim. "Must be a mistake."

"Maybe she sends her cards by computer," said Fran, and added, before he waded in, "I don't think it's a mistake, Jim. She named us on the envelope. I'd like to go."

"For crying out loud—Didmarsh is miles away, Berkshire or somewhere. We're far too busy."

"Thanks to your computer, we've got time in hand," Fran told him with a smile.

The moment she'd seen the invitation, she'd known she would accept. Three or four times in her life she'd felt a similar impulse and each time she had been right. She didn't think of herself as psychic or telepathic, but sometimes she felt guided by some force that couldn't be explained scientifically. A good force, she was certain. It had convinced her that she should marry no one else but Jim, and after three years together she had no doubts. Their love was unshakable. And because he loved her, he would take her to supper with Miss Shivers. He wouldn't understand *why* she was so keen to go, but he would see that she was in earnest, and that would be enough.

"By the way, I checked the computer," he told her in front of the destinations board on Paddington Station next Sunday. "We definitely didn't send a card to anyone called Shivers."

"Makes it all the more exciting, doesn't it?" Fran said, squeezing his arm.

Jim was the first man she had trusted. Trust was her top requirement of the opposite sex. It didn't matter that he wasn't particularly tall and that his nose came to a point. He was loyal. And didn't Clint Eastwood have a pointed nose?

She'd learned from her mother's three disastrous marriages to be ultra-wary of men. The first—Fran's father, Harry—had started the rot. He'd died in a train crash just a few days before Fran was born. You'd think he couldn't be blamed for that, but he could. Fran's mother had been admitted to hospital with complications in the eighth month, and Harry, the rat, had found someone else in a week. On the night of the crash he'd been in London with his mistress, buying her expensive clothes. He'd even lied to his pregnant wife, stuck in hospital, about working overtime.

For years Fran's mother had fended off the questions any child asks about a father she had never seen, telling Fran to forget him and love her stepfather instead. Stepfather the First had turned into a violent alcoholic. The divorce had taken nine years to achieve. Stepfather the Second—a Finn called Bengt (Fran called him Bent)—had treated their Wimbledon terraced house as if it were a sauna, insisting on communal baths and parading naked around the place. When Fran was reaching puberty there were terrible rows because she wanted privacy. Her mother had sided with Bengt until one terrible night when he'd crept into Fran's bedroom and groped her. Bengt walked out of their lives the next day, but, incredibly to Fran, a lot of the blame seemed to be heaped on her, and her relationship with her mother had been damaged forever. At forty-three, her mother, deeply depressed, had taken a fatal overdose.

The hurts and horrors of those years had not disappeared, but marriage to Jim had provided a fresh start. Fran nestled against him in the carriage and he fingered a strand of her dark hair. It was supposed to be an Intercity train, but BR were using old rolling-stock for some of the Christmas period and Fran and Jim had this compartment to themselves.

"Did you let this Shivers woman know we're coming?"

She nodded. "I phoned. She's over the moon that I answered. She's going to meet us at the station."

"What's it all about, then?"

"She didn't say, and I didn't ask."

"You didn't? Why not, for God's sake?"

"It's a mystery trip—a Christmas mystery. I'd rather keep it that way."

"Sometimes, Fran, you leave me speechless."

"Kiss me instead, then."

A whistle blew somewhere and the line of taxis beside the platform appeared to be moving forward. Fran saw no more of the illusion because Jim had put his lips to hers.

Somewhere beyond Westbourne Park Station they noticed how foggy the late afternoon had become. After days of mild, damp weather, a proper December chill had set in. The heating in the carriage was working only in fits and starts and Fran was beginning to wish she'd worn trousers instead of opting decorously for her corduroy skirt and boots.

"Do you think it's warmer further up the train?"

"Want me to look?"

Jim slid aside the door. Before starting along the corridor, he joked, "If I'm not back in half an hour, send for Miss Marple."

"No need," said Fran. "I'll find you in the bar and mine's a hot cuppa."

She pressed herself into the warm space Jim had left in the corner and rubbed a spy-hole in the condensation. There wasn't anything to spy. She shivered and wondered if she'd been right to trust her hunch and come on this trip. It was more than a hunch, she told herself. It was intuition.

It wasn't long before she heard the door pulled back. She expected to see Jim, or perhaps the man who checked the tickets. Instead there was a fellow about her own age, twenty-five, with a pink carrier bag containing something about the size of a briefcase. "Do you mind?" he asked. "The heating's given up altogether next door."

Fran gave a shrug. "I've got my doubts about the whole carriage."

He took the corner seat by the door and placed the bag beside him. Fran took stock of him rapidly, hoping Jim would soon return. She didn't feel threatened, but she wasn't used to those old-fashioned compartments. She rarely used the trains these days except occasionally the Tube.

She decided the young man must have kitted himself in an Oxfam shop. He had a dark blue car coat, black trousers with flares and crêpe-soled ankle boots. Around his neck was one of those striped scarves that college students wore in the sixties, one end slung over his left shoulder. And his thick dark hair matched the image. Fran guessed he was unemployed. She wondered if he was going to ask her for money.

But he said, "Been up to town for the day?"

"I live there." She added quickly, "With my husband. He'll be back presently."

"I'm married, too," he said, and there was a chink of amusement in his eyes that Fran found reassuring. "I'm up from the country, smelling of wellies and cow dung. Don't care much for London. It's crazy in Bond Street this time of year."

"*Bond Street?*" repeated Fran. She hadn't got him down as a big spender.

"This once," he explained. "It's special, this Christmas. We're expecting our first, my wife and I."

"Congratulations."

He smiled. A self-conscious smile. "My wife Pearlie—that's my name for her—Pearlie made all her own maternity clothes, but she's really looking forward to being slim again. She calls herself the frump with a lump. After the baby arrives, I want her to have something glamorous, really special. She deserves it. I've been putting money aside for months. Do you want to see what I got? I found it in Elaine Ducharme."

"I don't know it."

"It's a very posh shop. I found the advert in some fashion magazine." He had already taken the box from the carrier and was unwrapping the pink ribbon.

"You'd better not. It's gift-wrapped."

"Tell me what you think," he insisted, as he raised the lid, parted the tissue and lifted out the gift for his wife. It was a nightdress, the sort of nightdress, Fran privately reflected, that men misguidedly buy for the women they adore. Pale blue, in fine silk, styled in the empire line, gathered at the bodice, with masses of lace interwoven with yellow ribbons. Gorgeous to look at and hopelessly impractical to wash and use again. Not even comfortable to sleep in. His wife, she guessed, would wear it once and pack it away with her wedding veil and her love letters.

"It's exquisite."

"I'm glad I showed it to you." He started to replace it clumsily in the box.

"Let me," said Fran, leaning across to take it from him. The silk was irresistible. "I know she'll love it."

"It's not so much the gift," he said as if he sensed her thoughts. "It's what lies behind it. Pearlie would tell you I'm useless at romantic speeches. Hey, you should have seen me blushing in that shop. Frilly knickers on every side. The girls there had a right game with me, holding these nighties against themselves and asking what I thought."

Fran felt privileged. She doubted if Pearlie would ever be told of the gauntlet her young husband had run to acquire the nightdress. She warmed to him. He was fun in a way that Jim couldn't be. Not that she felt disloyal to Jim, but this guy was devoted to his Pearlie, and that made him easy to relax with. She talked to him some more, telling him about the teaching and some of the sweet things the kids had said at the end of the term.

"They value you," he said. "They should."

She reddened and said, "It's about time my husband came back." Switching the conversation away from herself, she told the story of the mysterious invitation from Miss Shivers.

"You're doing the right thing," he said. "Believe me, you are."

Suddenly uneasy for no reason she could name, Fran said, "I'd better look for my husband. He said I'd find him in the bar."

"Take care, then."

As she progressed along the corridor, rocked by the speeding train, she debated with herself whether to tell Jim about the young man. It would be difficult without risking upsetting him. Still, there was no cause really.

The next carriage was of the standard Intercity type. Teetering toward her along the center aisle was Jim, bearing two beakers of tea, fortunately capped with lids. He'd queued for ten minutes, he said. And he'd found two empty seats.

They claimed the places and sipped the tea. Fran decided to tell Jim what had happened. "While you were getting these," she began—and then stopped, for the carriage was plunged into darkness.

Often on a long train journey there are unexplained breaks in the power supply. Normally, Fran wouldn't have been troubled. This time, she had a horrible sense of disaster, a vision of the carriage rearing up, thrusting her sideways. The sides seemed to buckle, shattered glass rained on her and people were shrieking. Choking fumes. Searing pain in her legs. Dimly, she discerned a pair of legs to her right, dressed in dark trousers. Boots with crêpe soles. And blood. A pool of blood.

"You've spilt tea all over your skirt!" Jim said.

The lights had come on again, and the carriage was just as it had been. People were reading the evening paper as if nothing at all had occurred. But Fran had crushed the beaker in her hand. No wonder her legs had smarted. The thickness of the corduroy skirt had prevented her from being badly scalded. She mopped it with a tissue. "I don't know what's wrong with me—I had a nightmare, except that I wasn't asleep," she said. "Where are we?"

"We went through Reading twenty minutes ago. I'd say we're almost there. Are you going to be okay?"

Over the public address system came the announcement that the next station stop would be Didmarsh Halt.

So far as they could tell in the thick mist, they were the only people to leave the train at Didmarsh.

Miss Shivers was in the booking hall, a gaunt-faced, tense

woman of about fifty, with cropped silver hair and red-framed glasses. Her hand was cold, but she shook Fran's firmly and lingered before letting go.

She drove them in an old Maxi Estate to a cottage set back from the road not more than five minutes from the station. Christmas-tree lights were visible through the leaded window. The smell of roast turkey wafted from the door when she opened it. Jim handed across the bottle of wine he had thoughtfully brought.

"We're wondering how you heard of us."

"Yes, I'm sure you are," she answered, addressing herself more to Fran than Jim. "My name is Edith. I was your mother's best friend for ten years, but we fell out over a misunderstanding. You see, Fran, I loved your father."

Fran stiffened and told Jim, "I don't think we should stay."

"Please," said the woman, and she sounded close to desperation. "We did nothing wrong. I have something on my conscience, but it isn't adultery, whatever you were led to believe."

They consented to stay and eat the meal. Conversation was strained, but the food was superb. And when at last they sat in front of the fire sipping coffee, Edith Shivers explained why she had invited them. "As I said, I loved your father, Harry. A crush, we called it in those days when it wasn't mutual. He was kind to me, took me out, kissed me sometimes, but that was all. He really loved your mother. Adored her."

"You've got to be kidding," said Fran grimly.

"No, your mother was mistaken. Tragically mistaken. I know what she believed, and nothing I could say or do would shake her. I tried writing, phoning, calling personally. She shut me out of her life completely."

"That much I can accept," said Fran. "She never mentioned you to me."

"Did she never talk about the train crash—the night your father was killed, just down the line from here?"

"Just once. After that it was a closed book. He betrayed her dreadfully. She was pregnant, expecting me. It was traumatic. She hardly ever mentioned my father after that. She didn't even keep a photograph."

Miss Shivers put out her hand and pressed it over Fran's. "My dear, for both their sakes I want you to know the truth. Thirty-seven people died in that crash, twenty-five years ago this very evening. Your mother was shocked to learn that he was on the train because he'd said nothing whatsoever to her about it. He'd told her he was working late. She read about the crash without supposing for a moment that Harry was one of the dead. When she was given the news, just a day or two before you were born, the grief was worse because he'd lied to her. Then she learned that I'd been a passenger on the same train, as indeed I had, and escaped unhurt. Fran, that was chance, pure chance. I happened to work in the City. My name was published in the press, and your mother saw it, and came to a totally wrong conclusion."

"That my father and you . . ."

"Yes—and that wasn't all. Some days after the accident, Harry's personal effects were returned to her, and in the pocket of his jacket they found a receipt from a Bond Street shop, for a nightdress."

"Elaine Ducharme," said Fran in a flat voice.

"You *know?*"

"Yes."

"The shop was very famous. They went out of business in 1969. You see—"

"He'd bought it for her," said Fran, "as a surprise."

Edith Shivers withdrew her hand from Fran's and put it to her mouth. "Then you know about me?"

"No."

She drew herself up in her chair. "I must tell you. Quite by chance on that night twenty-five years ago, I saw him getting on to the train. I still loved him, and he was alone, so I walked along the corridor and joined him. He was carrying a bag containing the nightdress. In the course of the journey he showed it to me, without realizing that it wounded me to see how much he loved her still. He told me how he'd gone into the shop—"

"Yes," said Fran expressionlessly. "And after Reading the train crashed."

"He was killed instantly. The side of the carriage crushed him. But I was flung clear, bruised, cut in the forehead, but really unhurt. I could see that Harry was dead. Amazingly, the box with the nightdress wasn't damaged." Miss Shivers stared into the fire. "I coveted it. I told myself if I left it, someone would pick it up and steal it. Instead, I did. *I* stole it. And it's been on my conscience ever since."

Fran had listened in a trancelike way, thinking all the time about her meeting in the train.

Miss Shivers was saying. "If you hate me for what I did, I understand. You see, your mother assumed that Harry bought the nightdress for me. Whatever I said to the contrary, she wouldn't have believed me."

"Probably not," said Fran. "What happened to it?"

Miss Shivers got up and crossed the room to a sideboard, opened a drawer and withdrew a box, the box Fran had handled only an hour or two previously. "I never wore it. It was never meant for me. I want you to have it, Fran. He would have wished that."

Fran's hands trembled as she opened the box and laid aside the tissue. She stroked the silk. She thought of what had happened, how she hadn't for a moment suspected that she had seen a ghost. She refused to think of him as that. She rejoiced in the miracle that she had met her own father, who had died before she was born. Met him in the prime of his young life, when he was her own age.

Still holding the box, she got up and kissed Edith Shivers on the forehead. "My parents are at peace now, I'm sure of it. This is a wonderful Christmas present."

Other Titles in the Soho Crime Series

David Downing cont.
(World War I)
Jack of Spies
One Man's Flag
Lenin's Roller Coaster
The Dark Clouds Shining

Agnete Friis
(Denmark)
What My Body Remembers

Leighton Gage
(Brazil)
Blood of the Wicked
Buried Strangers
Dying Gasp
Every Bitter Thing
A Vine in the Blood
Perfect Hatred
The Ways of Evil Men

Michael Genelin
(Slovakia)
Siren of the Waters
Dark Dreams
The Magician's Accomplice
Requiem for a Gypsy

Timothy Hallinan
(Thailand)
The Fear Artist
For the Dead
The Hot Countries
Fools' River

(Los Angeles)
Crashed
Little Elvises
The Fame Thief
Herbie's Game
King Maybe
Fields Where They Lay

Karo Hämäläinen
(Finland)
Cruel Is the Night

Mette Ivie Harrison
(Mormon Utah)
The Bishop's Wife
His Right Hand
For Time and All Eternities

Mick Herron
(England)
Down Cemetery Road
The Last Voice You Hear
Reconstruction
Smoke and Whispers
Why We Die
Slow Horses
Dead Lions
Nobody Walks
Real Tigers
Spook Street
This Is What Happened

**Lene Kaaberbøl &
Agnete Friis**
(Denmark)
The Boy in the Suitcase
Invisible Murder
Death of a Nightingale
The Considerate Killer

Heda Margolius Kovály
(1950s Prague)
Innocence

Martin Limón
(South Korea)
Jade Lady Burning
Slicky Boys
Buddha's Money
The Door to Bitterness
The Wandering Ghost
G.I. Bones
Mr. Kill
The Joy Brigade
Nightmare Range
The Iron Sickle
The Ville Rat
Ping-Pong Heart
The Nine-Tailed Fox

Ed Lin
(Taiwan)
Ghost Month
Incensed

Peter Lovesey
(England)
The Circle
The Headhunters

Peter Lovesey cont.
False Inspector Dew
Rough Cider
On the Edge
The Reaper

(Bath, England)
The Last Detective
Diamond Solitaire
The Summons
Bloodhounds
Upon a Dark Night
The Vault
Diamond Dust
The House Sitter
The Secret Hangman
Skeleton Hill
Stagestruck
Cop to Corpse
The Tooth Tattoo
The Stone Wife
*Down Among
the Dead Men*
Another One Goes Tonight
Beau Death

(London, England)
Wobble to Death
*The Detective Wore
Silk Drawers*
Abracadaver
Mad Hatter's Holiday
The Tick of Death
A Case of Spirits
Swing, Swing Together
Waxwork

Jassy Mackenzie
(South Africa)
Random Violence
Stolen Lives
The Fallen
Pale Horses
Bad Seeds

Sujata Massey
(1920s Bombay)
*The Widows of
Malabar Hill*